HERETICAL FISHING

BOOK 5

HERETICAL FISHING

A Cozy Guide to Annoying the Cults, Outsmarting the Fish, and Alienating Oneself

BOOK 5

Haylock Jobson

Podium

Published in 2026 by Podium Publishing
www.podiumentertainment.com

To Pixie

Run free, my love

Previously on Heretical Fishing . . .

With Gormona's monarchy defeated, Fischer and the squad lead a raid on the Osnan family's coffee plantation, which they annex peacefully, giving them access to all the beans they could ever need.

Upon returning to Tropica, Fischer creates a coffee roaster, which he uses to infuse coffee with . . . more coffee? The resulting beans have too strong a pull on everyone, so Fischer stows them away. After some more experimentation, Fischer infuses some coffee with passiona (grown by Lemon in her new grove).

These beans let Sue discover her ideal as a barista, who subsequently facilitates the awakening of most of Tropica's citizens when they consume her artisanal beverages—including Paul, who hopes to become just like Fischer, if only the System hadn't put a temporary child-lock on his powers.

Maria, too, has a breakthrough when drinking one of Sue's passiona-infused lattes. She opens up to Fischer and reveals that she wants to use her power to heal others, though she hasn't yet found the inspiration to solidify her ideal, leaving the breakthrough incomplete.

Ellis continues to terrorize Tropica with his lust for information, whipping out a pad and pencil anytime he catches a whiff of a System-related advancement. His hubris and lack of self awareness lead to him using the semi-awakened Paul as a test experiment. Though Ellis believed his safety precautions were enough, Paul's muscular father (Barry) disagrees, issueing Ellis a one-way-ticket to the sun. Never one to let an opportunity for mischief pass her by, Corporal Claws shoots up into the sky, meeting Ellis just above the forest, where she kicks him over the horizon. The situation is the perfect storm for the devious otter—her desire for chaos and her lightning aspect combine, causing her to awaken as an elemental.

Wary of the power and wont for chaos Claws now wields, Fischer (lovingly) punts her even farther than Ellis, giving her some time to think about her actions. Claws embraces the impromptu flight, enjoying the many different scenes she soars past. An ancient, hibernating elemental senses Claws's awakening. He decides then and there to track her down, wanting to absorb her power before she can gain any more strength.

Meanwhile, Claws finds an injured and malnourished raccoon adrift at sea. She brings the mammal back to Tropica. Maria, assisted by the spirit of Sergeant Snips's pond, heals the raccoon. The raccoon, christened Rocky, Prime Minister (or RPM for short) by Fischer, has larcenous tendencies, letting it bond with Claws as her familiar. Similarly, the spirit of Sergeant Snips's pond gains an identity, becoming Maria's familiar and earning the name "Specialist Slimes."

Slimes insists, emphatically and often, that he is a boy.

Fischer gains a quest (In Defense of Tropica), which instructs him to defend Tropica against ten external threats. As a result, Fischer and Maria discover an ancient fish beneath their favorite lake. They attempt to heal it, but its core is too "evil" and pitted—much like Rocky, whose core was previously corrupted by the soul of an evil cultivator.

In Tropica's not-a-prison, Solomon and Francis are given permission to practice alchemy. The other not-imprisoned folk are less easy to appease. Tryphena (Trent's sister) rages continually against Maria's attempts at healing, and Penelope (Trent and Tryphena's mother, and the former queen of Gormona) remains blank and soulless.

Fischer and Peter (of Gormona's fishing club) throw everyone a lavish feast, successfully awakening the rest of the village with Peter's hearth-like chi. One of the newer cultivators, Bonnie, discovers her ideal as a pioneer—she is intent on pushing boundaries and discovering as much of the world as possible.

Deep in the ocean, the elemental being that is still hunting Claws collects ten (a divine number) natural artifacts, which shouldn't exist in a chi-started world. He then traverses the sea, seeking to meld with his brethren before he confronts Claws. Another being awakens, sensing the actions of the elemental that hunts Claws. This being refers to that elemental as his "oldest friend," and he hunts it in turn, his motivations unclear.

At the same time, Fischer continually grapples with how chaotic Claws has become. He is ostensibly pushed to the limit and repeatedly questions whether he needs to step in or not.

With Barry's blessing, Paul helps create a ship. The glorious vessel "Bob the boat" is born, decked out with red grass, flames, gothic lamps, and its very own golden toilet. As a result, Paul's breakthrough is further solidified, though the System's child-lock remains on his soul. Fischer gains insight into Paul's future advancement, wondering if he is a designer of sorts. If he hadn't known better, he'd have assumed Paul was some kind of tactician.

Fischer leads a deep-sea fishing expedition aboard Bob the boat with some of his friends. They catch squid, and something massive severs Fischer's line. Using a winch-like rod created by Bonnie, Fischer manages to hook the massive creature again. It tows Bob the boat across the ocean, and they pass Ellis, who waves politely from an island, declining Fischer's offer to take him back home.

Meanwhile, Maria and Slimes attempt to heal Gormona's "corrupt" cultivators, whose cores were further contaminated by their imprisonment in Theogonia. They possess a unique birdlike essence, borne from their desire to soar free of their confines. Maria's compassion—along with the assistance of Pelly and Bill, who want nothing so much as a flock of their own—help the corrupt cultivators become pelicans.

Snips undergoes her own internal struggles, recognizing the dissonance between her human-like behavior and her crab body and mind. She grapples with feelings of shame and inferiority. After a much-needed return to the ocean, she finally embraces her crab spirit, leading her to a stronger sense of self. She experiences a breakthrough as a result, transforming her rock crabs, Joel and the rest of the Church of Carcinization, and a swath of nearby shrimp. They all willingly gain unique forms and become her familiars.

Fischer lands the massive creature, an Ancient Monarch Swordfish. The sharp bill adorning its head has matured over thousands of years, becoming something that shouldn't exist in a world starved of chi—another natural artifact.

Having helped the corrupted cultivators become pelicans, Maria and Slimes attempt to heal Tryphena and Penelope. Maria discovers a single strand of corrupted chi that survived Fischer's cleansing. The parasitic strand jumps to Penelope, and Maria screams for help as the corruption spreads. Fischer hears the scream and transports the entire ship back home, using most of his chi in doing so.

Trent (who was out at sea and was the reason for Maria calling for Fischer) arrives at the not-a-prison and helps to heal his family. Maria harnesses his raging flames, harmonizing its power with her healing chi and sending Trent her (platonic) love. Trent realises Maria's intention and gives his mother and sister something to live for, reminding them of all the wonderful memories they have together. Combined with his flames, the love for his family burns the evil chi away, leaving Penelope and Tryphena cleansed.

Meanwhile, the elemental that has been hunting Claws has sprung his trap. The final battle has begun. Claws reveals to Fischer that she isn't as evil as she has been pretending to be. The elemental is revealed to be an amalgamation of earth elementals. The being following it is revealed to be an abyssal elemental. Once a cuttlefish and an octopus, they used to be brothers but became estranged because of multiple misunderstandings and the machinations of two divine tricksters.

Lots of other stuff happens. So much so that there would need to be another three recaps to go over it all. Fischer cleansed the divine tricksters from the world, who were poisoning the cuttlefish's mind. Most of the subjugated elementals chose to move on to the next life, with only the first sister (a lava slug) remaining. George and Geraldine bonded with the kraken, becoming abyssal cultivators.

Because Fischer "defeated" so many enemies and acquired so much hidden knowledge, he completes both his quests and earns bonus rewards—Tropica becomes a Tier 3 village, and Fischer gains *all* editions of the book *A History of the Kallis Wars* (which Ellis subsequently steals, having awakened as an archivist and gained a dimensional library).

After the battle, Fischer and Maria are sitting at the end of a new jetty that extends from Tropica. Sergeant Snips arrives, and her connection to Fischer grows stronger, letting her become his familiar.

HERETICAL FISHING

BOOK 5

CHAPTER ONE

Robbery

By every metric worth measuring—and even some that weren't—it was the perfect evening for a heist.

A blanket of clouds muted the moon's brilliance. A steady breeze blew over the dunes, creating just enough noise to hide any misplaced steps. And most important of all, the treasure keeper had fallen asleep, a foolish mistake by an otherwise flawless man.

One furry thief grinned. The second grinned back, then sprang into action. He rolled forward, leaped up toward the back entrance of the treasure keeper's castle, and silently tapped its handle. The entire locking mechanism vanished.

The first thief wasted no time; she slipped into the breach. The air inside was still, and a pungent stench floated up from her gloriously furred body, filling her nostrils. Though the alchemical concoction was terribly offensive to her refined tastes, it was entirely necessary. The mixture hid their presence from those with enhanced cores.

The second and more rotund of the burglars rolled in behind her, tumbling end over end in an exceedingly awkward but inarguably stealthy maneuver.

Impressive, the first thief thought. *He weaponizes his own spherical nature. This one is truly worthy of being my disciple.*

RPM agreed with a mental nod, neither missing a step nor letting his joy drift into his aura. He was hyper-focused on their task. Claws grinned and crept onward. Victory would be theirs. Side by side, then one behind the other, they slipped through the night unseen, only halting when face-to-face with another door. The first true trial of the evening had arrived—this lock couldn't simply be removed.

RPM jumped and landed on Claws's shoulders. He held his breath, paused for the beat of a cultivator's heart, then grabbed the handle and turned. It opened with a soft *click*. Nothing barred their way.

The treasure keeper has grown complacent, thought Claws, unable to keep a hint of a smile from her internal voice. *He underestimates us . . .*

The other didn't respond. He was too busy drawing on his power. He dropped down and clung to her like a larcenous backpack, limbs rigid as his core drew in the alchemical scent coming from their fur.

She paused a moment, letting him get a good hold on the weave, then flowed into the room, more liquid than living creature. She rounded a corner, and the final obstacle came into view. They were only steps away. So close to the treasure. Mere centimeters from . . .

Movement. To her right.

Claws froze, a razor-sharp fragment of shell forming in the pit of her stomach. A murky shadow sat up and stretched atop the royal bed, its hellish shape separating from the others sleeping there. The beast yawned. Its maw became visible against the gray walls behind it. Her worst fears had come to pass—the hound had stirred.

Neither of the thieves moved a hair. They dared not even blink. If the hound discovered them, it was over. The treasure would be relocated. They would never get this opportunity again. An eternity passed as the monstrous canine finished stretching.

Finally, Borks flopped to his side, letting out a soft grunt. Moments later, quiet snores came from his once-more-sleeping form. Borks hadn't detected their scent. Claws's backpack squeezed her a little tighter, communicating that he was ready. Once more liquid, she rushed forward, grabbed the handle of a sliding door, and pulled it open with silent ease—

Something fell. A silver object, shining and terrible and filled with meaning. It was a *pan*.

The treasure keeper was more formidable, more treacherous, than they'd assumed. He had laid one last trap, an unsophisticated-yet-effective measure she'd been unable to sense with her chi. It tumbled in slow motion. Its metal surface would make a terrible racket when it hit the ground.

Even if she caught it, could she do so silently? She would have to. This was it. The moment of truth. She stretched to her full height, narrowed her eyes at the descending item, and seized the adversarial kitchenware with both paws.

. . . Nothing. It made not a sound. Her disciple squeezed her again, his thoughts telling her the truth. It *had* made a sound—he'd stolen it from the air.

As expected of my familiar.

With that, Corporal Claws, lightning and chaos incarnate, reached up and stole the ornate chest her master had stored in his cupboard. She tucked it into her pouch, ripped RPM off her back, and stuffed him in there as well, then fled Fischer's bedroom, only pausing long enough to make a rude gesture at Brigadier Borks, who was once more snoring happily atop the blankets.

A kilometer away, nestled between two dunes, Claws withdrew her prize. There was a raccoon attached to it. She was a benevolent master, so she allowed him to continue hugging his treasure—for a few seconds, anyway. Then she shook him free. The cheeky little git would steal it for himself, given even half an opportunity.

She chirped an order. He readily obliged, slapping his paw against the padlock and sending a sliver of chi into it. The lock sprang free. With a flick of a dexterous digit, it fell to the sand.

My familiar is devious indeed, thought Claws. *He has robbed this lock of its very identity. It must have fallen open out of shame.*

"Actually, Master," he chittered back, "I just took the mechanism out of the—"

Smack.

"Don't ruin my phoneticism, squire!"

RPM appeared pensive as he rubbed the spot she'd struck. "Do you perhaps mean poeticism, Master? Phoneticism doesn't make any sen—"

Smack!

"You dare correct me, junior?"

His chittering laughter oozed out over the dunes as he rolled away, using the power of her blow to tumble around in a chaotic mix of somersaults and barrel rolls.

Claws took a second to savor the moment. Even if her master were to come, he would be too late; now that the lock had been removed, there was nothing he could do. Fischer should have stored it in Borks's dimensional space, just as he'd done with the naturally formed artifacts.

He had fallen victim to his own hubris, believing his senses strong enough to detect any thieves in the night. Claws grinned. He should have known better. She set the chest down and clutched the unlocked lid between both forepaws. She imagined the glittering riches it could contain. It was her master's—if it was tailored to him, what *would* be inside?

Gold? Iridescent stones? . . . Perhaps food? A never-before-tasted crab or even a handful of shellfish? She wasn't a monster, so she hadn't planned on actually stealing the contents—just peeking at it and taunting her beloved master. If it were a rare shellfish, though . . .

I'll need to have a little taste. Then I'll give the rest back. Unless it's really tasty, in which case Master will surely forgive one more bite. Two max. Okay, two and a half. Then maybe another half, but only because it would be rude to leave a partially munched mollus—

Light exploded out from directly beside her. He'd come. Claws cackled inwardly.

Foolish Master! How easy you are to trick! She'd had those thoughts intentionally, wanting to lure him in.

She wreathed her body in barbed lightning. It would be enough to hold his essence at bay for a fraction of a second—more than was needed for her to have a little peek.

"Gaze upon my majesty as I open the chest before your very eyes, Master! Your reward for reaching 100 Fishing, seen by my peepers before any other! You will forever remember the day that you lost this battle of wits against me, Corporal . . . huh?"

Her lightning was just . . . *gone.* Sucked away. She whirled, freezing when she saw the gigantic shape looming behind Fischer.

"Thanks for the assist, Claws." Fischer scratched her behind the ear. "I wasn't sure I could get it open without damaging the contents, so I thought I'd let you do it for me."

She was surrounded by light. Only when he'd grabbed the chest did he drop the walls of solid chi holding her still. At the same time, the being he'd brought with him stopped draining her power away.

"*Betrayer!*" screamed Claws at the kraken. "You're supposed to be on Team Elemental! Swine! *Pissant!* You smell like rotten fish thrice baked, over-chewed, then spat out again!"

His tentacles writhed in amusement. Fischer, she could forgive, but this *bastard*? She made a mental note to use some of the pranks planned for Barry's domicile on this creature instead. Her very soul demanded satisfaction.

"I welcome the attempt," he rumbled.

"Master!" She leveled an accusatory paw at the cephalopod. "He's stealing my thoughts! That's illegal!"

Fischer rubbed her head again. "I passed that one along because it was funny, but you're right. I should have asked. Sorry."

She sniffed and crossed her arms. *I forgive you. Unless it stops me from pranking him, in which case you will rue the day you gave me fish and helped me ascend.*

"I have no doubt, missy. If being forewarned was enough to stop him from being pranked by you, I wouldn't have shared. Your mischief is unparalleled, and I have full faith in your ability to inconvenience people."

She preened. Master always said the sweetest of things. It was one of the many reasons she loved him.

"And I love you too, even if you are an absolute menace to—" He cut off, having to backhand RPM, who'd tried burrowing up from the sand to steal the chest. "Society," her master finished, watching the raccoon sail over the southern mountain range. "Oops. Did I hit him too hard? I thought you had time to draw him into your core before he flew away."

"I did." She grinned, and he barked a laugh. The sound made the electricity in her limbs want to dance, so she gave a full-body wiggle.

"Come on, then," he said, kneeling down and grabbing the ornate lid. "Let's see what the System granted . . . me?"

Claws blinked. So did Fischer. The kraken let out a ponderous hiss of air. RPM returned in a flash, his neck craning to peer inside.

"Claws?"

"Yes, Master?"

"Did you actually pull off the heist?"

She shook her head. Neither she nor her familiar had broken the seal. The larcenously inclined raccoon felt around within the wooden chest, but no matter how much he tippy-tapped, there was nothing to be found.

"Well, I'll be . . ." Fischer said. "That's a bit *how ya goin'*. This world just keeps presenting more mysteries."

The kraken made a ponderous sound that could be confused with a belly rumble if Claws hadn't snacked all day. "I may know the reason for that."

Her head whipped around.

Fischer, however, appeared unsurprised. "Appreciate the honesty, mate. I could feel you drinking in your thoughts, but I wasn't gonna make you blurt it out."

"Which I appreciate in turn, Traveler Fischer. I am willing to inform you, but would you perhaps prefer to learn it with everyone else?"

"You mean tomorrow?"

"I do. It should be a part of Ellis's presentation."

"It's bloody annoying having to wait for Ellis to dole out the information he absorbed with those books. I never thought I'd be the one chasing *him* down for secrets . . ." Fischer sucked his teeth, then sighed in acceptance. "I can wait until tomorrow."

Claws glanced to the side as a wave of yearning came from her familiar. RPM's front grabbers twitched, his gaze locked on the kraken's center of mass.

Fischer noticed too; he shook his head. "Mate . . . I reckon you should have a long think about what you're considering. I'm willing to bet it's a terrible idea to try and yoink memories from an elemental whose power is *literally* a void. Did you stop to consider that the abyss might yoink back?"

Those words of wisdom from her flawless master did nothing to discourage RPM, so Claws drew him into her body, getting him to stay there via the promise of future shenanigans.

"Well," Fischer said, turning to the kraken, "that's that. Thanks for letting me bring you out here. And you, Claws . . ." He bent down to give her one last scratch behind the ear. She leaned into it so hard that she ended up gazing at the clouds above. "Thank you for your assistance. Appreciate you."

She chirped as she straightened, agreeing that her efforts were worthy. She had given it her all. It wasn't her fault that her master was flawless, kind, and so many steps ahead. Such things were to be expected.

With that, Fischer snapped his fingers, and they all vanished in a flash of light.

CHAPTER TWO

Dilemma

You're serious?" Maria asked. I smiled at her as she sat up and covered a yawn. "I kind of wish you'd woken me. The look on Claws's face alone might have been worth the lack of sleep."

"I knew you needed the rest after you healed, like, almost all the prisoners yesterday. You . . ." I trailed off, my mind going blank as she stretched. "*Damn.*"

"What?"

"Have you *seen* yourself? How do you wake up more attractive?"

She rolled her eyes, trying and failing to hide the faint blush rising in her cheeks.

I heaved an exaggerated sigh, gestured in her general direction, and shook my head.

"What now?"

"I just realized you're too good for me. What happens when a better bloke comes along?"

Laughter burst from Maria. It was as wild and free and intoxicating as the rest of her. "I know you're only joking, but let me set the record straight—I don't want a hint of doubt dwelling somewhere in that overactive head of yours." All timidity was gone when her gaze met mine. "Fischer, if you walked into hellfire, I'd grab your hand and leap in behind you. If you ascended from this realm, I would cultivate for a thousand years for the chance to join you again. You, my darling, are stuck with me until the day one of us dies. Actually, even that might not be enough. If I died first, I'd be tempted to do what those divine gods did."

"The whole spear-in-the-core thing?"

"Yeeeep."

"That's a wild move."

"Entirely necessary, though. How else would I ensure you don't find a *new* Maria? I reckon I'd make a pretty cute spear, too. Would I be the same color as them or pink because of my chi?"

"You *would* make a cute weapon, but aren't you worried about . . . I dunno, making me go insane?"

She blew air from her lips. "My inclusion couldn't be any worse for your mind than you are. If anything, I'd probably add some normalcy."

"You've got a good point there. What do you think, Borks? Can I trust her?"

The goodest of boys had shown incredible restraint so far. He was sitting at the end of the bed, his tail thumping away as he watched our exchange. But being addressed directly ruined his resolve. He sped forward, shifting into a form I'd not yet witnessed in Tropica. He struck Maria's chest with so much force that if he'd remained a golden retriever, he might have shot her into the next room.

"What is *that*?" Maria yelled, excited and confused and devastatingly beautiful. "Borks! What *are* you?"

He was too busy squirming in her grip to answer, a blur of tiny legs, darted licks, and a smooshed face.

"That, my love, is a pug."

She managed to keep hold of him as he rolled around like a crocodile. "Is this even a dog? It's more like a rat." Borks froze mid-spin, staring up at her from his back, the whites of his wide eyes making his face more comical than I thought possible. She laughed and pulled him to her chest. "That wasn't an insult, Borks. You're *adorable*. For a rat, anyway."

His vengeance was swift.

Maria let out a startled yelp as the rodent-sized animal cradled to her torso turned into a mastiff whose size was more horse than dog. The bedframe creaked as he squashed her back into her pillow. "I'm sorry! Please! It was a joke, Borks! I—"

All three of our heads darted toward the northeast as a pulse of essence washed through our home. It was ancient, of a nature we knew well after the events of yesterday, and held the undeniable feeling of ascension.

"Holy frack . . ." I said. "That was quicker than expected."

Borks turned back into a golden retriever and parked his furry tooshie between us. Maria sat up. "So much for going straight to the meeting . . ."

"Let's give them a few minutes, then we'll rush over." My mind started racing with countless possibilities. I had wanted longer to plan, but as so often happened in Tropica, the world refused to wait until I was ready. Something I'd thought of last night returned to my mind. It had been my first instinct, but now that I reconsidered it . . . it was *perfect*.

"Hang on . . ." Maria leaned in front of me, her eyes narrowed into a scowl. "*That's* why you want to go?"

"Hey! No peeking into my head!"

"Why am I not surprised?" She put an arm behind Borks's back and rubbed his head. "Your master is a real goose, Borks."

Ruff! he agreed, tongue lolled and tail wagging as we all stared to the northeast, focusing not on the blank wall but the conscious soul beyond it.

The sun was just cresting the horizon as we dashed across the dunes. Air rushed past our skin, its relative warmth hinting at spring's arrival and making my chi swirl in excited loops.

We had been unable to stay home a minute longer. We'd tried to control ourselves enough to travel at a slow clip, giving the others more time alone before we got there—and we had failed.

Rise after sandy rise, we chewed through the distance, called ever forward by the ancient essence still pulsing periodically. I nearly missed my footing as we strode over the last hill, realizing a little too late that I probably should have sought permission to approach. An unseen force pulled me closer, answering the question before I could ask it. With a grin, I leaped off, sailing through the air alongside my partners in crime.

I caught us with shifting walls of light that lowered us to the ground so we didn't spray sand all over those waiting.

The kraken arched a massive brow. "That arrival was . . ."

"Cool?" I suggested.

"Yes. *Cool*," he answered, tasting the word. "I believe that is correct."

"That's one way of putting it," George muttered to his wife.

"I'd have said he was being a show-off." From behind Geraldine's raised hand, I could see her lip curling into a smile. "I guess our new friends don't know him well enough to judge his actions accurately."

"Maria . . ."

"Yes, Fischer?"

"Mark George and Geraldine down for latrine duties."

"Right away, God-King! It's just . . ." She leaned toward me, hissing with false urgency, "*We don't have a latrine, sir!*"

"We don't? Belay that last order, then—mark them down for latrine-*digging* duties."

"Yes, sir!"

Beside the dark-skinned kraken of the void, another creature undulated its tentacles, two slitted pupils wandering over us hesitantly. It was an odd expression on a cuttlefish the size of a Volkswagen Beetle.

"I told you they were anomalous," said the kraken, which earned a slow nod from his brother.

"Uhhhh, octo-pal," I added. "Are you aware that you're both horrors from the deep, and that your bro is literally *floating in the air*? How are *we* the anomalous ones?"

"We are both oceanic animals, no matter our size and advancement." The kraken, entirely unperturbed, glanced at his gravity-defying kin. "And he is an earth elemental. Such things as floating are natural to him."

I opened my mouth to ask what the frack he was talking about—because why would something related to earth be able to *fly*—but I let out a sigh instead.

"I'm proud of you." Maria patted my back. "That showed great restraint."

"Thank you. It would have just taken us further off topic." I gave George and Geraldine some side-eye, my lips pouted conspiratorially as I pointed at their abdomens. "What's that?"

Geraldine frowned. George raised an eyebrow. "What's what?" he asked.

"The thing you're pushing into the center of your core. I know exactly what it is because I'm hiding something similar. I don't suppose that's something for our kraken pal?"

Black waves radiated across the kraken's sclera as he glanced back and forth between us.

Geraldine narrowed her eyes at me. "Were you poking about in our thoughts while we slept?"

"Nope! So you decided on it *before* you went to sleep, huh? Interesting. You must be pretty sure of it, then."

"We are." George released a fraction of his abyssal power as he prepared to unveil the secret. "Before we voice it, though, you said you have one too. Should we do it at the same time, to make it fair—"

"Absolutely not," Maria interrupted. "He's already chosen enough of them, and you've seen firsthand how *that* goes."

"Hey! My names are fantastic, thank you very much! You insult the brigadier!"

Ruff! Borks added, but not in agreement—he was just happy to be included.

"*Names . . . ?*" asked the kraken.

"Yes," George replied. "Forgive us for hiding it from you. We wanted it to come up naturally, but *someone* intervened." He glared at me, so I shot him a wink.

Geraldine took a half step forward and rested a hand on her husband's back. "We thought of a name for you, but we'll only share it if you want one. I know George's ancestors had a name for you, and I also know you haven't shared it for a reason. No—you don't have to reply to that. But say we *did* think of a name for you last night . . . would you want to hear it?"

There was no hesitation. Verbalizing it wouldn't have done his feelings justice, so he answered with a pulse of deepest longing, his core pulling the surrounding sand inches closer.

Though their chi was that of the abyss, George's and Geraldine's faces lit up like the sun. They both said a single word. It was filled with power and seemed to come from deep within, the noise reverberating as it flooded from their cores and out into the universe.

"*Fathom.*"

Every cell in my body and hair on my head vibrated. All at once, the sound waves were drawn away, disappearing into the void of a newly named being.

"Fathom . . ." he repeated, his voice and chi infused with awe.

The silence that followed seemed to extend out into the greater world; the otherwise-steady breeze died, no waves struck the shore, and the sparse clouds above ceased their endless march eastward. The universe itself had recognized the importance of the moment. And only one man was brave, stupid, and humble enough to interrupt such grave serenity.

"Fathom?" I asked, tasting the word. "Neat. I hate it."

"What?" Maria's head rocked back, and she studied me like I was an unsolved puzzle. Or a particularly colorful beetle. "It's a nautical unit of measurement, which is *perfect* for a kraken. And it also means to understand something difficult. Fitting, considering his knowledge and intellect. It's a double entendre. Why do you hate—"

"Triple."

"... What?"

"It's a triple entendre. His name comes from the Old English word 'fæthm,' which literally means the length between someone's outstretched arms, and Fathom here has a *lot* of bloody arms. See what I mean? It's . . . why are you all looking at me like that?"

George took the bait. "You just said the same word twice."

"*Fæthm* sounds the same, but it has that weird letter that looks like both an *A* and an *E* and hurts your brain if you think about it too long. Not to be confused with Fathom, which just has a boring *O*. Which spelling do you wanna use, by the way? Fæthm or Fathom?"

George pressed his thumbs into his temples. "One of these days, Fischer, you're going to have an aneurysm and no one is going to realize it. Anyone nearby will just assume you're fracking about."

"That's a risk I'm willing to take."

He sighed. "I already stepped in it, so I may as well ask the other question."

"Which one is that, mate?"

"Old English—what is that? A language from your previous world?"

"Oh, that one's easy. It's English, but older."

Geraldine pinched the bridge of her nose. "Let's get back on track. If Fathom has three different meanings, all of which are accurate, why don't you like it?"

"Another easy one. It has no alliteration, no misdirection, and *zero* cute factor." I shook my head. "I daresay it might just be the *perfect* name for a horror from the deep."

"So it's perfect?" Maria asked.

"That's what I said."

"But you hate it."

"They're not mutually exclusive. The name *did* remove a mental dilemma I'd been stuck on for a while, though . . . So maybe I *don't* hate it." I tapped my chin. "Mmm. Yes. That reframing seems to be doing the trick. I think I love it after all."

My verbal onslaught earned blank stares in response. Before I started to question whether I'd taken my shenanigans too far, I plowed onward. "Psst. That was a social cue for someone to ask what the mental dilemma was."

Again, I was met with silence.

Ruff!

"Thanks for asking, Borks! I came up with a name last night for our cuttlefish friend, but I felt bad about offering it if Fathom here didn't have one yet. Now, though . . ."

Maria groaned. "You haven't even spoken to him yet! All you've done is spout nonsense since we got here! How are you supposed to know his personality well enough to give him an accurate name?"

"Some things supersede personality, my love. Besides—he tried to kill me yesterday morning when he was still a mindless amalgamation of elementals . . . Wait, speaking of, where is the lava slug?"

"The first sister?" asked my cuttlefish compadre, the echoes of ascension still radiating from his body.

"Yeah. Her. Wait, was that rude? Sorry. I'm just *really* excited about your name. Err, if you like it, I mean. And if you want one at all. What was the question again?"

Each tip of the cuttlefish's tentacles flicked about in confusion. "It was *your* question. You asked about the first sister . . . ?"

"Ohhhh! Right! Where's she at? Is she all good?"

"She has gone to visit someplace close by with Rocky." His slitted pupils examined me with curious intensity. "Can you not feel her? Your level of cultivation. It's . . . *immense*. Even more than when you were witnessing our memories."

"I kinda absorbed a bunch more power yesterday. Or maybe it's more accurate to say the land did, which I'm low-key connected to? It's a *lot*."

"And your senses . . . ?"

"Oh. Right. I've been actively working on suppressing them. Given how sensitive my soul is, it was straight-up knocking me out if I focused on people's breakthroughs, and that's not even mentioning the sounds. Or the *smells*. Talk about a curse. I can hear and smell a coffee bean hitting the ground on the other side of town if I'm not careful."

"That's . . . fascinating, actually. I've never met someone who could mute their sense of chi so thoroughly. She's close. I can't stop myself from feeling the magma she's drinking."

"She's drinking *magma*? You know what, never mind. That's probably fine for her." I took a deep breath, then let it out with a slow sigh. "Where was I? Oh yeah. You tried to *kill me* yesterday. That makes us bonded by battle. Blood brothers, or something just as grandiose. And then there's the whole *freezing-time-and-going-on-a-spiritual-journey-into-the-past* thing. I reckon I know you better than anyone. Other than Fathom, of course. So what do you say, Cal? Reckon I understand you enough to give a name?"

". . . Cal?" the cuttlefish asked, his core and essence wavering.

My answering grin must have looked predatory. I didn't care. I'd been playing the fool since I got here for this very moment. "That's right, mate. *Cal*."

Maria squeezed the bridge of her nose. "You are *so* annoying sometimes, Fischer." I didn't miss the hints of amusement coming from her core.

"I know, right? In my defense, I haven't had a coffee yet."

"Go on, then," George said. "Tell us what it's short for."

"How do you know it's short for something?"

He just blinked at me.

"Okay, you got me. It's *totally* short for something." I looked at the currently nameless cephalopod floating across from me, his car-sized body refusing gravity's pull. I reached out with strands of my pure, unaspected essence, showing him the true, non-abrasive version of myself. Despite my antics this morning, I was the same man—the same *Traveler*—that witnessed his and his brother's memories yesterday.

Fathom, I thought to myself. *Damn. It really is a good name, isn't it?*

It is, the cuttlefish responded, surprising me.

Whoa! We can think at each other?

Apparently.

Neat. To be completely honest, I did *send that first one your way, but I didn't actually expect a response.*

I shook my head, returning to the present. "All jokes aside, do you want a name, mate? I won't share it unless you want me to."

"Didn't you already do that by calling him Cal?" Geraldine asked.

"Nah, that's just a nickname. The full version has too much *power* and *pizzazz* to be chucked around willy-nilly. Again, *jokes and shenanigans aside*, it is totally up to you. You've lived longer than I can comprehend, and I'm sure you've been given a whole bunch of names be . . . *fore?*"

With both amusement and sincerity swelling in his core, the elemental had raised a tentacle, gesturing for me to stop. "I would be honored if you gave me a name, Traveler Fischer."

"Are you *sure?*" Maria asked. "Are you aware of the other names he's given . . . ?"

"I am. I accept the consequences of my actions."

I grinned at the groan she made, grinned even wider at the anticipation she was actively hiding, then projected the name out toward the heavens. "Calamari! *Cadet* Calamari! Alliteration, cute factor, *and* misdirection! Now *that's* a damned name!"

A noise like rock splitting came from Cadet Calamari's earthen soul. And the name rushed in, filling the hairline fissures left behind.

CHAPTER THREE

Breather

Lovely bloody day." The sun beamed down upon us, hitting our backs as we left the ocean behind. I looked over my shoulder at the cephalopod hovering behind me. "Wouldn't you agree, Cal?"

Cadet Calamari wiggled his tentacles. "More than I can put into words."

"Glad *someone* is having fun," Maria muttered.

"See, I can feel through our connection that you mean it, but your tone made it sound sarcastic."

"Yes," she agreed, refusing to elaborate.

As we watched the monolithic shadows our bodies were casting across the dunes, a comfortable silence appeared. It settled on our souls like an old sweater—stretched, faded, incredibly cozy. And surrounded by that pleasantness, my mind drifted toward the future. It didn't have to go far. My future was right beside me, her hand held in mine. Maria and I had both agreed it was time to plan our wedding. No matter what Ellis revealed today, I doubted it would be more important than marrying the wonderful woman next to me. An unseen breeze tousled her hair, revealing blushing cheeks and an adorable smile.

Oops. I hadn't meant to share that thought. Before either of us could address it, we arrived at the village. A welcome mixture of scents wafted out from between the buildings ahead of us.

"Ahhh," I sighed. "It smells even better than I remember."

"Agreed!" came a voice as livid as it was familiar. "What took you so long? Your coffee would have gone cold if you had waited one more damned minute to . . . *oh.*"

Sue, Tropica's barista extraordinaire, had come barreling around the corner like a raging bull. When she spotted the house-sized kraken, she missed a step. When she spotted the car-sized cuttlefish floating beside him, she missed another. I reached out with tendrils of lightning-fast chi, but she caught herself at the same time.

"Sooooo," she drawled, attempting to play it cool, her eyes lingering on the recently reawakened elemental. "Who wants some breakfast?"

I raised the cup to my mouth as we strode into the very center of town. Upon first seeing Tropica's transformation to a Tier 3 village, I'd thought the layout hadn't changed all that much.

I was wrong.

Tropica now had a square. I pictured scenes from every fantasy novel I'd ever read. All that was missing were armored guards, a town crier yelling from atop a rustic crate, and perhaps a cutpurse or two, their cowled forms slipping unnoticed between the crowd.

Of all those elements, only the crowd was present. They poured into a giant structure, its entrance similar yet different to what it had once been. We received countless weird looks as we joined the procession of people—especially from those unexpectedly robbed of sun by Fathom's massive shadow—but nowhere near as many as I thought our peculiar group of cultivators and elementals deserved.

I stole a glance at Cal as we wandered into the giant cement and stone entrance. He was already looking my way, and I shot him a wink. His tentacles twitched. Our connection was . . . weird. He wasn't bonded to me like my animal pals, but neither was he completely removed like Rocky. The name I'd given him had linked us somehow, and I couldn't help but wonder what our friendship would look like in the future.

My thoughts were immediately forgotten when we left the stone tunnel's confines. Blinding light met us, its brilliance coming from the sun and reflecting off the white marble that the half-amphitheater's steps and seating were now covered in. As my eyes adjusted to the brightness, sound assaulted my ears, a susurration of soft conversations amplified by the structure's acoustic design.

I withdrew my senses until the stimuli were no longer overwhelming. My friends and I made our way down one of two staircases to the stage, and the voices lowered, discussions dying when their speakers caught sight of us.

Of you, you mean, Maria corrected in a mental whisper.

I gave her an audacious amount of side-eye, or tried to, at least—there was no heat in it. She just smiled back and squeezed my hand. On my other flank, a wet nose nudged my wrist, and I reached out to rub Borks behind the ear. His soft fur was a balm for the faint hints of self-consciousness so much attention was causing me.

When I saw the rest of my closest pals milling around down by the stage, I forgot all about the eyes of the villagers. I had to actively stop myself from running down to greet them, but as I stepped from the last stair, I gave up, launching myself at the largest silhouette.

Teddy's peepers dilated for only a moment, then his arms spread wide—just in time for me to hit his solid chest. The others were there a moment later, joining the cuddle puddle.

Corporal Claws got there first, using her lightning to zap herself into my side. Next, Cinnamon. She rubbed her velvety fur across my arm, making sure to give the corporal a playful kick or two. Borks appeared as a Chihuahua, squeezing in beside the bunny. Maria wasn't one to miss a good cuddle; she wrapped her arms around me and the three smaller mammals. Air washed down from Pelly and Bill as they landed somewhere above us—likely on Teddy's head—the rest of the pelicans remaining perched on the stage's roof.

My careful consideration of avian positions ended as a tiny crab came flying in from nowhere. Sergeant Snips's spikes were covered by dull caps of water chi, and when she hit me, she spewed a stream of contented bubbles. The rest of her crustacean squadrons sent small waves of salutation from within her core, happy to remain there for now.

I thought that was the last of those who'd join, but for the second time in so many minutes, I was wrong. A buzzing in my chest announced the impending arrival of two royal insects, and as Bumblebro and Queen Bee vibrated their wings in greeting, I let my joy at their presence flow out. I knew they'd been up to something for the last month or so, and as thankful as I was for the upgrade their efforts had granted their progeny, I was even happier for them to be present more oft—

An insect slammed into my back. And another. *And another.* So many of the Buzzy Boys hit me that I lost count of their little bodies. Some of them must have flown from far away, because they'd not yet transformed—the event that happened when they touched one of their enhanced brethren. At least a dozen of them shook, then evolved, releasing small *pops* of pressure as plated chitin grew, mandibles extended, and stingers appeared.

Teddy had wrapped his arms around us all, but they abruptly opened, making way for . . . something. I was a little confused at first, but then I saw Pistachio and the boy atop his sturdy back. The lobster reached up, carefully grabbed the half-ascended lad, and chucked him at us. Teddy easily caught him. He lifted Paul onto his shoulders, whose eyes went round like coconuts. "Whoa! Teddy! You're *so tall!*"

Last but not least, a tiny hole appeared below. A single root shot up, which swiftly became ten, widening as they wrapped everyone present in a careful embrace.

"Hi, Lemon," Maria said, rubbing a cheek against Lieutenant Colonel Lemony Thicket.

I could sense two nearby sources of elemental chi, their abyssal and earthen aspects unmissable. I'd of course hoped they'd join in, but it was okay if they didn't—we'd eventually get Fathom and Cal to partake of their own free will.

Agreed, Maria thought.

Agreeeeed! a squeaky voice echoed into our minds. His crystalline form became squishy as he hit Maria's shoulder from above. He burbled there, information streaming from master to familiar. "Ooooooh. Cadet Calamari . . ." His body stretched as his head extended to look at the newly named cuttlefish. "I'm Slimes! Nice to meet you! I'm a—"

Someone cleared their throat, cutting him off. The sound was easy to ignore, but the chi that came along with it wasn't. Ellis's ideal pressed down on all of us, the knowledge his metaphysical library contained lending an unquantifiable weight to his request.

"Thank you," he said, giving us, then the rest of the crowd, an affable smile. "Would everyone please be seated? I must ask for stillness before I begin."

CHAPTER FOUR

God-King

As you all know by now," Ellis said, the left side of his face lit by the rising sun, "upon Fischer's completion of two quests yesterday, the System gifted him several rewards. Most obvious are the changes to the village—including the upgrades to the theater you currently sit within. But that's not why you're all here . . ."

Tension rose as he trailed off. No one said a word, yet the accumulated scrape of feet and shifting of bodies bounced off the half-amphitheater's walls, the individually quiet sounds becoming a roar. Only when it settled did Ellis continue.

"Whatever you might assume, let me assure you, the breadth, scope, and implications are likely beyond your most ambitious of estimations."

He paused again. This time, there wasn't a single sound. I craved the knowledge more than I could describe. In spite of that need, something else tugged at my thoughts.

He's saying the same words with the same cadence as before, Maria whispered into my mind, voicing it for me. *But it seems* cool *now.*

Right? How is he doing that?

As if he'd heard us, he removed a pipe from his pocket. The bowl lit itself when he puffed on it, a soft red glow visible even beneath the day's brightness. He filled his chest, savored the moment, then exhaled a thin stream of smoke to the side in an annoyingly cool manner. So fast that only those with advanced cultivation could notice, he shot Maria and I a wink before returning his attention to the crowd.

"Unfortunately," Ellis said, "I cannot reveal *all*. Not yet, anyway. I will be vague with some of the details, but that is by design. To ease your minds, let me say this: The information I withhold is not just being withheld from you, but the rest of Tropica as well—especially Fischer. Please confirm, Theo."

"*Truth!*" the Truthsayer cheerily called.

"With that out of the way," Ellis continued, "there are many things that I can reveal. First, as some of you might have already heard following the events of yesterday, the water gods betraying this world is a lie, but not a complete one."

Hundreds of exclamations and mutterings answered this claim. Ellis had expected it; he let the clamor rise and fall before speaking again.

"They did not turn their back on this world, but they *did* betray the divine gods—only, however, after those treacherous ascendants abandoned their oaths, the heavens, and every soul living in the Kallis Realm."

I already knew that much, but as the din once more swelled and died, I found myself leaning forward, drawn in nonetheless.

"The gods of the divine . . ." Ellis's mouth twisted in disgust. He took a tiny puff of his pipe, circulated chi through his core, then let out a slow, calming sigh. "Those supposedly righteous forces wanted more than they already had. For the sake of brevity, I will summarize a few points.

"Gods in this realm gain power not only from the world as cultivators, spirit beasts, or elementals do, but also from their faithful. The more followers they have, along with the capability of said followers, the stronger they grow. Factions can also be formed. Say five gods are separate, and each has one follower, they will be better off forming a faction if they are closely aligned. They won't each receive one hundred percent of each follower's faith—the calculation is both exceedingly complex and still up for debate—but one thing is certain: The more followers a faction has, the swifter its gods can ascend. So if a planet's pantheon were able to form a single, unified faction . . ."

Gods above, I thought as implications sprouted then bloomed like bloody roses.

"I see that most of you understand the gravity of what I just said, but let me state it plainly for clarity's sake: The divine gods spearheaded a campaign to unify this entire realm under one faction. It is unclear if the gods of water—those called the allied forces—were only pretending to go along from the start, but . . ." Ellis trailed off, glancing behind me.

Cal, in a gesture entirely too adorable for a horror from the deep—but just the right amount of cute for a bloke named Cadet Calamari—had raised a tentacle.

"Yes, Cal?" Ellis asked.

"May I add context to that statement?"

"So long as it only pertains to the knowledge of this realm . . ."

Cal nodded. "From what I have learned, the gods of water went along with it willingly at first. It was presented as a worthwhile risk. A gambit for power that, if it failed, would be abandoned. But then . . ."

"The divine gods did not stray from the path. Even when it started to hurt the realm's citizens, they didn't abandon the course," Ellis surmised.

"Just so."

The man before us swallowed to hide his anger, the emotion alien on his stoic features. "As I thought, but I digress." He resumed circulating his chi, letting his anger fall away. "Just as gods of water were generally ascended from spirit beasts and elementals, the divine gods almost exclusively came from human cultivators. When it became clear that spirit beasts and elementals could not become the faithful of this new faction—whose identity too closely resembled human sensibilities—a solution was presented."

"*Frack me* . . ." I said, already suspecting where he was going with it.

Ellis's gaze was rich with meaning. Sadness, fury, acceptance, and countless other emotions roiled behind his eyes. "You recall your deduction from weeks ago, Fischer? The one about why spirit beasts were feared by cultivators?"

"They go mad like old Rocky. He awakened by nibbling on that bloke who, despite having already carked it, hitched a ride within Rocky's core. It was only a part of him, but it was the *worst* part."

Ellis nodded. "As with all troublesome propaganda, there is a grain of truth in that, which the divine forces then twisted beyond recognition. Some spirit beasts and elementals *did* go mad, but only when they adopted the minds of those they ate. Some were evil to begin with, of course—that is just how any population works." I could feel Ellis's stare boring into me; he knew I was connecting the dots. He exhaled a cloud of smoke, his mouth trying to tug into a snarl as his calming circulation of chi fell apart. "Aye, Fischer. It's as you suspect."

My mind raced. The shock of it all made me lose hold of my otherwise controlled senses. Waves of confusion washed down from all around me. Ellis was still grappling with his emotions, so I explained.

"Self-propagating and self-fulfilling propaganda. The divine gods set up spirit beasts and elementals as the bad guys, suggesting they were inferior and untrustworthy. As a result, people hunted them down—especially those that were already a little loopy and inclined toward violence. If the cultivators win, great. One less spirit beast to contend with. If the cultivators lose and get eaten . . . the spirit beast might become changed by their personality."

"Which then becomes another example of a corrupted spirit beast for the divine gods to point to," Ellis continued, "drawing ever-increasing numbers of humans to their side. As Fischer so eloquently said: 'Self-propagating and self-fulfilling.' Brilliant, really. With each spirit beast and elemental eliminated, it would leave more natural chi for human cultivators to absorb, further pushing divine traitors toward the peak of ascension, and increasing the overall power of the faction."

Fathom nodded, glancing at Cal beside him. "We reached the same conclusion and later confirmed it. Your tomes are factual, Archivist Ellis, and your reasoning is sound."

"Truth," Theo repeated, his earlier exuberance replaced by numb certainty. "All of it."

I barely heard him. My core had latched on to something Fathom had said: the title he'd given Ellis. *Archivist.* Something resonated within me, acknowledging its veracity. Ellis had gone full circle and become an archivist again, but this time, it wasn't just a profession—it was a purpose, the ideal his very identity had used to facilitate his recent breakthrough, along with the creation of some kinda soul library.

Absentmindedly, I felt whispers of the myriad emotions washing down from everyone filling the stands. I closed myself off to them and returned to the present, forcing myself to focus on the dire revelations. "How long did all this go on for? Centuries?"

"Millenia, actually," Ellis replied. "The divine gods were careful. They methodically hid their actions by disseminating these lies through countless cults, all of which they started themselves by wearing false faces, pretending to be fledgling gods. I believe you know the pair behind it . . ."

"Dolos and Apate," Fathom and Cal hissed before I could, their cores and tentacles writhing.

"We will come back to them. First, we need to go in a different direction for a moment." A plume of smoke left Ellis's mouth, the biggest I'd seen him release. Despite everything, he wore the hint of a grin. "There is a single thing revealed in the tomes that I have been leaning on above all other positives to ease my troubled thoughts. Care to take a guess, Fathom? Cal?"

I didn't need to extend my senses to tell they knew exactly what he was talking about.

"Archivist Ellis . . ." Cal said, the tips of his limbs twitching about. "I believe you should have the honor. I cannot imagine how hard it has been learning all you have in so little time."

Fathom rumbled his agreement. "We know what you speak of, and we are glad it grants reprieve. I hope it does the same for everyone."

Abruptly, Ellis's grin appeared in full, his teeth glowing under the rising sun. "I will happily share. The revelation I adore most is the method with which the allied forces enacted their 'betrayal.' By the time they realized it was the divine forces behind all the upstart cults, it *should* have been too late. So many of the realm's spirit beasts and elementals had been driven mad or snuffed out that if they split from the singular faction, they'd have been annihilated immediately. They lacked followers and faith. Instead of accepting their fate, however, they got creative.

"It's something Tropica has used extensively, actually. Something . . . *beautiful.*" His eyes swam with amusement as he glanced around, his stare settling on me.

"No way," I said. "Don't tell me . . . Anime was right all along?"

Ellis blinked. "What?"

"Extensively used and beautiful. You're talking about the power of friendship, aren't you? I bloody *knew* it."

"Uhhh. No."

"Damn. Thought I was onto something there. Might need another hint, then, mate."

Ellis rolled his eyes at my ham-fisted injection of levity. "Very well. How is this for a hint?" He leaned forward and peered down at the three animals in my lap. "Corporal Claws is quite fond of—"

"Clams!" screamed Claws, so loud that my brain vibrated. "Are clams the key to power? Is that why I'm the strongest of all the animal pals? I—"

"Not clams," I interrupted, finally realizing. "*Oysters.*"

"Ohhhhh!" Maria clapped her hands together. "Iridescent stones. Is that right? They were the method of counterattack?"

"They weren't always the currency that they are now?" I asked. "That actually makes so much sense. Pearls forming in their environment is way too much of an advantage."

Ellis nodded. "Precisely. They were highly prized once, but only because of their beauty and scarcity."

Cal cleared his throat. "That is only half true. If you would allow it, Archivist Ellis and Traveler Fischer, I can share a relevant memory."

"Hell yeah," I answered. "I was just getting bored with Ellis's yapping."

"Please do," Ellis replied at the same time, his smile turning into a scowl as the end of my sentence came tumbling out.

A second later, thick tendrils of power flowed from Cal and into Fathom's core. There, it shifted, changed, and was ejected back out. That darkness engulfed the theater, allowing us to look through the eyes of another.

Cal was but a tiny little spirit beast in a wonderfully warm patch of ocean. He swam over the oyster beds below with great curiosity. He'd seen nothing like them in the weeks since his awakening.

He'd been listening to the cultivators that guarded and worked these beds, and had learned much about the world. A treaty existed between the denizens of land and sea, protecting and sharing the natural resources of each. Oysters were one such protected product. Or rather, the items they produced were. Iridescent stones had suppressing capabilities, allowing cultivators, spirit beasts, and elementals to coexist with beings of varied power. Without them, one might lose their temper and hurt or kill someone important, which could start a downward spiral of violence and vengeance.

From the whisperings of the cultivators present, all of whom belonged to the Church of Tides, Cal learned that the iridescent stones now being harvested were far more potent than they used to be. No longer would a crown of stones be needed to contain a cultivator's power—a few rings would do. And no longer was the Church of Tides sharing its bounty, instead storing the iridescent stones in the fathomless depths, where no divine would dare tread.

They told those who came seeking the gemstones that the oyster beds were diseased and no longer producing. That excuse worked for a time. After some years, however, the Divine Church discovered the duplicity, and they answered with significant force.

Hidden between the racks of oysters, Cal witnessed it all.

"For the crime of embezzlement, the Church of Tides is hereby disbanded!" a man in golden armor yelled, his legion of soldiers circling the shore. "All members and faithful are to face the judgment in the capital!"

Standing atop a wooden dock, only one man faced the army. His patchwork robes were threadbare, held together by sun-bleached twine and a crust of salt. "Wh-what? There has to be a mistake!" His eyes were wide, his body trembling as he gazed at the legion surrounding him. "We're a peaceful clergy! We serve the tides and all that dwell within! The ancient accords demand that you turn and—"

"Speak no more of your lies, betrayer! The gods know all!" A spear of light appeared in his hand, its tip pointing unwaveringly at the lone man on the dock. "Will you surrender willingly, or will you bring yet more shame to your fallen order?"

"The gods know all, you say?" The man's meek facade melted away, revealing a sharklike grin. "Those bastards you speak of aren't worthy of the title. The only thing they know is how to serve themselves."

Faster than Cal could register, the spear shot out. He had never seen the divine aspect unleashed, and in that moment, he hoped he'd never see it used again. The deadly point buried itself in the torso of the salt-crusted man, vanishing into his body rather than exiting out the other side. Terrible waves of hungering power radiated out and washed over Cal.

But judging by the face of the golden-armored man, something was wrong. His legion seemed to recoil, some even taking a step back. The man on the dock cackled, his arms raised in rapture, the waves of hunger growing stronger. "If your 'gods' knew all," he bellowed, his voice resonant with the desire to consume, "they would have sent more than the likes of you!"

"Abyssal cultivator!"

That was the last statement Cal heard. The world descended into chaos as he fled, his retreat aided by the shockwaves of countless attacks as a legion fought a lone cultivator.

The surrounding ocean wavered, then faded entirely, revealing a stage lit by the morning sun.

It took me a moment to realize the vision was over. "That . . . *Damn*." I shook myself as I got used to the sensations of my human body. "Was that the first time you heard about abyssal chi, Cal?"

"It was. If not for that chance encounter, I might never have learned of its importance in combating the divine."

Much to my delight, Ellis's cool disposition had melted away like butter on a hot pan. He was furiously scribbling in a notepad, and when I cleared my throat, he sniffed, stood upright, and sent the book back into his dimensional library with a flick of the wrist.

"A fascinating revelation," he said, once more circulating chi as he puffed on his pipe. "Thank you for sharing, Cal. My records were incomplete."

"No problem. The issue with first-person accounts is that . . . *is* . . ." Cadet Calamari dropped, half losing his mastery over gravity.

"Brother!" Fathom lunged forward, his tentacles a blur.

But Cal caught himself. "I'm—I'm fine. Sorry. I just had a moment of . . . I don't know what that was. Call it a side effect of my previous affliction."

I frowned at Cal's core. His *essence* felt fatigued. I didn't even know that was possible. Maria's connection to me flared with shock, then excitement, and finally shame. I squeezed her hand and sent reassuring thoughts her way. There was no need to be ashamed of her eagerness at the prospect of healing others.

Ellis took a single step that made him appear before the cuttlefish. "Are you okay for us to continue, Cal?"

"I am."

"Very well." Ellis stepped smoothly back onto the stage—damn it was annoying how cool he made that look. The cheeky bastard shot me another wink. "Thank you again for showing us. It is one thing to know what happened, but seeing the fervency of the *Divine Church* through your eyes really hammers home how effective their gods' propaganda was. The Church of Tides cultivator was right: If those holy forces knew he channeled abyssal chi, they would have sent far more than a legion his way. I'd bet my pipe on it."

I was nodding along with Ellis up until that last bit. I choked back a laugh. "Bloody hell, mate. Phrasing."

"What do you—*oh, hah-hah, Fischer.* Grow up."

"No."

A handful of soft laughs came from the crowd behind us. Maria snickered, too, abruptly stopping and averting her eyes when the archivist leveled a glare at her.

"So how did they, uhhh, do it, Ellis?" she asked.

"Increase the power of the iridescent stones?"

"Ya-huh. I get they were gods or whatever, but still . . ."

"Self-sacrifice," Ellis answered. "But also theft."

"*Oooo,*" cooed Claws and RPM, enamored by the merest hint of larceny.

I smiled down at them. "I'm guessing I know where at least some of that power was taken from. Would you mind, Borks?"

With a ruff, a wag of his tail, and a dozen rapid-fire licks to my forearm, he ripped open a small portal, from which I drew an unlocked item. I held it above my head for all to see. "Whatever was supposed to be in this chest, which is granted when people raise a skill to level 100—they stole that power, right?"

"And more, but that was the 'betrayal' part of it, yes. They also sacrificed their own bases of cultivation in order to save the world from becoming an autocracy— funny how that was not included in the histories the divine forces left behind."

"I bloody *knew* the water gods were the good guys. What a bunch of homies. Okay, so that explains why pearls are so useful for powering transforma—"

"Iridescent stones, you mean," Maria corrected, her face entirely too pleased.

"I've just thought of a new royal decree: They're called pearls for short now."

She snapped off a crisp salute. "Yes, God-King Fischer!"

"Wonderful. Also, anyone correcting me is sentenced to public quartering via Sergeant Snips." I tapped my chin in exaggerated thought. "Is that too harsh?"

"I believe so, God-King. Perhaps allow them to repent for their sins by delivering a delicious pastry to you? Or a tasty fish to Snips? We need to reward the sergeant for all the possible quarterings, you see. Executions are hungry work."

"A wonderful suggestion. Let it be law." I clapped my hands twice above my head like an absolute wanker before relaxing again, done with the charade. "As I was saying, we know why *pearls* are worth so much. One thing I still don't get is how all this led to the gods having to leave."

"I am hesitant to elaborate, Fischer," Ellis said. "If you would like to know, ask. If I have the knowledge and it does not exceed the scope of this realm, I will answer."

"You keep saying that. 'The scope of this realm.' That means you have knowledge of the . . . what did they call it? The heavens beyond?" I shook my head, stopping myself from diving into that rabbit hole just yet. "Never mind. What I don't get is, the pearls gave more power to the water gods, right?"

"Yes."

"And before that, the divine gods were trying to gain more power by forming a single faction, then straight-up icing anybody or anything that couldn't provide utility to said faction?"

". . . Icing?"

"Yeah, mate. Snuffing out. Dispatching. Putting someone on ice. Same same."

"I see," he said, his face telling me he absolutely didn't.

"Wonderful. Back to my first question, how did that cause all the gods to leave? Was that not what the divine gods wanted, hence their attempts to skip steps on the path of ascension or whatever?"

The archivist's eyes sparkled. "It is so refreshing talking to you, Fischer."

"I . . . I don't know what to say to that. Thank you?"

"Not surprised," Maria muttered to Claws. "People usually express the exact opposite."

I'd just started giving her an impassioned pout when Ellis shook his head, drawing my attention. "I cannot answer that question yet. I have theories, but they are out of scope. Still, your thinking is on the right track. It is a pleasant surprise compared to those I spoke to earlier . . ." He glanced meaningfully toward a section of the crowd, where Gormona's fishing club was seated. "Some of my frie—er, best to call them *colleagues*—are not so quick-witted."

"Keith . . ." someone asked in the silence that followed.

"Yes, Theo?"

"He just insulted us. Twice in one sentence."

"He did."

"He was joking."

"I thought so too . . ."

All four members of Gormona's fishing club stared up at the stage with expressions ranging from blank to confused to impressed.

Theo blinked. "It . . . it was actually *funny.*"

Ellis smirked. "Call it a joke if it makes you feel better."

"Theo . . ."

"Yes, Keith?"

"He just did it again."

Theo pinched his arm. "Perhaps we're dreaming?"

"That seems more likely . . ."

Barry cleared his throat handsomely—I wish he'd stop doing that—and stepped forward. "Before we get off track, Ellis, may I ask something?"

"Please do. I will answer if I can."

He paused for a short—and muscular—moment. "Am I correct in assuming we're all descendants of the divine gods' forces?"

"That is true, yes. I would not feel bad about it, though. Your ancestors could hardly be faulted for trusting their gods. There *is* one more revelation I wanted to broach, though . . ." The archivist trailed off, his eyes roaming before landing on his target.

"Ellis?" Theo asked.

"Yes?"

"Why are you staring at me, and why do you look so happy about it?"

He shook his head as if the knowledge he bore caused him great distress. "Do you recall Fathom's response to thinking you had lied?"

"I do . . ."

"The thing is, not everyone can become what you are. Auditor. Truthsayer. There are many other names for people with the skills you possess. Its origins transcend this world, which is perhaps why it lingered despite the absence of chi for millennia. By some accounts in the texts, it's a recessive gene. Others claim it's a power granted by the heavens, passed down by divine inspiration, not blood." The archivist shrugged. "I cannot say for sure, but that matters little compared to what I *can* say."

The look in his eyes grew taunting. Claws chirped softly, both she and RPM resonating with power as the tension grew. I grabbed Claws by the waist so she wouldn't get overexcited and zap someone.

Ellis's eyes drifted, leaving Theo to land on another. "Would you care to enlighten him, Fathom?"

"Falsesayers . . ." both cephalopods answered without missing a beat, their voices rumbling the ground. They glanced at one another, a slight sense of camaraderie taking the edge off their visceral reactions.

Fathom explained. "Falsesayers are Truthsayers that forsook—*tainted*—their very souls. It is hard to put enough emphasis on how twisted one's spirit becomes as a result. For those of you who have solidified an ideal, think of your purpose, then imagine poisoning your core until it became the exact opposite of what it is now."

I shivered. The idea of it made me sick.

Cal spat a squirt of water onto the ground—which was actually quite cute despite his intent—and shook his many tentacles. "I came face-to-face with one once. I could show you with my aura, but it's unnecessary. You'll know if you meet such a being."

"Okay," Theo said. "That's pretty fracked up, but I fail to see what . . . *Ohhhh.*"

"Indeed. I was planning on letting you sweat a little, but I can see you've already worked it out. A shame."

Theo grinned, the two men sharing a moment.

"Uhhh," I said, frowning as I ruined said moment. "Is this what it feels like when I keep you guys out of the loop?"

"Yes," Maria answered. "How does it feel?"

"Terrible."

"Does that mean you'll stop?"

"What? No. I can just declare a new decree. Henceforth—"

"No leaving God-King Fischer out of the loop?" Theo interrupted.

"Yes. But also, no finishing God-King Fischer's sentences. It's rude and it hurts my feelings."

"Aye, sir!" he yelled, snapping off a salute so crisp it couldn't be anything other than mocking.

"Good. I love when my peons learn from their mistakes. Now, before your benevolent leader starts lopping off heads—or sentencing people to quartering by crab—can you please share with the class the subtext of your conversation?"

"Ellis was implying that I am descended from the forsaken. You said you were going to loop Dolos and Apate back in. The two trickster gods. They created Falsesayers?"

"Correct."

Theo nodded. "Good."

I raised an eyebrow at him. "Good?"

"Yep. It clears me of any guilt, even if I am their direct descendant. Just like with the misled faithful to the divine forces, you can hardly blame people for being fooled by their deities. The fault rests solely on the shoulders of the gods."

I expected Ellis to continue, but he puffed at his pipe instead. Twin streams of smoke flowed from his nostrils, dissipating as they hit the wooden stage and curled outward. "I believe that is almost all for today." Since the start of his lecture, he'd been focused on those of us closest to him, only shooting passing glances at the rest of the villagers. Now, he watched them intently, his affable demeanor replaced by something firm and cold. "We have arrived at the reason for this meeting. Please listen well to what I say next."

His words drew on our cores. Everyone leaned in, going silent. He knew he'd hooked us, yet it brought him no joy. Anticipation coursed through my veins. Claws shook in my arms, her jolts of lightning crawling across my chest and tickling my skin.

What he said next exceeded my wildest expectations. "Tropica is not safe." His tone was blasé, almost conversational. Only his eyes betrayed his true feelings, weighing our reaction with silent intensity.

I turned to gaze up at Theo, already knowing what he would say. He gave the slightest of nods. "Truth . . ."

"I apologize again for being vague," Ellis continued, his casual words penetrating the silence. "It is as necessary as it is regretful. If this village—this *world*—continues on its current trajectory, we will one day be conquered. It is likely a distant threat, but a threat all the same."

My mind sped away from me. Tropica in ruins, its buildings decimated. My friends fleeing, my power insufficient against a rising tide of faceless attackers. Fear and doubt swelled all around me, the village's emotions overwhelming my senses. Maria's hand brushed up against mine, a lighthouse in the storm. I breathed a shaky sigh as I forced most of the crowd's despair from my core, leaving only mine.

Ellis let out an uneven breath of his own. "I am sorry I had to share this burden with you. If I could, I would have gladly kept it to myself. If we want to retain control of our lives, however, it is imperative that we all know what is at stake."

Without realizing it, I had gotten to my feet. "You still won't tell me what's going on, Ellis?"

He gave me a sad smile. "I cannot, for telling you will hurt our chances of success."

Anger flared in the pit of my stomach, a bitter storm that scoured away all the levity and joy of this morning. I thought of forcing Ellis to give me the books in his library. I weighed the morality of it, considering the books were a reward for a quest *I* had finished. How would a fight between us go? Before I could stop it, my mind envisioned it, enacting different avenues of attack, seeking the one that would do the least amount of harm.

Maria squeezed my arm, and I returned to myself. Across from me, Ellis's gaze flicked toward my tensed fist, then back to my eyes. "You consider making me tell you?"

"I have a Domain's worth of chi flying through me, mate. I consider a lot of things without meaning it. My thoughts tend to race out ahead of me."

A smile played across his lips. "You would not need to force me, Fischer. If you demanded it, I would tell you."

His words calmed my rage. Abruptly, I realized I wasn't angry with him at all. I lacked control of the situation, which made me feel unsafe and triggered a fight-or-flight response. I knew Ellis. He was my friend. The archivist was just as aggrieved by the idea of losing Tropica as I was.

"So you would tell me . . . but it would hurt our chances of success," I finished, relaxing my fist and letting out a long sigh. "What do we need to do, mate? How do we keep everyone safe?"

"Oh, that's simple. For everyone other than you, anyway. *Crafting.*"

He ashed his pipe, letting his proclamation sit with the crowd. Dozens of murmured conversations sprang to life around us. Only when they died down did I continue.

"Crafting?"

"That's right." Eliss repacked his pipe with a pinch of material. "What we need is more stats. More levels. The future of this village—of this entire *realm*—is bright, but only if we advance even faster than we have been. The best method of doing so is by raising our System-granted professions."

"And me?" I asked. "How do I keep everyone safe?"

"Your task is a little more challenging, I'm afraid—you have to let them."

". . . Let them?"

"That's right. Let them succeed. Let them flounder. Let them *fail.* You are unimaginably strong, Fischer. Your existence is the reason we have come so far. But if you want Tropica to soar to new heights, you can't always be there. Just as a baby bird needs to risk hitting the ground if it wishes to fly, the people of Tropica must be allowed to spread their wings."

"I've already been doing that."

"You have," he agreed, "but only up to a point. You step in if anyone's life is ever in danger."

"Uhhhh, yeah. Of course I do. You're ordering me to let my friends die?"

"I am not ordering you to do anything. You're the god-king, remember? I am merely suggesting that, if you truly wish for the people around you to reach their full potential, you have to give them the agency to try."

I sucked air through my teeth. "Damn. That *is* more challenging."

"If you think that is bad, wait until you hear about the other task."

"Come again?"

"There is something else you have to do. I cannot tell you yet."

"Mate . . . you've gotta give me *something*."

"If I inform you now, it will hurt our—"

"*Chances of success*," I interrupted, unable to hide my frustration. "That's not enough, Ellis. I'm serious. I can't just go along with your every whim."

He raised his hands placatingly. "Peace, Fischer. I swear on my life that I will share it with you as soon as I can. Until then, I suggest you focus on the idea of letting people fail. Danger is coming. It is only a matter of time. If you continue to coddle everyone, they might not survive the eventual storm."

If his words were meant to make me forget about the second task, they worked. The air grew still as not only me, but everyone in the stands chewed on his message. I started to wonder what I could say to dissolve the rising tension, but then a familiar voice did it for me.

"What about us? What profession do we . . ." Bonnie trailed off and cleared her throat when she realized she'd broken the silence. "Errr, can I ask a question, Archivist Ellis . . . *sir?*"

He laughed. It was rich and filled with all the joy missing from the last few minutes. "Go ahead, Bonnie. No need for titles or honorifics."

"Which professions should we focus on, and should we go all in on one, or branch out into a bunch?"

"A wonderful question, as expected of such an adventurous soul. It doesn't particularly matter. As with most things related to advancement or creation, listen to your instincts. Spend time doing whatever makes you happy."

"Fu—er, frack yeah, I mean. Cheers, Ellis!"

I had to pinch my lips, lest my laugh escape. I'd clearly influenced her during our time at sea.

"No," Ellis replied. "Thank you for listening—and that goes for everyone. Now, what do we have to say?"

I frowned up at him. Was he expecting everyone else to give their thanks? It seemed a bit . . . *wanky*, if I was being honest. Where had the calm and collected Ellis . . . *gone?* He stared back at me, his eyes aglow with mischief. What was he—

"Thank you, God-King Fischerrrr," the villagers all droned with the slow, inflectionless cadence of students addressing a teacher.

I rolled my eyes. "Mate, I've already gotten over the whole leadership complex. I'm the one who started jokingly calling myself that. If you think I'm gonna get flustered over a harmless prank, you've got another thing com—"

Something pressed into my core. Like an ephemeral hand, it reached through me, only solidifying right in the center of my being. The spot grew warm, then scorching as a mark was stamped onto my soul.

I stared within for a long moment, waiting for it to fade. It didn't. I looked up at Ellis. The more my eyes narrowed, the wider his grin grew.

"Ellis . . . ?"

"Yes, Fischer?"

"What the frack did you just do to me?"

"Nothing you would not have agreed to. Though I am sorry that I did not warn you in advance. Your ignorance was imperative."

"Truth," Theo said.

I groaned and ran my hands through my hair.

"But you should not worry anyway, *God-King*," Ellis continued, a devious smile making its way to his face. "As you said, 'twas nothing but a *harmless prank*."

Theo cleared his throat and leaned forward, ensuring I didn't miss an inch of his amused smile. "Lie."

CHAPTER FIVE

Empress

Far, *far* away, an empress sat in deep meditation, her core temporarily deconstructed, mind focused on examining the hidden pathway her chi tended to travel. It was a precarious road to walk. A single misstep would leave her crippled if she were lucky, dead if she were not. It was fortunate, then, that oceans separated her kingdom from the meeting now concluding on a distant continent—such knowledge, if learned in this moment, would end her.

Empress Aletheia let out a controlled breath as she finished tracing the length of her core in its entirety. She'd originally succeeded in separating it months ago, her usually spherical nexus of power shifting to resemble a knot of roots, but this was the first time she'd managed to explore it all without needing a break. She thanked the heavens for this victory, remaining in the moment for a score more breaths.

Finally, she opened her eyes. At the state she found her five attendants in, confusion threatened to extinguish her lingering peace. "Might I ask what you're all doing?"

"Forgive me, Empress!" Evan yelled, not looking up from his prostrate position. "I almost let the veil slip!"

"I'm not trying to place blame here, but wasn't it Grace that almost faltered? You saved it."

Grace flinched, but it was Evan who replied. "As head mage of the Prime Cadre, the fault is mine, Empress! The fact you were interrupted enough to identify where the error began only further incriminates this lowly servant!"

"I'm not sure that's the case. With that logic, wouldn't it then be *my* fault? It was I who chose you all for this task, was it not?"

"I would never imply such a thing, Your Holiness!" Evan somehow got even closer to the ground. "On the service my family has given House Veritus over the centuries, I beg your forgiveness! I will accept any punishment necessary!"

Aletheia frowned, sending out tendrils of essence to check if the man derived pleasure from chastisement. He didn't, of course, and when she realized what she'd just done, she laughed—which only made Evan, and the rest of the Prime Cadre, flinch.

Her meditative haze remained, allowing her to see the humor in this one-sidedly fraught exchange. She shook her head and reached out with her senses again, this time with thick tendrils, sharing her thoughts and feelings. It was taxing, especially after hours of mindful examination, but she owed it to them—the least she could provide was reassurance after accidentally inflicting panic upon such reliable followers.

All five of the hooded attendants inhaled sharply, their bodies snapping upright, their eyes wide.

"Empress . . ." Evan swept his hood back, revealing dark shoulder-length hair. "You offer too much. Kindness and effort both."

"Nonsense. This introspective method of advancement is only possible because of your efforts. If not for you mages, it would be too dangerous to even consider."

"But . . ." Grace cleared her throat. "If my failure had caused you to get distracted. If you'd lost control of your chi the way I had—"

"Then it would have been the will of the heavens." She gave them a wink. "And I wouldn't be the divine bridge after all. Wouldn't that put a burr in the Seers' breeches?"

Grace laughed, as did her twin brother, Esmond. They swiftly realized their error, faces going still.

"Please," Aletheia said, getting to her feet. "How many times have I told you all that you need not be so formal in private? Loath as I am to admit its necessity in public, there's no one else here right now."

"We understand your position," Evan replied, "and, as ever, we appreciate your kindness. But—"

"'But it's best to err on the side of caution, lest decorum slip,'" she quoted, reciting the thoughtful and carefully worded response she'd heard a thousand times. "Very well. You win this round."

"I look forward to the next," the head mage replied, flashing a cheeky grin for so short a time that only a divine cultivator could catch it.

Aletheia got to her feet and stretched, enjoying the sensations of taut muscles and warm skin, the latter coming from the sun that beamed through mosaic glasswork high above. The ritual room they occupied was near the top of the castle, dozens of floors from the ground, and though that was not much distance when it came to celestial bodies, it made her feel closer to that burning giver of life. She sank into the moment, staring directly at the star, its brilliance not damaging her enhanced—

A soul called out. Kilometers from the kingdom's walls, right at the distant edge of her influence. The panic in its wordless plea melted away the pleasant sensations, along with any meditative peace still lingering. "Evan!"

"At once, Empress!"

Aletheia rushed to sit, this time on the outside of the ritual circle she'd left only moments ago. "You have the strength?"

"Yes, Empress!" they called in perfect unison, their self-reproach gone, their gazes fixed and cores reaching for power.

"Here, or . . . ?" Evan asked.

"Here."

The head mage's eyes flicked toward her, displaying a hint of a question, but it passed a fraction of a second later. No matter how much Evan cared for Aletheia's safety, he knew now wasn't the time to voice suspicion about her agents.

Riddled with fatigue and worry, the empress raised her arms high, drawing in the sun's divine rays as she pictured her target's face. The ritual circle shifted and swirled, its intricate lines writhing like so many snakes. The moment they ceased dancing, a feeling of rightness flooded out. Aletheia opened her core, instantly powering the ritual. A flash of light. A consoling warmth. And a man appeared, back arched and limbs splayed in ecstasy at being directly touched by the will of the heavens.

As the golden aura disappeared from the room, the spy shuddered, falling to his knees, taking a gasping breath. Aletheia took a single step that sent her to the middle of the massive ritual circle.

"Empress!" Evan yelled.

Aletheia didn't listen. She caught the man, actively stopping her muscles from squeezing him too tight. "Sven . . ." she said, eyes darting from her trusted agent's eyes to his bare chest. The artifact. It was *gone*. "Your amulet . . ."

Hating that she had to do it, she let her divine chi flood out and suffuse his skin, the essence ready to cleanse her spy from his realm if evil had taken root in his soul.

"Lost," Sven groaned, his throat sounding as dry as his chapped lips looked. "At sea, Your Holiness. I'm not . . . corrupted . . ."

It was the truth—the *complete* truth. Aletheia didn't suppress the tears of relief that swelled in her eyes. "Fetch this man water," she said to the room. "Food, too. The thin soup from this morning, if any remains. Bring nothing too heavy."

"At once!" Grace replied.

"Yes, Your Holiness!" Esmond added, the twins sprinting away.

Aletheia smiled weakly at Sven as she lowered him to the ground. "Forgive me, but I can't let you eat too much, no matter the strength of your cultivation. Even I can be hurt by prolonged malnourish—"

"Unimportant, Aletheia," he interrupted. "I bring *news*—" He broke off with a hacking cough, anger flaring from his core at his body's failure.

She couldn't help but raise a brow, neither bothered by the interruption nor lack of honorifics. For this particular agent to drop them, his tidings must be dire.

A displeased noise escaped Evan's throat, and Aletheia shot him a look before returning her attention to the man she'd sent to a faraway continent. "Save your strength, Sven. You're already weeks past your reporting date. We can wait ten more minutes."

The spy must have known it would take no longer than that to recover, yet his eyes remained panicked. "Weeks? Spirit beasts in the capit—" He coughed once more, dry and sharp and pained.

Spirit beasts? Aletheia thought, not allowing herself to speak, lest Sven feel pressure to reply.

"Sorry!" Grace yelled, flying into the room. "No water jugs this high up! Had to go all the way to the kitchens!"

She was at Sven's side in an instant, her limbs aglow with thin strands of golden chi. The entire time, Aletheia's enhanced mind raced. *Spirit beasts in the capital—that was what he'd tried to say.* She had sent Sven to the capital city of Gormona, on the continent of the same name. Ostensibly, he was a honey merchant. In truth, he was a spy assigned to investigate the royal family, along with the existence of ancient relics.

Her gaze flicked up, eyeing two such artifacts. So long had they sat inert that they were just another part of the room. Phostheia, capital of the Kingdom of Light, had once owned a vast horde of the treasures, amassed by ancestors and exploits long forgotten. What wasn't forgotten, however, was why Phostheia no longer possessed them.

Gormona.

They had stolen them by force, employing methods of cultivation that defied the low level of chi suffusing the world. The records spoke of enslaved cultivators, which Aletheia, if she was being honest, had suspected was a lie—propaganda deployed to instill hatred of that antagonistic kingdom. Until Sven's first trip there almost two years ago had confirmed the disgusting truth of it. To think humans, beings shaped by the heavens, could do such a thing to others of the divine form . . .

Spirit beasts in the capital, she repeated internally, centering herself.

If that wasn't heavenly punishment, she didn't know what was. For Sven to return so panicked, these spirit beasts he spoke of clearly weren't weak. Gormona's royal family had fled or fallen—it was the only possibility that made sense.

Which boded well for the requisitioning of artifacts. Spirit beasts were mindless creatures of consumption; they wouldn't go out of their way to destroy or steal anything they couldn't gain power from. As soon as that thought passed, Aletheia felt a wave of vitriolic self-disgust. What kind of woman would celebrate such a tragedy? People had *died.* Even if the royal family had remained to fight the beasts before fleeing, the collared cultivators would have been sent in first.

Anger flashed through her core. She had wanted to free them. Their safety was the only reason she hadn't raised the banners of war and sailed for Tropica the moment she had learned of their enslavement.

Her abdomen turned radiant, a tiny sphere mirroring the sun's brilliance.

She had delayed in hopes of attaining another breakthrough first. She knew her forces were already strong enough to shatter that continent's seat of power, but without hurting a single of the collared? It required overwhelming might. Enough potency to disarm every cultivator there. She had been too late.

The star within doubled, tripled, doubled again. Aletheia wished she could take it all back. She should have gone to Gormona earlier. She should have toppled the royals, even if it meant their destruction. If she hadn't clung so tight to her peaceful intentions, the slaves would have lived. In denying violence, she had caused suffering.

"I was a fool," she declared, her voice resonating with truth. There was something here. A bridge toward the heavens, paved with stones from the rubble of her folly. Taking a deep breath, she listened to her soul, stating that which her new worldview demanded.

"If something does not serve me or humanity, it is my obligation to burn it away." Her core hummed in agreement, urging her to continue. "Discard old ideology if it no longer suits." That was on the right path, but there was more to it. A brutal truth sitting in the back of her mind, waiting to be voiced. In trying to save everyone in Gormona, she had doomed them all.

She swallowed, shutting her mind off and letting the words flow. "Kill the few, save the many."

Radiating heat and fury and regret, her abdomen thrummed alongside her thoughts. Suddenly, it unwound, turning into a familiar knot of roots. Incandescent passion—a desire to save humanity—flowed in, racing along the infinite loop of her soul. Her ideal. She had found it. And all too late, she realized her error.

Aletheia focused on the outside world. All eyes were on her, their faces lit by the deepest gold imaginable. Her breakthrough. It had already begun—and it would destroy them. Her Prime Cadre of mages and her finest spy, all burned away by her lack of care. Her heart should be shattering, but all she could feel was ecstasy, her soul rejoicing at the ideal she'd finally found. To rejoice in such a moment . . . it was *wrong*.

Were the Seers' predictions incorrect? she wondered. *Has evil infected my spirit, creating another weapon of war instead of a unifying bridge?*

No, her very identity replied, urging her to actually *see* them—her allies, her *friends*.

A grin on Evan's face, shock on Sven's, resolve on all the others. The ritual circle from earlier. They were touching it. Reshaping it. Esmond had just run into the room. The bowl of soup he'd fetched was in free fall. Even as it tumbled to the ground, its contents spilling, his foot brushed the ritual's edge, his essence flowing down and powering the only thing keeping Aletheia's breakthrough from incinerating them all.

The lines snapped into place. Divine light raced along the infinite path of her core. Not a knot of roots at all—a serpent eating its own tail. Ouroboros, the endless cycle of life and death. She finally understood. This was what she had been missing. One could not flourish without the other.

There was no sound as her core's new form solidified. Golden rays shot in every direction, passing through stone and mortar like the sun's light through mosaic glass.

She felt every one of her subjects. Echoes of their surprise, joy, love. All understood what had happened. Thousands of them, each stunned by the weight of her brilliance. She sent them her thanks. If not for them, she would be nothing. Above all else, a single word came her way, repeated sporadically, then all at once, her followers' voices combining as they chanted.

"Empress! Empress! *Empress!*"

The golden light returned, knocking the wind from her lungs as their intention slammed into her core. *Empress.* She could feel the title within, a brand upon her identity. No longer was it an honorific. She had been recognized—by the System, her subjects, and the very heavens.

"Your Holiness," Sven said, eyes wide and vigor returned. "Empress Aletheia. Please forgive my insolence. I bring dire news from the capital city of Gormona. Spirit—" He cut off abruptly, every head turning to look at a far wall.

Despite her lingering breakthrough and recently discovered ideal, she was also stunned into silence. A whirring sound came from two artifacts, the twin prizes her forbears had managed to hide from an invading force. The noise was soft, yet it grated at her enhanced hearing. Both screens flickered, lit, and enacted their ancient directive, the leftmost producing a result sooner.

Local Domain detected.
Effect: 20% Suppression, 20% Bolstering, 20% Growth

A Domain. *Her* Domain. She'd long known about it, but never had the effects been quantified. It was no wonder her forces had been progressing so swiftly. How long had the growth been—

More lines printed out below the others.

Warning! Foreign Domain detected

. . .

[Error: Tier 3 Village]

"Gormona?" she wondered aloud. Surely it could be no other. What was the significance of its tier? Had the royal family survived after all if their Domain remained? "Sven, what were you going to—"

More words in bold interrupted her. This time, they were directly in her field of view.

New Quest: In Defense of Phostheia
Objective: A Tier 3 Village has been detected. Are its citizens enemies or allies to your cause? Gather relevant intelligence.
Progress: 0/3
Reward: Domain evolution

She blinked, clearing her vision. A grin tugged at her lip, but it wasn't just because of the System's direct contact. Gormona's royals might have lived after all. If they'd survived, perhaps the collared cultivators had, too.

She opened her mouth to speak, but then a surge of chi caught her attention, the other relic fulfilling its purpose for the first time in centuries, if not millennia.

Phostheia, capital of the Kingdom of Light, has chosen a ruler!
Long live Empress Aletheia of House Veritus!

She had to look away. Her breakthrough being acknowledged by the heavens was too much. She stared up at the midmorning sun, its brilliance and warmth embracing her. The brand on her soul seemed to tingle. It was just as the Seers had said— she, Aletheia Veritus, empress of Phostheia and ruler of the Kingdom of Light, was the divine bridge that would connect this lower realm to the heavens above.

"Sven!" she yelled, voice exuberant as her eyes darted toward her loyal spy. "Tell me all about what you saw! There might yet be time to save the collared! I got a *quest*! If I can learn three secrets, our Domain . . ." She trailed off, confusion shining from within. "Sven? What's wrong?"

He remained unaffected by her words. His core was numb, and only when she focused in on it did she sense the vaguest hint of fear. She followed his gaze to stare at the screen which had him transfixed. The second relic. More lines had appeared below those that referenced her breakthrough. She read the first.

Tropica, capital of Gormona, has chosen a ruler!

Before she could continue onto the next, the System spoke directly to her again.

Quest: In Defense of Phostheia
Intelligence gathered: Tier 3 Village is named Tropica
Progress: 1/3

She flailed, sending that message—a direct missive from the heavens—hurtling away as if it were trash. She had to read the rest of the information displayed on the relic. Who had Tropica chosen as a ruler? Had King Augustus somehow used the spirit beasts in the capital to leverage a breakthrough?

She read the rest of the screen. Then she read it again. And again. And *again*.

Another heaven-sent missive arrived to commandeer her vision.

Progress: 2/3

If she learned one more piece of information, her Domain would evolve. She found she didn't much care. The joy of its impending completion had turned to ash in her mouth.

She stepped to the side, an empress reduced to a child of the heavens, seeking the sun's guidance from what light shone down through the stained-glass windows about. Those brilliant rays provided neither warmth nor comfort as she read the screen once more, hoping—*praying*—they had changed.

They hadn't.

Tropica, capital of Gormona, has chosen a ruler!
Long live God-King Fischer, [error] of [error]!

CHAPTER SIX

Planning

Sir!" Theo boomed, his heels clicking together as he snapped to attention. "Forgive my impropriety! I didn't expect your greatness to walk the streets with us commoners!"

I rubbed my temples. "For the love of any non-divine gods that might yet be hiding away in this realm, please stop doing . . . whatever this is."

"At once, sir!" He snapped off an antagonistic salute. "Anything the God-King demands! Long live God-King Fischer!"

"*Long live God-King Fischer!*" the exiting crowd echoed, dozens of Tropica cultivators taking up the call. Even Cal and Fathom joined in from down the street, immediately stabbing me in the back with tentacle-gripped knives.

It was too soon for me to laugh about the events of the so-called "meeting." Ellis's declaration that Tropica was in danger had knocked me off balance, then whatever he'd done to my core had pulled the rug out from under me, but the surrounding smiles did wonders for my spirits. As did Claws, Cinnamon, and Snips, who were still cradled in my arms.

I tried to take solace in the fact that pranking me had lifted Tropica's spirits. It worked until the self-satisfied giggles of an archivist oozed from somewhere within the mass of awakened humans around me. His somber attitude had vanished the moment his "prank" had come together. I wasn't sure if it genuinely tickled him pink, or if he was playing up his amusement for everyone's sake, doing what he could to lift their spirits. One thing was certain: It was annoying as hell.

"Maria?" I asked.

"Yes, dear?"

"Do I deserve this?"

"Afraid so."

I let out an exaggerated sigh. "Like Icarus, I silly-goosed too close to the sun."

My followers—my *taunters*—smiled all the more. One was particularly egregious, and I raised a brow at her. "What's so funny, Bonnie? You looking to get latrine duty?"

She cocked her head. "We have latrines?"

"You know what? I'm not sure. I *did* order some built. Maria, how goes the creation of . . ." I sighed again, dragging it out until my lungs were empty. "I can't even use the god-king joke anymore. It just doesn't hit the same when I actually am one."

"Oh noooo," Maria drawled. "Whatever will we do?"

Despite her words, she sent a soothing pulse of essence my way, checking if I was okay. I replied in kind, trying to reassure her, but I could tell by the look in her eyes that she sensed the undercurrents of worry. With no small amount of reluctance, I temporarily closed our connection. Maria, knowing my reasoning, followed suit. I didn't want to talk about it here. Not in front of everyone.

So I sighed instead. "You could at least pretend to feel sorry for me."

"I would, dear," she said, going along with it after a slight pause. "But I can tell you don't really care."

"Maria! I'm trying to make Ellis feel bad!"

She glanced to the side, eyeing the archivist now visible through the thinning crowd. "I don't think it's working."

"It is not," he confirmed, trotting off northward with a skip in his step. "If anybody needs me, I will be in the alchemical workshop. Will I see you there, Solomon? Francis?"

"Aye!" both called.

I watched the cheeky bastard and his two alchemical associates go. Getting one over on me had made him shine with joy. A warm gust blew past, its touch tickling my hair and skin. All around us, similar conversations were taking place, Tropica's citizens planning, debating, and verbally processing which profession suited them best.

Despite the brand now seared into my very soul, I felt an immense sense of gratitude as the discussions washed over me. An otter's whiskers brushed my cheek, Corporal Claws giving me a soft little smooch before bolting away. Hopefulness poured from her core. I wondered what it was about, but then I got a second whiskered kiss on the other cheek. Cinnamon leaped off and was caught by Pelly, who'd swooped down to collect her.

Part of me wanted to ask what their plans were—their cores were practically screaming with purpose—but my mind was busy replaying Ellis's words. The only creature remaining in my arms blew a stream of reassuring bubbles. Sergeant Snips wiggled into the nook of my elbow. She had no intention of leaving.

Maria grabbed my hand. "Shall we go find a quiet place to do some planning of our own?" Her heart fluttered with meaning; mine thumped in response. Snips blew a single anticipatory bubble, which floated up, its rainbow sheen beautiful under the morning's rays.

"Walk or teleport?"

"Hmm. Usually I'd say walk, but you *did* just become god-king. I think you owe it to the village to show your power off."

"Agreed!" Bonnie said. "You know what would *really* show everyone how powerful you are? If you send me to the smithy, along with a half dozen croissants. And a passiona treat or two."

I shot her an askance look.

"What? A woman has to eat. Smithing is hungry work."

"Smithing, huh? I should have known you'd settle on that." I needed to see how my essence felt now anyway, so I raised both hands and clicked my fingers. There were two surges of power, both accompanied by flashes of light, one beside me, the other on a street over.

Damn, I thought, wincing. The mark on my soul had altered my chi. Each strand now had a sort of "weight" to it, for lack of a better word. Stronger. More capable. Much harder to control.

A startled noise came from the other street. It was Sue, clearly unhappy with the pastry-stealing flashbang I'd just bombed her bakery with.

"Time to go," I said, nodding my head toward the ocean. We vanished in another flash of light, my essence becoming further known to me, the strands more . . . *something*. Confined, yet authoritative? It was hard to put it into—

"Thank you!" Bonnie yelled, loud enough for me to hear from the smithy halfway across the village.

"*Fischer!*" Sue bellowed even louder, the sound waves reverberating off the buildings near the dock's entrance. "Steal pastries like that again, and there won't be coffee for a week!"

I blinked at Maria. "Think she means it?"

"Are you willing to test her?"

"Nope. I might be a god-king, but . . ." I trailed off at my own reminder of the things that had happened this morning. Now that I wasn't surrounded by Tropica's citizens, fears and doubts crashed against my psyche like a tsunami.

"Come on," Maria said, abruptly grabbing my hand and leading me away.

"Where are we going . . . ?"

"To do the one thing I *know* will help you sort through your emotions. Besides . . ." She glanced back at me, then out at the ocean, squinting against the sun's brilliance. "It's a perfect day for it."

CHAPTER SEVEN

Fishing

Waves crashed against the rocky shore. A serendipitous gust of wind whipped the salty droplets skyward, and as they spattered against me, my gratitude grew like sugarcane under the summer sun.

Maria had been right. It was a wonderful day for fishing.

We were down on the headland, standing on the slick rocks by the mouth of the river. We'd originally headed for the stone pier, but after spotting Peter, his apprentice chefs, and Theo already fishing there, we decided on somewhere a little more private.

I realized my thoughts were drifting, so I focused on the sensations of my body—the ocean's mist kissing my skin, the line taut against my index finger, the warmth of my future wife resting against my side. All the worries plaguing me less than an hour ago suddenly seemed unimportant. They drifted further away when the smooth section of an otherwise spiked claw brushed against my leg.

I smiled down at my trusty guard crab. "Are you unsure of your purpose, too, Snips? Is that why you didn't dash away like our other pals?"

She shook her carapace, blowing negative bubbles.

"Oh. Why are you here, then?"

Her eyes were narrowed in befuddlement. "Master . . . are you dumb?"

"Well, yes, but—"

She cut me off with a torrent of bubbles, their meaning clear.

"I love you too, Snips," I said, bending down to pat the top of her mighty shell.

"Hey now . . ." Maria leaned over from my other side with an exaggerated pout. "First you lock me out of your mind, now you're confessing your love for another woman? What gives?"

I wrapped my right arm around her. "Forgive me, darling. Snips is just so . . . carapacey, and I lose myself around her." I kissed the top of Maria's head. "I promise I'll change once we're married."

I expected her to quip back. To either double down on the allure of Snips's shell or joke about leaving me for Rocky. Instead, she went silent.

"Maria . . . ? You know I was kidding, right? I'm sorry if I went too far with—"

"It's not that," she interrupted. "I just . . ." She took a few beats to gather her thoughts before continuing. "You don't need to avoid the truth with jokes, Fischer. I can handle it."

I started to laugh but trailed off when Maria remained stoic, her eyes glued to the spot where her line entered the water.

I peered down at Snips. She gave me the crabby equivalent of a shrug, which was *still* impressive given her lack of shoulders. I turned back toward Maria. "Uhhhh, just to be clear, I do love Snips, but she's a *crab*. An adorable, lovely, trustworthy crab, but a crab nonetheless."

Now it was Maria's turn to look confused. "What in Eris's winged sandals are you talking about?"

"What—" I cut off as a fish bit down on my hook and sped away. I set the hook, started reeling it toward the shore, and repeated my question. "What are *you*—"

"Fish on!" Maria yelled as her line cut through the water, her reel screaming, her rod bent almost in half. "Sorry, Fischer. What were you about to—"

Snips cut her off with an exasperated hiss, gesturing emphatically at our rods with both snippers.

I couldn't help but laugh. "She has a point . . ."

"She does," Maria agreed, a smile tugging at the corner of her lips.

The creature she had hooked tugged even harder. As it took a screaming run out toward the horizon, like a bolt fired from a crossbow, I realized how much bigger it was than mine. A moment later, her foe changed direction, darting back toward the river mouth. Maria didn't miss a step. She reeled with expert precision, not letting her line go slack.

I leaned down and lifted a well-fed creature up onto the rocks. Its description leaped out at me.

Mature Shore Fish
Uncommon
Found along the ocean shores of the Kallis Realm, this fish is a staple source of both food and bait.

As the description lingered in my mind's eye, I recalled the first time I'd caught one of these fish. It had been such a challenge, making me put in the work with my old bamboo rod. It was just me and Snips back then. She'd sprinted around me like a maniac as I fought the fish, then flicked it up onto the shore with her mighty clacker. We'd cooked it on a campfire and eaten it together. That meal had caused Snips's first breakthrough, which was when she'd gotten her spikes.

A part of me missed those times. Everything had been so fresh, so unknown, and fishing had been far more difficult.

I shook my head, smiling at myself. I wouldn't trade my current life for anything. So what if I didn't get the same amount of adrenaline from fishing as I once had? Perhaps I could find ways to make it more challenging for myself.

I was still holding the shore fish, so I thanked it, leaned over to let Snips give it a gentle lil' pat, and slid it back into the water. With a few kicks of its tail, the fish was gone. Usually, I would have kept it. But I recognized the movement of Maria's line, the way it raced out to sea, and the speed with which it returned to shore. I knew what it was, and that Maria was skilled enough to land it.

She danced along the shore, Snips and I stepping and scuttling out of the way. Minutes later, the fish started to tire, and after one last run that left it just beyond the river mouth, the battle was decided. Maria brought the now-exhausted creature toward the rocks.

When I caught sight of its silvery scales beneath the water, my suspicions were confirmed. Snips leaped into the waves with a soft *plop*, then lobbed the mackerel from the bay and into Maria's arms. Words occupied our vision.

Mature Bluefathom Mackerel
Rare
Found in the deep waters of the Kallis Realm, this fish is prized for both sport and the quality of its flesh. Rarely seen, some say that consuming this creature provides a temporary boost to Luck.

A laugh boomed from my chest as I shook my head and returned to the present. I expected to find elation and triumph on Maria's face. Instead, her brow was furrowed, and she chewed the inside of one cheek.

"What's wrong?" I asked.

"It's nothing. Sorry." She stepped forward, lowering the fish toward the water.

"Whoa," I said. "What are you doing?"

"Letting it go. I caught it, didn't I?"

"I mean, yeah. It's your call, but don't you want to keep it?"

"Of course I want to keep it!" she snapped. "It would have been the perfect bloody ingredient for our perfect bloody wedding, okay?" She sighed in frustration. "We came down here because you needed to think, but I can't hide my disappointment no matter how much I try to push it down."

I blinked in confusion.

"I'm sorry, Fischer. It's not your fault, and I know you're disappointed, too. We *finally* decided to plan the wedding. You were thinking about it only this morning, and you were being so sweet. I couldn't wait to marry you. But then Ellis"—she gestured toward Tropica with the Bluefathom Mackerel she still held—"did the thing. I'm just disappointed, and of course we can't focus on it now. We have more important things to consider. And then I caught *this*." She held up the fish, scowling at it. "It feels like the universe is taunting me."

Snips and I shared a bewildered look, then I turned toward Maria. "When I joked earlier about changing my ways when we were married, and you got quiet . . ."

"I know. I'm sorry." She set her burden down, removed a metal spike from her pocket, and humanely dispatched the fish with a single thrust. "I'm being selfish. There's no reason we can't all enjoy my catch, and I shouldn't have let my feelings out when you've already had such a hard morning. I don't . . ." She trailed off, frowning at the soft squeaks escaping from Snips. "Why are you laughing?"

The question made Snips's amusement boil over. She hissed and bubbled as the situation's hilarity consumed her, all eight of her legs scrambling for purchase on the rocky shore. I couldn't stop my laugh from joining in, but before Maria could get even more of the wrong idea, I swept forward, pulling her body into mine and pushing open the imaginary door sealing our connection.

"You . . ." She swallowed, her eyes watering as my thoughts assailed her, showing her the truth. "You don't want to delay the wedding . . . ?"

Snips made a choking noise and gave up on remaining upright, her spiked legs splayed outward as mirth consumed her.

"Maria." I smoothed her hair down with one hand, stopping when it rested against her cheek and neck. "If Ellis told me the world would end tomorrow, I'd marry you today. If he told me Tropica would explode in a few hours, I'd marry you *now*, consequences be damned." Her lower lip quivered as she stared up at me. "That meeting shook me to my core, but there is nothing more important to me than you. I can't wait any longer. I *refuse* to." Heat flared from the mark on my soul, and for the first time since I'd received it, the sensation felt *right*. "As far as I'm concerned, you're already my wife, and I'll not let anything stop me from making it official."

The tears swelled in her eyes, and she bit the inside of her lip to stop it from shaking, her potent relief and joy threatening to overwhelm her. Before she could reply, another voice called out into the silence.

"Mistress is *dumb like Master*!" cackled Snips, smacking the rocky shore with one of her powerful clackers.

From anyone else, it would have been poorly timed, if not outright rude. From Snips, a crustacean who had cast aside her human traits and completely embraced her identity as a crab? She was just calling it how she saw it.

Maria laughed, pulling herself tight to my body and pressing her head against my chest. "When you closed yourself off back in Tropica, I thought . . ."

"You thought wrong. I'm sorry it caused you so much stress, but it's kinda nice not being the one to make assumptions for once."

Snips let out a long hiss, finally regaining her composure. "So many times Mistress warned Master not to keep things to himself, then she falls into the same trap. You are both so *human*. Be more like a crab. Take what you want. Do what you please."

I nodded sagely. "I see what you're saying, Snips. I'll commence immediately."

Maria frowned as I let go of her and took a step back. "What are you . . . ?"

I dropped my tooshie low, adopted what the Church of Carcinization called the "perfect form," and clacked my claw hands in her general direction as I scuttled sideways at her. "Marriage! Marriage *now*!"

"Too much crab! *Too much crab!*" she yelled, giggling as she backed away.

I got back to my feet and tried to pull her back into a hug, but she held me at arm's length, suddenly growing serious. "Before we laugh it off, how are *you* feeling? I hope I didn't make your worries worse . . ."

"If anything, you helped. Fishing always keeps me in the present, and I realized I was getting caught up in things I can't control. I have some big decisions to make.

They for sure need to be considered, but agonizing over them constantly is only beating myself up. And though I'm sorry for the wedding misunderstanding, it just reminded me how fortunate I am. If the price I need to pay for living a life by your side is an existential crisis or two, I'll happily pay it."

She frowned and tapped her chin in thought, an amused glint flashing in her eyes. "How about *three* existential crises?"

"Still worth it."

". . . Four?"

"Yep. That's my lucky number."

"Wow. You must love me after all."

"More than I can put into words."

We stared at each other, a million different sentiments and thoughts passing between us. A flickering flame of desire swiftly grew, flaring across my chest. Before it could burn out of control, Maria closed our connection and pulled away, taking three steps back.

"You really meant it?" she asked. "You want to get married today?"

"I did, and I do."

Her breaths came shallow. Her pulse quickened. I took a step forward, my entire being wanting to embrace her, but she skipped back the same distance. "We've already broken the custom of not seeing each other—the least we can do is keep away from each other until the ceremony. Mental connection included."

"I mean, for sure, but . . . what are the other customs? Is there anything I should know?"

"Nope!" She grinned. "We're not supposed to be involved in the planning. Traditionally, the bride and groom's family members take care of everything." Her grin widened as her eyes drifted past me. "If only we had one such family member nearby . . ."

I followed Maria's gaze and found Snips shaking again. This time, it wasn't mirth assaulting her. She did her best to tamp down her emotions, but try as she might, her excitement couldn't be contained. She took off so swiftly that she lost contact with the ground, and as her legs scrabbled for purchase, she unleashed waves of billowing chi that blasted her along the shore and around the headland.

Hundreds of crustaceans appeared in her wake. The recon crabs shot toward the village on streams of water essence, looking more like surveillance aircraft than aquatic creatures. The little shrimpy boys—who I'd taken to calling assault prawns—flicked their tails and rocketed away. And the formerly human Church of Carcinization crawled atop one another to form a tower, which almost fell over when the bottom crab sped away, taking them around the headland and out of sight.

"Should we be worried?" she asked.

I blinked at the now-empty shore, then shook my head. "What's the worst that could happen . . . ?"

CHAPTER EIGHT

I Do

Sweet summer child, I thought to myself as I considered my dismissive words from earlier today. It was my fault for assuming nothing bad would come of letting them make the announcement. I hadn't been thinking creatively enough.

"Hey!" called an annoyed and feminine voice from behind me. "Why are you tensing up? You'll ruin our masterpiece."

I let out a slow breath. "Sorry, Rubes. Just recalling what Roger did earlier."

She leaned around to my front, her eyes sparkling with mirth. "I heard about that."

"I mean, we literally heard it, too," Steven added from my left side as he measured my cuff. "Hard to miss the sound of a building being cut to splinters."

"I'm surprised he reacted so poorly," Ruby said, vanishing from view to fuss over something behind me. "I thought he'd accepted your relationship."

"As far as I know, he has. The problem wasn't so much the message, but the way it was delivered."

"Oh? What did you say?"

"*I* didn't say anything . . ."

She leaned forward again, giving me a quizzical look. "Don't tell me . . ."

I grimaced. "Yep. The Church of Carcinization told him."

"You let your future father-in-law, who is famously short-tempered and wields swordlike chi, find out about his daughter's wedding from a crab." She shook her head and returned to my back. "I'm not surprised the old Roger came out for a second."

"It was a stack of crabs, actually. All of them were there. I'm not sure if that makes it better or worse."

"Worse."

"Definitely worse," Steven agreed, now measuring my right cuff.

Ruby draped something over my shoulders. "What were you thinking?"

"I wasn't. I got swept up in the moment. Snips wanted to take care of it, and the crustaceans all just . . . sped off."

"Remind me not to annoy Roger. An explosive reaction makes sense, but to destroy a building over it . . ."

"One and a half buildings, actually," I corrected, straightening my back at Ruby's prompting. "The grouchy bastard loses control, tears his own home to pieces—and half of his neighbor's—then blames me for it. Deklan only made things worse."

"Wait." Ruby pressed two fingers to my spine to hold whatever she was doing in place, then leaned around again. "Deklan is the neighbor whose house got damaged?"

"Yuuup."

There was a moment of silence, then Ruby barked a laugh. "Goodness. How did he take it?"

"Poorly."

"Thought he would. So, which method of attack did Deklan go with?"

"Damn, Rubes. You know him better than I thought. He chose aggressive forgiveness."

"Stop it! He didn't!"

"He did. It was . . . *effective*."

Ruby cackled, and Steven cleared his throat. "I regret to inform you that some of the tools in this building aren't as sharp as the others. This one is rather dull and finds himself lacking the edge to comprehend what's so funny."

"Oh, shush, husband. You'll always be my better when it comes to measurements. And taxes. And growing facial hair. Don't put yourself down just because I'm the people person." She tutted, the fabric over my shoulder blades pulling together as she started pinning pieces of cloth. "Deklan is extremely kind, but also has a trickster's heart. I'm sure he was at least a *little* annoyed about his home getting reduced to rubble."

Steven smiled to himself as he moved back to my left cuff and slid a series of sewing pins into place. Or strands of chi. Perhaps both—I couldn't be certain. "I need more clues, dear."

"I was going to continue. I just need to . . ." Her deft movements connected fabric down the length of my spine in mere seconds. "*There*. If Deklan wanted to give it to him, he could have gone on the offensive, pointing out that Roger, the one always preaching self-control and discipline, had lost himself to anger."

"But you said he chose 'aggressive forgiveness'?" Steven asked around a mouthful of pins as he shifted to my right sleeve. "Stand still for a second, Fischer. Relax your arms. Just like that." I stood as a statue, letting him do the same to my other cuff. When he finished, he inspected his work, nodding to himself. "So? What is 'aggressive forgiveness' and why was it effective?"

I took a deep breath now that I could move again. "He showed Roger understanding and compassion. I honestly can't tell if it was intentional, but if it was—"

"It was," Ruby concluded. "I'd bet my hat on it."

"You don't have a hat, dear."

"Then I'd bet Fischer's hat on it."

Steven whistled. "You *must* be sure if you're willing to risk the wrath of God-King Fischer."

"Guys . . . It's fine to give me shit, but can we at least finish teasing Roger first?"

"Deal," Steven said, "but only because it's your wedding day. You were saying?"

"I was saying Deklan is godsdamned *diabolical*."

"Imagine, dear," Ruby said. "You slip up and lose control of the very thing you have been preaching about for *months*. Then, the person whose house you destroyed, instead of getting understandably mad, only shows you kindness."

He snorted in realization, gaze focused on my upper torso as his precise hands pinned the different materials together. "He exhibited the exact traits Roger lacked. I get that being annoying, but it doesn't seem all that diabolical. What am I missing?"

I shook my head, remembering Deklan's slight smile—the only warning of the volley to come. "I haven't mentioned the follow-up barb yet."

Ruby was before me in a blur, moving faster than seemed possible for someone so heavily pregnant. She supported her abdomen with one hand, the other resting on my shoulder as she stared up at me, eyes manic.

I nodded. "His exact words were: 'You're correct, Roger. I *am* understanding. I take pride in controlling my emotions, you see. If only everyone in Tropica showed the same restraint . . .'"

Ruby cringed at the verbal attack's potency.

"Roger almost destroyed three more houses in response," I said. "He went so far as to scan the surrounding buildings to check there were no people inside. If he'd actually let the bladelike chi fly, I would've had to suppress him—which would have for sure delayed the marriage. I don't wanna wait a minute longer, but I also won't allow a grumpy Roger to skulk about in Maria's memories of our wedding day."

"That's one of the few downsides to having a cultivator's mind." Ruby rolled her shoulders. "An almost-flawless memory can be a curse."

Both tailors stood back, assessing the clothing they'd just created. Not wanting to stare at and distract them, I allowed my gaze to wander around their new workshop. I'd seen it in passing, but the view from outside didn't do it justice. I was in the rear of the building—the utilitarian area used for crafting. There was a stoppered bottle nearby that I lingered on for a second, but it wasn't interesting enough to stop my eyes from drifting toward the storefront.

Racks and racks and *racks* of different clothing lined the two distinct halves of the retail section. One side was filled with free items: everyday garments, profession-related equipment, and more hats than there were oysters on the headland. The other side was for specialty clothes, most of which were System-made and came with random, if minor, stat bonuses. I smiled. Seeing the results of their hard work made my heart sing.

But then I spied the color of the sky through the front entrance. "Uh, I don't mean to rush you guys, but aren't we pushing it for time?"

"Not at all," Ruby said. "You're the last customer."

"Right. But the sun has just now set, and we're not even half done."

"You underestimate us, Fischer. Your suit is finished."

I blinked, peered down at my legs, then back up at them. "I'm not wearing any pants."

Their faces were both graced by small smiles that sent a shiver down my spine—they were just like Deklan's earlier today.

"Have you not noticed we've used no chi?"

"No, actually. I'm still getting accustomed to whatever Ellis and the rest of my trai-torous followers did to me this morning. Snips made me promise I wouldn't snoop around the shore, so my only option right now is to seal off my senses completely."

"Well," Steven said, "we haven't." He turned to Ruby. "Ready, dear?"

Her eyes danced with glee that may or may not have been at my expense. "Ready."

"Wait just a min—"

Power slammed into my chest and spread out. My core's senses were muted, so I witnessed with my physical ones as a soft-brown light flowed from them, engulfing me. As it took shape, the chi stopped streaming from Ruby, Steven having to pour out double. She flicked her wrist, the gourd from earlier popped open, and count-less threads rushed out. They wove themselves through Steven's essence, becoming enmeshed with the cloth covering me.

It was over in the blink of a cultivator's eye. Forgetting all about the crafting, I dashed forward to catch Steven. Ruby tried to do the same but stopped when I beat her to it.

"Mate . . . you good?"

He . . . *laughed.* It came from the depths of his core, holding nary a hint of fatigue. "Good? I'm *great*!" He stood of his own power, running a hand down the length of my arm. "Unbelievable. The taper. The *silhouette.*"

"Steven, my man, I'm about to get married and your pregnant wife is right here. Show a little discre—"

Said wife interrupted me with a whap on the back of the head. "Shut up and appreciate the *art* my husband just made for you."

"The art *we* made," he corrected.

She blew a raspberry. "You're the one who almost fainted. I just got to stand here looking radiant."

I already had a good idea of what I wore from the glimpses I'd caught, but as I looked down now, I let out a soft whistle. All they'd had to go on were my vague instructions, and they'd absolutely knocked it out of the park.

"Look in the mirror!" Ruby insisted, badgering me all the way there. "Do you like it? The cut? The palette? Most of the stylistic choices were hotly debated today, but the colors were an exception. It— Listen to me, blathering on! What do *you* think?"

I'd barely heard her words, my eyes locked on the stranger in the mirror. "Guys . . . *how?*"

"How what?"

It was a basic suit, its material the color of sand. I had a white button-up beneath the open jacket, tucked into pants of the same sandy hue as the top. Despite not being stylistically unique, it was the effect it had on *me* that I still couldn't quite comprehend.

I gestured at my reflection. "You made *me* appear stylish. I know you won't get the reference, but I look like the main love interest from the cover of an enemies-to-lovers romance book set on the seaside."

"Steven . . . ?"

"Yes, dear?"

"Fischer just forewarned that we wouldn't understand what he was talking about."

"He did."

"Without intentionally trying to confuse us."

"I noticed—he might be unwell."

"Or maybe he *really* likes the suit?"

"Seriously," I said. "I look like Barry if he focused on calisthenics. As much as I joke about being handsome and humble, this actually makes me *feel* handsome. Are you sure there aren't any bonuses to attractiveness or something? I can feel it trying to draw me in, but if I open my senses to it now, I might find whatever Snips forbade me from seeing."

Ruby's brows knotted above an amused smile. "Remember all those times I said your physique matched a tapered fit, but you made me create oversized clothes anyway?"

"What can I say—I love having enough room for the breeze to flow through my shirts." I opened the jacket and twisted to the side, the form-fitting shirt sticking to my skin and showing off washboard abs. "For Maria, though? I'd wear a clown suit if she was into it."

Ruby patted me on the shoulder. "You don't need an outfit for that, sweetie—you're enough of a clown already." I pouted, but she continued. "That aside, it's time we get going."

"I have one more question." I nodded toward the now-empty gourd. "What the frack was in that?"

"Secret." Steven met my eyes, giving me a grin that told me he would not relent.

"Boooo." I released a slow, steadying breath. "Fine. Let's go."

"That's it?" His grin faltered. "You aren't going to push—"

Ruby shut him with a soft *whap*, then looped her arm through mine, leading me outside. "We can't leave Maria waiting at the arbor!"

I frowned. "Don't you mean alt—"

"*Onward!*" she interrupted, her expression not betraying a thing.

As I stepped into the chilly night air, I took a deep breath, looking around when I realized just how dark it was. Most of the lanterns had been extinguished, only a single line of them lit, a beacon leading me to my love. "Nice touch," I said, my pulse quickening and palms suddenly clammy.

Neither Ruby nor Steven replied, marching off ahead of me so we didn't arrive together.

Though my steps were calm and measured, the rest of me wasn't. Time passed at a crawl as I traversed one street, then raced by along the next, my perception and thoughts varying. A single person kept me grounded—memories of Maria flashed through my mind as I trekked across paved roads, between rows of sugarcane, and over sandy dunes.

Soft chatter came from just over the crest ahead. I glanced down, suddenly aware of the cold sand beneath my feet. I . . . I wasn't wearing any shoes.

I suppose it is *a beach wedding . . .*

The thought was a comforting one, but not comforting enough to completely banish that nagging doubt. I fought the urge to fetch a pair of sandals, only the risk of accidentally discovering Snips's surprise stopping me from reaching for my chi.

When I caught sight of the ceremony area—and the people within—I stopped. "What the *frack* . . . ?"

All eyes turned to me as a yawning silence settled over my closest friends and family. Their attire was . . . *Hawaiian*. Like they were attending a party with the theme 'your fun uncle's comfiest clothes.' All the blokes sported baggy shorts, bright floral shirts, and not a single item of footwear. The women were the same, however, some had swapped shorts for skirts, and others wore flowing summer dresses. Though the colors were varied, they were all of a pastel hue, somehow complementing the light-brown benches and sand beneath them.

On the other side, with the ocean as its backdrop, stood an arbor so ambitious only a spirit beast could have dreamed it. A solid ring of ice floated upright in the air. Two meters tall, its almost-clear outline was as thick as Corporal Claws. Countless semi-opaque flowers sprouted from it, their petals all dancing as if blown by different breezes. Red and orange and yellow and blue, they were living flames, each soft color reflected in the nearby ice.

Between the arbor, the outfits, and the smiles of my loved ones, I wasn't even sure if Maria was here. Perhaps she was going to let Roger walk her down the aisle after all. I strode forward, scanning the crowd, releasing my senses now that Snips's wondrous surprise had been revealed.

In retrospect, it was obviously a mistake—a tidal wave of love and compassion crashed into my core. I had to stand still for a moment to ensure I didn't fall to my knees under the assault. In that second of weakness, my oldest enemy made an opportunistic attack, delivering a blow that passed right through my defenses and into my vision.

Matrimonial Suit of the God-King
Mythic
Created for a god-king, on the day of his marriage, by his nation's leading tailors. The god-king's followers have imbued threads of gratitude and love into this suit. So long as their faith holds true, the only thing capable of damaging it is a blow possessing even greater faith.

Time froze as I read, reread, then read it some more, my mind desperate to explore the implications. I focused elsewhere, knowing now wasn't the time. Fortunately, I already had the perfect thing to ground myself with, and as I pictured Maria, nothing else mattered.

Except . . . it did. I frowned internally, unsure why the description was lingering. There was an invisible tag there, the end of a thread just begging to be pulled. A little frustrated, I slammed my will into it, annoyed the damned System was bothering me today of all days.

Almost immediately, I found the string's end. I tensed my physical and meta-physical cores, then yanked. Dozens of loops ripped free, a patch of obscuring fabric falling away from the rest of the outfit. The description flashed again in my mind's eye—this time, there was an additional line printed at the bottom.

. . .

[Hidden Ability]

That was it. No elaboration, just the confirmed existence of something hidden.

Steven and Ruby, I thought, returning to the present, my eyes flicking toward them.

Those dastardly tailors had done it on purpose. They'd intentionally concealed the ability by stitching something over it. This knowledge brought with it even more of those pesky implications, but, thankfully, now that the main mystery was solved, focusing on Maria made me forget all about them.

"*Daaamn!*" Barry cupped one muscular hand to his mouth, the other pointing at the still-tensed abdominals my form-fitting shirt was clinging to. "Look at those obliques! Have you been working out?"

"*Daaang!*" Paul yelled—in a clearly rehearsed manner, judging by the look he darted at his dad. "Fischer is looking *whacked*!"

"*Jacked*," Barry whispered out the side of his mouth.

"*Daaang!*" Paul corrected, louder this time. "Fischer is looking *jacked*!"

I grinned, the well-intentioned blunder only bringing me even more joy. My skin prickled as I strode between the seats, my eyes and senses wading through the crowd in search of my bride. She wasn't yet here. As I made it to the front, I gazed at the arbor, finally close enough to feel the source of its chi—or, rather, *sources*.

Trent and Keith stood amongst the others, wearing light-blue shirts with red swirls, their concentration the only visual clue they were contributing. The rest of them, though . . .

I shook my head and snapped my fingers, making two royals and five former handlers appear in a flash of light. "I appreciate the thoughtfulness, but Maria will have my hide if I leave you out in the dunes while your chi powers the . . . flames? Flowers? Whatever you call them, they're bloody stunning."

Tryphena and the handlers, their eyes wide at the sudden teleportation, stared back. The queen, however, was a picture of regal poise, her raised chin and benevolent smile commanding attention. "It is no trouble, Fischer. We really don't mind—"

"Denied!" I waved dismissively. "God-King Fischer *demands* your attendance." I leaned close, covering my mouth with the back of my hand. "There are far too many *poors* here, you see? They're my friends and I love them, sure, but someone of your regal bloodline will *surely* elevate them. You might even motivate them to better themselves."

"But of course, sire." She curtsied and fanned out a skirt—whose colorful palette, the same as Trent's and Keith's, didn't escape my notice. "With any luck, they'll start chasing the things that actually matter in life, like wealth, physical appearance, and looking down upon your lessers."

I barked a laugh. "Jokes aside, Penelope, I'm glad you're here. We haven't had much of a chance to speak, but I reckon you and I will become good mates."

Her lip tugged up so slightly I almost missed it.

"*Fischer!*" Trent said with mock indignation. "That's my *mother!* And what about Maria?"

"What are you— Oh, *hah-hah*, Trent. You know that's not what I meant, you cheeky bastard. And you, Penelope! For *shame!* I expect as much from your son, but from the former queen of . . ." I trailed off, jaw falling open as I turned to look at the procession just now cresting the same dune I'd arrived over. They walked with purpose, all radiating positive emotions. My brain wanted to ask so many things, but one question rushed out before the others. "*Where the frack did you guys get clothes?*"

Sergeant Snips headed the parade, wearing a giant bow made of coral-colored materials atop her spiky carapace. She opened her connection to me, and as her love came flowing through, I sent mine back, along with my gratitude for the flame- and flower-covered arbor she'd surprised me with. Rocky was beside her in the same cloth . . . but his was in the shape of a whole damned *suit*. Bowtie, layered jacket, and sleeves included. He winked at me and took a drag of his cigarette, looking even more suave than usual.

Next came a wedding transport bus—or, more accurately, a wedding transport lobster. Pistachio wore cuffs, *only* cuffs, of a pale blue that covered parts of his snippers. Riding his head, hundreds of winged creatures waved at me, all wearing a royal purple that complemented their yellow stripes. Queen Bee and Bumblebro's matching garments were akin to Snips's and Rocky's, while the Buzzy Boys—over half of them here for the ceremony—wore sashes over their armored exoskeletons. Behind all the insects, Bill and Pelly rode the stoic lobster's back, all sporting smart vests with holes large enough for their wings to poke through.

After I'd locked eyes with all of them, I glanced up at the gigantic form behind them. Teddy was walking on his rear legs, standing upright with immaculate posture, a massive colorful tie attached to his neck. Corporal Claws perched on his shoulder like a queen, wearing the top half of a suit. RPM sat on the other shoulder, wearing the bottom half of said suit. It was unclear if their fashion choice was by design, or if Claws's thieving familiar had simply stolen her pants.

Of all the half outfits I'd seen, Borks's had to be the funniest. He was in the form of a toy poodle, his suit tailored for the pants to be on his front legs, and the approximation of a dress shirt attached to his neck and chest, complete with fake suspenders. As he saw me, he went full wiggle-worm, his tail wagging so hard his entire body joined—

A ripping sound tore into the night. Borks, now in his golden retriever form, froze, ears alert and eyes wide as he peered down at the remnant strips of his cute lil' outfit. He'd gotten too excited and lost hold of his shape—he couldn't have cared less.

His mouth snapped down, collecting the pieces of his suit and placing them on his back. Well, he tried to, which resulted in him spinning in circles, never quite getting the right angle. A giant root parted the sand beside him, grabbing the strips and tying them to his neck so they wouldn't fall off. The extension of Lemon waved in greeting, a thin and flexible ribbon of colored material wrapped around her.

With Lemon's arrival, all of my animal and spirit pals were here. Together, they stepped aside, a thick cloud of their intent dissipating to reveal . . . *her*.

I lost track of everything else, mouth open as I gaped at the woman descending the slope behind them.

Her dress was simple. Strapless. The same oceanic color as her eyes—and just as effortlessly beautiful. A string of seashells divided her hair, a see-through veil coming from it to cover her features. Her loose curls, chaotic and flawless and shining, reflected the lantern light that had guided her to me. Which was how it truly felt—like the universe had brought her here for me, and me here for her. The more I stared, the surer I became.

I soaked in all the perfect little imperfections that made her so intoxicating. The smattering of freckles across the bridge of her nose. The natural flush of her cheeks, enhanced by the surrounding lanterns. The shallow yet swift rise and fall of her chest, reflective of the adrenaline coursing through both of us.

A grumpy man stood by her side. Roger was a soldier, a farmer, and a husband. But above all else, he was a father. I couldn't miss the pride radiating from him despite my eyes never once leaving *her*.

I did what I could to keep our connection closed, knowing we'd both go temporarily catatonic if our emotions started enhancing each other right now. My chi was harder to control and feel, but the new weight it possessed seemed to help.

Then she was next to me. Our animal pals were fanned out to each side—when had they gotten there? Roger said something, but all I noted were the hints of joy and pride and adoration in his voice. We shook hands. At least I think we did. It was difficult to remember touching anything else now that Maria's slight yet strong fingers were held in mine.

She lifted her veil. My heart beat so hard the whole continent might hear it. She spoke. Asked a question.

"Sorry?" I croaked, clearing my throat after hearing myself. "What did you say?"

She laughed, the sound like . . . some kind of really nice analogy I was too preoccupied to find. A mixture of angels and bells and the trickle of a shallow creek, perhaps. Her hand drifted up to cover her mouth, but she stilled it halfway there, squaring her shoulder and lifting her chin to meet my eyes. "I asked what you thought." She removed her hands from mine and twirled on the spot, her hair and the silken bottom of her dress swishing outward. "So?" She gave me a teasing smile. "What do you think?"

I pointed directly down at the ground. "I'm really glad you're also barefoot. I was second-guessing my lack of shoes earlier."

Our now-seated friends laughed, as did she, but that hadn't been my intent. My brain couldn't figure out anything else to say—no combination of words existed that could do the rest of my thoughts justice.

"Greeeeat," someone said. Ruby, maybe. "You've broken him, Maria. Who's gonna be god-king now? You up for it, Ellis?"

"Unnecessary," he replied from my side.

I turned toward him, a small part of me recognizing that I would normally feel surprised at being snuck up on.

He grinned. "I believe Fischer's affliction is temporary. The sooner we marry him to Maria . . ."

He kept speaking after that, but at the mention of her name, I'd looked at her once more—and everything else had, once again, fallen away.

Her beautiful mouth smiled, and she said: "Ellis asked if we're ready," which I only "heard" by reading the velvety lips I just happened to be staring at. I nodded, not trusting my voice, doing my best to focus on the man beside me. Maria helped by grabbing my chin with both hands and guiding my face toward him.

"*Shanks*," I said, her fingers garbling the words.

"You're welcome, my love."

Ellis raised a brow. "No questions or accusations, Fischer? You do not mind me being the celebrant? I expected at least one wisecrack."

I shook my head. Or Maria shook it for me. I couldn't be sure.

"In that case, let us begin." The archivist and former leader of Gormona's fishing club—who was apparently also a celebrant—raised his arms. Strands of essence flooded from his back, flaring different colors as they brushed against the red and orange and yellow and blue flames of the arbor. Sounds of awe came from the gathering. A half dozen spikes of panic stabbed out from nearby cores, receding a moment later as the cultivators regained control of the fires Ellis was actively contorting.

"We are here today," he continued, "to consecrate the marriage of Maria and God-King Fischer."

A small part of my subconscious wondered at his use of that newly gained title, but the rest of me was lost in *her*.

"Before they make their vows, I implore the couple's loved ones, familiars, followers, and any other witnesses to declare the objections they might harbor. Speak now, or hold your tongue for all eternity."

That same tiny voice at the back of my mind reacted, but it remained unnoticed, a single droplet in the waterfall of emotions crashing against my heart and core. Maria was the same, her attention only for me, just as mine was for her.

A silence spread, lingering for what could have been milliseconds or minutes. I felt a pang of impatience, my unruly essence sick of containing our emotions.

"None have objected. Thus, I declare my intention to bond Maria and God-King Fischer together." I'd forgotten about the strands of chi flowing from his back. They were thick tendrils now, spread wide and looping in to form a half sphere.

"Holy frack," Maria said, blinking at the colors and power fanning from him like giant wings. "Where did that arbor come from?"

I laughed, becoming more aware of my surroundings than I had been since her arrival. "You just noticed it? I'm glad my beauty is also distracting."

"Your beauty, huh?" She gave me a dangerous smile. "What makes you think it was your beauty bewildering me?"

"Because you're only human."

"What if it's only your strength I'm interested in?"

I grinned. "Then I'll never have to worry about your gaze straying. After the last few months, I'm guessing I'll only grow stronger."

"Hmmmm." She tapped her lips, failing to stop a smile from shining through. "You've got me there. I guess I'll just have to work on getting more powerful myself. Can't have my god-king husband constantly distracting me with his glory."

It had gotten harder to listen with each passing word; the slight curve of her mouth was demanding my attention. I saw a hint of the same impatience growing within me. She also couldn't wait. She wanted to be married *now*. We stared at each other, both drifting forward, my eyes stealing glances at her flushed lips, her gaze flicking down toward mine—

Ellis cleared his throat. *Loudly.* "I imagine there will be plenty of time for that. Perhaps later? After you are married?"

I stood upright once more, and Maria did the same, grinning unabashedly. "Apologies, Ellis. I was lost in my future husband's *beauty*."

A smattering of laughter came from our loved ones. Ellis reached wider, his hands and fingers splayed. All at once, his half sphere of chi went rigid, its multicolored form holding even without his active instruction.

"God-King Fischer," Ellis calmly said, the words amplified by his construction, each syllable clear and booming. "Beneath the heavens, and before so many witnesses, do you take this woman to be your wife? Do you willingly pledge your soul to her, accepting all that will follow, till death do you part?"

Despite his unnecessarily ominous phrasing, I didn't need to think about it. "I do."

"Maria," Ellis continued, face a little strained. "Do you willingly pledge your soul to God-King Fischer, accepting all that will follow, till death do you part?"

She swallowed, her brow knitting as she stared up at me. And my heart threatened to shatter into a million pieces. She was worried. Was it the phrasing? Was she about to say no? Had I misread the tension in her visage all along, assuming impatience when it was actually fear? Doubt? *Regret?*

Before my thoughts could spiral any further, my worry was confirmed. It hadn't been impatience. Her entire core trembled, shuddered with the effort to keep it hidden, but then the truth came hurtling out for all to see.

"I'm really sorry—" *Slam!* "—please forgive me, I—" *Thump!* "—tried my absolute *beeeest!*" Slimes screamed in a rush as he was violently ejected from Maria, struck the inside of Ellis's construct, then bounced off the sand below, circumstance and his own gelatinous body conspiring to send him rocketing westward over the mountains.

Unstoppered, Maria's emotions came flooding out, hitting me with tenfold the force Slimes had whizzed away with. It wasn't impatience, but neither was it fear, doubt, nor regret. It was her love. It hadn't just been the weight of my chi keeping our connection closed. I willingly admitted my hubris as the magnitude of her feelings threw both doors open, shattering them into countless splinters. I felt all-powerful at times, like there was nothing in this world I couldn't accomplish if I set my mind to it, but I could barely contain my own emotions—why had I thought I could also contain hers?

My yearning for her flooded out through the endless pool that was our bond. They whirled around one another, combined, built. Just before I lost my sense of self, she spoke, her voice breathy and strained and, somehow, making my love grow even stronger.

"I do . . ."

CHAPTER NINE

Mark

Fifty meters from shore, in the calm swell just past the breaking waves, two horrors from the deep observed. Other beings might have been offended that their absence wasn't noticed, identifying it as reflective of their social standing.

Cadet Calamari and Fathom knew better.

Though it paled to the bond between the couple about to be married, the brothers had both spent time connected to Fischer's mind—they understood just how strong his feelings were, that glimpse into his awareness confirming the affections wrought clear on the bride's and groom's faces whenever they saw one another.

"It's still a slight shame we weren't invited," Cal said, bobbing over an unbroken wave.

"Oh?" Fathom asked. "Why is that?"

"It was a perfect opportunity to show off. The outfits are all wonderful, but can they do this?" Cal, without using a drop of essence, made his skin swirl with the myriad colors visible on the shore.

"Ahhh, I finally comprehend Roger's reason for placing us here." Fathom gave Cal a meaningful glance, his body emulating the same pattern with inhuman perfection. "Our glorious appearances would have detracted from the beauty of our tyrant god-king, which would have surely resulted in our heads adorning Tropica's walls."

Their eyes shone in shared amusement, twinkling brighter than the stars above. Then, before either could release another quip, the true reason for their position arrived.

"I do," Maria said, sealing the pact.

Fathom slammed his core open. A yawning void appeared in one of his mighty tentacles. It felt so right to embrace his ideal, his very soul wishing to pause and rejoice as the world's chi streamed into him—but his work wasn't done.

Ellis dropped to the ground, revealing the fist-sized hole he'd left in the half-sphere structure behind him. It looked like an amplifier. Something that essence or sound could bounce off of just like Slimes had. But that couldn't have been further from the truth.

It wasn't for boosting power; it was for stealing it.

Fathom created a second void on this side of that small opening. It was the last component necessary for Ellis's funnel, but as the abyssal elemental pushed for its completion, his strength waned. Forming an external vacuum was always possible, but doing so while maintaining an internal one? It was far too much for a single soul to handle. He would lose control of both, resulting in a detonation that would consume everything for kilometers.

Fortunately, he wasn't alone.

Cal's will flew out into the night, their bond—and the cuttlefish's experience with abyssal essence—allowing help that shouldn't be possible. The second void solidified just in time to catch the brilliance that erupted from the consecration of husband and wife. Oceanic currents of chi flowed into the endless abyss, the funnel working as intended. The flame cultivators joined in, their beautiful flowers flaring, reinforcing the structure. The rest of the congregation, all forewarned to release their power when the consecration occurred, also opened their cores. Countless elements and aspects formed a solid net, corralling the light coming from Fischer and Maria toward the closest void.

It was just as Ellis had predicted. If not for their intervention, the truth of what happened here would have flowed up into the heavens, echoes of the monumental event bouncing around before broadcasting beyond. Every strand of that far-reaching power was contained and absorbed. The localized storm of emotion, however, wasn't.

Fischer's and Maria's feelings for one another poured out for all to witness, somehow aided by the suit Fischer was wearing. *Curious*, a part of Fathom thought, but he set it aside for later, instead focusing on the immeasurably deep bond assaulting his senses.

Human philosophers and poets spoke of love as if it were flawless. An experience that finds kindred souls if they are so fortunate, elevating them. That view, in Fathom's ancient opinion, was a trap.

Love is not something that happens to you. It is a series of choices, the small and large decisions one makes every single day to put the other first. But neither is it the complete abandonment of self. Love is a *dance*. A constant give and take, only made possible when done with grace, humility, and compassion.

These two souls, a god-king and his wife, knew all this and more. They were free of misconception. They understood exactly how much hard work it would be to remain dedicated to one another, especially with how long cultivators lived. This knowledge could drive some to despair, but not them. Maria and Fischer saw it as beautiful. A task they were both willing to dive headfirst into, its difficulty making it all the more desirable.

They'd seen each other's souls. Weighed the good and the bad and the ugly. And chosen each other time and time again, just as they would forevermore.

As the countless currents of brilliance flowed into his external void, Fathom dismissed these musings. Filling something endless should be, by definition, inconceivable. It was one more impossibility facilitated by Fischer, and predicted by Ellis. Which was why there was a second black hole. Fathom focused. The hard part had arrived.

He connected the two abysses, his chi not needing physical proximity to interact.

The magnitude of the consecration's power hit differently now that it was passing through his tentacle, but he didn't let himself get distracted. What came next should have been unworkable. It definitely would have been if it were just him and his brother handling the distribution.

But as Cal reached for the slew of earthen elements below, another rushed to assist. A volcanic elemental, the second sister, helped carve a tunnel directly down, its width tapering as it got closer to the planet's core. Magma was solidified by Cal's intent, becoming the solid walls necessary to—

It happened in an instant. The final wave from Fischer and Maria was stronger, larger than any other, and it flooded into the first void. Which Fathom then merged into the second, the transition so swift his body hadn't yet registered the pain of his tentacle rupturing.

Now!

An arcing blade of Roger's chi severed the limb. Deklan and Dom surrounded them all in a protective shield, just in case. Fathom released his hold on the only remaining abyss, and as a spear of agony shot through him, he poured every remnant ounce of will into a third void—this one kilometers underground.

Cal and the first sister, two elementals of similar aspects, handled the rest. They carved tunnels underground in the shape of a vast root system, which the pure-white currents of Fischer and Maria's love exploded into. The incandescent tempest was pulled down by the distant void, then carried onward by momentum when Fathom dismissed his power.

Perhaps he should have experienced a moment of fear. The main trunk was hurtling toward the planet's core, after all. But all he felt was excitement, fatigue, and the deep pleasure of a job well done.

The light struck. The realm shook as it noticed the offering, then absorbed it all in less than an instant, the impossibly vast tide just . . . *vanishing*. Fathom held his breath, waiting for something to go wrong. Instead, Kallis stored it away, and the world fell silent.

A few heartbeats later, Cal let out a slow hiss. A stream of contemplative bubbles breached the ocean's surface as he looked up at the sky. "How long do you think it will take?"

"Logic dictates that it will be millennia. Centuries, at the very least."

"I didn't ask what logic dictated, brother."

"I know." Fathom studied the stars for a pregnant moment, his discarded limb regrowing to drift in the waves. "I dare not speak a timeline, but things seem to progress rather swiftly around here."

"Around Fischer, you mean."

Fathom burbled in agreement. Neither brother said a word more as they bobbed up and down, weary and weightless, both content to gaze at the stars high above.

I let out a shaky breath as strength and warmth flooded me, refilling my core. Maria did the same, our hearts pulsing in tandem as we leaned against each other. The only sounds were small waves crashing against the shore, gulls crying from above, and the hiss of sea foam as the ocean retreated, only for it to return and begin anew.

It was serene. A little slice of heaven for us alone. If I hadn't experienced it first-hand, I never would have assumed we'd both just released multiple nuclear bombs' worth of power.

"Shame about everyone else," Maria said, standing back.

"It's their own fault," I replied. "Serves them right for keeping secrets."

There was a zapping sound, and Maria and I both spun.

RPM. He'd dashed toward Claws, making a play to steal her suit jacket, but he lost hold of his chi during the approach. His body flopped uselessly over her. She lifted a paw to slap him but gave up halfway, letting it fall to the sand. Behind those two miscreants, the rest of the congregation members were in similar states of exhaustion. They had all been pushed to the absolute limit. Each man, woman, beast, spirit—and even a child—using every drop of essence they possessed, ensuring the power that had just flowed from us wasn't sent flying up into the heavens.

Ellis groaned. He had one hand on his knee, the other on the ground as he struggled upright. "You may now . . ." he wheezed, his core absolutely spent. ". . . *kiss the bride.*"

A sliver of will left him—a loose thread that hung in the air, waiting to be har-nessed—and he crumpled, hitting the deck like someone had replaced his kneecaps with jelly.

It was objectively hilarious, but neither Maria nor I uttered a peep. Everyone's selflessness had sobered us; Ellis's words had made our intoxication return.

We stared at each other, both more knowledgeable about *us* than ever before. Earlier, we'd expected *something* to happen when we got married—especially with Ellis's intentionally grandiose verbiage. Now, though? We understood what this meant. On an instinctive level, we comprehended exactly what would occur when we sealed our marriage.

I lost myself in her beautiful eyes, more green than blue in the low light surround-ing us. "Are you sure you want this, my love? I—"

"Shut up and kiss me, Fischer."

I didn't have to be told twice. I grabbed her by the waist, one hand drifting up the side of her torso to rest on her neck. The movement was carefully measured, my brain fighting the urge to squeeze her tight and never let go.

Maria was . . . less controlled. She seized me by the back of the head and pulled herself up with all her strength. When our lips met, something in my core trembled, broke free, and flew across our bond.

The stamp. That mark branded on my soul. Part of it was gone, moved to the woman across from me.

The woman, I repeated internally, amused by my own language. *My wife. She's my wife.*

And you're my husband, Maria replied, disbelief lacing our mental voices.

Together, we inspected the permanent marks now etched into our cores.

CHAPTER TEN

Love and War

A blanket of pinprick lights covered the sky, each star's individual brilliance combining to create a pattern so beautiful it could be a master artist's magnum opus. They reminded me of Maria's freckles. Had I ever made that connection before? It was hard to think of the past when the present was so perfect.

She gave me the mental equivalent of a kiss on the cheek, reminding me of the task at hand.

I'm sorry, I thought, looking into her core.

No, you're not, she replied, sending me love as her gaze joined mine.

The brand drew us in, proud of its existence. It was familiar, but only vaguely so, an echo of the intricate tapestry it had once been. Maria and I—my *wife* and I— shifted, going to inspect the place it had originated from.

We both paused when we saw its shape. The lines now gracing her soul hadn't been copied from mine—they'd been *taken*. There had been two marks on my core. No wonder I'd lost control of my chi.

We had both known something like this would occur. It was part of the intrinsic insight we'd gleaned following the ceremony. But neither of us had expected it to feel so . . . *right*. We weren't just bonded by title; we had truly become one. Two sides of a coin, entirely distinct in uncountable ways, yet indisputably made of the same mettle. And the System, with the help of some meddling villagers, had acknowledged it.

I exerted some chi, testing my agency over pure essence now that Maria's brand no longer fought my own. It was *stunning*. Great trunks of solid light wound from me, curved and chaotic when I willed it, smooth when I didn't. Gone was the need to rely on somatic movement for control. I raised my hand anyway, curious to see just how much power I could wield by using such a gesture, but decided against it at the last second—best to err on the side of caution.

"I appreciate you not accidentally blowing up Tropica," Maria joked, unable to decide between staring up at me and resting her head on my chest. "Or the world, possibly."

I kissed her forehead, the contact making my body flush with heat. Warmth radiated through her as well. It was so strong that, before this moment, it would have caused our emotions and need for one another to spiral.

With our marriage, however, we'd gained authority over our bond. I sent a spike of desire her way, a playful little jab. Or at least, that's what I'd intended. Her soul responded in kind and knocked the air from my lungs.

"Okay," Maria said, her flushed cheeks only partly caused by embarrassment. "Lesson learned. Don't do that."

"Agreed," I replied, hoping my face wasn't as visibly reddened as hers.

If anyone noticed, they made no mention. Someone *did* speak, however.

"Success . . ." Ellis groaned, making us both glance his way, surprised he was conscious—he looked half dead.

"What do you think, wife? Should we help him?"

"Hmmmm. I don't know, husband." She tapped her chin, her eyes sparkling with understanding and all the joy in the world. "It's debatable whether he deserves it—on account of all the misdirection and scheming he committed to get us to this point."

"Couldn't have said it better myself. The outcome, though . . ." We both leaned back, staring into each other's eyes rather than at the man lying at a comically askew angle. "I think the end might have justified his means."

"I daresay it did." She swept in to grace me with a swift peck on the lips, which then turned into at least two dozen more, each rapid touch more enjoyable than the last. She let out a controlled breath, fought to regain her composure, and failed in spectacular fashion. "I can't believe we're *married*!" She hopped up and down on the balls of her feet, letting out a high-pitched squeal. "I'm your *wife*! You're my *husband*!"

I grinned at her, drinking everything in. "I gotta say, the moment is a little ruined by all these complaining peasants."

Most of our friends were either unconscious or too drained to move a muscle. Of those still operational, soft noises escaped, the most dramatic of which came from Corporal Claws. She had a forelimb haphazardly draped over her eyes, leaving just enough of a gap for her beady little peepers to peer from.

Maria started a theatrical sigh, but it cut off abruptly. "I'm too happy to feign annoyance. Let's try this out . . ."

She opened her core, letting a pink cloud of chi billow out. When I sensed the difference the mark made on her spirit, I whistled softly. My change had been notable, but it was *nothing* compared to the magnitude of Maria's alteration. I'd *maybe* doubled my control and power; hers was tenfold stronger than before. If I was god-king, she was god-queen—and not only in name. I still had the edge when it came to raw output, but she'd reduced the canyon between us to a thin ravine.

I wasn't the only one who noticed her enhanced capacity. I sensed his approach before I heard it, and only after he slammed into Maria, whizzing through the air like an intercontinental missile, did the sound waves arrive.

"Ooooh," Slimes cooed, his body shifting as his master's strength flooded through him. "Oh. Oh! O—" He cut off with a choked noise as his form roiled. "*Help.*"

I barked a laugh, reaching out with a mesh of light, the strands helping him stay whole. He would have been fine, but my reinforcement made it a much less painful experience than exploding and re-forming might have been. Maria giggled, her clouds having paused with his arrival. Fractions of a second passed, and he turned himself into a gem, taking up a crystalline structure as he dropped toward the sandy ground.

Before he could reach it, Maria's pink haze engulfed everyone—including the two horrors of the deep currently bobbing up and down nearby on unbroken waves, not to mention the molten slug dwelling just below the seafloor. Time stood still, and I let my awareness drift away from my body, focused entirely on what my wonderful wife was doing.

Her billowing chi sought out ailments. Surprisingly, she actually found some. A muscle in Fergus's shoulder, a long-ago fractured bone in Peter's arm, and an over-used tendon in Steven's wrist. That cultivators still had bodily injuries was a stunning revelation—common knowledge stated that awakening fixed such things—but I didn't have time to consider it.

The moment said ailments were healed, her chi looked for something else. It assessed their cores, finding them all exhausted, except for Corporal Claws and RPM—who'd stolen chi from somewhere—and Ruby, who hadn't overexerted herself because of her pregnancy, but was doing an impressive job at pretending to be unconscious.

Though I didn't actively shape it, I could feel my core contributing, faint wisps of purpose guided by my miraculous wife. She used them to strip her own healing aspect from the pink clouds. Now pure, her essence flowed into our enervated friends and family, allowing everyone, even those with antithetical natures, to absorb the functionally endless chi.

They shot upright like reanimated zombies, each fevered by the events of the last few minutes. I was beyond thankful for my previously unknown level of self-control. If not for it, their waves of emotion probably would have knocked me on my ass. Instead, it was their actual bodies that knocked me on my ass, the vast majority of those present unable to stop themselves from joining the affectionate assault.

Neither Maria nor I said a word, both bathing in the onslaught of unspoken sentiments, rushed sentences, and bestial noises that assailed us. But then a threatening blade of aura stabbed out into the night. Like a busload of tourists driving past a train wreck, we all turned to stare, creating a sea of wide-eyed faces that couldn't look away.

Rocky had intentionally overshot the group hug. He rested on the sand beside a seated Ellis, the former holding a lit cigarette out toward the latter. Neither archivist nor crab were the source of that violent intent.

"Explain yourself," Roger demanded, the tip of a chi-blade held to Ellis's throat. "You did *not* mention this in your plans."

Ellis shrugged, his right hand reaching over to pluck the cigarette from Rocky's claw. Roger's blade was a blur. It twisted and lashed out, severing its target in two. Unperturbed, the archivist caught the top half of the bisected cigarette and took a drag. "I did mention this part of the plan, just not to you."

Roger seethed, not hiding his core's belief that Ellis was a threat, his killing intent as cold as it was clear.

Rocky let out a placating hiss and gestured with one claw for Roger to relax. In response, the sword-chi cultivator sprouted a second blade from his other hand and pointed it directly down at the unfazed crustacean.

But Rocky wasn't swayed. He reached behind his back—retrieved a cigarette from literally fracking nowhere, lit it on his shell, and raised it toward Roger, all the while giving me a questioning look.

"I consent," I said. "As long as you tell me where those keep coming from."

He blew negative bubbles.

"Ah, well. Worth a shot."

"What of the leaf?" hissed Rocky.

"What? Oh, I don't care. I know I made you promise not to give it to anyone, but I'm not about to make my father-in-law ask for permission to smoke. Seems like a great way to have a blade of chi aimed at my neck." In truth, I thought it might actually help Roger, but I wasn't about to tell him that—it would only make him refuse it. Maria agreed, squeezing my hand ever so slightly.

"So?" hissed Rocky, raising the "leaf" toward the sword-chi cultivator. "Will you try? I believe it could benefit—"

"I don't want drugs, *crab*. What I *need* is for this wretched archivist to take responsibility for his actions."

"Would you accept a wager, Roger?" Ellis asked, puffing on . . . *When did he light his pipe*? He breathed so deeply that the unprotected skin of his neck pressed into the sword, a single bead of blood forming around the tip. But Ellis just exhaled, a serene expression coming to his face. "If you partake of . . . What do you call them, Fischer?"

"Cigarettes."

"Yes. Thank you. If you partake of a cigarette, Roger, and meditate with Rocky and I, you can hit me. As hard as you want."

Roger's eyes narrowed. "That isn't a wager."

"Sure it is. The wager is upon your resolve. I bet that once you inhale the exalted leaf and practice the technique passed down to us, you will no longer wish to strike me. If I win, you don't hit me. If you win, I am struck."

Another time, Roger might have considered the bet for longer. But the fury in his soul was barely letting him breathe, let alone think straight. "Deal," he said, holding out a rigid hand.

Ellis shook it. "We must go, then."

"What? Where?"

"The technique may only be passed down by its master practitioners. We must go to the isle."

"That wasn't part of the deal. I won't leave my daughter's side so soon after you *forced* her to become some kind of fledgling deity!"

As they spoke, the cuddle puddle had slowly disassembled. Each of us stood and watched the spectacle. One woman in particular had been inching forward, and with those words from Roger, she finally made her move.

Sharon slammed into his back, her arms wrapping around his torso, hugging him tight. Rather than doubt or fear, she radiated surety and contentment. He retracted his blades, and she squeezed him tighter. "This was what Maria wanted, dear. I knew about the plan, and I also agreed to hide it from you. We needed your full strength to contain the resulting, uhhh . . . *love?*"

"It was an *explosion*! An explosion that came from our *daughter!*"

"Roger . . ." She spun him by the arm so they faced each other, his movement only occurring because he allowed it. "It's what she wanted. What she *wants*. How many times has she told us she will follow Fischer if he ascends? How many times has she come to us and expressed the depths of her affection for the man beside her? A *good* man, by the way—one who feels exactly the same as she does. *Hera's beautiful gaze*, you felt their bond not two minutes ago! We all did!"

Rocky, taking one last puff on his cigarette before throwing the butt into his mouth and chewing it to mush, blew bubbles of approval. "You know me to be an honorable crab, swordsman Roger. I promise you this: The thing we intend to share with you, the wisdom of the isle, will assist you in growing stronger, protecting your family, and seeing things as they truly are."

It was a ridiculous statement from the formerly belligerent crab, yet Roger mulled it over for a long moment. Contrasting expressions flashed across his face, vanishing as fast as they appeared, until, finally, he nodded. "I'll follow you. Don't be surprised when I still choose to strike you over the horizon, Ellis."

"Hey now," I said, "let's not rush into things. Maybe Roger *should* stay close. Why not teach him here? Where I can, uhhhh, watch from a safe distance, you know? Make sure nothing goes wrong?"

"I am sorry, Fischer." Ellis shook his head. "It must happen on the isle. And no, you may not come."

"Yeah? Well, maybe I'll just follow you, then! I can teleport there in an instant!"

"You will not do that."

I sniffed. "Why not?"

"It would be a grave insult, one egregious enough for you to be unwelcome on the isle forevermore."

"Are you hearing this, Maria? They deny a god-king. On his wedding day."

"Precisely," Ellis replied, already walking toward the shore. "Are you implying that the alleviation of momentary ignorance is more important than spending time with the woman you have finally married? Your god-queen? After making her wait so, *so* long?"

I pointedly avoided glancing at Maria, whose expression was no doubt sharper than her father's blades.

"Besides," Ellis continued over his shoulder, "you have to stay here and fill the tunnels."

"The what now?"

He turned on the spot, giving me a rueful smile and pointing down. I saw nothing, so I reached out with tendrils of essence. My eyes went wide when I felt the cavernous structure below. The tunnels created by Cal and the first sister had fused with the network of my Domain. They were empty of . . . everything. Neither air nor chi filled the kilometers of winding paths. That vacant space called out to me. It remembered my chi and wanted more. The marks on our souls buzzed in response. A deep desire to fill it with essence washed through me. Instead of capitulating, I focused on the outside world, leveling an accusatory gaze at Ellis.

He was already raising his palms in supplication. "Apologies, Fischer, but I promised to tell you as soon as I was able. This is the other task I mentioned."

"Why couldn't you just tell me this morning? Why spring it on me now? I'm all for pranks, but . . ." I frowned at the sheepish expression he was giving me. "There's more, isn't there? Go on, then. Out with it."

"I really am sorry. But yes, there is one more thing. Once you start channeling chi into the network, you cannot stop. Disconnecting yourself for even a moment will damage the tunnels, possibly beyond repair."

"How long will it take . . . ?"

"I do not know. Maria can accelerate the process by also channeling her essence into it. Unlike you, she should be able to pause at will."

"*Should* be able to?" Maria repeated.

"Yes."

"How much of my chi will it take?" I asked.

"I do not know."

"And we need the tunnels because . . . ?"

"I cannot tell you."

"Let me get this straight: I have to sacrifice an unknown portion of my chi for an unknown amount of time, you can't tell me why—other than that it will help Tropica—and if I stop for even a second, the whole thing might permanently fail. Is that about right?"

"Yes."

I turned toward Maria. "Would it make me a bad person if I slapped Ellis through a mountain or two?"

"You know, I'm not sure. On one hand, he just married me to the man of my dreams. On the other, he's being a dick."

"Right? Something about his manipulation is really rubbing me the wrong . . ." I trailed off as I noticed something not far from shore. "*Oh, get fracked, Ellis!* You can't just take a man's boat without asking!"

Bob the boat, my trusty vessel of the deep, sailed parallel to the coastline, sails unfurled to catch the blasts of wind essence from Bill and Pelly's pelican family. That's why I hadn't seen them earlier. They'd been waiting by *Bob*, ready to bring him here at a moment's notice.

Roger had a similarly visceral reaction. If looks could kill, Ellis would have been cut down where he stood. "You planned this, didn't you, bastard? All of it?"

Ellis took a deep breath, his guilt leaving him as salty air entered his lungs. "If I did, do you not wish to learn the technique that allowed me to calm my thoughts and scheme so thoroughly?"

"I am going to savor hitting you after all this is over . . ." Roger turned to Sharon, his edges nowhere to be seen as he embraced her, his wife clinging to him and rubbing his back reassuringly.

Maria's vise grip on my abdomen tightened, and we held each other as Roger, Ellis, and Rocky leaped onto *my* boat, the latter having hissed something at Snips that left her blushing.

A tension had been rising between Maria and me, an itch that had only gotten more demanding the longer it remained unscratched. I looked down at my wife. "Shall we?"

"I thought you'd never ask."

We moved through space in an instant, appearing on Bob's deck, which wasn't far from shore. Both Maria and I caught one of our tormenter's wrists as the light of our arrival receded.

"Wha—What are you doing?" Ellis demanded, his cool demeanor wilting beneath the strength he had conspired to grant us.

"Just giving you our thanks," Maria replied, her voice sickly sweet. "For *everything* you've done."

"You don't—you don't have to do it!"

"Whatever do you mean?" I asked, giving him a caustic smile.

"The task! You can do what you want! You don't have to fill the tunnels with power! It's only if you *want* to!"

"I know that, mate. I also don't have to throw you over the ocean, but that doesn't mean it's not the right thing to do."

Roger gave me a respectful nod from behind Maria. Ellis swallowed and tried to circulate his calming chi, but it fell apart without the smoke he used to center himself. Rocky scuttled up before us. Hope flooded from Ellis's core when he spotted the crab, assuming he'd come to intervene.

But then Rocky pointed up at the archivist's head. "May I?"

"Be my guest, mate! See, Ellis? It's not hard to communicate. You should try it sometime."

Rocky leaped onto the archivist's noggin, produced a lit cigarette from nowhere, and took a drag.

"Rocky!" Ellis said, eyes pleading, still failing to circulate his chi without access to his pipe. "Please! My friend! Might I take a hit off—"

We launched him.

Rocky's telltale "EEEEEEEEEEEEEEEEEEEeeeeeeeeeeeeeeeeee—" was music to my ears, as were his mount's terrified screams, the archivist flipping end over end countless times before disappearing beyond the horizon.

A Little Spicy

The following morning, I woke to wonderful scents and even better memories. A riot of wings fluttered in my stomach, the sensation so overwhelming I had to roll around, my arm drifting over in search of . . .

"Maria?" I asked, blinking bleary eyes to find her side of the bed empty.

Soft footfalls fled from the lounge room, growing louder as they approached the door. It swung open a moment later and light came flooding in, the sun having risen more than I'd expected.

"What time is it?"

"Closer to noon than sunrise." My wife didn't move from the doorway, her silhouette intoxicating despite being obscured by a robe. "You clearly needed the sleep after last night."

"You should have woken me."

Maria stepped forward, the scent of what she held almost as entrancing as she was. "The sky was already light when you fell asleep. Mid-sentence, by the way." She laughed at the memory, then offered me the cup. "Coffee? Sue's finest."

I let out a pleased *mmmm* as I took a sip, the earthy, rich, and slightly bitter notes perfectly contrasted by the slightest hint of passiona husk. "Are those pastries I smell?"

She'd retreated to the doorway, still facing me. "They are. I had Rocky create a little oven outside to keep them fresh for when you woke." There was a whisper of teasing in her voice. Before I could ask about it, she continued. "You have two courses for brekkie. Second, Sturgill's best creation."

"I can smell the buttery croissants, but what's the first cour . . . *Oh.*"

In a single lithe movement, she'd untied her robe. It parted, yet the blinding sunlight obscured the soft curves and hard lines of her body. A taunting shrug, her lungs expanding, her robe falling. She stretched and twisted oh so slightly. The side profile of her chest knocked the air from me.

"I thought you might want something more . . . indulgent for your first course," she said. "As befits a god-king."

Unable to help myself, I pointed over her shoulder. "You know that anyone walking past the front window would see your perfect little tushy, right?"

She grinned. "Good thing I have the Buzzy Boys holding a perimeter in every direction. Wouldn't want us getting interrupted."

"You . . . you created a demilitarized zone around the house?"

"I did."

"That might be the single most romantic thing anyone has ever done for me."

Her answering laugh was lilting yet filled with desire. "Really? I'm only getting started."

"Gods above, I love you."

"Is that so?" She stepped back, a third of her body shyly disappearing behind the doorframe. "You seemed more worried about people walking past than taking me up on my offer. Maybe we should have brekkie and—"

"*Here*," I commanded, sitting up, letting a fraction of my need for her flood out. "*Now*."

She gasped, chest heaving as she stepped forward, full silhouette once more lit from behind. Her heart raced even faster than mine. Her yearning was just as strong. The four steps she took to the bed seemed to take an eternity.

She raised one knee to the mattress; the other swung over me. I grabbed her waist. Her smooth skin consumed my senses. She lowered herself, but I rolled us both over, planting my arms to either side of her. Beneath me, her freckles were almost invisible against the red flush of her face.

I moved even lower, my forearms bulging, elbows pressing into the white sheets. We were so close I could hear her pulse, feel her breath, hot and sweet and pleading.

Like universes colliding, their many stars, planets, and moons reduced to shimmering clouds of interstellar dust, we became one.

CHAPTER ELEVEN

Collaboration

High above Phostheia, an empress exhaled slowly, doing what she could to calm her racing thoughts. She'd hoped it was all a terrible dream—a vivid nightmare whose impact would begin to fade the moment she awoke, becoming a distant memory by this late-afternoon hour.

No such luck.

As Aletheia extended her recently enhanced senses, scanning the words of her faithful below, her mood darkened still. They spoke of her ascension. Some sang— literally *sang*—of the glory that House Veritus had bestowed upon the Kingdom of Light. One and all, their intentions were pure. Pious, even.

It made her sick.

None of them knew of the terrible discoveries. They were blessedly free of that burdensome knowledge, having neither witnessed the revival of ancient artifacts, nor heard Sven's recounting of the events he'd seen—which, rather than provide illumination, had only further clouded the truth.

There really had been a spirit-beast attack on the capital. And in the dark ashes of that atrocity, an unknown cultivator had somehow come out on top.

God-King Fischer . . .

Even thinking that name made bile rise in her throat. This should have been a week of celebration. She should be moving through the people atop a palanquin, casting the brilliant light of her breakthrough down each of Phostheia's streets. Instead, she sat alone in her sleeping quarters, her mind and future cast in bitter shadow. She thrashed under the covers, frustration building until her eyes watered. It wasn't fair. None of this was how it was supposed to be. She had succeeded, damn it!

So consumed were her thoughts that she did not sense Evan's approach. The soft rap of knuckles on her chamber door twisted the blade of dread already stabbing her abdomen, making the anguish flare even brighter. She had ordered nobody to attend to her. For the head mage to defy her request? Something severe must have occurred.

She refused to be seen by Evan this way. It would only cause him more grief, and if his unshakable foundation cracked, hers might crumble with it. "So much for being the divine bridge to the heavens . . ." Aletheia placed her hands in her lap, relaxed her shoulders, took one last deep breath, and adopted the regal mask she so hated donning.

"Come in," an empress ordered.

But when Evan opened the door, his eyes were already red, his resolve on the verge of breaking. Disconnecting the latch had canceled the chamber's nullifying rituals, and the depth of his worries assaulted her, threatening to tear the mask free. He made to talk, but she stalled him with a raised hand. "Get a hold of yourself, Evan." *Please,* she didn't add. *I cannot support both of us right now.*

Her most-trusted servant nodded, taking a moment to box in his doubts. "I apologize, Empress Veritus. I bring news."

"Speak it."

His chi wavered, threatening to spill, but he hammered the sides back into place. "Best you see for yourself, Empress."

"The relics?"

Again, the brittle walls surrounding his core threatened to fall. "Yes, Empress."

"Very well." She stood, crossing her arms to ensure her hands didn't shake. "Let us go."

With each step she took through the castle, a bit of her composure returned, each brick of optimism built upon the others—only for the structure to come crashing back down when the reality of her situation struck. This cycle repeated three times before she focused on the outside world instead, no longer trusting her thoughts.

"Did the screen light up last night, Evan? Hours before midnight?"

Genuine surprise leaked through the gaps between his walls. "Yes, Empress. You knew?"

"A hunch." Her brand had tingled. She'd thought it a figment of her imagination. Evidently, it wasn't. "Why didn't you come straight to me? Someone was watching the artifacts, were they not?"

"We . . . we did not want to defy your orders, Empress."

She cast a sidelong glance. He hadn't bothered hiding the lie. Or perhaps he was no longer capable now that she'd successfully attained her divine ideal? "You used my words against me. You wanted to let me rest, and it was a convenient excuse."

"Yes, Empress."

"Did only some of you agree on this course of action, or was it unanimous?"

"Unanimous, Empress."

"Never do it again," ordered the mask, chin raised and eyes forward. *Thank you, Evan,* thought the woman behind it.

"Yes, Empress!" He dropped to a knee. "This I swear, on my soul and cultivation: I will never repeat such an error, lest I be unmade." He was already upright before she could even think of stopping him.

The mask slipped; Aletheia slapped him on the back of the head. "Release that this instant, you idiot. I won't have you dying the next time you make a mistake. I absolve you of your oath."

Blinking, he let her strands of divine chi cast the words away. He clearly didn't know she could do that. To be fair, she hadn't either. Not for sure, anyway, though her instincts had assumed it possible. She allowed herself a small smile at the reminder of her newfound power over the universe—it was enough to override her many fears, if only temporarily. Then she slipped the mask back on.

Evan took a few hurried steps to catch up with her stride. "Yes, Empress. Thank you, Empress."

Neither of them spoke as they climbed the last few stories. They passed more and more serving staff, each of whom radiated such reverence that Aletheia's stomach twisted anew.

But I am not Aletheia, she reminded herself. She was indistinguishable from the mask she wore. *I am the Empress.*

Her nausea turned to glory as her ego burgeoned. She held on to that feeling with white-knuckled intensity, refusing to let go of the only thing keeping her afloat, no matter how unbecoming it might be.

The other mages of the Prime Cadre must have heard or felt Evan's oath. When they saw her enter the ritual chamber, they dropped to their knees—but this time she was ready.

"No," commanded the mask.

All returned to their feet. Without preamble, the *empress* strode to the screens, seeing the words from halfway across the room.

Fischer, god-king of Tropica, has chosen a wife!
Long live God-Queen Maria of House [error]!

Before her racing mind could pick apart the implications, the chamber faded, her vision commandeered by the heavens.

Quest complete: In Defense of Phostheia
Intelligence gathered: God-King Fischer has married God-Queen Maria
Progress: 3/3
Reward: Domain evolution
. . .
Domain has gained passive: Threat Specialist
Effect: Detect foreign Domains up to two stages above your own
Aletheia licked her lips and dismissed the words. She felt numb as she glanced down at the lines appearing on the screen.
Local Domain detected.
Effect: 20% Suppression, 20% Bolstering, 20% Growth
Evolution: Enhanced threat detection.

She waited for the foreign Domain's information to display. Nothing happened for a long moment. Each blink of the screen's cursor forced her closer to the edge of a cliff. Below, the abyss awaited. Her hands started to tremble, so she clenched them and squeezed her eyes closed, shutting herself off from the outside world. When she opened them again, the screen had changed.

Warning! Foreign Domain detected.

Effect: 40% Suppression, 40% Bolstering, 40% Growth, 500% Range.
Evolution: All effects doubled.

The ground seemed to crumble beneath her, and she hurtled down into the abyss, the sun's rays getting farther from reach with each passing moment. A second god-tier ruler, aligned with the god-king and recognized by the heavens, had been terrible. The effects of Tropica's Domain were catastrophic. She plunged deeper and deeper into the surrounding depths, the sun's divine light becoming all but a memory.

Her ideal faded from view. Within the span of a day, she'd been acknowledged by the heavens, then tossed aside like trash. It had been a rollercoaster of emotions, her mind cycling through higher highs and lower lows than she'd fathomed possible. Despair settled on her sternum, forcing her even further down. An old emotion arrived, acidic and demanding consideration.

Fury.

How *dare* she be treated so. Was Aletheia not the divine bridge between heaven and the Kallis Realm? Was it not Aletheia's face in all the visions? Her ideal responded, pulsing high above, flashing the faintest glimmer of illumination—of *hope*—across her body.

"If something does not serve me or humanity . . ." she recited. "It is my obligation to burn it away."

The glimmer became a solid ray, which multiplied into dozens, then hundreds of warm beams. They shone into and through her. Those words, the sentences she had spoken to facilitate her breakthrough . . . they extended beyond her mistake of allowing Gormona's rot to fester by delaying action. Just as she'd let good intentions cause the razing of a kingdom, she was now letting her own thoughts threaten her purpose. And by extension, her faithful.

So, beneath the divine light of the heavens, their brilliance once more acknowledging her, she cast aside what no longer served.

Fear, worry, doubt. Those feelings lingered for a reason. Each was necessary for self-preservation, a remnant attribute of evolution that had ensured the survival of her ancestors. Such emotions were undoubtedly human—which Aletheia was not. She was the divine bridge. She was the one who would connect this lowly realm with the heavens.

All at once, everything clicked into place. Of course the heavens had shared the existence of these detestable upstarts with her. *Fischer and Maria* . . . they probably thought themselves on the path to godhood, only a short distance from sitting atop the empty throne high above. Aletheia knew the truth—they had been sent to test her. They were nothing more than obstacles created for her to overcome. A final challenge to conquer. For what was light without shadow? How could you be good without denying evil?

She was the brilliance, and she must cleanse these villainous heretics from the world.

That incessantly nattering part of herself rallied one last time, desperately clawing its way up her throat, trying to force the regal mask from Aletheia's face.

She met it with her own ideal. *Kill the few, save the many.*

Those words beat the voice back, her divine illumination forcing it to the darkest corners of her soul. The mask fused itself to the best parts of the empress. She transcended the bleak pit, drawn ever upward by golden light, leaving behind the weak girl she had once been. When she opened her eyes, she'd returned to the ritual room. It was aglow with glorious radiance.

No longer hiding, the empress spoke, giving voice to a new title. Her faithful heard. All across the city, they repeated her proclamation with tears in their eyes as they screamed it into existence. Lines printed across a relic. She didn't need to gaze upon its screen to know the words, but she did so anyway. Such was her right as god-empress.

Phostheia, capital of the Kingdom of Light, has witnessed the divine!
Long live God-Empress Aletheia of House Veritus!

No sooner had she finished reading the last line than more words appeared. This time, they were directly in her field of view. She grinned as she read them.

New Quest: The Best Defense
Objective: Go on the offensive. Identify and annihilate a [severe] threat to humanity and the Kingdom of Light.
Reward: Variable

Beneath the late-afternoon sun, I gazed at the river mouth, taking solace in the small waves forming where it met the ocean. I took a deep breath, reached out for the mark on my soul, and hesitated.

Maria rubbed my forearm, her gentle touch centering me. "You don't have to do it."

"I know." I laced my fingers through hers, lifted her hand, kissed it. "I want to."

And I meant it. The mark had itched all day, growing more insistent the longer I endured. That wasn't the reason I was gonna do this, though. If filling the network below would strengthen Tropica, I would do it. Still, weakening myself temporarily was a terrifying prospect, as was knowing that I couldn't stop without repercussion.

Ellis had gone about it in all the wrong ways, but I believed the scheming bastard. I trusted him, and that he had good reason for keeping me in the dark.

So, with my god-king mark encouraging me to continue, I cast my hesitation aside.

A thrill ran through me as my first tendril of chi flowed into the empty cavern. Regret followed soon after, the tunnel ripping more and more of my essence away. Head pounding, vision wavering, senses dimming, I breathed a sigh of relief when the flow stabilized. My headache receded and vision returned, but my senses stayed diminished.

"Damn . . ." Maria said. "That's most of your chi. How do you feel?"

"Not great, though I'm glad it didn't leave me completely helpless." I frowned, reaching for my essence. My own core disobeyed me at first, the network below demanding that any spare chi get sent down into its empty tunnels. But after a few seconds, my core obeyed, letting me harness what little chi I could. It was only a trickle of my former strength. "That delay is gonna take some getting used to . . ."

"Best we get this over with as soon as possible, then."

"You don't have to—"

"I know," she interrupted, throwing my words back at me. "I want to."

Her mark rejoiced as she consented to its desires, and the same percentage of chi flowed down into the ground. Identical symptoms to mine hit her, so I held her by the waist, helping what little I could.

"Huh," she said, blinking. "That's not so bad. Having muted senses is actually a little refreshing. It's nice not having to consciously suppress them."

"Huh. You're right. That *is* nice. Trust you to see the positive side of things." I offered her my arm. "Shall we go see how everyone's doing while we get used to this?"

She looped her elbow in mine. "I'd love nothing more."

Just before we reached Tropica, I paused mid-step as an odd tingling hit the god-king mark on my core. Curiosity bloomed, and a million thoughts raced through me. I let them float past like so many clouds. The anomalous feeling in my soul was all but forgotten as I stretched my arms toward the sky, soaking in the sensations of warmth, taut muscles, and a cool breeze gusting from the east. The network below could have my power, but it couldn't have my peace.

"Agreed," Maria said, having also felt and discarded the unexplained tingle in favor of a good stretch. We were both so lost in the bliss that we bumped into each other, motor skills momentarily absent.

"Well, well, well," interrupted a booming voice. "Look who finally—" Duncan cut off with a grunt as a gelatinous form slammed him to the cobbled street.

"Hiiii! He was about to say something silly. I took the liberty of flattening him!"

"Thank you, Slimes," Maria replied, holding out a hand. Her familiar leaped onto it, wobbled with delight, then merged back into her core. Evidently, his abilities weren't diminished by Maria channeling most of her chi into the tunnels.

"I regret nothing," Duncan groaned. Regretfully.

Beside him, Fergus shook his head. "Forgive me."

"It's hardly your fault, mate."

"I encouraged his oddities, Fischer. I hoped to foster out-of-the-box thinking, assuming it could lead to creative innovation . . ."

"Bullshit," Duncan wheezed, dusting off his clothes as he stood. "You're even more of a jokester than I am. You should hear the things he says in priv—"

Clap.

"Ow! What was that for?"

"For running your trap, you cheeky git. Run along back to the workshop. If we leave Claws and that damnable raccoon alone too long, there won't be a smithy to return to."

"She's taken up smithing?" I asked.

Fergus snorted and shoved Duncan, firm but without ill intent, sending him stumbling off in the direction of their building. "If by 'taken up smithing' you mean zipping around the workshop, watching everyone a little too closely, and only stopping her familiar from stealing half the tools he tries to pocket, then sure, she has taken up the profession."

"She's just . . . watching? *Why?*"

"*Inspiration*," Fergus quoted, twisting his burly mouth into a grin approximating hers, complete with a tilt of the head and slightly crazed eyes.

"Damn, mate—that's actually a really good impression."

"Thanks. I've had all day to brush up on that devious little rat's expressions."

"How has it been otherwise? I can sense a *lot* of cores that way."

This grin was genuine. "We have more apprentices than any other profession. Ellis's speech yesterday morning lit a fire under the entire village, and most gravitated our way."

"Really? That's wonderful, mate. What are they all working on?"

"Perhaps you should come see it for yourself. Have a moment?"

Maria and I shared a look, both too curious to turn it down. She nodded. "Lead the way, dearest smith! The god-king and his wife wish to assess your workshop's, er, *efficacy!*"

Even before we reached the crossroads that led to the smithy, the sounds of its workers rang out, echoing off the empty streets. The rhythmic clang of metal on metal might have been annoying for some, but it reminded me of the various projects I'd worked on with the smiths, making a sense of calm wash over me as I recalled my Zen-like state when operating the bellows.

It was like finding an old friend on your doorstep. I couldn't help but smile at the unexpected arrival. But then another friend came from behind, shoulder-checked the Zen-like memory, and exploded the metaphorical doorstep into a million splinters.

Corporal Claws had sensed my distraction. She seized the opportunity, flying out, loading her lips with potent chi, and planting a kiss right on my forehead. The weak jolt of electricity zapped my brain. Claws paused there for a second, frowning as she felt how much essence the tunnels were taking. Then she grinned like the maniac she was, squeezed my cheeks together, and pressed the top of her noggin against my forced pout, making me smooch her back.

She retreated into the smithy on an arc of lightning, her head swiveling like an owl so I never lost sight of her cheeky smile.

I shook my body to dispel the lingering current and strode forward to peer through the workshop's double doors. Claws hadn't stopped moving. She zipped around, eyeing the dozens of humans lining workstations. There was a moment of confusion when I spied what they were creating, but when I noticed the object mounted on a far wall, I realized what they were trying to emulate.

A third of the building's occupants were crowded around one of five furnaces. The person holding their attention removed a glowing chunk of metal with giant tongs. The gathering parted, letting her move to an anvil. She held the metal in place and raised a massive hammer overhead, preparing to strike.

I cleared my throat. "Bonnie?"

"Huh? Oh! Hey, Fischer!"

I waved to gesture at the room. "Is this your doing?"

"Is what my— *Oh!* A little no, a little yes. Chat later." She turned back to the anvil, glancing up at the apprentices watching her. "You give it a good ol' smack right here, see? Keep spinnin', keep smackin'. Only return it to the furnace when it's as long as your forearm."

I blinked at the swift dismissal, confusion rising, only to be washed away by relief. Between Claws and Bonnie, I had at least two friends who wouldn't start treating me differently—no matter the strength I attained.

"It wasn't her idea," Fergus elaborated, also smiling at the intensity on Bonnie's face. "I hung the winch as a trophy of sorts, and when the rest of the apprentices learned it was created by a novice . . . ? Well, it gave them a goal. Something to aim for."

I peered around the room, looking at the workstations manned by fledgling smiths. All were producing long lengths of metal that tapered off to one end. Duncan supervised, his gaze serious, his lackadaisical demeanor forgotten. In the far corner, a small stack of completed winches were piled atop a bench. I pointed at them.

"Why aren't there any reels? Did they give up, or . . . ?"

Fergus's eyes twinkled in delight. "Not at all. Follow me." He led us from the building.

As we approached the structure next door, I cocked my head at the sounds coming from the building.

"We decided to make it a group project of sorts," Fergus said, gesturing with one hand for us to look inside.

I already knew what we'd find, but that didn't stop a wide smile from splitting my face as I saw the woodworkers. There were almost as many apprentices working the stations here as there had been in the smithy. They were in the early stages of crafting reels. Unlike next door, varied materials were in use, some opting for pine, others for hardwood.

"Ho, Fischer!" Brad called, which his brother Greg echoed even louder.

"I've told you guys not to call me that." I shot them a wink. "Not in public, anyway."

They snapped off rigid salutes. "Yes, God-King!"

"On second thought, maybe the former was bett—"

"No," Maria interrupted. "Don't even joke about it."

"Yes, God-Queen!" I mirrored the woodworkers' salutes. "Forgive me!" She gave me a warning glare, which only made me laugh. "Ohhhh, you don't like that, huh?"

Her glare deepened. "No comment."

"Noted, God-Queen!" the brothers yelled, their bodies stiffer than the firmest of planks. "You hate being called god-queen, *God-Queen!*"

Maria responded with a sweet smile that turned saccharine as she extended a hand, palm up, a certain familiar jiggling out of it.

Before they could respond to the wordless threat, a pulse of chi suddenly came from the east. My muted senses made me question whether I'd imagined it. But then a cacophonous droning shook the world. The Buzzy Boys, one of whom was just outside, vibrated a warning. I whirled eastward.

A moment later, Teddy roared in fury, the primal sound racing across our connection and into the center of my soul.

I reached for my essence—it didn't respond.

CHAPTER TWELVE

Consumed

The Church of the Leviathan, Tropica Branch, five minutes earlier

The mind of a lobster is simple, yet impossible to comprehend. Because of their ostensible lack of problem-solving skills, many assume conscious thought to be beyond the average cricket's capabilities. Which might seem true if one compared them to humans or other seemingly intelligent beings, but was false nonetheless.

Even with a body the size of a finger, this particular runt of a cricket knew all too well how wondrous her living situation had become. She possessed flashes of memories of the time before, stored in her nerve clusters—not that she was aware of said clusters, of course; she was a lobster. All she understood was that the before had consisted of retreat, hiding for her life, and scavenging what little sustenance could be found.

Every moment had been fraught. So when some unknown attacker had scooped her up, she acknowledged her fate, a calm acceptance flooding her body as she was dragged to the surface. No sooner than she'd been trapped, however, she was freed once more, dropped into the den she now called home.

In the present, there were no more predators to avoid, lobster or otherwise. She could smell them nearby, their scent wafting over the sheer cliffs surrounding her. But with each passing day, she grew less afraid of their appearance, learning to trust the walls of her paradise. Caution was still observed, of course, which was why she'd dug a cave in the sand under said walls, large enough to conceal her entire body and then some.

There she rested, her antennae waving about in the currents, in wait for *it* to happen. Her favorite moment. It arrived multiple times a day, each instance so exciting she forgot all about her need to hide—if only for as long as it took to drag the falling prize back to her dwelling.

Food. Delicious, irresistible food. Sometimes it was firm and savory. Other times it was sweet, squishy, and released juice that colored the water purple, making her cave smell incredible until the next time food came from the heavens. She far preferred the sweet ones.

As wonderful as each day here was, today was even better. Rather than a single source of sweet juice, three of them drifted down onto the sand before her.

They were flawless. They called to her very soul. And they were all for her.

She dragged the first back to her lair and raced through her usually thoughtful consumption, not caring how much of the pulp fell to the sand—she could finish what remained later.

She was halfway through the second and already shifting to grab the third when a flash of color caught her eye. The hint of orange was there only a moment, and she scooted backward, hoping it had just been her imagination, her cave suddenly feeling too small to contain her. But then the color appeared again. There could be no doubt.

A massive claw bent over the lip of her sheer walls. A second followed. The lobster's antennae came next, trailed by the rest of it, the crustacean tumbling over the precipice in its rush. She went incredibly still, hoping it would eat the food and leave.

The invading creature's legs caught hold of the lower section of wall and raced forward, barreling for the meal it had clearly come for. With the faintest of movements, she started eating the rest of her sweet fruit, partly to destroy as much of its scent as possible, but mostly in defiance. How *dare* this young male invade her paradise—her *home*.

She recognized his odor. He had pursued her once in the before, chasing her until she wedged herself in a hole only she could fit within. His claws, almost twice the size of hers, had reached again and again into that crevice. When he eventually left, it wasn't out of compassion. Food had arrived nearby. It was her least-favorite variety, salty and firm, yet she would have sacrificed a limb for a few bites. Instead, she'd needed to find a new hiding place, knowing her tormenter would return when next he grew hungry.

Something occurred to her in that moment, her thoughts coming clear and concise. If spoken in English, the sentiment could roughly be translated to: What a bunch of *bullshit*. In the before, there had been too many other lobsters to count. Despite their number, they'd left each other alone, only ever ganging up on *her*.

Things were peaceful if their stomachs were full. Otherwise? The second they saw her up close and realized the disparity in their size, they chased like starved creatures, their intent clear.

Back in the present, she looked at the invading lobster, seeing the same ceaseless gait and unerring intensity it had used when chasing her. That's all she had ever been to him. Food. She was his sibling, yet he saw her as nothing more than a snack. For the crime of not representing a credible threat, she'd earned a death sentence. Close as he now was, she could see that he'd grown even larger than before. He had been eating well . . .

Before she knew what she was doing, she moved, her antennae leading the charge out of her den. He saw her coming, slowed a moment, then raced the last few steps to the spherical fruit. His pincers ripped and tore, pulling a large section off, which he then shoved into his undulating mouth. Worse, he started retreating with it, dragging her prize farther away.

Incensed, she raced forward. She cared not for the threat he presented. Her rage demanded retribution. The ground blurred past, and as she got closer, the analytical part of her mind registered that he wasn't so big after all. His snippers, so mighty from afar, seemed smaller than her own . . .

He never changed his course of action. Even when she was almost upon him, he slowly retreated, most of his awareness focused on shoveling as much of *her* food into *his* mouth as possible. Her powerful claws, fully cocked, shot forward.

He must have assumed she was aiming for the berry—she wasn't.

All too late, his muscular tail tensed, fibers preparing to contract and send him rocketing away.

Crack.

A cloud of grit billowed up, and as the grains slowly drifted back to the sandy floor, so, too, did both halves of his body. She reached out tentatively, picking one up, her antennae smelling its flavor. Her invader was certainly edible. She considered consuming him, her roiling emotions urging her toward such action. There would be justice in that . . .

But no. She wouldn't stoop to his and the rest of her kin's level. She made to drop him and return to her berry—which she now somehow knew her sweet treats were called—but she felt a pulse come from the larger half of her felled brother. Leaning closer, curiosity blossoming, she touched a small colorless orb. It was only as large as a pebble, yet contained an inordinate amount of strength.

It was in the same spot, centered below his thorax, that her own rage had seemed to originate. Her orb wanted to devour his. *Needed* to feel its power. She didn't fight the compulsion.

It tasted of nothing, then everything grew warm. She shook as the vitality became her own, lost to the sensations until a series of terrible sounds arrived—the scrape of carapaced legs on sheer rock.

She gazed up just as the first of them crested the walls of her paradise. Her brethren, the spineless scavengers that they were, had smelled their bisected brother and come to feast.

She stood as tall and proud as a cricket reasonably could. She'd not give up a single inch of ground—which was an odd notion for a regular lobster to hold, considering their general lack of knowledge regarding measurement systems. But she had more important things to worry about right now.

Let them come, she thought, spreading her snippers wide.

Technical Officer Theodore Roosevelt's mind was . . . elsewhere. He was all too happy following this daydream, his imaginary limbs at ease as they padded over loamy earth and across cool grass. Verdant trees surrounded him, another source of pleasant relaxation, but he barely noticed them—he'd just caught the smell of something far more intoxicating.

Honey.

Its scent was an almost physical thing. He imagined it as a yellow stream, opaque and bright and all-encompassing. His nose moved incessantly, twitching in all directions to follow the trail of golden goodness drawing him along. It grew stronger with each trunk he passed. It—

Crack.

A tree crashed to the side. He must have bumped it with his sturdy rump. He ignored it.

A soft buzz murmured out through the forest, and Teddy's mouth watered. If this was in the waking world, he wouldn't dare harm innocent insects. Those were the actions of the unawakened bear he once was. But in this vivid dream? No creatures would be harmed. He could indulge to his heart's content.

His salivary glands started working overtime in anticipation of the feast to come.

Clack.

Another tree fell. Teddy didn't care. He sprinted through the many trunks, embracing his animalistic instincts. He was on the hunt.

Clack. Snick. Clack.

He neither cared nor really noticed the odd sound each obliterated tree made in his wake. His hackles shivered. A part of him dreamed of a rival mammal being there in his path. Of his fangs and claws and brutal strength forcing the other away, leaving Teddy alone to tear into the beehive.

Branches rained down, leaves, sticks, splinters bouncing off the forest floor.

Snick. Snick.

And there it was. A horde of drones had surrounded their home. He could sense chi coming from them. They were spirit beasts. A hive mind, much like the Buzzy Boys, except far weaker. Teddy could just ignore them as he devoured their hard work. Their pathetic stingers wouldn't be able to puncture his thick hide.

He lowered his head, huffing and snorting, warning them to flee. They vibrated in response, their cores sending out a wave of essence. Teddy exploded forward, his mighty paw descending to pulverize dozens of them in a declaration of war.

But his limb found resistance, freezing in place as his claws dug into something stronger than stone. They were no mirage. Had he thought this was a dream . . . ? These upstart bugs stood between him and what he'd *earned.* They—

Crack!

A wave of potent power struck Teddy. He whirled, eyes opening, the verdant scene replaced by uniform bricks, lacquered wood, and . . . water? It sloshed under him, pooling in the giant grooves his deadly claws had carved into the church's floor, before becoming stuck. The liquid was clear at first, but then sand, gravel, and glittering shards of glass flowed by.

The crickets. Their tank. It had broken.

Two of said crickets came to a stop right under him—except it wasn't two at all. Both halves of the single lobster lay lifeless, its tiny body sliced right down the center. Everything went still. Had he done this? Teddy followed the trail of carnage, bile rising in his throat as his eyes passed over the dozens of dispatched lobsters, each a creature he'd been charged with protecting.

A trickle of water dribbled down the tank's wooden stand. His gaze traced it back to the shattered corner it spilled from, finding as many murdered crickets within the tank as on the floor. They'd become trapped in the isolating walls of stone crafted to protect the runt—the undersized creature he'd identified with—so she got enough food. Especially passiona berries. They were her favorite.

One of the crickets stirred. What he thought for a moment was an entire body was only a claw. He recognized her. It was the same adolescent crustacean he'd protected. How had she gotten so large? Her limb picked up one half of a murdered pod-mate, plucked something from its abdomen, and raised the orb of power to her mouth.

Layers of realization struck Teddy, each adding a boulder to a tomb of his own creation. Before he could fully comprehend the consequences of his actions, a wall of light and euphoria shone out from the lobster.

He had failed them. Each slain creature was a result of his inattention, and the undersized female he identified with had become a kin slayer, her soul burdened forevermore. He shivered as the light of her ascension consumed him, suffusing his body with rapturous elation he didn't deserve.

Teddy roared.

CHAPTER THIRTEEN

Enthusiastic Destruction

I cursed the tunnels below. The seconds they delayed me felt like an eternity. The moment my chi obeyed, I appeared in a flash of brilliant light, holding on to my essence, ready to strike whatever had caused Teddy such wordless anguish. His roar shook everything. There was a flicker of power, the same essence I'd noticed before hearing Teddy's call. Something shot *through* the cricket tank, rocketing away from the bellowing bear faster than a bullet. I caught it in one hand, glanced down, and stared into the eyes of an unknown lobster.

"Uhhh," Maria said.

"Uhhh," I agreed.

Teddy's roar continued shaking the world outside my barrier. A voice called out to my mind, so I brought him here. My essence tried to slip away. I didn't let it. Pistachio appeared in a smaller flash of light, his intense gaze locked on the regular-sized lobster I held out in front of me.

I passed it—no, *her*—to Maria, knuckled Pistachio's claw in thanks for his timely assistance, and dashed to Teddy. His eyes were pressed together, wicked jaws facing the heavens, lantern light reflecting off his deadly teeth.

In the time it took me to wrap my arms around him, I understood his red-hot flashes of anger. They were self-directed, containing the memories of what assailed him, so strong that even my disobedient chi could sense them. Teddy had been lost in thought for only minutes, but that had been enough for almost all the lobsters to be destroyed.

I squeezed him tight. "Mate . . . this isn't on you."

"My fault!" roared Teddy, sending glimpses of the daydream he'd been having. Shame fed his guilt, which further fueled his distress, a vicious cycle of self-castigation he couldn't escape.

My chi was slipping away from me, so I swiftly used it to give Teddy's brain a lil' slap, imagining and trying to mimic the way Claws's lightning had stunned me earlier, outside the smithy. It worked, Teddy's mind going blank for a brief moment. But because of my wavering control, I accidentally broadcast the image to another.

"On my way!" screeched Claws, misinterpreting my message. I emphatically declined her offer and returned my attention to Teddy.

Before he could swirl back into a spiral of punitive despair, I wrapped him in another hug and clutched at the last vestiges of my fleeing power. It almost escaped, but then Maria bolstered my will. Our fondness for him flooded into his core. The others joined, too. Love from all my bonded pals assaulted him, each of us broadcasting our genuine feelings and showing him the grace he wasn't giving himself.

It took a moment for us to break through, but when we did, I could tell it—

A fucking otter crashed through the building's southern wall.

"Master calls!" trilled the corporal. "I answer!" One forepaw was already drawn back, and with as much power as she could muster, Claws launched her payload. RPM's eyes were aglow, his larcenous little grabbers grasping, ready to apply a five-finger discount to anything he could get a hold of. The fun-sized bastard was going to steal the very anguish from Teddy's soul.

I caught him before he made it. "Sorry, buddy. I appreciate the sentiment—really, I do—but this is something Teddy has to work through on his own."

I had sensed the currents lurking beneath the surface of Teddy's core over the past weeks. He'd come here in search of purpose. This temple had been a refuge, a harbor in which he could weather the emotional storm. In letting most of his charges get dispatched, the currents had breached the seawall.

Teddy stood up, head hanging. "Walk," he growled, his tone and spirits at rock bottom.

"A bit of a stroll is a great idea. Is it okay if some of the Buzzy Boys accompany you, though? I'd worry otherwise."

"Don't care."

One of the Buzzy Boys, who'd already made it halfway into the building, froze mid-flight and let out a sad note. He'd wanted to ride behind Teddy's ear.

"Me!" screeched Claws. "Ride on *me!*"

The armored insect readily obliged. With a raccoon pulled back into her core and an awakened bee happily buzzing behind her ear, Claws trotted out through the hole of her own creation, chest proud and chin high.

Her pomp made Teddy's massive lip tug up into the facsimile of a smile, but it was for show. I patted him on the shoulder. "Take as long as you need, buddy. When you're ready to talk, you know where to find me."

He nodded, let out an apologetic growl, and cast me a meaningful glance.

"Happy to oblige. Just need a few seconds." I passed the time by giving another pat for good measure. The moment my essence obeyed me, I sent him far to the west and withdrew my senses, giving him space.

Maria had wasted no time in wrapping the newly awakened lobster in a cloud of pink essence, then running to the rescue of the unsnipped crickets. She scooped a couple off the floor, returning them to a section of tank free of bodies and broken glass.

The damage to the now-regular-sized lobster's core had been healed, but it was still in a state of distress, its form frozen as it took in the size of the leviathan holding it.

Pistachio gave her a *sup* nod.

Sup, she immediately nodded back, politeness overriding her terror. The token gesture seemed to boost her confidence.

Thick tendrils descended from the heavens, and unimaginable amounts of information streamed into the confused creature. It reminded me of Pelly's awakening so long ago—of the complete dissociation her face had momentarily shown. But it was over in the blink of an awakened lobster's eye. If they had eyelids, that is.

She peered at Pistachio, at Maria—stole another quick glance at Pistachio—then gazed up at me. As our gazes locked, something familiar and entirely unexpected occurred. We bonded. It wasn't the laborious and exhausting process as it had been with the rest of my animal pals and Maria in the sky. We still communicated the same depth of memory and meaning, though. It just . . . happened.

She knew all about me, and I all about her. The time in the tank. The hunger, retreat, and indignation of having her little patch of paradise invaded. The first male she'd severed in two. She understood the weight of what she had done. Part of me feared she'd go full introspection like Teddy, Snips, and . . . well, *me*. I couldn't have been more wrong.

She held no regrets. They had tried to end her when she was smaller, and when the tables turned, she decimated them, painlessly executing any of her brethren that scuttled overtop the walls of her home. Would she do the same with the knowledge she now possessed? No. Not at all. But neither did she hold her past self accountable for ending any interlopers and eating their spheres of power.

"Wait, *what?*" I shook my head, clearing her memory of those translucent orbs. "They had *cores?* Cores you could *eat?*"

I couldn't yet interpret her sounds as words the way I could with the rest of my animal pals, but the meaning of her soft hiss was nonetheless clear. *Delicious.* Again, she felt not a hint of self-reproach. It was a fact. The bubbles of gelatinous essence were tasty.

I broadcast all of this to Maria. Unfortunately, the other being bonded to my wife's soul also caught the message.

"Hiiii!" He jiggled atop her palm. "I'm Slimes! I'm a—"

"What about him?" I interrupted, pointing at Slimes. "You can feel how much chi he holds, right? Does he smell delicious?"

The lobster seemed to chew on this statement. The cogs of her mind whirred, every last grain of newly acquired knowledge used to reach her decision. She pointed up at Slimes and hissed. *Not food.*

Pistachio blew an affirmative bubble. "Good."

The homie was playing it cool, but through our bond I could feel the emotions he was hiding deep beneath his mighty shell. Maria did, too. We exchanged a flicker of a glance, our excitement building.

But then the moment was ruined.

The leader of the church we stood within came barreling *through* the front door. Thick bands of ornate metal warped around Gary's face, hips, and leading leg. It was a well-constructed entrance. Perhaps a little *too* well constructed. The frame and part of the building's facade came with the Gary-shaped strips.

Pistachio had to grab two massive stones from the air before they could destroy what remained of the compromised tank, and the female crustacean who'd only recently lived within stared at him in open awe. To her senses, he must have basically teleported, moving with far more haste than something his size should possess.

I tore my eyes from the two lobsters and grinned at Gary. "I've got good news, even better news, and a little bad news, mate. Which would you like first?"

He also had to tear his gaze away. He answered my question with a soundless nod toward the lady lobster.

"Wonderful. She's the 'even better' news. Looks like you have a second leviathan in the making, my man."

He licked his lips, staring at her once more. "What's the good news?"

"That's simple." I gestured all around. "Despite your church having lost two load-bearing walls, it's still standing. Definitely made of sturdy stuff."

"What are you— *Oh*." He spotted the side breach first. Maria gestured over his shoulder, pointing out what he'd done to the front door. "I did that?"

Maria barked a laugh. "You seriously didn't notice you tore the frame off the wall?"

"The first one was Claws," I added. "The front door, though . . ."

He frowned, his eyes flicking around at the different piles of rubble strewn all over, gaze always returning to the lady lobster before leaving once more. When he spotted the dispatched crickets, his face fell. "The bad news . . ."

"No, actually."

It wasn't just Gary who gave me a confused look—both lobsters did as well.

I held up my hands. "Okay, don't get me wrong. It's objectively bad that they're dead. But it was also what facilitated the awakening of Pistachio's lady friend. The bad news is related to that essence running through your veins right now."

Gary's eyes drifted toward his abdomen, lingering there before tracing lines up his chest and down his arms. "What? Where did . . . ?" His mouth hung open as he searched for the correct words. "*How?*"

I gestured all around us. "I've felt the power of this building before. Next door is the same. Since Ellis and the rest of my treasonous followers stamped me with this damned god-king mark, I now know for sure what I'd only suspected previously. Both the Cult of the Leviathan and the Church of Carcinization are separate entities from mine . . ." I held up a finger, needing a second to gather my thoughts.

Gary blanched, his enhanced mind latching on to the worst possible interpretation and sprinting away with it. "Do I have to leave Tropica . . . ?"

"*What?* No, you goose. You're still a part of the village—and a member of my church—but there's a different source of chi flowing into this building." I nodded toward his navel. "For whatever reason, it flooded your body with that strength, possibly so you could get here and defend your new leviathan? I can't say for sure."

He tensed his arms, assessing the palpable power still coursing through him. "If I don't have to leave . . . what's the bad news?"

"You're on the edge of a breakthrough, mate. That alone is *great* news. The negative bit, though, is that I have to sign off on it."

Of all the outcomes I expected from this revelation, his immediate acceptance wasn't one of them.

"That makes sense, actually," Gary said, troubled thoughts nowhere to be found. "We're in your Domain. If the System still sees me as your follower, of course you'd have to give me permission to become even higher in a different church."

"Huh." Maria pouted, a brow slightly raised as she looked at me. "He gets it."

"He does . . ."

Pistachio just nodded, clearly understanding the man better than either of us.

"Can I ask why, though? Why do I have to wait?"

"My every instinct is telling me it isn't the right time to let it happen. Even if it was, I reckon it's only prudent to confer with Ellis . . ." I trailed off, tilting my head in thought. "Actually, there might be another pair who knows."

After the requisite delay, my chi shot across Tropica in an instant. I found Fathom and Cal in the alchemical workshop. Both recognized me, acknowledged my presence, then sent me the mental equivalent of "scram."

"Never mind," I said, rolling my eyes above a slight smile. I filed their secrecy away for later consideration. "Guess we just leave it for now. You want a hand fixing the church up, Gary? Happy to help."

"No," he immediately replied. "I think I should do it myself. Both for penance, and in hopes of better understanding the power coursing through me."

It was the second rebuff of a friendly offer in like ten seconds, but that bothered me none. I took a deep breath of the fresh ocean air and let it wash over my senses. I grinned at Maria. "You know, my love, I was really worried about the work this whole god-king and god-queen predicament would lead to, but nobody wants a damn thing from me."

"It's wonderful, isn't it?"

"It is. Almost as wonderful as the weather this afternoon . . ."

Maria snapped to attention, understanding the subtext of that last sentence. Pistachio nodded, agreeing with the implied course of action. The smaller lobster cocked her head at me, curious. Though she now possessed the world's knowledge, she was still acclimatizing to it, mapping her different areas of understanding.

"Clear your schedules," I said with a grin. "We're going fishing."

CHAPTER FOURTEEN

Potential

With Maria's arm looped through mine, a fishing rod in one hand and an inordinately intelligent lobster in the other, I marched across the dunes, smiling at the world. The sun appeared to grow larger as it neared the horizon, its light taking on a reddish hue that did nothing to combat the cool breeze blowing in from the coast. We climbed the last sandy peak between us and the bay's waters, and I finally caught sight of the shore.

Pistachio blew thoughtful bubbles, speculating out loud for the smaller lobster's sake.

"He's right," I agreed. "The sun is setting, the wind isn't too strong, and it looks like the tide's about to change—the conditions are *perfect* for fishing."

The crustacean in my palm nodded. She knew as much from the memories running through her. She gestured low with her claw, cocking her head in question.

"Yep! It's low tide. Did you get that from your memories?"

She gave a so-so gesture. *Life*, her hiss seemed to say, and she pointed at the boulders surrounding the jetty, their exposed surfaces peppered with snails, limpets, and patches of seaweed.

Maria gave Pistachio a suspiciously emotionless glance. "Considering she just awakened, your lady friend is brilliant. Don't you think that's really attractive?"

He faltered, missing three steps.

"In friends, I mean," Maria continued. "Nothing like an intelligent *friend* to bounce ideas off of."

"Yes," hissed Pistachio, pointedly fixing his gaze on the ocean.

Choosing to take pity on him, neither Maria nor I doubled down, instead joining him in watching the waves. They crashed against the rocks, white and chaotic as they disappeared between the boulders to rejoin the comparatively calm waters below.

The momentary flashes of chaos gave me an idea. I flexed my will and isolated my senses, testing what I could manipulate without wielding my chi. Vision faded, scent and taste were forgotten, and even the feeling of my body fell away. Only sound remained. The wall of noise loomed, towering ever higher the more I focused on it.

I could hear the quiet components of each wave—the contact of unbroken water sliding along slick stone.

The cacophony poured overtop like a hundred drummers: the sharp clap when a flat rock face was hit head-on; the spray of thousands of droplets as they descended from their momentary flight; the churn of countless bubbles, each indistinguishable pop combining to create a sound so potent it hijacked my senses. Those pockets of oxygen seemed to caress me, roll over my skin, lift me toward the heavens, a force I couldn't hope to descri—

"*Fischer!*" Maria called, her voice urgent.

A sudden pang of loss jolted my core as I dropped back into my body, letting out a shuddering breath. "What? What's wrong?"

She made a similar sound, swaying to the side before righting herself. "You were sharing the . . . whatever that was. The sound. The *bubbles*."

"Oh. My bad. I was seeing if I could manipulate my senses without chi."

"Well, it worked. You sent it out across our connection."

"Sorry. Are you okay?"

"Okay? It was wonderful." She pointed down. "It was a little much for some, though . . ."

Confused, I glanced at my hands—and abruptly recalled that I held a lobster, whom I'd accidentally gifted an existential crisis. She was staring into the middle distance, her antennae rigid.

I took the time to gather then apologize with a soft pulse of chi, not wanting to add any more sound to the mix. While I waited, I learned it wasn't just a few of my connections I'd broadcast the sound over.

"Thank you!" trilled Claws. "Loud! Very loud!"

"Thanks," bubbled Snips in agreement.

"BIRDS!" screeched Cinnamon, sending an image from her point of view, riding Pelly's back as her adoptive mother soared high over a flock of gulls. They were off scouting, apparently.

My chi finally obeyed, and I found the lady lobster's core remarkably calm. The sound had been entirely too much, but more than anything, my unintended over-sharing had excited her.

Potential . . . she seemed to hiss. Whether it was about me, her, or just in general, I couldn't say.

After a long moment, I cleared my throat. "You sure you're good?"

Slowly, effortfully, she nodded, her mind still poring over the experience. Beside me, Pistachio's core swam about riotously. I'd have missed it, given my chi was playing silly buggers, but his addled state let hints of it pour through our connection. The homie was working overtime to challenge what he thought to be an illogical belief.

Attraction.

Just like when I'd first felt the beginnings of a crush coming from him, it had nothing to do with her physical attributes. Pistachio was enamored with her *mind*. She'd ascended not a half hour ago and hadn't yet charted the universe's knowledge. Despite this, she was already thinking rationally, exhibiting reason beyond what was expected.

Maria and I shared another look, and again chose to take pity on our leviathan pal.

"Come on, gang," I said, gently passing the yet-unnamed lobster pal to Maria, then bending to bump Pistachio's closest claw. "We're wasting daylight."

Given it was her first time witnessing fishing firsthand, I gave her the full experience. "Normally I'd just put a hunk of eel on this hook and send it out, but I thought it best to show you how we catch bait." I tied one of my *sabiki rigs of the fisher* to the end of my line, drew back the tip of my rod, and flicked it out into the northern side of the jetty, where the current was weaker.

A bait fish hooked itself before the sinker reached the bottom, but I didn't rush to retrieve it. "When you feel the first bite, wait a second before reeling. More sometimes follow the fir—" I cut off, lifting the rod high as something large hooked itself. Swift and gentle, I raised them from the water.

"I was going to say that more can follow." I nodded toward the eel now writhing on the stones. "But if you're lucky, something even better might come along."

I dispatched it in an instant and held it out, letting her inspect the fully grown creature.

Pungent Monkeyface Eel
Rare
Found in the brackish waters of the Kallis Realm, this mature variation of the Common Eel has high oil content and a pungent scent, making it unpalatable food but excellent bait.

With my other hand, I slid the bait fish off the barbless hook, raising it beside the lifeless eel.

Juvenile Shore Fish
Common
Found along the ocean shores of the Kallis Realm, this fish is a staple source of both food and bait.

As soon as her eyes focused on it, I tossed it back with care, ensuring it landed at an angle that let it dart back into the depths with ease. The lady lobster nodded and blew bubbles of approval, my actions deemed both kind and logical.

The next half hour was spent in sheer bliss, interspersed with acute moments of excitement. The seasonal fish no longer graced our shores, making way for the year-round species that was our usual fare—mature shore fish. Though they were only uncommon in rarity, each one Maria and I caught made our pulses and hopes rise.

Potential, Pistachio's lady friend hissed again as Maria set her hook and started winding.

I raised a brow, grinning down at the half-submerged rock she resided on. "Exactly. Is it probably another mature shore fish? Ya-huh. But there's always the possibility that it isn't. It could even be an entirely new species. Until you actually see the fish, you can't say for sure."

Addictive, she seemed to hiss.

My grin widened. "It is."

Silver flashed just below the surface, and Maria lifted another shore fish my way.

I caught it. "Plus, even if it's not some rare new fish, it's dinner—sustenance for those I love." I unhooked the recent catch, glanced back to confirm this one was smaller than the six we'd already caught, then returned it to the water. Having not enjoyed its oxygen-based adventure, it kicked its powerful tail and glided from sight.

I stared down at the place it had disappeared from. The water swirled in a distinct pattern, seeming to get sucked back out to sea. I knew exactly what this meant. "Looks like the tide has changed," I said, standing and stretching. "I reckon we cast farther out into the river mouth. Good chance of finding some monsters feeding there." I laughed at the twinkle in the lady lobster's eyes. "To be clear, I don't mean *actual* monsters. I was referring to larger fish."

She turned around to face me and scuttled to the edge of her slick rock, the twinkle remaining.

"You knew that?" I asked.

Her head dipped in agreement.

"You're excited about the possibility of catching something bigger?"

Again, her head dipped.

"Do . . . Do you wanna try?"

She paused for only a moment before nodding repeatedly, each more insistent than the last, then blew thoughtful bubbles, their meaning obscured by my human mind.

Pistachio, who was sitting in the splash zone beside her, translated for me. "Worry. She noticed you created your fishing rod and doesn't want to damage it."

"Ohhh! Forget that. I can just fix it. You know what to do, right? How to fish?"

She bustled up onto the jetty's stone path. A slew of affirmative bubbles streamed in her wake. Passing such a long object to a relatively small creature felt a little odd, but she easily held it, her body more than up to the task.

"I have two rules," I said. She was focus incarnate as she stared up at me. "First— and this is just to make sure—we dispatch any fish caught, swiftly and humane . . . er, kindly, I mean." Affirmative and sincere bubbles came in answer. "Good. Second, and just as importantly, have fun."

More earnest bubbles.

Maria, having re-baited her own hook, dashed to the river-mouth side of the jetty and cast her line out. "Biggest fish wins!"

With the spirit of competition joining the lady lobster's already motivated core, she pinched a sliver of eel and attached it to my Bamboo Rod of the Fisher. Her right claw drew the pole back, her left claw flicked the reel forward, and she cast the line out, using both antennae to keep tension as the tackle gathered speed. The sinker led the charge high over the bay. She blew apologetic bubbles as it arced back down and landed atop Maria's line, but my wife just laughed and ducked under it, shifting positions to remove the potential tangle.

Not skipping a beat, the lady lobster reeled some line in, only stopping when it grew taut. She remained completely still, all senses focused on the fishing pole before her. I willed the universe to reward her bravery; if she caught something now, she'd be hooked on fishing.

But it was Maria's bait that got hit first. "Fish on!" she yelled, lifting her arms to set the line.

Her rod was arguably better than mine, and as I watched it bend under the fish's efforts, its description filled my field of view.

Bamboo Rod of the Fisher's Apprentice
Rare
A bamboo rod paired with an ironbark reel. This fishing rod provides boosts to both fishing and luck. The stats provided will grow with the skill of the user.
+? Fishing
+? Luck

I snorted at the useless reminder. When it had popped up without my prompting, I'd assumed I was going to be shown its hidden stats—no such luck.

I rolled my eyes, preparing to voice a suitably sassy diatribe against the System and its shenanigans, but a high-pitched squeal beat me to the punch. The lady lobster was hauled across the stone walkway, a creature catching her by surprise, her legs only finding purchase when she enhanced them with essence.

My eyes darted around as soon as I knew she wasn't about to be dragged out to sea. The rod was bent almost in half. The hooked fish seemed massive, but I could see neither headshakes nor kicks reflected in the rod, its length remaining relatively stationary.

I almost immediately understood what was on the end of her line, as did Maria. Pistachio had his suspicions, and they were confirmed when the creature sucked itself onto the sand, doing everything it could to stop the diminutive yet powerful lady lobster from pulling it to shore.

It was rare that I knew exactly what someone else had hooked, so I didn't waste the opportunity. Rather than witnessing the details of the fight, trying to guess at the species, I watched my newfound pal: the slightly awkward but still effective manner in which she retrieved line; the improvements that happened by the second, her body rapidly growing accustomed to the motions; and best of all, the pulses of pure joy that came from her core.

I turned for a fraction of a second to grin at Maria. Despite being engaged in her own battle, she was already grinning back. If my wonderful wife had fought her fish months ago, she'd likely have lost the battle. All things being equal, hers was the hardest to land of the two.

But things weren't equal. Maria's dedication to fishing, along with a skill level approaching 100, all but ensured her victory. She systematically brought it to the rocks, letting line out when it ran, only to regain that ground, and then some, when it tired. All the while, she watched the lobster beside her, also enthralled by the first timer's jubilation.

Silver flashed just below the surface a meter away. Maria hopped down onto the rocks, retrieved a little more line, then bent to grab it by the gills, only stopping when she saw the creature. She changed tack, flicking open the reel and setting the rod down. This time, she grabbed it with both hands—one on its gills, the other holding its body for support.

My eyes were drawn in.

Mature Giant Trevally
Rare
Found in the oceans of the Kallis Realm, this fish is a prized sport fish for anglers everywhere. Its flesh is undesirable, and it is considered bad luck to harm them.

I shook my head, returning to the present.

Maria had forgotten all about our new lobster pal's exuberance; she was too busy with her own.

"Fischer!" she yelled, core thrumming. "It's *huge!*"

"It is!" I yelled back. It really was.

Preoccupied as we were, we still didn't miss the *kerplunk* of a leviathan-sized lobster leaping into the river mouth. We turned toward the splash, only to find something even more surprising. His lady friend had also brought her foe to the rocks, and rather than the deep-brown we'd expected her hooked creature to be, it was the color of sand, interspersed with electric-blue dots that were the size of a small grape, or an even-smaller crab.

Despite Pistachio's aerial entrance, the hooked creature was too exhausted to flee. He lifted it onto the rocks a half-second later.

Juvenile Blue-Spotted Ray
Rare
Found in the coastal waters of the Kallis Realm, these stingrays are elusive despite their striking color. Their flesh is said to be identical to the common stingrays they live amongst.

"You actually did it!" I yelled, eyes flicking between the lady lobster and her catch. "I knew it was a stingray, but we've never caught one of these! You landed a new species!"

She blew wondrous bubbles as she stared down at it—swiftly turning shocked when she spotted the fish in Maria's arms. She shot from side to side, her entire body rotating to look at her own catch and the gigantic creature held against my wife's chest. Maria smiled down at her and moved to the water, intending to release the giant trevally, but froze when a deadly spike of killing intent lanced out.

It pinned us in place, stabbing its jagged edge deep into my core. I instinctively slammed solid walls of chi into place—or tried to. The network below didn't release its hold on my essence. As I battled to regain control of my power, not having a second to spare, I realized where the intent was coming from.

The blue-spotted ray had lashed out with its tail, aiming the venom-filled barb right at Pistachio. The part of my brain playing tug-of-war with my own damned chi sighed in relief. Pistachio was fine. Such a weak attack couldn't hope to breach his mighty carapace.

The lady lobster extended a claw. Despite the ray broadcasting its violent intent, she knew how feeble it was compared to her own capabilities, let alone mine. Her counterstrike was measured. She used all of her focus to minimize the damage done to the ray—sparing no attention for the object between her and the creature.

Her claw sliced through my fishing rod like a blade through butter, then continued on, severing only the tip of the ray's envenomed barb.

My heart sank.

CHAPTER FIFTEEN

Threat

The blade of energy continued on, cutting into the water before dissipating when it struck the sandy floor below with a loud *thump*. The attack was like a mixture of Pistachio's and Snips's original powers, the precision of the former combined with the deadly edges of the latter.

What remained of my rod clattered to the rocks, the dull thuds of hardwood and bamboo underscored by the soft pinging of metal components that tumbled from my bisected reel. Even the waves seemed to pay their respects, their endless assault on the jetty momentarily ceasing.

In that stillness, I knelt and picked up the pieces of my favorite . . . How best to describe it? "Tool" felt too impersonal a word for something I'd shared so many moments with. Its power leaked out and lingered in the surrounding air, but there was no putting it back together—it couldn't be fixed.

I let out a slow breath, torn between processing or letting go of the complex emotions welling up within.

The one who'd destroyed it scuttled into view, a picture of remorse. She lowered her entire body to the rocks, claws and legs outstretched, kowtowing to place herself in as vulnerable a position as possible. *Sorrow*, said her body language. *Regret.*

I gave her a reassuring smile. "Not your fault."

She lifted her gaze, intent on debating my dismissal, but I forestalled her with a raised hand. "Before we get into all that, are you going to keep the ray?"

She was at its side faster than a lobster had any right traveling. She let out a questioning hiss, her vision lingering on the severed barb.

"Yes," replied Pistachio. "It will regrow."

With a nod to herself, she slipped under its massive body, scuttled to the water's edge, and let it slide into the darkened waters. She didn't need to say anything—I understood why she'd chosen to set it free. She considered her attack a lapse of judgment, so the only equitable outcome was to allow it to live.

Maria, who had returned the giant trevally to the water, pushed it out toward the river mouth. The trevally's powerful tail sent it sailing away with ease, and the stingray's wings undulated across unseen currents, its blue spots contorting hypnotically.

When they were gone, Pistachio's lady friend picked up where she'd left off. She whirled, hitting the deck with splayed limbs. Even if I couldn't physically see how remorseful she was, I'd have felt it in her core. Earlier, she'd easily forgiven herself for past errors, but she no longer had the justification of being an unawakened animal. Her actions were now those of a spirit beast—an ascended being.

I shook my head. "It really isn't your fault. Don't give me that look, missy. Either stop kowtowing like a chastened disciple or stop glaring at me. You can't do both."

She declined my suggestion, her glare and posture deepening.

"I mean it! Show yourself the same grace you did earlier. You have the knowledge, sure, but you've yet to absorb and process it all. I also specifically told you to try fishing despite your worry of damaging my rod. Besides . . ." I bent to grab the severed pieces. "I'm extremely grateful for the adventures we had together, but at the end of the day, it's just an object. One I loved, for sure, but an object nonetheless. There's nothing anyone can do to fix it."

My arguments were chipping away at her reasoning but had yet to convince her. I grinned and launched my final strike. "You should be proud of your choice. Not only did you defend Pistachio when you sensed killing intent, but you also did so with care, despite the perceived threat."

Like someone had flicked a switch, she got up, nodding along as she released a few bubbles, their meaning clear.

Pistachio translated just in case. "She agrees it was your fault. Being a vastly superior being, you accepted responsibility for any damage done to the fishing rod when you dismissed her concerns."

A laugh exploded up from my chest, booming out into the night to join the sounds of waves once more slapping against the rocks. There was no accusation in her response—she was simply stating a fact. As the de facto leader of this little troupe, it was, indeed, my fault. A recently awakened spirit beast couldn't be held accountable in this situation.

Her antennae waved around, tasting the air. She seemed to consider something.

"Ah-huh," I said, which drew a curious look from her. "Go ahead. If you can consume it or whatever, have at it. Otherwise, it'll just drift away."

Needing no more permission, the two appendages extending from her head shifted even more, twitching as she felt the System-sourced chi that had flowed from my severed fishing rod and lingered in the surrounding air.

With a sudden inhalation—made all the more impressive by the lobster's distinctive lack of lungs—she sucked every last strand of essence in. I marveled at the process. Her core rejoiced, and not only because of the power it was harnessing; the very act of absorbing chi felt in alignment with who she was. Who she would *become*.

Maria, Pistachio, and I shared a glance, each of us knowing that her insight could well lead to a future breakthrough. But we were wrong. Her insight wouldn't lead to some future advancement at all. The breakthrough was happening *now*.

I reached for my essence again, mentally glowering at the tunnels below that drew from me. There was no need, however. A small wave of force pulsed out from her. It was . . . minor? I still had no idea how to classify these things, but it wasn't a complete advancement—it was only the beginning of one.

The power settled into her core, its surface shivering as it came closer to what it would eventually become. It felt wonderful, but it was the look of dissociation and abject confusion on her face that made me smile.

I picked her up and set her atop Pistachio's mighty carapace. "Would you take her back to the house, mate?"

He blew bubbles of assent, his visage stoic and unreadable—well, that was his intent, anyway. Maria and I could both feel how his lady friend's proximity was affecting his thoughts. "What will you do?" hissed Pistachio, seeking distraction of any kind.

"Just gonna process these fish. This'll be her first proper meal since awakening, so I want to start off with the basics."

Maria and I beamed at each other as we leaped up onto the walkway, where the half dozen mature shore fish waited.

"Are you sure?" my wife asked as I lit the fire beneath my barbecue on my back deck. She leaned down to hug me from behind, her hair falling to tickle my neck.

I thought about how to reply, then decided actions spoke louder than words. I picked up what remained of my rod and reel, then flexed my arms. The bamboo made a horrific sound as it broke in half, and an even worse sound when I doubled the lengths over and did the same again. I dropped them into the flames, along with the pieces of my reel.

Already the frayed splinters were turning black. The reel's hardwood wasn't so fragile, but it would only be a matter of time until it, too, was consumed. I didn't look away as fire surrounded my favorite rod. I was putting on a brave face for our new friend's sake, but I couldn't deny the sadness now welling up. This was a tragic end for something that had brought me so much joy.

My subconscious chose that moment to consider the doubt I'd been harboring since it happened. I had tried to shield everyone, and the tunnels below had stopped me. It'd worked out this time . . . but what about the next? What if the creature was stronger? What if its venomous barb was sharp enough to pierce Pistachio?

All I had lost today was a rod—what if I had lost a friend?

And an innocent creature had been injured. I didn't blame the lady lobster, but I certainly blamed myself. Some pain was the harsh truth when it came to fishing. In my mind, that was justifiable. I fished to provide myself and my loved ones with nourishment. But this felt different. I could have easily protected the ray if I hadn't temporarily surrendered most of my power.

Maria rubbed my back, sensing my troubled thoughts. "Do you want to talk about it?"

I filled my lungs, imagined my fear and anxiety as a black cloud in my chest. Nobody had forced me to start filling the network. I'd made the decision of my own free will, knowing that it was the best long-term choice for Tropica and my many loved ones who called it home. I exhaled the noxious fumes filling my lungs. I would stay the course.

I stood and wrapped my arms around Maria, taking solace in her lithe form. "I'm fine. Promise."

"Good, but I wasn't asking for your sake. I just don't want you to bottle up your emotions and turn into a ticking time bomb again. With how powerful you are now, you might blow up the whole damned planet."

"Hmm. That would look pretty cool, though. For the few that survive, I mean."

She gave me a fiercely histrionic glower. "No blowing up the planet, mister."

I sighed with just as much excess. "Yes, dear. I'll write it down so I don't forget."

To her confusion—and my enjoyment—I removed a notepad and pencil from my back pocket. I scribbled swiftly in the written language Snips had taught me.

Maria squinted at my messy handwriting as I showed it to her. "No fun allowed," she read, then grinned and shot me a wink. "And don't forget it."

Dual hisses cut through our merriment, and as I looked the lobsters' way, I found two very different moods. Though both were ostensibly expressionless—neither felt guilt for interrupting to let us know the fire was ready—Pistachio's core was flustered, barely containing the blush hidden just below the surface of his carapace.

Maria spoke in my head. "*He's so lucky it's us here and not C—*" She cut herself off. "*Better not to speak of the devil, lest we summon her.*"

I smiled at the prospect of Claws arriving and teasing the absolute shit out of the otherwise-stoic lobster, then banished her from my mind when I realized she might somehow hear my thoughts.

"Okay!" I said, doing my best to think of anything other than mischief. "Let's get cookin'!"

I'd seasoned all the fish fillets with salt, and a few with pepper as well, keeping the flavors plain. I scooped a dollop of tallow onto the hotplate. It sizzled and spread, bubbling as it melted across the metal.

"Demeter's bountiful bosom," Maria swore. "It already smells delicious."

Pistachio and his lady friend both hissed in agreement, the former shooting a furtive look at his new companion.

The corner of Maria's mouth twitched, and she sighed into my mind. *If there's an afterlife, we're both going to heaven for not teasing him.*

Right? I replied. *It's taking all my strength.*

Her forehead bunched up, a line forming between her brows as she considered something. "Do you think it reflects poorly on us that our friend is experiencing feelings of attraction for the first time in his life, leaving him confused, and our initial instinct is to make fun of him?"

My frown joined hers, and we pouted at each other as we did the math.

"Naaah!" we both decided aloud, drawing confusion from our crustacean compadres.

Before either could question it, I laid a fillet on the barbecue, using it to spread the melted tallow before adding the rest of the fish. I'd already thanked each creature whilst processing them down by the ocean, but I took a moment to express my gratitude again for the strange world I now called home.

"Thanks, fishies," Maria agreed, hugging me by the waist. "And thanks, world."

Fat bubbled up around the meat, juices dripping out to hiss when combined with the tallow. Steam rose as a result, the vapor rising skyward before swirling in the breeze, further spreading the potent scents. Mouth watering, jaw aching to bite down into the succulent flesh, I forced myself to wait before flipping them.

When I finally did, my patience was rewarded—the skin was brown and crispy, cooked to perfection. I ran my metal tongs along them; the scraping sound made a delightful shiver run down my spine. I wondered how I was going to distract myself for the minutes required for the other side of the fish to cook.

The answer arrived a moment later, making terror and adrenaline course through me.

"Cultivator!" declared the Buzzy Boys, echoing the call of a single armored insect far to the northwest. It was a warning. A call to action.

Meal forgotten, I launched my awareness to the outskirts of Tropica, honing in on the Buzzy Boy that had raised the alarm.

CHAPTER SIXTEEN

Protector

Dusk, the merchant's road to Tropica

Though the man was still getting used to his new body, not one of his steps strayed from their intended placement, each footfall even surer than . . .

Than when I was still a human, he thought, forcing himself to face that terrible truth.

All knew how calamitous it was to be contacted by the System, but only some understood just how terrible it truly was—he was one of the unfortunate few that had seen it firsthand. He hated cultivators. *Despised* them. And now he'd become one, doomed to go mad, get collared, or both.

He could come to terms with that, given time. He'd likely stop caring after he went insane. What he couldn't accept, however, were the consequences for those he loved most. The cultivator who'd once been a man glanced back at his children, watching their careful passage. His blood set to boiling.

His son carried his daughter, the boy's muscular frame making hers look small despite the many layers of surrounding blankets. She should be curled up by a hearth. The sweet scent of medicinal herbs should be all around, their healing properties wafting up from a kettle sitting beside the fire. Instead, she was being hauled through a forest far from home, forced to breathe cold air that aggravated her already-weak lungs.

As if to confirm his thoughts, a cough escaped her, the sound harsh from such a young girl. *My own daughter.* His boiling blood turned to liquid metal, his heart a crucible, his fury the furnace. It grew ever hotter, threatening to consume him.

"Dad?" His son's voice seemed to dump a bucket of soil atop the fire, starving the flames of oxygen.

He glanced back. The worry and stress he found lining the boy's face almost brought back the flames, but the innocence in his son's eyes soothed them once more. Countless memories replayed in the father's mind, his newly enhanced consciousness recalling past events with perfect clarity.

He focused on those times long gone, on all the wonderful moments that had made his heart sing with joy, the chorus even now echoing through his body. This rage . . . it was impossible to know how much was because of his System-induced madness and how much was reasonable—the reaction of the man he'd once been when seeing injustice heaped upon his children. He balled his fists until they hurt. His jaw trembled, and before he clenched so hard his teeth shattered, he hissed a breath between them.

This fury didn't serve. Not tonight, anyway. He had to get his daughter to safety. Only then could he find an outlet for his anger. Jaw still aching, fists wanting to lash out, he reached for instincts earned through decades of hunting and patrolling.

All he had to do was put one foot in front of the other. One step at a—

His step landed on something hard and curved. His leg slid out from under him, the object shooting forward as he fell to the ground. His enhanced vision witnessed it all in excruciating detail. The glass bottle, of a kind usually used to store wine, was drab beneath the forest's leaves.

Then it shattered against the base of a tree. Its countless shards glimmered as they caught what light filtered through the canopy above. The sound was deafening to his amplified senses, but it was nothing compared to the vibration that shook the world a moment later. At first it came from nearby, a single source of noise that vibrated through his chest and abdomen. Then it came from *everywhere*, dozens, hundreds of others joining the chorus.

If he was alone, the father might have remained there, content to let his powerful attackers end his life. He considered doing as much. But two faces flashed in his mind. Not the teenagers they now were—the children they'd once been. His daughter, endlessly kind despite her chronic ailment. His son, responsible, protective, reliable.

Their visages transformed, traveling through the years until they were the present. His son's harried face. His daughter's sunken cheeks. The internal furnace flashed again, red, hot, all-consuming.

He forced himself to exhale, focusing on the soft hiss of air passing between his clenched teeth. The cultivator wasn't alone. As expendable as he might be, he had two souls to protect, each more precious and unique than all the gold in the world.

"To the road!" he yelled, signaling his son with hand gestures in case the buzz was too deafening.

The boy nodded. Both dashed to the merchant's trail they'd been shadowing. It was only ten meters away, but even that felt like an eternity to his enhanced senses, each trunk they passed providing cover from which an attacker could spring.

As he skidded to a stop on the well-worn path, he felt an immense sense of discomfort at being so exposed, making the coals of his furnace spit and crackle. *It is the best option*, he reminded himself. Cover would be a liability if he was facing multiple enemies—which gave him an idea . . .

The cultivator reached over his shoulder and gripped a well-worn pole. Even decades after the war, it felt *right*, and as he held it forward, he channeled his fury into it. The spear glowed in the fading light, his madness made manifest. Hating how good it felt, he swept a circle around his children, the deadly tip of his weapon passing through trees like so many stalks of wheat.

Lost—perhaps more so than when he'd begun—Teddy wandered. Far and wide he roamed, knowing neither where he traveled nor what he looked for.

Purpose . . . he growled to himself, sounding more crestfallen than intended. It came so easily to some, yet still evaded him, his core unable to find meaning in everyday life. This hollow feeling wasn't eternal. It didn't haunt his every waking hour. But always it lingered, ready to strike at a moment's notice.

Only two events in recent memory had left him free of the self-inflicted torment: the wedding and the battle to defend Tropica from Gormona's forces. He considered them, his enhanced mind pondering each in search of answers. Both just confirmed what he already knew. He was a protector. He found great meaning in defending his tribe and seeing them flourish.

So he had thrown himself into the work of the Church of the Leviathan, hoping that caring for the crickets would give him that same satisfaction. How wrong he'd been. Watching over the baby lobsters hadn't brought fulfillment. Within those walls, his mind had meandered, leading to ascension, yes, but also to death.

Part of him wished for another attack to arrive, for Tropica to face some existential threat that required the use of his full power. It was objectively selfish. What kind of monster would wish, even secretly, for their friends to become imperiled?

Trapped in this endless loop of pressure and shame, he didn't recognize the warning drone at first. Only when the other Buzzy Boys joined the chorus did Teddy snap back to the present. A threat. An enemy had arrived. And based on the original call, they were close.

A tiny part of the massive bear felt a pang of humiliation, acknowledging that this was just a convenient method of distraction. The rest of him didn't care. Flooded with a desire to protect those he loved at any cost, Technical Officer Theodore Roosevelt barreled forward, body glowing red and charging through trees like they were paw-high weeds.

Chi flared ahead. Young, lacking control, bolstered by a rage so deep it matched Teddy's own. He imagined one of the Buzzy Boys being on the receiving end of it. His fury manifested, hair bristling, hackles rising to form reddened spikes whose luminosity bloomed across the endless storm of splinters, branches, and leaves cascading in his wake.

When he charged into the circular clearing, his limbs shattering felled trunks, the only thing that saved the cultivator's life was that none of the Buzzy Boys were in immediate danger. And when Teddy caught the scent of the human bundled up in the arms of another, a dozen or more spears of shock ran Teddy through.

It . . . it smelled like *her*. He scanned the cocoon of blankets with his senses. A single curl was visible, auburn in the fading light, just as wild as he remembered. It wasn't possible, yet there could be no doubt. It really was her. All these years later, he'd found her.

But her blood was wrong. She stank of sickness. He huffed a great breath, his heart breaking when he discovered the depths of her illness. Not just sick, but dying.

Teddy, shoulders hunched and head lowered, tore his gaze from her to look at the cultivator. Again, sharp points of disbelief stabbed him from all directions, this time bringing the memory of pain with them.

The weapon and the face of the man who wielded it . . . Teddy had seen both before. It made a terrible kind of sense. Of course she was with one of those men, the same tyrants who had trapped and killed his mother, the deadly tips of their spears used with disgusting efficiency.

It no longer mattered to Teddy that his mother and the humans they'd stumbled upon had been playing out their roles: a mother bear defending her cub, a hunting party defending themselves. All that mattered was that this man, this cultivator, was one of them. The aura of sheer fury flooding from the spearman proved how dangerous he was.

It was the logical part of Teddy that weighed these thoughts. Perhaps if it had occupied more of his mind, he'd have reconsidered his assumptions. Unfortunately for the cultivator, that portion of Teddy's consciousness was but a seedling, a tiny whisper of growth surrounded by a forest ablaze. Each time a leaf grew, flames washed overtop, burning it away.

Teddy's muscles flexed and bulged, his form expanding, filling with his desire to protect. His was the rage of a sleeping bear. Of a den mother who'd been backed into a corner. This thought drew forth memories of his own mother, and Teddy took an involuntary step forward, his forepaw doubling in size by the time it landed. Rocks crumbled. The ground shook. Teddy strode on.

Red spikes spread from his hackles to create a mane, and smaller tufts bunched around his elbows and knees. His upper canines extended, protruding from his jaw, tips glowing and casting crimson light across the entire clearing. His head was now the size of the cultivator's torso. The rest of his body was equally engorged. Insensate as he was, Teddy still recognized how ghastly a sight he must now present. He rejoiced in it.

Let this spearman know fear.

But the man remained unaffected. He was crouched low, backing closer to the two adolescents, his spear a snake ready to strike. Though he was a cultivator, he'd not have stood a chance against the Teddy of before. This version, muscles bulging and claws sharp, could tear the man to shreds with a single blow. Such an end, however, was too good. Too clean.

Teddy bounded forward, his paw descending sluggishly. The cultivator reacted faster than expected. He stepped back and his spear shot out, its deadly point twisting so that Teddy's limb would find only its jagged edge. Far too slow. Teddy adjusted, batting the weapon down with a lazy flick that lodged the armament in the earthen floor. He watched for a reaction, for an acknowledgment of the difference in their strength, but all Teddy sensed from the man was renewed rage, his anger burning like a furnace.

The cultivator advanced. He freed his weapon and circled his captives in retreat, the spear ever lashing out, its tip glowing red against the crimson of Teddy's spikes. Teddy beat aside every attack with the faintest shifts of his body, working to ensure the man knew just how futile his pathetic strikes were.

If asked, Teddy wouldn't be able to say why he was toying with him. He hadn't paused long enough to consider it. In his current state, he was nothing more than a bundle of muscle and instinct, for which he was thankful—it was bliss compared to the suffocating pressure and shame from earlier.

As the farce of a battle dragged on, Teddy grew frustrated with the cultivator's tenacity. He started returning half-hearted attacks, but the man somehow dodged each swing, moving with impossible speed to slip out of the way at the last second. The look in the cultivator's eyes, that of a predator refusing to abandon his kill, stoked the wildfire that was Teddy's rage.

After one particularly rapid exchange, in which the man evaded a blow by ramming his spear into the ground and slipping away, Teddy decided that enough was enough. A feeling of rightness, one previously only glimpsed from afar, came forth to greet him. It was there, barely beyond his reach, telling him his violence was justified. He could end this man and feel no remorse.

He hadn't yet seen the fear and regret he craved, so when he unhinged his colossal jaw and dashed forward, it was neither flesh nor bone that he crunched down on. The man's spear exploded. Splinters flew in all directions. And Teddy stared at the cultivator's face, waiting for the terror to show.

The bastard didn't so much as flinch. Teddy's terrible canines had missed his hands by only centimeters, but his enemy's only response was to retreat a step, still circling his captives. Chi poured from the endless furnace of anger that was his foe's core, and he raised the two ends of his spear like clubs, a sense of injustice joining his fury.

Injustice . . . ? Teddy exploded forward, his gaze pinned to the malevolent cultivator as his deadly paw descended for his foe's torso, too swift to dodge.

He must have seen his death in that strike. His gaze darted away, finally showing the doubt Teddy had been wanting to see this entire time. But it wasn't doubt. Bone-weary sorrow and regret flashed in the man's eyes as he looked not at Teddy, but at his captives.

Something was wrong.

Teddy let out a roar so loud that the world shook. He drew back what power he could and twisted his forelimb, letting it slam into the ground instead of the cultivator's chest. As clumps of soil flew up into the air between them, Teddy's conscious mind barreled to the forefront of his awareness, calming his bestial instincts.

The man's eyes weren't those of a predator. They were those of a den mother, a parent prepared to sacrifice themselves for even a slight chance of helping their young survive. He saw the signs now. How had he missed them before? That same hair on the father, though his was cropped and hers was wild. The lines between eye and temple, visible when the father scowled and when the daughter laughed. The young man, too. He was her brother.

This was no insane cultivator. Teddy's thoughts spun.

He'd almost ended an innocent life, the father of the first human to show him kindness. Worse, he'd drawn it out, intending on causing the man as much grief and pain as possible before ending his existence. This was what had called out to him? His ideal had finally come forth, encouraging him to brutalize a man who was only trying to protect his family. Teddy was no better than the men who had killed his mother.

His abdomen shook as he railed against his own ideal. He felt like he was being split in two, and when the fault lines appeared on his core, Teddy welcomed them. That glimpse of who he'd become was all he needed to see. He would rather cease to exist than become a mindless force of cruelty.

The faces of his friends flashed through his mind, appearing between the cracks, his nexus of power preparing to shatter. *Forgive me*, he thought. They would understand. Fischer would tell them what had happened. Would they loathe him, as he loathed himself? This only made him reject his ideal with even more vigor. Oblivion couldn't come soon enough.

A presence appeared. If Teddy had control of his body, he would have whimpered.

Do not stop me, Master.

Fischer's will swelled all around. Despite most of his power being feasted on by the tunnels below, he could wave a hand and halt the sundering of Teddy's core. Fischer's emotions built, becoming known. The god-king was conflicted. He wanted Teddy to live but wouldn't stomp on his wishes to save his life. Teddy's request was tearing him apart.

Leave me, begged Teddy.

It was one thing to know that his destruction would hurt his friends. It was another to be present for their grief. The agony in his abdomen spread to his chest. This was all his fault. He wished he had never come to Tropica. The world would be better off without him. He—

Fischer released a rather undignified noise from his throat. "Get over yourself, mate. Not everything is about you."

The joking tone made Teddy pause. Before his self-recrimination could resume, his master did.

"Don't get me wrong, I *am* over here fighting for my life, but it's against my own demons, not you. I'm stuck on the whole 'letting my friends fail' thing. It's already super self-absorbed of me, and you soaking up the blame like a lamington absorbing triple-choc icing is making me look even worse." Fischer paused. "And now I'm hungry. Great. I wonder if Sue knows how to make lamingtons? We'll have to check when your breakthrough is finished. You'll love them. I bet it wouldn't be hard to make one with honey."

Teddy huffed. He knew what Fischer was doing. This was his master's signature move—throwing people off balance with a barrage of well-intended nonsense.

"Ouch. Nonsense is harsh. Did it work, though?"

Teddy snorted across their connection. No. It had been a welcome distraction, however, if only a temporary one. Teddy lacked the presence to speak with words, so he sent a wave of affection. This was how he would remember his master and friend. Teddy reached for his ideal, preparing to shove it away for good.

"Yeah, yeah," Fischer drawled, his strange accent heavy. "Love ya, too, big guy. You've got it all wrong, though. You think throwing people off balance with a barrage of endearing larrikinism is my signature move? This isn't even my final form. My *real* signature move is to double down with even more nonsense, maybe make a reference from Earth that nobody would understand. If I'm feeling extra fancy, I'll even accuse my target of doing something they didn't do, then finish it all off by sprinkling in some big words right out of a thesaurus. I'm talking *mad* synonyms, mate."

Fischer paused for effect.

"I only use this signature move on my best friends, though. I won't just go Super Saiyan 3 for everyone, ya feel me? And no, I will *not* acknowledge Super Saiyan 4, Teddy. I can't believe you said that. As far as I'm concerned, GT was a fever dream— a discombobulating reminiscence from which I apply gratuitous separation."

When it was clear that Fischer wouldn't continue, the bear equivalent of a laugh rumbled from Teddy. The pain in his chest was gone, and though it still lingered in his abdomen, its edge had been blunted, his synapses numbed to the shock. The cracks running through his core had shrunk but not healed. Teddy shook his head at his master. He would miss these moments.

"No, ya won't. I haven't even told you the best part." Fischer's awareness leaned closer, looming over the clearing. "I lied before. I don't finish this move with a bunch of synonyms, mate. I finish it off with a *truth bomb*."

He ended the sentence with dramatic flair, voice booming, arms spread wide. When nothing happened, Teddy blinked, and Fischer unleashed a string of colorful expletives that would have made even the old Rocky blush.

"I can handle not having control of my power. Really, I can. But to rob me of my dramatic moments? Have you no shame, tunnels? Let me . . ." Fischer grunted. "Do the *thing . . .*"

Again, nothing happened, and Fischer let out a sigh. "All right, I'll just bloody tell you. Hold on to your hat, Teddy. This is gonna hit harder than a Polynesian forward."

Teddy didn't know what that was, and he didn't have a hat, but he did pay close attention. This would likely be the last thing he'd ever hear from his master.

"You're not some kind of bestial masochist, mate. You didn't let that battle stretch on out of cruelty. What's that, you say? *Then why did I want to see despair on his face?* Bit rude of you to interrupt my impassioned speech there, so I don't feel bad answering your question with a question. If your only goal was to terrorize him, why didn't you actually injure him? He's a slippery bloke, I'll give you that, but let's not pretend you couldn't have extended your claws at any point to slice up a limb or two. Even when you finally unleashed the killing blow, it came from a place of compassion. It would have been *instant*. Painless, as far as deaths go."

Confusion burrowed through Teddy's numbness. He had been slowly regaining control of his body the more Fischer distracted him, and he felt his head twist in thought. His fractured core started to itch.

"Ahhh. You're getting it already. I told you, Maria!"

"Hey! We agreed not to let him know I was here!" The mistress's presence flared up beside Fischer. "Sorry, Teddy. You know how he is. Good luck! You're doing great!" With that, she disappeared, falling back from his awareness.

"Point is," his master continued, "you see the flaw in your thinking, don't you? I had way more to say, but you don't need it. You've got it from here. I'll just leave you . . . *this*."

Fischer slammed his entire will down on the clearing. Despite the power still being drawn in by the tunnel below, the world acquiesced. The image of a raging bear appeared in Teddy's mind, its body covered in deadly spikes that glowed red. It took him a moment to realize it wasn't just any bear—it was him. His legs were thicker than trunks. If he stood upright, his height rivaled the surrounding trees. That wasn't even mentioning the ominously glowing spikes, claws, and canines.

His new form was even more terrifying than he'd imagined.

But he didn't understand the point of the image. Why had Fischer shown him this? He reached out to ask, but his master was nowhere to be found. Teddy was alone. He took in the features of his transformation again, a welcome distraction from his increasingly itchy core.

As he pondered the red mane of jagged spikes adorning his neck, realization struck, simple yet profound. This new form would strike fear into the heart of anyone who gazed upon it, and fear was the entire point. Aggression wasn't some animalistic ideal for spirit beasts to leave behind. It was in his blood. It was a tool. Like a mother-bear bluff charging a hunter, Teddy had sought to instill terror. All so he could reach his goal: *despair*.

The cracks lining his core started to close, glowing with the same crimson light that shone from him. The itching was terrible. He ignored it.

Despair, he pondered. Though he didn't want to cause it, he had looked for it on the man's face because it was something measurable, a metric with which he could judge success and failure. To be seen as ruthless and brutal was preventative. It would lead to less death and destruction, even if a life had to be taken. And the cultivator's life *had* been worth taking, but only because of the assumptions Teddy had made. He'd thought the man a kidnapper. Next time, he wouldn't make assumptions. He would control himself and learn the facts before delivering judgment. Anything else could invite retaliation, risking harm to those he sought to protect.

Teddy's core vibrated, its cracks stitching back together, its red light getting sealed within.

He hadn't wanted to be seen as scary. He wanted to be liked. Wanted to be part of a family, which was why he was always so polite. But that came from a place of weakness. He didn't want to be kind out of fear. He wanted to be kind because it felt good, and because his friends' smiles were even sweeter than honey.

So what if he looked terrifying? This was something nobody else could do. Deklan and Dom could protect with their ideal, but that was a shield, not a deterrent. Borks had nightmare-inducing appearances—like his original form, and the weird little creature Fischer called a chi-wow-wow—but they were *nothing* compared to Teddy's imposing form. He would transform into a monster far more grotesque than this if he had to.

For Tropica and the happiness of his friends, Teddy would give the world.

His core bulged, bloodred needles coming from the sutures holding it together. They banished the itch that had plagued him, replacing it with euphoria. Power swelled all around. Orbs of faint red light coalesced, then slammed down into Teddy.

Everything went white.

CHAPTER SEVENTEEN

Illumination

Above, the sky had darkened. Shadows spread all around me, growing larger as the sun's light retreated behind the western mountains. I smiled and took a deep breath, absorbing the scents of fish, tallow, and sweet victory.

"Go on," Maria said. "Just say it. Get your gloating over with."

"Told you so," I stated—very ungloatingly. "You never should have doubted Teddy."

She gave me a slight pout below an even slighter frown. "I didn't doubt him. I was worried, and who wouldn't have been? Teddy was halfway through a breakthrough, you are struggling to control your chi . . ." She trailed off, rolling her eyes at the look I gave her. "*We* are struggling to control our chi, and if you severed your connection to the tunnel—which you nearly did, by the way—the whole thing might have been irreparably damaged. That's not even mentioning Rodger with a D, who was using a normal spear to attack a *four-meter-tall bear*! The bloke is certifiably insane. He was one bad decision away from getting filleted."

"Ahhh, I get it now." I nodded to myself. "You didn't doubt Teddy or me. You doubted Rodger with a D."

Maria raised her hands. "Wait. Pause the conversation. He told us people called him Rod, right? I know that's a confusing name in Tropica, but are we really gonna keep calling him 'Rodger with a D'?"

"Hmmm. We can't call him just Rodger because it sounds too much like Roger *without* a D. It'll undo whatever calming technique your dad is learning on that island with Ellis. And *Rod*? Way too confusing. It'll drive us all mad, him included. Pass the rod, Rod. Poor bloke will think people are always calling his name."

"So we just call him Rodger with a D?"

"For now. We'll ask him about it when the time is right. Deal?"

We shook on it, and Maria picked up right where she'd left off. "Are you saying I *shouldn't* have doubted Rodger with a D? The man who, despite being a normal human back then, snuck up on and greeted us with a spear to the throat the only time we met him?"

Okay. He and his son *had* snuck up on us back when we were making our way to Gormona during the early stages of Operation: Sticky Fingers, so maybe she had a point. I wasn't gonna tell her that, though.

"I can hear your thoughts, Fischer."

"I don't know what you're talking abou— Oh, look! Teddy's waking up!"

She whapped me on the upper arm, but I barely felt it. I was too busy watching the scene unfolding to the northwest. Back within the clearing, Teddy blinked, his eyes slowly focusing. Through our connection, Maria and I both sensed how powerful he'd become. Not that we needed to feel it to understand—our lovable bear was the size of at least five outdoor dunnies. He seemed to have unlocked some kind of aura power, too. It was similar to Deklan and Dom's ability to shield, but I got the hint that it was offensive rather than defensive.

The cultivator—Rodger with a D—stared at him in disbelief. He'd witnessed Teddy's breakthrough and knew he was no longer a threat. "You . . . You know Theresa?"

Teddy sat up, his rear legs splaying outward, his body shrinking back to its previous size, though the tips of his red spikes remained. He nodded.

The young man, Toby, looked like he'd aged years rather than the months it had been. He blinked in absolute shock. "Little Bear? You're *real?*"

"Teddy," growled Teddy—quite politely, in my estimation—and gestured to himself with one paw. By the looks on their faces, they had no clue what he was trying to say.

"I . . ." Rodger with a D said. "We . . ." He wobbled, adrenaline making way for fatigue now that he and his children were safe. Teddy caught him before his unconscious form could hit the forest floor.

Rod woke from one dream to arrive in another.

The former had been a chaotic blend of time, only scant seconds passing before fading once more. Each glimpse showed his daughter cradled in the arms of a giant bear, surrounded by a faint-pink cloud. There were weird crustaceans as well, one colossal, the other the size of a cat. Their forms were nightmarish, yet he got a sense of calm compassion from their compound eyes.

It was a surprisingly pleasant string of visions, but they didn't hold a candle to the sound he heard on repeat: Theresa's laugh. Even in his favorite memories, it wasn't so rich, so full of life. It drifted over him, her breathless giggles seeming to cover him in a fur blanket that was velvety, warm, and . . . *breathing?*

His blanket licked his chin, and Rod opened his eyes, frowning at the realism of the sensation. It licked him again and disappeared, cold air rushing in to fill its former position, goose bumps rising from atop his exposed sternum.

He couldn't see a thing. The sun was streaming in through a giant window, overwhelming his enhanced vision. Only when he squinted against the light and actively focused on his surroundings did the room come into view. He was in a building constructed of shockingly opulent materials. Beneath him, a collection of blankets sprawled, forming a makeshift bed atop a wooden floor.

Theresa's wonderful laugh was gone now. The dream had fled, leaving only emptiness in its place, a vacuous void that threatened to swallow him whole. Yesterday flashed in his mind, but addled as he was, he couldn't discern the truth from imagination. *The bear can't have been real, could it?* His head spun. He had to find Theresa and Toby. Nothing else mattered. The facts would unravel the more he—

A shape froze in the doorway, a shadow, and it looked so much like her. But it couldn't be. She hadn't stood for months. A lump formed in his throat, his still-waking mind lacking the mental fortitude to control his emotions.

"Dad . . ." came the voice, so sweet, so angelic that he *had* to be dreaming.

Theresa's shape swept forward and left the blinding sun behind, revealing her face.

Formerly gaunt cheeks were covered in a layer of plump skin. Her sunken under eyes, darkened with fatigue for so long, had filled out, her youthful features returned. Her entire visage was filled with life, highlighted by an anticipatory smile so beautiful he didn't care if it was a dream.

Let me linger here forever.

Theresa hopped in place, her feet unable to stand still. "Come on! You have to see this!"

He just blinked at her. His mind had gone numb. He dared to hope this was real.

"Dad!" she yelled with the endearing annoyance only children could invoke. "*Get up! You're missing it!*"

She reached out a hand, and when he grabbed it, his heart broke. It was tiny, just as small as he remembered. Below the skin, however, fat and muscle covered her bones, her body having filled out alongside her face.

"Daaaad," she groaned, still annoyed, still endearing. "You're seriously going to miss it!"

She tried to pull him to his feet, but even with her strength returned, she was only a young girl. He pushed off the blankets with one hand and stood, telling himself this was still a dream, lovely as it might be.

She dragged him outside. He barely felt his steps or the pain of the sun's assault— all he could focus on was the tiny hand in his own, her grip squeezing two of his fingers with ferocious intent. As overwhelming as the brightness was, it was nothing compared to the sensation in his core. There were cultivators nearby.

He braced his core, made to rush past her and become a physical barrier, only to freeze in place.

The two creatures waving at him couldn't be any more different.

The first was the bear—the same one he'd seen yesterday. Its deadly hackles and glowing spines had vanished, replaced by coarse hair that blew in the breeze. His raised paw was larger than a man's head.

The second creature didn't look violent in the least. Silken fur covered a lithe form, and as she smiled at him, a forelimb drifted up shyly, covering a mouth set below eyes that wouldn't meet his gaze. Her other forepaw rose, waved in greeting, and sprouted claws like miniature scythes.

Rod balked at those gleaming blades, but it only got worse from there.

She dropped her limb to reveal needle-sharp teeth. Electricity danced over her body as if she were a living storm. The lightning crackled and shifted around her, vanishing, only to reemerge again.

The memories that weren't his identified it: This creature was an otter, a semi-aquatic mammal that lived in—

The fiend cut his thoughts off by becoming an opaque blue, reaching one paw into a built-in pocket and removing another, smaller mammal. She launched it at the bear. This new arrival, his core incredibly powerful and somehow linked to the otter, curled into a ball. Electricity shot from him. He moved faster than Rod could track. And he hit the bear right in the chest.

The collision could be called nothing other than a detonation.

Blue and red light clashed, the former from forked lightning, the latter from the bear's many spikes. And then, as fast as it began, it just . . . ended. They drew their respective powers in, the bear smacking the smaller animal—which Rod's mind was referring to as a raccoon—on top of the head when it tried to steal some red light.

The man, presented with what could only be three different spirit beasts, found himself struck dumb. He could separate neither truth from fiction nor dream from reality. The likeliest scenario was that he'd gone mad even sooner than expected. None of this could be true. Should he attack? But what if his daughter was standing over his prone, nightmare-locked body? If so, she could be right in the line of fi—

A sound ripped his thoughts apart, shredding them like grain before the powers of the mighty spirit beasts only meters away.

Theresa's laugh.

It flowed over and through him, a magical salve to heal any ailment of the mind or body. Her tiny fingers, stronger than they'd ever been, slipped from his grip. Her legs buckled and she fell to the sand, but when she gasped for air, it wasn't in the breathless manner that always broke him—it was in joy, her laughter so potent it sounded painful. Tears formed in her eyes as she stared between the creatures and him, wordlessly checking if he'd seen it.

A man strode out to join them on the sand. Unlike other cultivators, Rod couldn't feel a single hint of his power.

"Morning, mate," Fischer said. He'd not seen the strange man in months, but he still wore the same curiously amused expression as the last time they'd met.

"How . . ."

Fischer beamed, both figuratively and literally. His index finger shone with white light. "This should explain everything. Had to fight tooth and nail with that damned tunnel, but I'm pretty sure I've—"

He cut off when a woman popped out from behind him and whapped the back of his head. "What do you think you're doing with the power in your finger, mister? Did you not think to at least run it by your wife? I could have helped, you know. Oh. And hi, Rodger. Sorry about the reception. My darling husband might be trying to do something foolish."

"There's no 'might' about it. This is unabashedly foolish. Worth it if it works, though."

Rod blinked at them, too overwhelmed to say anything. This was starting to feel less and less like a dream. He looked down at Theresa, who was gazing up at him with adoring eyes, her hands absentmindedly playing with the sand beneath her.

Maria sighed. "Okay. I think you're right."

"I can illuminate him?"

"May as well. You've already done the foolish bit by gathering the power."

Fischer bowed at the waist. "As my god-queen demands!"

"God-queen . . . ?" Rod asked, his mind spinning. Illuminate? That was ominous. "What—"

Fischer touched him.

As light rushed in, flooding his body and spirit both, Roger had to admit how apt the word "illuminate" was. He saw it all. What Fischer had been doing here. The friends he'd made, spirit beasts included. The formation of a church. The assault on Gormona, the freeing of slaves, the defense of Tropica. All the trials and tribulations that had gotten in his way. Gods. Actual divine gods, but he cast the memory aside. There was a healer. Maria. *Maria was a healer.* She could fix—

She already had. Last night was no dream.

She already has . . .

Rod's eyes found Theresa again. She peered back with a wide smile, eyes still swimming with mirth. He didn't feel himself drop to his knees. He reached out, his hands hesitating just before making contact, scared she would disappear. "You . . ." He swallowed. "How do you . . . ?"

She cocked her head, a patch of chaotic curls flopping to the side with the help of a slight breeze.

Fischer cleared his throat. "I think your father wants to know how you feel."

"How I feel . . . ?" Her face scrunched in thought. "Hungry. Do you have any more passiona pastries, Uncle Fischer?"

The existence of passiona pastries would have normally left him reeling, but with his daughter before him, hale and healthy enough that hunger was her biggest concern, he found he didn't much care.

He wrapped Theresa in a hug, squeezing her as tight as he dared. Someone else came running. Toby crashed into them, tried to wrap them both in an embrace, but Rod was swifter, his arm scooping the teen in.

For the first time in years, he believed everything was going to be okay. He wasn't going mad. Theresa was healthy. Both his children were safe. He held on to them, the morning sun seeming to bless them as his vision swam, tears of joy and despair and countless other emotions blinding him.

CHAPTER EIGHTEEN

Mischief

Hours after that heartwarming reunion, the midday sun shone down from above, ready at any moment to begin its slow descent toward the western mountains. Its position caused shadows to darken the features of the man before me, his muscular brows enhancing the effect.

Barry glanced at the bloke to my right, then back at me. "We can't have two Rogers."

"We don't. This is Rodger. With a D."

"Rodge, maybe?" Barry suggested, but shook his head a moment later. "Still too close."

"How about Rod? He told us that was his nickname, but Maria and I figured it was too confusing. It *is* short and sweet, though. Just like him."

"That's what most call— What do you mean, *short and sweet?*"

Barry clenched his already-firm jaw. "Rod is even worse. Do you have any idea how much the word rod gets thrown around in these parts?"

Rod's brow knitted—as did mine. "Rod" really didn't suit him.

"Why would the word rod get thrown around . . . ?" Rodger with a D asked.

Barry's forehead joined the knitting party. "I thought you said Fischer showed you everything?"

"Wait!" I raised my arms and shot to my feet. "This is gonna get *way* too confusing. We need to pick a name, like, now." I peered at Rod. Or Rodge. Or Rodger with a D. "It's ultimately up to you, mate. If you wanna go with Rod, go with Rod, but just know that we handle a *lot* of rods, so you'll have *stiff* competition. Don't look at me like that, Maria. Get your mind out of the gutter."

"Huh? I didn't—"

"Sorry about her. She can't help—" I ducked as Slimes sailed through the place my head was a moment earlier. "—herself."

The man in question watched the familiar-turned-missile sail over the river and slam into the other bank, tons of sand spraying from the impact site in a great arc. "Uhhh."

"That's Slimes," Maria answered. "My familiar. He helped heal Theresa."

"*I'm a boy!*" Slimes called from the newly formed crater.

I cleared my throat. "Seeing as you need a new nickname, I have some suggestions . . ."

Barry and Maria both flung their heads back and groaned up at the sky.

Before he could question their visceral response, I let the words fly free in a rush. "The problem is Rodger with a D sounding too close to Roger without one, right? What if we keep it similar so it's not so confusing for you and everyone else, but just change it a little so you won't get confused with Roger without a D, who is easily bothered and just so happens to have chi made of blades."

All three blinked back at me for different reasons. I forged on.

"It's simple, really! We change the first letter so it rhymes. Here are three I prepared earlier: Codger, Lodger, or my favorite, *Dodger*."

Again, they blinked.

"That . . ." Maria squinted. "I can't tell if you're brilliant or stupid."

"Both, probably. If his little tussle with Teddy is anything to go by, his eventual breakthrough will have something to do with dodging stuff."

The man in question was rubbing his chin and staring off into the middle distance. "I thought that was my imagination . . ."

"Nope. You were slippery as frack. Kept avoiding strikes that absolutely should have hit you for six."

"Dodger . . ." he repeated. His core vibrated a little, seeming to like it but not quite convinced.

Barry looked like he was trying to swallow a lemon whole, and when he felt the slight hesitation from the man's soul, he let out a relieved sigh. "Oh, thank the gods. Fischer would have been unbearable if—"

"Dodge!" I interrupted. "Not Dodger, but Dodge! Short and sweet!" *Just like him,* I didn't add, thinking it at Maria instead.

"Dodge . . ." he repeated, tasting it. His core *shook* in agreement.

By the time my gaze had drifted toward Maria and Barry, I wore a shit-eating grin. "Well, well, *well*. Look who's done it again."

I expected unbridled annoyance from them both, but Maria nodded along, her eyes glittering with meaning. "It *is* short and sweet, isn't it?"

Barry, however, was annoyed enough for ten men. His cheek muscles grew so taut they looked like little biceps. All at once, he relaxed, blowing air through his lips and letting his irritation go. "I hate to say it, but the name suits you. Even if it didn't, it's not up to us." He pointed at Dodge's radiant abdomen. "It clearly aligns with you, and now that we've worked out the naming debate, we can pick up where we left off . . ." His predatory gaze settled on me. "I believe you were about to tell Dodge that you omitted certain *details* when you showed him what we do here in Tropica . . . ?"

"Wellll." I indulged the acute compulsion to inspect my fingernails. "I might have forgotten to mention some things."

Dodge—*man was that a sick name*—frowned, taking a moment to reorient to our previous conversation. "Rods . . ." He gave me some seriously judgmental side-eye. "If the word 'rod' is overused here . . . were you telling the truth back when we first met?"

"By 'telling you the truth,' do you mean that most of our village enjoys fishing, and that we were on a fishing and camping trip to the capital?"

"Yes."

"Ding-ding-ding!" I shot to my feet and threw my hands up in the air. "Got it in one!"

"You're serious?"

"Why are you so surprised? We literally showed you our fish skeletons."

"Well, yeah. But after you showed me the rest of those memories, I assumed the trip was a lie, and the remains were a cover."

"We're heretics to our cores, mate. No trickery here."

He'd accepted everything prior to this with more grace than could be expected. My sharing of past events had laid down a solid foundation, and Maria's healing of Theresa had built atop it, as had Teddy's affection for Theresa.

Fishing was the straw that broke the cultivator's back—he frowned so hard I worried his face might fall off. "Why do you seem like you're telling the truth?"

"Because I'm serious as a summer storm, mate—fishing is where it's at. If you think that's bad, though, wait until you learn about Borks's true identity."

Barry gave me a confused look. "Why didn't you tell him about Borks?"

"Because Borks was there in the forest and reacted *really* poorly to Maria and I being held at spearpoint. I figured it may be overwhelming to learn our growling dog was actually an ancient hellhound who could've torn him to pieces."

Dodge had gotten paler with each word, and he inspected everyone present, scanning faces in search of amusement. All he found was sincerity. "I think I might have made a mistake in coming here . . ."

"Oh, c'mon. How are fishing and an ancient hellhound where you draw the line? You were fine with *him*."

They all looked at where I was pointing. Teddy waved back from his seat on the sand, a vision of politeness and genteel poise.

"There's purpose behind Teddy's ferocity," I said. "And if I'm being honest, it's the same with Borks. You threatened me, his master, and he reacted."

Dodge nodded, accepting the explanation.

"So you have no regrets in coming here?"

"Regrets? No. You healed Theresa. It's just . . . What can you get from fishing that you can't get elsewhere? You're surely not wanting for food. I could track a wild animal in minutes, then quarter it with a single strike. And you're all stronger than I am—*much* stronger, might I add."

"First, thank you. I *am* rather strong. Second—and I can't emphasize how important this is—please don't go around punching wild animals into quarters."

He gave me a flat stare. "You're the one that showed me I wasn't insane. What makes you think I would do something so cruel?"

I rubbed my chin, completely disregarding anything he said. "Actually, I take it back."

". . . Take *what* back?"

"The 'wild' qualifier. Please don't go around punching *any* animals. Or kicking.

No head-butting, either. You know what? No striking at all. No, don't look at me like that—I shan't change my mind, mate, no matter your natural inclinations or established proclivities."

His flat expression had slowly returned with each word I said. "You know, I'm starting to see where Corporal Claws gets it from."

"Her adorable looks and pattable tushy? Thanks, Dodge, but I'm happily married. I hope you'll remain in the village despite your love being unrequited."

He turned away from me. "Was he always like this?"

Maria shrugged back. "This is just how he is, I'm afraid. There's nothing I can do about it. In sickness and health, as they say—which I assume includes the mental affliction clearly haunting him."

"Afflic*tions*," I corrected. "Probably, anyway. I'd be shocked if it was just the one."

"You know," Dodge said, "that might be the first sane thing you've said in the last hour."

"Agreed. And while I'm spouting insane ideas anyway, I have another. How do you feel about going fishing?"

"I should probably go check up on my kids."

"Don't worry about them, mate. They're in good hands."

He opened his mouth to reply but froze, considering for a long moment before turning toward Barry. "It's nothing against your son. I just don't feel comfortable leaving them with anyone I don't really know, especially, *er* . . ."

Barry's answering laugh was rich. "You don't need to pretty it up—my son is around the same age as your daughter, but because of his half-awakening, he has the strength of at least twenty men. You're right to be wary, but I promise you this: that's only because you don't know Paul."

I nodded. "If he presented any sort of threat, we'd have him watched all hours of the day. Actually, now that I mention it, he *is* being watched, but it's out of curiosity, not vigilance. Here. Check this out."

I reached for my essence. There was a momentary delay as the tunnels below fought against my will, wanting every last drop of chi for themselves, but then they relented. I sent a tendril of power across the village, through an outer wall, and into the rafters of a previously unused building. The lone Buzzy Boy perched there gave a nod of approval, so I copied his vision over to Maria, Barry, and Dodge.

In retrospect, I probably should have checked what the insect was witnessing before passing it on.

The good news was that we'd located Claws; the bad news was that she'd constructed a child-sized furnace and was actively encouraging Paul to shove his bare hand into its glowing heart.

Barry flinched, preparing to leap across the village, but I held up a mental finger, forestalling his jump. I had to physically grab Dodge's shoulder to stop him from doing the same.

Paul, unaware any of us were watching, shook his head. "I know it won't hurt me, but it sets a terrible example, Claws." He pointed at Theresa and Toby. "They're still regular humans. They'll be healed when they awaken, but that won't help the pain. Even if I didn't promise Fergus I'd be the only one using it, my dad and Fischer are both counting on me to make good choices. I gave them my word."

If Claws had even thought of arguing against such wholesome words, I would have joined Barry in leaping over there and smacking her fuzzy little butt over the mountains. Thankfully, it wasn't necessary. She cooed in adoration, scooting forward to leap onto his shoulder, where she used both forepaws to mess up his hair.

RPM, however, was absolutely keen to debate. His upper half rose from one of Claws's pockets, and he started saying something about stealing scars and pain away from them, but cut off abruptly when his master violently head-butted him back into her own soul.

"Bad familiar!" she screeched, then rubbed Paul's face all over in apology. With that, her task was done. She fled the building backward while flashing a cheeky smile at Theresa, who was still giggling from the slapstick routine.

Paul cleared his throat and adopted an air of maturity. "The purpose of our work here is to explore, and to build . . ." He trailed off with a subtle inflection that invited the siblings to enquire.

Toby took the bait. "Build what?"

"Anything and everything. Whatever you might find interesting. The goal isn't material objects or gaining power, but finding professions that resonate with you. Your dad was directly opposed to forcing your awakening, which we'll respect. That said, we won't actively avoid activities that *could* lead to your ascension."

"Why here?" Theresa asked, a finger twirling absentmindedly through a loose curl. "It's kind of . . ." She looked around at the bare walls. "*Boring.*"

"It is, but only for now. It's too dangerous for you both in most of the workshops. Besides, I chose this building on purpose. It's far from the other crafters, so we won't disturb them. Here, we can freely express ourselves. We can *play.*"

Toby, being the teenager he was, looked a little aggrieved at that last word, but Paul plowed onward.

"We'll also be contributing toward Tropica by discovering our purpose." This made Toby's eyes light up, and Theresa's lose their luster. "We'll start as soon as I finish giving some safety instructions."

Theresa groaned. "But we're just watching! Can't you show us by doing it? I wanna see metal turn into water like you said!"

"Sorry. I promised. I'll go as fast as I can, okay?" He marched carefully toward the small table beside the furnace and picked up a brand-new crucible. "Do either of you know what this is . . . ?"

I abruptly severed the tendrils of essence that were relaying the scene to us. The Buzzy Boy dipped his head in shame, feeling a deep sense of remorse for his role in spying on the overtly responsible young man. He raced across the rafters and back outside, departing through the small gap he'd used to enter.

Dodge took a little longer than the rest of us to regain equilibrium. When his eyes finally focused, he looked up. "You've raised a good kid, Barry, I . . . Are you okay?"

"I'm fine." He clearly wasn't. "Got sand in my eye." He turned away and wiped at his cheek. "Oh, *frack it*, I'm proud of him, all right?"

I slipped forward and placed a hand on his shoulder. "You should be, mate. Dodge is right. You've raised a damn good kid . . ."

Even if he's a cheeky little bugger, I added to myself, keeping the thought concealed. Maria sent a wave of amusement. Surprisingly, so did another. Claws cackled in my mind from afar, having also seen right through him.

As the meticulously planned and practiced words spilled from Paul's mouth, he did his absolute best to keep his core under control. His chaperone had retreated, the not-so-subtle insect flying far from the building. His scheme had *worked*.

He abruptly stopped talking, looked around conspiratorially, then leaned forward. The siblings mirrored him, subconsciously drawn in by his body language.

"I lied about three things," Paul said.

Toby and Theresa went wide eyed, their curiosity only rising as the silence stretched on—which was exactly the point. Paul was well aware this could be interpreted as manipulation. So what? Intent was all that mattered, and his intent was even sweeter than his mum's famous pie. They would all benefit from working and playing together.

Though his awakening and breakthrough were partially restricted by the System, his mind whirled as he let the silence stretch. He was so, *so* thankful that the two before him had arrived. Ever since Ellis's dire warning at the town meeting, his stomach had been twisting in knots. Even thinking about it now made the sensation return. He cut the silence short before the knot could fully form.

Paul raised a finger. "The first lie: I never got permission from Fergus to build this, so there was no such promise of not letting you use it."

Toby gaped. Theresa beamed. Paul's worry retreated.

He lifted another digit. "Second, the reason I chose this building isn't so we don't disturb the other crafters. It's so *they* do not disturb *us*. I don't want anyone finding out what we're actually doing."

Toby's mouth formed a thoughtful pout. Theresa's brow lowered. "What we're actually doing . . . ?"

A third and final finger joined Paul's other two. "I said I didn't know what we'll make. That was also a lie. I've identified a hole in Tropica's defenses, and I'd like for us to be the ones to fix it. I don't want anyone finding out until it's finished, which is why we need to be so far away."

He studied their faces closely, hoping his words had the desired effect, fearing they wouldn't. He needn't have worried. As an expression crossed their features, he returned it, all three grinning like exactly what they were.

Three kids in the early stages of mischief.

CHAPTER NINETEEN

Direction

Eustace, holy seer of Phostheia, arrived in a flash of gold that did nothing to lighten her dark thoughts. She had tried to see Aletheia at least once a day since her awakening as god-empress, and had been turned away each time. She had pushed her way past the guards last night, having grown sick of their polite refusal, only to be met by Evan seconds later, the head mage turning her away with a promise that "God-Empress Aletheia" would see her tomorrow.

Devious bastard, Eustace thought, eyeing the mages now marching into the amphitheater in groups of five. Evan had expertly misled her into believing it would be a one-on-one meeting. He was more formidable an opponent than she'd assumed.

"Would you relax, Eustace?" Holy Seer Anius asked, fanning himself with an ingenious creation of wooden sticks and folded paper. "You're going to give me indigestion."

Eustace glowered at the only other living seer. They often engaged in verbal jousts, their many decades together transforming once-bitter enmity into only-sometimes-bitter companionship. A few choice responses sprang to mind, but she swallowed them, lacking the stomach for such levity today. Her charge—her *friend*—could be in danger.

Eustace was nothing if not self-aware; she knew it was more than worry for her friend twisting her core into knots. She recognized the sharp pangs of rejection and betrayal dwelling beneath the surface of her concern, but being able to identify it did nothing to alleviate her distress.

Seeking distraction, Eustace focused on the outside world. She and Anius sat on a private balcony above and to the side of the tiered seating below. Despite being openly visible, nobody dared gaze their way. The last of the mages marched down the stairs and filed into position. The Twenty Hands of Phostheia stood unmoving in ten rows of ten—two hands of five per tier—as they awaited their god-empress and her Prime Cadre.

Eustace's lip twitched. The mages' rigid backs, blank expressions, and mindless obedience were everything she hated about Phostheia and the Kingdom of Light. This thought made her think of Aletheia and all the conversations they'd bonded over, so she banished it by circulating divine chi, decorum be damned. It wasn't like anyone would sense it, anyway. The ability to hide one's essence was one of the first secrets all seers were tau—

Golden brilliance exploded from the stage below, filling the entire amphitheater. Where Eustace's flashiness had been a side effect of her chi, this was a cheap trick. A gimmick better suited to a charlatan than a god-empress. And the sheep below ate it up, their basic levels of cultivation not letting them see through the thick wall of light as six figures dashed onto the stage. By the time the essence faded, Aletheia and the Prime Cadre were pictures of regal poise, appearing as if via teleportation—a god's method of travel.

The audience gawked in open-mouthed awe. Eustace bit her tongue, circulating her chi. Anius snorted, using his own divine essence to hide the sound from all except Eustace. But then Aletheia's eyes flicked up toward their platform. Her gaze seemed to impale them on the spot, and when those golden irises finally drifted back to the masses below, Eustace almost lost control of her core.

Anius helped her recover, shooting her a warning glance that she barely registered. Aletheia's eyes . . . gone was the sweet girl she'd once known, her ever-curious expression replaced by something far more cold and severe and calculating. As that dreadful truth coursed through Eustace, the god-empress started to speak.

"Good morning, everyone." Her voice was reminiscent of the former queen's, each syllable enunciated with care. "As you know, I recently experienced two breakthroughs."

Aletheia paused, raising her chin almost imperceptibly, prompting the hundred mages to clap and cheer her name. It was perfectly timed, masterfully done, and it sent Eustace tumbling further into despair. Where was the shy princess, whose cheeks flushed when faced with praise from a single subject? What had happened to the older version of the frail little girl with golden ringlets, who used to wander over despite her bashfulness, knowing that at least one of the seer's many pockets hid a sugary treat? In a matter of days, she had so easily shed her timidity . . . it left only one possibility.

Aletheia had fallen victim to the same often-fatal disease of the mind as her progenitors.

The wider implications—that it had happened after a breakthrough, which confirmed her and Anius's theory that these delusions of grandeur were an inherent risk of channeling divine chi—should have been even more troubling. But it was nothing compared to the grief of losing a friend.

The god-empress cared not for Eustace's devastation. "Thank you," she continued, giving her audience a slight nod. "I heard all of your voices over the past few days, and though I could not respond, know that I would be nothing without you— no, do not deny me—my advancement is as much yours as it is mine." She dipped her head, appearing to gather herself. "It is the boon we have waited all these years for, and it *should* have brought only celebration and prosperity . . ."

She paused, letting the "should" hang like a noose around their necks.

"Instead—" She lifted her face, meeting the eyes of the hundred. "—we have been granted a chance to prove our righteousness."

The crowd forgot themselves, a great many leaning forward, feet shuffling and divine cores shining. Eustace and Anius shared a glance. This was abnormal, to say the least. No previous Veritus had shown such tact when gripped by the delusions.

"This power . . ." The god-empress created a miniature sun above an upturned palm. "It was granted by the heavens, following the ascension of another." She grabbed the celestial facsimile in her hand and squeezed; it exploded into countless beams of divine essence. "This other being, who ascended before me, is named 'Fischer' by the System. He hails from the faraway kingdom of Gormona."

Gormona, Eustace thought, recognizing the name from her teachings long ago.

Anius whispered the name, recalling it. "The kingdom that stole the relics . . . ?"

The hundred mages whispered, too, but they had latched on to something other than the existence of a foreign state or another ascendant.

"The System . . ."

". . . acknowledged by the heavens . . ."

". . . the divine bridge!"

Their god-empress merely watched and listened as their hushed exclamations became a roar within the amphitheater. With measured ease, she raised a hand, drawing their attention. The susurration died in an instant.

"There is more, and there is no hiding its ruinous meaning. Though I cannot say with absolute certainty, I believe that Fischer and his wife, Maria, both possess abyssal chi."

The only sound to be heard was the soft hiss of wind as it swirled around the building. Aletheia didn't continue, and when nobody below voiced the question she was expecting, she nudged Anius and Eustace with an invisible pulse of chi.

Eustace could hardly breathe, let alone speak.

"*W-what?*" Anius asked after a beat, his voice cracking. "What makes you believe that?"

She acknowledged his question with a gracious nod. "Months ago, the capital city of Gormona was assaulted by a united herd of spirit beasts, and it fell." Sorrow and regret gathered on her brow. "One of my agents saw it with his own eyes, and bless the heavens, he managed to escape. I have verified the truth of his account. Gormona, as it once was, is no more. Now, it is ruled by two humans and their . . ." Her lip twitched. "Pets."

Anius didn't need to be prompted this time. He swallowed audibly, his mouth sounding dry. "This Fischer you spoke of. And his wife. You believe the spirit beasts obey them . . . ?"

"I *know* they do. The royal library contains many entries regarding beasts. Their way is to conquer and remain, not to flee. But neither do they cooperate. For so many of them to work together? It only happens when united under a cultivator." This revelation alone seemed to knock the air from the building, but she wasn't done. "And according to the dozens of entries I found, humans who successfully subjugated spirit beasts have historically possessed one of two aspects: divine or abyssal."

The crowd rocked as if physically struck. The god-empress let her power leak out. It prickled at first, too brilliant for them to handle. But then it grew warm, a blanket to shield them from what had to be done.

"And," she continued, jaw tense, shoulders firm, "if these two cultivators were of the divine, the System, the very voice of the heavens, would not have given me a quest to annihilate them. Make no mistake—they are our enemy, and they *must* be cleansed from this world."

Eustace felt the truth in Aletheia's words, and another possibility occurred to her, a thin ray of hope shining down upon her despair. Golden light flooded the amphitheater, coming not just from the stage but the crowd, too; a god-empress had lit the beacon, and her followers had answered the call, duty and purpose flaring from their cores. When Eustace saw and felt their response, her thin ray of hope became a solid beam.

She reached out and held on for dear life.

Aletheia was putting on this facade for the sake of her kingdom. She had selflessly donned the hated mask of a ruler, seeing the wisdom, the *necessity*, in it. Eustace's childish feelings of rejection—*for what else could they be called?*—turned inward, her own assumptions making bile rise in her throat. What sort of friend could so easily lose faith in someone they loved? The seer let whispers of her platonic affection flow out in a controlled stream. But before it reached Aletheia, the god-empress denied it, throwing it back at Eustace. The feeling of rejection flared up again, but it turned into guilt when she remembered Aletheia's true nature. It was likely hard to maintain the facade, and Eustace's admiration might have threatened to crack it.

Lines streaked many faces below. The Twenty Hands of Phostheia had been moved to tears by their god-empress, yet all of them were back at attention—and Eustace, just this once, decided there might be good reason for their rigid backs, blank expressions, and mindless obedience.

"I see you understand," her friend said, voice making the city tremble. "Thus, let me tell you what needs to be done. First, we are doubling the Twenty Hands to become the Forty."

Involuntary gasps escaped both Seers.

"Yes," the god-empress replied, nodding at them. "You guessed right, Eustace, Anius. It is time to cast aside the doctrine of old, for it no longer serves humanity. This foreign kingdom of heretics and spirit beasts must be cleansed from this world before they can gain more power, and if we wish to cross the ocean, we need enough mages to man each vessel in the Divine Fleet."

Eustace gazed down at the crowd, waiting for their reaction and terrified of what she'd find. *Forty Hands?* It went directly against the Divine Church's doctrine to settle in these lands—a religion the hundred mages were functionally acolytes of. Sure, Aletheia was their holy leader . . . but was that enough? Would they accept her order to do that which was explicitly forbidden?

Eustace didn't have to wait long. She saw it in the lines of their faces, heard it in their quickening breaths, and felt it radiating from their cores. To a man and a woman, Aletheia had them. She wasn't just the Divine Church's leader—she was its deity, the being who would become a bridge to the heavens and usher in a new age for humankind.

"Damn," Anius whispered, hiding his mouth with his fan. "She actually did it. Shame it took her going mad to—"

"She's not—" Eustace barked back, only to cut herself off when she realized her volume.

A mistake.

Aletheia's golden irises pinned them down for a second that felt like an eternity, and when she finally looked away, Anius shot her a warning glare. Eustace ignored him—she could explain later.

"The Prime Cadre will handle the recruitment," the god-empress told her mages, "but your task is just as important. If not for your direct efforts, we wouldn't stand a chance." Each word increased the luminosity coming from them. "Your directive is twofold: increase your power . . ." She let them hang, a master musician plucking their strings. "Which you will achieve by channeling your divine essence into, and filling up, certain containers."

There was a long moment of silence, their cores flickering like so many candles in the wind as they realized what she was talking about. If restoring the Forty Hands was ignoring doctrine, using the relics she spoke of was akin to spitting on it. Even *if* the ancient containers were redeployed to the Divine Fleet they'd been decommissioned from, only the chosen faithful of a divine deity were supposed to fill them with essence. None present were chosen.

"Yes," Aletheia declared, spreading her arms wide and raising her chin so she faced the heavens. "I *am* God-Empress. I am the divine bridge who will connect this lower realm to the heavens above." She paused, her eyes weighing the crowd. "And you . . ." Their god-empress's attention was as a shield against the winds of uncertainty threatening to extinguish their cores. "You—all of you—are *my* chosen."

The hundred mages roared, as did their souls, Aletheia's proclamation fanning the flames within. The light of their devotion became blinding, a singular pillar of brilliance that grew by the second and outshone the glorious sun above.

Aletheia cut them off with a quick burst of her divine will, the prickle of discomfort vanishing before it could become painful. "Forgive me, my chosen," she said, gracing them with a smile. "Time is of the essence, and I must depart. Head Mage Evan will explain in greater detail."

She gave a slight bow, held it for a moment, then disappeared in the same flash of brilliance that she had arrived in. It no longer seemed like a cheap trick. It was a stroke of genius. A selfless performance from a leader who knew it would inspire awe in her followers.

But still, a shadow of doubt lingered in the far reaches of Eustace's mind. She had to talk to her friend. Had to know for sure. Anius, understanding her better than any other, tried to grab her as she dashed forward and leaped over the balcony. She batted his hand aside, flew for the stage as a streak of light, and raced past the Prime Cadre before they could stop her.

She found the god-empress in the tunnel just beyond. Aletheia's outward emotions were completely controlled; her body was not. She leaned with one hand against the stone wall, her other held to her face, back racked by sobs. Eustace almost missed a step, her doubt and hopes banished by the acute need to comfort the former princess.

"Aletheia . . ." Eustace said. No response came, so she reached out to touch her young friend's arm. "*Aletheia.* How are—"

The god-empress whirled, pulling away, meeting Eustace's care with fire and brimstone. "*Do* not *call me that!*" Some of the true feelings of the fledgling deity before her leaked out. Gone was the careful composure. Gone was the kind facade.

Gone was her friend.

The seer froze, her mind trying to reconcile the woman before her with the one she'd once known. In her desperation, she reached for comforting lies. This had to be a side effect of the ascension. Aletheia was merely overwhelmed—understandable, given the quiet girl's distaste of public speaking. But the longer they stood staring at each other, the more tenuous those explanations became. Seeking comfort, Eustace channeled her essence, once more hiding her thoughts from the world.

The god-empress's eyes, golden and hateful, flicked down toward Eustace's core. "Pray tell, Seer, why do you conceal yourself?" She took a step forward, gaze returning to Eustace's. "What truth do you fear revealing? Do you harbor animosity, I wonder?"

The words were like a knife in the gut. If not for the chi she circulated, she might have buckled under the blow. She had told Aletheia that in confidence, and now the god-empress used it against her, wielding it like a blunt weapon.

"I told you that as a friend . . ." was all she could say.

The woman snorted, an ugly sneer appearing on her face. "I am not the foolish girl you once knew. I am not your *friend,* nor will I indulge your whispers. If you wish to keep your venomous tongue, I suggest you never again use it to speak my birth name."

The rejection and betrayal dwelling beneath the surface of Eustace's core tried to consume her. They writhed like snakes, twin serpents entwining her, wrapping around her neck. They constricted, forcing the air from her lungs. But other emotions boiled up from within. Rage and disgust and incandescent fury, more brilliant than the mage's cores from earlier, roiled through her.

Outwardly, she merely nodded and bowed. "Apologies, God-Empress. I will never again call you anything so familiar."

And she meant it. Aletheia, the kind and curious and peaceful girl she'd once loved, had been smothered. Not by the hand of the delusions that had claimed her progenitors, but within the grasp of something much, much worse—a sickness of the mind that was as conniving as it was arrogant.

The god-empress studied her for a long moment, then turned and left, her footfalls making not a sound against the stone passageway.

"That was foolhardy, Eustace," Anius whispered, appearing at her side.

Another joined them. Eustace spun when she felt his presence. Evan reached out for her, but Eustace pulled away, much like the Veritus brat had done to her only moments ago.

"You forget yourself, *mage*." She opened her mouth to say more, intent on spewing forth the vitriolic grief building in her chest, then bit it back when she saw a hint of something hidden in the lines of his face. Despair. The very same that gripped her soul.

We both mourn the loss . . . she realized.

Before it could take root in Evan's soul, he tensed his jaw and hid behind duty. "You must not disturb Her Holiness further, Seer. She has a lot to work on before we depart."

It should have stoked her fury. She should have bristled and spat—Anius certainly expected her to, judging by the way he took a subtle step forward—but her heart felt carved out, a gaping hole of nothingness left behind.

Eustace, Holy Seer of Phostheia, trudged away, her passage just as directionless as the world around her.

CHAPTER TWENTY

The First Disciple

Fischer?" Maria asked, her voice a welcome addition to the harsh sounds of wood being sawed, sanded, and filed. I breathed deep, letting the room's aromas wash over me, hints of pine, lacquer, leather—and crab—creating a surprisingly pleasant amalgamation.

"Fischer!" Maria repeated in a yell.

"Sorry—was lost in the moment. Yes, sweetheart?"

"You know I love you, right?"

I cracked an eye. "Why do I feel like that sentence has a 'but' attached to it?"

"Because it does." She pointed down at my modest collection of items. "Those are your materials?"

"Yep!"

"That . . . that doesn't make sense."

"What are you talking about? Of course it does."

She raised a brow and picked up a long strip. "Leather."

"Yes."

Next, she lifted a palmful of jagged offcuts. "Metal spikes."

"Ya-huh! Good for offense *and* defense."

"Oh, they're offensive all right, just not in the way you think." She grabbed more offcuts, these of the long and wooden variety. "And *this*? The first two make sense on their own, as does that spool of string, but what in Zeus's barbed beard do you plan on doing with this bamboo?"

"Stuff."

". . . Stuff?"

"Maybe I'll need them, maybe I won't. Are you saying my last ingredient isn't worthy of a few bamboo poles? What if bamboo is vital and I have none on hand?"

"Yeah!" hissed the last ingredient. "What if it's vital?"

Maria narrowed her eyes at the section of sturdy carapace visible beneath the rest of the materials. "Which brings me to the crux of the issue." She flicked a strip of leather away and lifted the palm-sized crustacean from the pile. "Why are *you* included as a material?"

Snips let out a few bubbles that drifted into the air, her eyes glinting. No words were necessary. Our connections told me the simple truth: She was a crab, and crabs enjoyed hiding.

"As to why she's here," I said, "instead of hiding out in the ocean with her crustacean familiars—don't give me that look, Snips. You're my familiar. Even with most of my power being absorbed, I can sense where you're at." I patted her head, then turned back to Maria. "Snips is here because the item I'm trying to make is for her."

She smirked at me. "I already knew that."

"You did?"

"Duh. Why do you think I'm so confused by the bamboo? Speaking of, care to enlighten me? No need to be so secretive if I already know what you're creating."

"Nope." I gave her a toothy grin. "I have to keep at least one surprise."

"Fiiine," Maria drawled, spinning. "What about this, then?" She gestured at the surrounding room. "What the frack is this?"

"This is our workshop," Brad replied from behind his bench.

"And watch your swearing!" Greg added. "Our apprentices are impressionable!"

Maria rolled her eyes, ignoring them. "You know what I mean, Fischer. Why are you doing this here and not with the tailors? They made the last one, right?"

"I'm here for inspiration, of course!"

Snips nodded along.

Maria squinted at us. "Riiiight. Inspiration. Guess I'll just have to take your word for it."

I glanced up with a soft smile and caught her sporting the same expression. Neither of us needed to voice the fact she could barge into my mind and plunder the knowledge if she wanted to. That would be a terrifying prospect for many, but not me—I trusted her unconditionally.

"I love you," I said.

"And I love you."

"Love," agreed Snips from the crook of Maria's arm.

Behind us, Greg turned and grinned at Brad, then mimed being sick. A pink blur slammed him into the wall with a *boom* that shook the building, the workshop going silent as all heads whirled.

"*Bad* Greg!" Slimes chastised, sticking to the bricks above the woodworker's crumpled form. "*Very* rude!"

Greg groaned as he struggled to his feet. "Couldn't . . . help myself . . ."

"Back to your projects, everyone," Brad said. "And let my brother's lesson be yours, too. Our god-queen rules with an iron fist." They did what they were told, many sharing amused looks with their neighbors.

I laid my materials out across the bench, and with a nod to myself, I picked up the bamboo. Maria's curiosity washed over me, as did Snips's, woman and crab both unsure of its purpose. I grabbed a chisel, pressed it into one end of the fibrous plant, and split it right down the middle.

"*Oh!*" Understanding bloomed from Maria as she finally realized my goal. "Wait, are you sure that's going to work?"

"Nope!" I set the chisel under a tiny bunch of fibers, separating it carefully at first, speeding up as I approached the end. "I don't see why it wouldn't, though. Ruby gave me the idea with her weird rod made of stitching. If she can make string rigid, why can't I make bamboo more flexible?"

I held up the foot-long strip and focused my awareness on it, extending a single tendril of chi.

"The only issue is time. It took Ruby *weeks*, and she's more aware of tailoring and its intricacies than I am of . . . woodworking? Leatherworking? I don't even know what this really counts as."

I willed the wood to soften. Nothing happened, and I smiled at myself. Part of me had secretly hoped this was one of those things I could brute-force.

Maria patted me on the shoulder. "You'll be fine, dear. I'm sure you'll find some other impossible task to complete before the end of the . . . *day?*"

Resolved to make some mistakes, I'd flooded dozens, then hundreds more branches of essence into the bamboo fibers as she spoke. I half expected the bamboo to explode—they flowed in all at once after the now-customary slight delay caused by the network. Instead, my microscopic strings echoed the will I'd woven into the first. They contorted, twisted, and changed, each attaching to and mimicking the shape of a fiber.

"Huh." I raised my now-bendy length of wood and jiggled it about. "How about that?"

Snips leaped down onto the bench, her lethargy replaced by open wonder.

Maria sighed. "Well, you're as annoyingly competent as ever."

"Naturally. I wouldn't embarrass my lady wife with incompetence. She's overtly violent, you see."

"Hmmm. Quite." Rather than violence, she leaned to plant a tender kiss on my cheek. "Now that I know you won't cause me shame, I'll take my leave."

I grabbed her softly by the arm before she could go. "You're sure you don't need me there?"

"I'm sure." She swooped back in, gave me another kiss, gifted my butt a quick slap, then patted Snips atop her sturdy carapace.

"Say hello to Pistachio and his lady friend for me."

"Will do," Maria's eyes lingered on me for a moment, then she turned and dashed from the building.

I returned my attention to the workbench in an attempt to banish the thoughts of her silhouette from my mind. It worked. Mostly.

Holding two vaguely eye-shaped pieces of leather, I started sewing with the stitch Ruby and Steven had shown me so long ago. I already knew exactly what I wanted to create, so my will flooded out. Though it probably wasn't necessary, I leaned on my old trick of partitions, using one side to envision this garment's purpose, the other on suffusing the materials with reinforcing and pure essence.

It wasn't easy, but neither was it difficult. The countless tendrils extending from my core and Domain strained me terribly, most of the power still being drawn into the ground. Despite the drain on my resources, my body was light as a feather. The process felt *right*. This item was for my trusty guard crab. The earliest of all my animal pals to awaken. My first disciple.

Fond memories flashed through my mind.

The sickly, clawless crab covered in scars I'd discovered in the shallows. The one-eyed crustacean with deadly clackers who greeted me at my door the following morning. Countless meals. The shock and awe when she showed me her ability to shoot godsdamned energy blades like some kind of anime protagonist.

Skirmishes with Corporal Claws. Her general distrust of birds. The way her legs kicked out when I tickled her, seeking purchase on the sandy shore. Bubbles popping against my arm to wake me up. Her stalwart leadership of Tropica's spirit beasts. Her loving reluctance—sometimes overshadowed by genuine fury—as she yeeted Rocky over the horizon, into low orbit, or both.

She was the best friend I'd always wanted. The companion I didn't deserve. The crab I couldn't live without.

There weren't enough words to express how much she meant to me.

I faintly registered cold metal against my fingers as I started integrating the off-cuts with the rest of the materials, but it remained at the edge of my periphery, the bulk of my awareness focused on things far more important.

Snips's recent transformation coursed through my mind. Her willingness to cast aside her crablike tendencies had reflected just how far she was willing to go for Tropica—how far she was willing to go for *me*. Ultimately, it was an error, but that didn't change the intent behind it.

Which made me consider her soul in the present. She was something unknown. Neither spirit beast nor elemental. Our bond was unyielding, yet distinct from master and familiar. She sat on the precipice of an advancement. I could feel it in my core.

Her future self—the crab she'd become—was beyond my comprehension. But it caused me no grief. Just like Maria, I trusted Snips as much as I trusted myself.

I offered that thought up freely, only for a similar sentiment to flood back across our connection, our streams of belief forming twin currents of equal strength.

To her, I was like an elder female, a mighty matriarch whose size and majesty scared most from her den. To pair with such a crab meant giving one's spawn the greatest of chances, for none could provide as much safety, defense, and genetic advantage.

It was certainly a unique way of viewing things. *Thanks, Snips. I think.*

She sent a mental nod back, a hint of amusement joining her sincerity.

With that confusing message running through me, I focused in on the item I was crafting. My deft fingers had stitched the metal spikes between layers of leather, their tips poking out in places, jagged ends ready to snag and rend.

I stole a peek. It looked terrible, the different-sized offcuts ruining its uniformity. I couldn't give it over like this. It was nowhere near good enough for my trusty guard crab, and I'd have to start again if its shape wasn't altered upon completion. That was okay. I'd repeat the process a thousand times, happily scrapping any attempts that weren't perfect.

Luckily for all involved, such an eventuality wouldn't come to pass. Power swelled all around us. Some chi drifted in through the building's walls as a haze. Thin tendrils joined them, this essence latching on to others, bearing the same pure power. Bubbles flowed up from underground, permeating the floor. It didn't matter that most of my essence was being drained by the network. This act of creation had taken on a life of its own.

My attention wandered toward the room's occupants. All were in the middle of building their own projects, yet every pair of eyes watched me, their work momentarily paused. They wanted to see the fruits of my labor. I'd have felt it in their cores even if it wasn't plastered on their faces.

Curious, are you? A smile crossed my face as I placed the very last stitch. *Then witness . . .*

All at once, the frozen moment ended—bubbles, tendrils, and clouds of suspended essence slammed into the item before me. Like a reverse firework, the shapes grew brighter the closer they got, their power condensing.

I abandoned my senses and dropped into myself. Darkness surrounded me as I tumbled, ever downward, and only when I reached the center of my partition did I allow my mind to open. My feelings for Snips poured out in ceaseless torrents. The memories from earlier returned, flickering before my eyes, each flowing into the next. All were fuel.

The item stretched, warped, then shrank in my mind's eye, mirroring its physical form. Not once did I let go of what I pictured. Both the System and the world obeyed, bending to my will. The item's outline sharpened, stabilized.

It gleamed like a miniature sun into the room, and with it came a sense of ecstasy, every cell in my body exulting in the sensation. Terror raced up my spine and filled my chest, sharp and sickening following the euphoria. It wasn't a miniature sun—it was the beginning of an explosion, bearing enough to level more than just this building if left unchecked.

I instinctively reached for my essence to raise barriers of solid chi. The network defied me, continuing to devour my essence. Time crawled to a stop as calm certainty suffused me. I had to sever my connection to the tunnels. It was the only way. I pictured it as a giant faucet, and I mentally grabbed its handle, ready to turn it off.

Before I could, a stalwart companion arrived at my side, her awareness tapping at mine.

"*Help*," hissed Snips, her slew of bubbles holding neither doubt nor hesitation.

That was all I needed. I ceded my will to her, returning her trust.

She started forming a blast shield with our combined chi, but stopped when she realized it wouldn't have as much strength as my pure essence—if a single side failed, all the force could leave as a concentrated cone. Redirecting our intent, Snips did something remarkable. She willed the detonation to appear elsewhere, picturing a location where none would be harmed.

I'd never considered using my power to teleport force . . .

The resulting explosion rocked me. My eyes told me it was happening here, the beams of light brilliant and blinding. Every other sense, however, told me it was far above the building, almost all the force appearing in the sky hundreds of meters above us. The sound hit a moment later, as did the wave of pressure that shook any items not nailed down, tools tumbling from benches and walls alike.

Snips expelled remnants of my essence with a cute little burp, made all the more adorable by a few bubbles that drifted from her mouth to float in the air before her. I probably should have praised her, rubbed her shell all over while making a huge fuss. Instead, both Snips and I glanced down, looking at the System-made item sitting between us. Nobody said a word. The workshop was bathed in silence, broken only by the soft tap of carapaced legs scuttling forward across the bench.

Snips dipped her head, paused, then positioned herself between the leather straps. Without so much as a whisper of warning, the item shrank, snapping into place around the soul it had been created for.

Before I could inspect my guard crab's new eyepatch, my oldest nemesis appeared, drawing me in.

CHAPTER TWENTY-ONE

Yearn

Most times the System spoke to me, it was a source of frustration. Each instance harkened back to my arrival in Kallis, when the only words I'd received were about errors, superfluous systems, and how much they were offline.

I rarely liked the messages sent my way. It was a fleetingly scarce experience, and I grinned as one such experience appeared, the description of Snips's eyepatch rising to fill . . .

Wait, what?

I absorbed the first line, then skim-read till the last.

You have learned Alchemy!

. . .

You have advanced to Alchemy 64!

I caught the coin-filled sacks that appeared behind me. "Okay, how the frack does a leather eyepatch have anything to do with alchemy? That makes literally zero—"

More letters in bold arrived, cutting my words off. My core grew warm with anticipation when I saw the first line.

Transformative Eyepatch of the Traveling Fisher
But then I saw the rest of them.
[Authorization error: protected asset in lower realm]

I looked up at the ceiling, imagining the System in the sky beyond. "At this point, you're for sure just fracking with me." I paused, waiting for a response, some snarky comment like I'd seen once before. Nothing came. I let out a sigh and, looking for a pick-me-up, peered at Snips's new item.

It fit perfectly, the previously oversized strips contoured to her carapace. The leather had been dyed pitch black, and metal studs speckled the straps, their gleaming tips only just protruding.

I let out a soft whistle. "Was anyone able to inspect . . . Why are you all staring at me like that?"

Sergeant Snips, looking particularly sharp with her new garment, grew. The eyepatch transformed with her suit. She reached forward with a single claw and pointed at my navel.

"Oh . . ." I said, blinking down at my abdomen. It was glowing. Like *glowing* glowing. Shining-like-I-had-eaten-a-*star* glowing.

I lifted my shirt to reveal a bright white mark in the place I'd first felt my core. I poked it. Warm. Fading by the second. Before I knew it, the mark was gone, as was what I had assumed to be an anticipatory heat but was evidently something much more.

"Huh . . ." I said. "Neat."

Movement had yet to return to the workshop. Everyone seemed to struggle with where to look, their expressions landing between incredulity and shock as they assessed me, Snips, and her new eyepatch.

"Guys, c'mon . . ." I shook my head. "I know abs like mine are usually reserved for Grecian gods, but you're going to make Maria jealous if you continue staring. And that's not even mentioning Barry. I do my best to keep my jacked bod under covers. His identity as Tropica's muscleman might be threatened if he catches you salivating like this."

Some of the women's—and a few of the men's—faces flushed red. Most knew me better and simply rolled their eyes, trying to hide their amusement with feigned annoyance. Greg and Brad, however, were genuine in their loathing.

"Shut up, Fischer," they said in unison, followed by "Jinx!", "Under a roof!", and twin *thumps* as both brothers punched each other on the shoulder.

I smiled at them, but it grew strained. "Every time the bloody System speaks, it only makes me more confused. Alchemy?" I shook my head and blew air through my lips. "What the frack, man?"

"It really gave you levels in Alchemy?" Brad asked, rubbing the arm his brother had struck. "Was that where both sacks of coin came from?"

"Yeah. I shot from zero to sixty-four."

Snips hissed.

"Right? And then it doesn't even give a proper description for the eyepatch! All I learned was the title. Transformative Eyepatch of the Traveling Fisher. The only thing close to being descriptive is 'transformative,' and we already know it grows bigger and smaller with you, Snips."

She shook her carapace.

"Huh?"

"That's not all it does," hissed Snips.

"What are you trying to—"

Shink!

In an instant, the metal studs sprouted from beneath the blackened leather, becoming lengthy spikes resembling an off-center mohawk atop her mighty carapace. The bottom strap did the same, and those deadly needles skewered the table, lifting her inches into the air.

With another *shink*, they retracted. She landed gracefully on the workbench. Snips's visible eye sparkled.

Some of the nearby cultivators took an involuntary step back. They no longer gave a shit about my shenanigans—all gazes were locked on Snips. She spun slowly, showing off her new garment, the metal spikes sounding like a sword in its scabbard each time she sheathed and unsheathed them.

"Snips, you beautiful, sturdy crustacean . . ." I picked her up and raised her slightly, showing off her gleaming tips. "Forget about Rocky. You are, without a doubt, the coolest crab on these shores."

"Yes," hissed Snips in agreement, nodding sagely as she preened under the attention.

"I was gonna get started on my next crafting project, but this changes things. Shall we go show you off a bit?"

She resumed nodding, then went stiff as an oyster, a thought striking her. She blew conspiratorial bubbles, gave me some side-eye, and sent me an idea. I grinned back. It was a downright *devious* prank, made all the more fitting against its intended target.

"Bye!" I yelled, waving a hand over my shoulder as I snatched Snips and strode from the building.

In my haste to leave, I almost ran into a trio of metal-plated dwarves. All five of us froze.

"Uhhh," I said.

"*Umm?*" hissed Snips.

"Errrr," Paul and Toby and Theresa said. Paul's oversized armor clinked as he raised a visored helmet from his eyes.

I pointed down at their suits. "How . . . I don't even know where to begin. Where'd you get those? Where are you going?" I rubbed my chin with one hand. Snips mirrored the gesture from the crook of my arm. "And can we come too? It looks like a great time."

Paul let out an awkward laugh. "Oh, uhhh, yeah? You can come if you want . . ."

"We're going *venturing*!" Theresa yelled. I was pretty sure it was Theresa, anyway. Her oversized armor hid every one of her features. "We got the suits from Uncle Danny!"

I grinned at hearing the quartermaster referred to as "uncle." "Adventuring, huh? Sounds like fun. Do you have a direction in mind?"

Toby fit his armor better than the other two, but he was nonetheless awkward, his fingers fidgeting with a small axe strapped to his waist as he replied. "The mines . . ."

"The iron ore one?"

"Yup!" Theresa yelled, stabbing a wooden sword skyward, the training weapon only just shorter than she was. "We're gonna—"

"Don't! Don't tell me! You'll, *uhhhh*, ruin the surprise!" If they told me the specifics, I might have to warn Barry. I stood at attention and snapped off a salute. "Dismissed, soldiers! Do Tropica proud!"

Theresa bellowed and charged away. Paul followed soon after, both kids raising their respective weapons as they sprinted away, armor clanging like metal sheets in a spin cycle. Toby gave me an embarrassed smile before running off after the others, his weapon and suit only mildly quieter.

"Huh," I said. "How about that?"

Snips cocked her carapace in question.

"The children . . ." I mused, watching them go. "They really do yearn for the mines."

CHAPTER TWENTY-TWO

Pocket Crab

Corporal Claws grinned as she slipped between rows of sugarcane and emerged onto the sands south of Tropica. To most, she was a being of pure chaos. It was a reputation she had carefully cultivated, occasionally exaggerating to a cartoonish extent. But was that not also mayhem? Did it not add to her mystique? How could anyone hope to comprehend her next course of action if they didn't know where her bedlam ended and her facetious pandelirium began?

"Pandemonium, mistress," hissed RPM, unhelpfully.

Claws froze mid-step, then sighed her annoyance out. She would let that one slide—their subterfuge of the last few days had been a success.

Nobody had questioned the chaos-aspected mammals as they'd flown around the smithy, propelled by barbed lightning and an endless thirst for knowledge. Their subjects were all too happy for Claws and RPM to watch their crafting; it was preferable to being zippity-zapped by lightning, kicked in the shins, or sprayed with debris should Claws choose to enter the building through a wall rather than the boringly functional door.

Among all of Tropica's denizens, only a few select souls truly knew Claws. They were the ones she had to avoid for a while—especially her master. Only they could discern her secret mission.

RPM agreed from within. He steepled his fingers, grinned in her mind, then tickled her core with his tricksy little digits. The traitorous bastard. She reached into her right pouch, withdrew his upper body, then head-butted him back down.

The scoundrel chittered with laughter as he tumbled into her core, his soul holding nary a whisper of regret. She rolled her eyes yet didn't deny her amusement—it *had* been funny.

"But don't do it again."

"Yes, mistress."

She resumed her sneaky sneaking, each step silent as she padded across the dunes, avoiding their peaks where at all possible. So serious was Claws that when an explosion rang out from Tropica, she dropped to the floor, sand parting to conceal all but her face. There was a bird soaring high above her. Had Pelly, Bill, or one of the other pelicans scouted her out and warned Fischer?

But no. The explosion wasn't one of teleportation, and the shape flying away was a regular seagull. She glowered skyward, reemerging, shaking a paw in threat. If stealth wasn't the name of the game, she might have zapped up there and given the feathered oyster stealer a piece of her mind.

The goal, mistress, RPM reminded with a thought, which earned him some of her ire, its veracity undermined by her lack of internal brows with which to express disdain. He was smart enough, or averse to headbutts enough, that he didn't mention it.

Smoother than river-tumbled stone and faster than . . . something really fast that she was moving too swiftly to think of a proper analogy for, Claws sneakily snuck once more, body tracing the dunes. She didn't use her senses, not wanting to broadcast her position to her blessedly and frustratingly powerful master.

An explosion rang out above Tropica, and Claws buried herself. After a minute, she reemerged and sent her familiar an order—best to keep him occupied, lest he tickle her again—and he nodded in assent. He started going over the many techniques and methods he'd stolen from the apprentices in the smithy, seeking those that were most applicable.

Claws smiled at his exuberance as she let his devious mind churn, her own focused on their silent passage. She didn't need to rely on chi, and as she crested the final dune, her heart fluttered. Or would have, if she still had one.

This was it. This was the place.

The coastal winds so common to Tropica had hidden their prize, the sands swallowing it over time. Still, it was here. There could be no doubt. Even with her senses retracted, it called out to her, resonating with the power suffusing her soul. Which made sense, of course. The treasure they sought was of her own creation.

She summoned RPM forth, and together, they dug.

They could excavate it in a flash with their vast reserves of essence, but they took their time. Hours passed by, and day faded to night as they dug with care, evenly spreading any displaced sand to hide their efforts. Being discovered was unacceptable. When her nails first brushed against the hardened object buried below, it made a dull sound. In Claws's internal world, however, it chimed like a hollow bowl of crystal, seeming to resonate with her core in a way that—

Her familiar tried to steal the resonance. The result was an explosion within the center of his mass, the force inflating him like one of those funny fish that turned spherical when poked. She would have ignored it, as she so often did when RPM attempted larceny, but force rippled out from her familiar, broadcasting their location.

Her fur stood on end as she waited for her master's arrival. He would sense the strange chiming resonance and come investigate. Seconds passed, and her anxiety retreated. Maybe powering the tunnels below had left him too weak to—

Light blossomed behind her, and a formidable figure arrived, his silhouette making her stomach drop.

"Stupid fracking network," Fischer swore. "Making me wait to use my own— Oh! Claws! I've been looking everywhere for you! Here, *catch*!"

An oblong being sailed through the air in slow motion, thrown underhand by the last person she'd wanted to encounter. He *had* sensed the resonance in her soul, using it to locate her. There was bitter yet fitting irony in this ambush. He, too, had helped create the prize she'd come to excavate.

One side of Claws's mouth tugged up as the spiky shape continued tumbling end over end, growing ever closer. Before Claws's grin could fully form, it transformed into a scowl. Why did they have to come? She was trying to do something *cool!*

Claws moved as a blur to catch the airborne crab, flooding enough electricity into her forelimbs that—

Thunk.

Claws's vision bounced. She blinked. Where had Snips gone? Why hadn't the crustacean landed in her waiting paws? And, more importantly, what was up with the stabbing pain atop her furry head?

"Oh . . ." Fischer said, eyes wide, face blanching.

There was an amused hiss, followed by bubbles of the same emotion drifting down into Claws's field of view. She glanced up, saw nothing, then used her connection to her master to see what he did.

"Hi," hissed Snips, legs twitching in delight, a row of spikes having grown from a new eyepatch, whose pointed ends seemed to be lodged in Claws's *fracking head*!

Her indignation started in the muscles of her jaw and radiated out from there, her entire body shaking, flashing with lightning. Snips's visible eyestalk suddenly filled with regret. She retracted the metal spikes, beginning to flood billowing power from her joints, already zooming away.

Claws was, all things considered, rather proud of her communication skills. Certain words sometimes evaded her, but that was their own fault for being too long, or not punchy enough to keep up with her flawless and *imasculate* intellect. The noises that escaped her throat now, however, held no discernible meaning.

She screeched and growled and spat all at the same time as she launched a haymaker. It connected with the already-fleeing Sergeant Snips, who released a hiss similarly devoid of meaning, an involuntary sound that came from the depths of her being in response to losing agency over her passage.

So fast did Snips travel that, if not for their master, she would have conquered heights previously unseen by crabkind. But Fischer was as bothersomely competent as usual. His chi took a second to obey, and just as Snips started fading from view, he made her reappear before him in a flash of light.

Snips slammed into his chest. All the lightning Claws had flooded into the blasted crab transferred into him, making his limbs go rigid and consciousness waver. Both man and crustacean tottered, barely staying upright. Claws had actually done some damage to her master . . .

It didn't make her feel any better.

"Leave," she ordered, crossing her arms and glowering at them. RPM was atop her shoulders, mirroring her glower as he tippy-tapped his paws across the place she'd been stabbed. *Stabbed!* In the head! *By a fracking crab!* Every one of her silken fur follicles stood on end.

"I, uhhh, sorry." Her master took a step back. "Didn't mean to actually hurt . . ."

He trailed off, his brow furrowing, his finger pointing down at the excavation. "Wait, isn't that—"

"***Leave!***" bellowed Claws, her familiar, and the very sky. Thunder boomed as lightning struck a nearby mountain.

"*Sorry!*" was all Fischer got out before his chi obeyed him. He vanished, and light flashed on the far side of Tropica to announce his arrival there.

Claws took a deep breath, smoothing her fur down as she exhaled, then shot RPM a look both blank yet filled with meaning. He returned the same expression, an almost imperceptible grin appearing a moment later.

She rocked back on her paw pads and scoffed. As if something so mundane as a metal spike could cause her pain, made by her master or not. Her feigned outrage had been the perfect cover—a way to stop Fischer from questioning her purpose here.

It was actually quite enjoyable seeing Snips stuck up there like a prickly seed. Though it would have been far more satisfying to see the crab-turned-conker lodged in someone else's noggin.

"It was enjoyable," agreed RPM, sending the view from his perspective. Claws usually would have given him a soft smack for that unsolicited cheek, but he'd earned a little leniency—his performative fury had been perfect.

"But don't do it again."

"Yes, mistress."

They grinned at each other in full. RPM started giggling first, but Claws wasn't far behind, the deviously kindred souls chittering under their breath at the joy of a plan coming together.

Without another word, they resumed their excavation, this time with much more fervor. Silence was no longer necessary. Fischer wouldn't return.

I shook my head as the light of teleportation vanished, leaving only the crescent moon above to illuminate the surrounding rows of cane. I gazed down, raising a brow at Snips. She stared back, her lone stalk somehow mirroring my dubious expression. And we cackled.

My eyes bugged out as I covered my mouth, smothering the sound lest Claws hear. Snips did the same with one claw, her limbs twitching, her hisses cutting through the night's silence.

"She's definitely gonna dig that up, isn't she?"

Snips hissed in agreement. "For crafting, yes?"

"I'd bet my hat on it. The cheeky little rat thinks she's so clever." I extended a tendril back her way, willing my sense of hearing into it. I forwarded the noises found there—chittering giggles and energetic digging. "Your plan was more effective than I could have hoped, Snips. You should have seen her face when you got stuck in her forehead. I might have to commission a statue."

Her carapace shook in amusement at the suggestion, and I filed it away for later.

"Should we go check up on Maria? Not to help, of course. Just to, ahhh, witness?"

Snips sobered in a flash, giving me a warning glance.

"I was joking! Sheesh, Snips. I promise I won't help."

"Good. Strength must be earned."

"I do have some things to offer, though. Two—"

"No helping!"

"Let me finish before reprimanding me! They're both methods of distraction should their attempt not go well. Here. Have a peek."

I sent her both. One was a concept I'd been mulling over all day, having had to keep it carefully concealed. Snips perked up a little. The second was something I'd only thought of just now, but that didn't make it any less enjoyable. She blew a stream of happy bubbles, nodded emphatically, and leaped into my open pocket.

I patted her through the thin material. "Get nice and comfy. We'll leave as soon as they arrive . . ."

With that, I pressed two fingers between my lips and whistled, letting out a tone that was silent to most and unmissable to some.

CHAPTER TWENTY-THREE

Just the Thing

Maria took a deep breath of the damp air trapped beneath the canopy. It was cold against her throat and settled heavily in her chest. Evenings in the vast forest beyond the western mountains were always rather bland, especially when compared with the vibrant colors, cheerful birdsong, and droning insects so prevalent during daylight hours.

As they got closer to their destination, however, it grew even more bland than usual.

The haunting hoots of the occasional owl vanished entirely. The unseen crickets, who usually only ceased their chirping when one strode nearby, were nowhere to be heard. Even the wind had disappeared, as if it, too, was fearful of the clearing ahead.

Maria and her two crustacean companions, however, were more excited than scared. The closer they got, the more they fidgeted, their nervous energy growing. The lady lobster scuttling along between Pistachio and Maria was particularly intrigued. Her antennae waved about, tasting the surrounding air in search of what caused the forest's critters to flee.

Taking another breath, the moisture-laden oxygen filling her lungs, Maria cast a glance at Pistachio, only to find him glaring back in accusation. She averted her gaze and stared up through gaps in the canopy, using the crescent moon above as a grounding force to stop herself from chortling.

Touché, Pistachio. Touché.

Slimes hummed in her core. *He's leaning into his annoyance at you to distract himself from his own infatuation.*

He is. It's quite brilliant, really . . . but there's a hole in his defense. She locked eyes with the massive lobster again, and rather than run from his accusatory stare, she accepted the gambit, waggling her brows suggestively.

He missed so many steps that he careened into a tree.

The sound snapped his lady friend from her reverie, and as she stared at him, Pistachio's carapaced cheeks actually blushed.

Maria choked, and her laughter broke free. She transformed it—masterfully, in her humble opinion—into a cough, concealing her amusement. "Please focus on your steps, Pistachio. We're almost there . . ."

Only when his lady friend fell back into contemplation did he look over at Maria. If looks could kill . . . well, he wouldn't actually end her life, but his gaze certainly wished her ill. Perhaps a stomachache. Or a few stubbed toes.

She winked and gave him a thumbs-up. Slimes did the same, his approximation of a hand jiggling from Maria's shoulder for only a second before retreating to her core.

Much to the delight of everyone—but *especially* Pistachio—the endless trunks finally came to an end, black water and darkened skies becoming visible between the mighty trees.

They had arrived.

Maria removed the block on her senses, and she immediately understood how the lady lobster had slipped so easily back into distraction. Clouds of chi suffused the entire forest. It was . . . weak, which gave her a moment's pause. Her first reaction was to assume the source of it was fading in power, its life draining away, but the truth was far more gratifying.

It hadn't gotten weaker at all. She'd gotten stronger. *Much* stronger.

She flexed her will, and pink essence billowed from her after a slight delay, the clouds of foreign chi fleeing from her restorative aspect. The origin of that sickly haze, however, had different plans. The placid water before them grew turgid, the spirit beast within its depths stirring from its slumber in response to her claim. It struggled against the bars of its prison, and though it couldn't hope to break free, the effect on the lake was immense.

The surface bulged and roiled, small waves cascading out to crash against the shores. Pockets of air released a sea of bubbles. The odor they delivered was wretched, and Maria instinctively covered her nose as she muted her sense of smell, knowing her chi would take a moment to obey.

The lobsters were far less bothered by the scent, which wasn't all that much of a surprise considering they delighted in the taste of raw, sun-ripened fish. Neither did they appear pleased, however; they lowered their carapaces to the grass, profiles low and clackers prepped for violence.

Maria let out a slow breath through pursed lips as she channeled more of her power out into her burgeoning clouds of pink. The surroundings became tinged with the color, growing less visible as her chi condensed.

"Disgusting," hissed the lady lobster. "Wrong, wrong, *wrong.*"

Maria couldn't help but smile at the words. This was the first time she'd understood the crustacean so clearly. "Yep. Its core is absolutely abhorrent. Poor thing."

The smaller lobster seemed to consider this. After a few seconds, she nodded, understanding. This giant spirit beast, the same creature Fischer had tried and failed to cleanse months ago, was something to be pitied. Its soul and intent were vile through no fault of its own.

"Based on what we now know of spirit beasts—and their tendency to turn evil after consuming humans—it's highly likely this fish is a victim. The other creatures found in this lake were created by the followers of Ceto, so its corruption could have been intentional. Maybe it was just a regular fish before they found it. Or perhaps it was already an awakened spirit beast, a kind creature turned evil by the humans that tried to hunt it down."

"Which do you find more likely?" hissed Pistachio with a slew of thoughtful bubbles.

Maria shrugged her shoulders, a soft smile playing on her lips. "I mean to find out for sure." She sent her pale chi billowing over the water, its color condensing, the moon above infusing it with an ethereal light.

The fish thrashed. Railed at the power it could feel encroaching on its Domain. But it was entirely outmatched in this battle of wills. If desperate, Maria could have reached for Fischer, could have used what reserves he wasn't feeding into the tunnels as if they were her own. Such action wasn't necessary.

Her husband sent the faintest pulse of acknowledgment from somewhere to the southeast when he sensed her thoughts drifting toward him. He was on his way, sprinting leisurely through the forest, a pair of animal pals by his side.

Maria's soft smile turned into a sharp grin; she would finish before they arrived.

Her clouds covered the entire lake now, one giant sheet of shimmering color. Below, the spirit beast grew frenzied, its battering against the bars getting stronger, more desperate. Yet the water's surface remained still, the soothing aura of her healing power so strong that the very environs were affected.

Faster than the piteous creature could fathom, her chi engulfed the lake. It flew in from all directions, absent one second, ubiquitous the next. A mistake. She reeled, struggled to regain her equilibrium as the awareness of every organism calling the ecosystem home swarmed her.

Pistachio pressed one of his giant claws against her leg, helping her remain standing. She didn't waste a moment, immediately trying again, this time limiting her scan to only those creatures larger than her palm. It took a second to detect them, and another second to go over the results. Both the jungle mudminnows and alligator gars remained, the two species somehow surviving the spirit beast's reawakening.

She wanted to thank the universe that they'd lived, but she swept that gratitude aside for later. She had more important things to do. The ascendant beast trapped within the solid bars of Fischer's light was stunned. Maria conquering its waters was so shocking that its fury, otherwise mindless and without end, had faltered.

In that moment of nothingness, its awareness empty and malleable, her essence poured in. Slimes squealed in delight, his will exploding outward to join with Maria's. Master and familiar were one. Both sought to heal the poor soul trapped in physical and mental prisons not of its own design.

In some ways, the process resembled the cleansing of Theogonia's cultivators; like the pelicans, its imperfections were scoured away. What differed, however, was the scale of the task at hand.

Firstly, rather than boulders, the afflicted beast's defects were mountains, each belonging to a single cultivator. The breadth of its corruption was staggering. Hundreds of peaks lifted free, their bases running so deep they seemed lodged in its very center. Maria forced herself to ignore the sheer number, instead focusing on the other difference between this fish and the would-be pelicans.

The gaping rents left behind were too vast to be filled. She severed her connection to the tunnels momentarily, and she gasped as her vast power slammed back into her. Feeling more alive than she had in days, she sent every drop of chi flowing into the fish. Waters flowed up from the cracked lake bed of its core, pooling in great canyons, never quite reaching the surface. Even her full strength wasn't enough. Panic coursed through her, and she grasped out with a mental hand, seeking Fischer's spare power. She would allow herself to fail, but not if it endangered a creature too insane to consent. Before she reached her husband, however, she realized the terrible truth.

It was no good. There was nothing more his light, brilliant and purifying as it was, could do here.

Maria inspected the result of her attempted healing. The spherical nexus was pitted, damaged. Her hopes died a little, but not entirely. This was one of the better outcomes. In a perfect world, she could have healed it back to full health, but its trauma made that impossible for now.

Though she could accept the outcome, it still niggled at her, a single question repeating over and over.

Why?

Why was this creature so different from Fathom and Cal? The pair of cephalopods had experienced things that would drive anyone mad, yet Fischer's cleansing light had helped burn away their spiritual wounds—along with two literal *gods*.

The unknown was sometimes a source of wonder, a mystery whose possible discovery fueled exploration and advancement. This wasn't one of those times. She suspected that any illumination of this spirit beast's past would be smothered by shadow.

Maria withdrew her chi, curing scratches, internal injuries, and even a few mud-minnow limbs as she went. The lake was once more mired in darkness as the last plume flew into her, and though the lake remained still, she could sense movement below.

From behind, too. Three shapes strode between trunks, having kept their distance while she worked. Borks zoomed forward and licked her hand. Teddy cocked his head, staring down at the water. And Fischer rested a reassuring palm on her upper back. He opened his mouth to speak, but then another arrived.

The top of the beast emerged from the murky pool, one inhuman eye taking them all in. It was no longer mindless, but neither was it kind. It communicated nothing, simply lingering, watching, then sinking once more, its tail barely moving as it returned to the depths.

"I'm sorry." Fischer squeezed her hand, the small touch making a world of difference.

"It's okay. I'm glad we came, even if it never recovers more than this. We've at least freed it from an eternity of directionless wrath."

"*You* did, Maria. You freed it." He squeezed again, his skin warm. "Well done."

"Thanks, but it really was a team effort." She turned to Pistachio. "I appreciate your help earlier, especially after I was so antagonizing."

He just shrugged. Of course he'd helped. Her statement had brought confusion to the lady lobster's face, so Maria swiftly changed the subject. "What did you think? Did you feel any alignment with healing?"

Though it was her reason for coming along, the smaller lobster blew unsure bubbles. Maria gave a tight smile. She'd hoped her own purpose would strike a chord within the newly awakened crustacean, but perhaps it wasn't meant to be.

Fischer felt her despondency. "You know, I might have just the thing to cheer you up."

He had sensed her mood, but she could also sense his. She frowned at him. "Careful, husband. I love you, but if the barely restrained mirth pouring from you is related to an impending prank, I'd really rather you didn't—"

"Nope!" Fischer reached down and collected something from his pants. He opened his fist to reveal a small, stylish, and decidedly spiky crustacean. "Check it out! Pocket crab!"

Shink! went the pocket crab, proving Fischer right. He *had* possessed just the thing to cheer her up.

CHAPTER TWENTY-FOUR

A Whole Pile of Clams

On the shore beside the headland, I smiled at the world, my hands held forward and palms facing the campfire, soaking in the warmth. A small breeze swept by, making the orange tongues dance. I was surrounded by friendly faces. Most stared at the flames while two lobsters, one big and one small, collected clams from the gathered pile and placed them on the red-hot coals.

One might wonder why we'd chosen to start a gathering on the rocky shore, whose jagged and slick surface was much less inviting than soft sand, and whose proximity to the water made wind and ocean spray far more likely a prospect. The answer was simple: It just felt right.

Teddy and Borks looked like they could be brothers. They sat on their haunches, backs to the waves, noses twitching and gazes distant. Maria was to my left, using my body to shield most of the spray, delighting in the few droplets that reached her.

The clams hissed and bubbled as they cooked swiftly in the campfire's incandescent heat. One popped open, and Maria skewered the morsel within. Rather than throw it into her mouth, she held it out to me.

"Does anybody object to our benevolent god-king having the first? I don't want him growing violent with hunger, you see. He's very abusive. Someone could die."

Borks and Teddy let out assenting growls. The lobsters nodded their heads. And my pocket crab, who was clutched in Maria's hand, one of her eyepatch's spikes being used as a skewer, blew affirmative bubbles.

I reached out to grab it, but Snips slightly retracted the metal spike it hung from, her eye twinkling with mischief.

"With your mouth," Maria ordered, emphasizing her point by jiggling Snips—and, by extension, the clam.

"The things I do for love . . ." I leaned over, grabbed it with my teeth, and forgot about everything else as its umami flavor exploded across my awareness, each bite flooding my body with warmth and—

Boooom!

The world shook, a wave of sound striking my chest with so much force it would have knocked the air from a regular human's lungs. Even through my closed eyelids, I couldn't miss its blinding glory. I tried to blink away the jagged lines of lightning burned into my retina, but the authentic version replaced them, crackling up from the being whose arrival had caused the explosion.

Corporal Claws looked like a furry reincarnation of Zeus, her brow enraged, body and eyes aglow. She cast an imperious look across all present. "You *dare?*"

"You *dare?*" repeated RPM, appearing from her pocket, mirroring her posture and ire.

"Fish is one thing," continued Claws, lip twitching. "But clams? A whole pile of clams! You know they're my favorite!"

I sighed. "You were invited, you peanut."

"Are you calling me a liar?"

"No. Well, I mean, yes, you *are* a liar, but—"

RPM let out a wordless squeal and tried to dash forward, but Claws caught him by the waist. "Master is right. Lying is fun. But that doesn't change the facts!" One of her paws jabbed out in accusation. "I was left uninvited! To a feast of *clams!*"

The raccoon crossed his forearms and growled menacingly—but only succeeded in looking cute, his grumble squeaky, his body hanging limply from Claws's arm like a restrained toddler.

"Claws . . . I invited you with the smell. You forbade me from bothering you, so I let the scents wash your way. If I didn't want you coming, I wouldn't have . . ." I trailed off mid-sentence as she released hold of her chi, all of it rushing back into her core.

"Why didn't you say so?" She marched up, plucked two cooked mollusks from the fire—and a third after her familiar stole one of the first two—then raised both remaining shellfish to her mouth. She slurped them noisily, juices and all.

With the wildcard mammals satiated, I gazed over at the lady lobster, a plan days in the making finally coming to fruition. I said not a thing as she tried the cooked clam, clearly finding it to her liking. Only when everyone was on their second mouthful—or tenth, in Claws's case—did I clear my throat to get their attention.

"So, do you want a name, Specialist Shell?"

You'd think I had just walked into a funeral and sucker-punched someone's grandma. All eyes went wide, faces tinged with surprise and a hint of outrage, the latter more prevalent on one in particular.

"Among the sea of confusing and, frankly, sometimes insulting names," Maria said, "this might be the worst yet."

"Don't listen to her, Shelly! Close your— Wait, you don't have ears, do you? Damn, talk about inconvenient. Can't even pop in some earplugs when your upstairs neighbor starts tapdancing on their hardwood floor—"

"Fischer!" Maria yelled, cutting me off.

". . . What?"

"Explain yourself!"

"I mean, you know what hardwood is. The upstairs-neighbor part is pretty self-explan—"

"The name," she interrupted again, more disappointed than upset. "You said *Specialist Shell,* then you said Shelly!"

"Well, yeah. Specialist Shell is a mouthful, so Shell for short, and Shelly for shorter."

A shape emerged from the gloom just in time for Maria to redirect her confusion. "Barry! Thank the *gods*! I need someone sane to back me up. Did you catch all that?"

"Unfortunately." He gave me an odd look from above his muscular jaw. "Shelly *is* longer than Shell."

"But shorter than Specialist Shell. It's a matter of perspective."

Barry ignored me. "If anyone can explain how his brain works, Maria, it's you. I thought your marriage would make you understand him more—weird names and all."

"It only made it *worse*." She rubbed the bridge of her nose. "I could at least hold on to the hope that there was some greater meaning behind it before, but now I know the truth."

"Which is . . . ?"

"There isn't one. He just goes with the first thing he thinks of. He *pretends* to consider it, feigns mulling it over for days, but *always* just ends up going with the original."

"First off, how dare you reveal trade secrets? More importantly, I won't apologize for being decisive and trusting myself. Isn't that what's needed from a leader? What Ellis *specifically* told me to work on?"

Maria groaned. "He's right. I *hate* when he's right."

I grinned at her, knowing those weren't her true feelings. She could protest all she wanted, but her trust was unconditional.

Barry, however, wasn't ready to surrender. "Why not, I don't know, 'Major Michelle' if you want to call her Shelly?"

"Dunno. I like Specialist Shell better."

"But *why*?"

"I already told you—dunno. Why is Maria so beautiful? Why does your jaw look like it could crack stone? How does Claws keep sneaking sand into your bed without being noticed? Not every question has an answer, mate."

"Okay, look," he tried again. "I get the shell thing. Really, I do. It pairs well with Pistachio"—this made the mentioned leviathan jolt and Claws's eyes twitch in response—"but Michelle follows your usual convention of title followed by an actual name."

I snorted. "An actual name? Like Claws, Snips, Borks, Pistachio, and Lemony Thicket? Each suits them perfectly, but they're absolutely *not* normal names."

"You know what I mean. Those with nicknames—Warrant Officer Williams for Bill, Theodore Roosevelt for Teddy—they follow that convention."

"Barry . . . they're both blokes."

"So?"

I leaned forward, giving him a measured look. "Are you implying that Shelly looks like a man?"

Snips let out an appalled hiss.

"What? No. I didn't mean—" His jaw moved silently, searching for any way out. "RPM!" he yelled.

"What about him?"

"Abbreviation! You could do an abbreviation!"

"Of Specialist Shell? Heavens above, Barry. I didn't take you for a racist."

"What in Hades's clammy thighs are you talking abou—"

Borks bolted upright, ears alert, head gazing over the river. Teddy did the same. My doggo pal opened a portal, leaped into it, and sealed it the moment Teddy was also through.

I threw my hands up. "Great! You offended Borks and Teddy so much that they left—are you happy with yourself, Barry?"

His stupidly muscular jaw chewed on that for a long moment. The look on his face suggested he'd realized I was messing with him and was now considering whether to swallow my words or spit them back at me.

Unaware or unsympathetic of Barry's concerns, another hissed first. "Sergeant Shell . . . Shelly for short . . ."

"You like it?"

Shelly nodded, antennae waving, core radiating delight as a stream of contented bubbles spilled from her mouth.

"Another win for God-King Fischer. I can't keep getting away with it."

Maria patted my arm. "Yes, dear. All bend the knee before your mighty naming ability."

Snips wiggled farther into the nook of my elbow. She was the only other soul I'd shared it with, and she was as pleased as I was that the name had stuck. In a perfect world, I could sit and enjoy the rest of the evening, eating copious amounts of clams and dwelling on just how damned lucky I was to have so many friends—even if one of them might be a closeted racist. The world, however, was far from perfect. There were shenanigans brewing.

Corporal Claws, ever on the lookout for a screw to twist, had noticed Pistachio's reaction earlier when Barry mentioned his name pairing with Shelly's. From across the fire, the troublesome otter was doing well to conceal it, but I didn't miss the twitching of her fuzzy little brows, a physical tell of the devious machinations forming behind them. One corner of her upper lip tugged into the beginning of a smile, but she swept it away, not yet wanting to reveal her hand.

I launched a preemptive strike. "What were you up to earlier, Claws? When we found you on the sand?"

Her brows flew up, her jaw unhinging in panic. I half expected her to respond violently—which was rather graceful of me, considering the *actual* chance of her responding with violence was far higher than fifty percent—but Claws surprised me.

"Who, me?" she chirped, shrugging and waving a paw dismissively. "Psh. Nothin'."

I'd normally have smirked and left it at that, but Pistachio's happiness was on the line, and I was already shipping the idea of him and Shelly forming a power couple. I frowned at Claws, lips pursed, letting distrust flow from my core. "You're acting a little *too* nonchalant there, missy. I'm starting to think you're actually chalant."

"Chalant . . . ?" Maria asked.

"You don't agree?"

"No, I mean, yes, it's just . . . I don't think that's a word."

"Don't be ridiculous. It's a perfectly cromulent word."

Wisely, she chose not to engage, pivoting instead. "So what are you going to do about the kids, Barry?"

"The kids? How did you know?"

Maria and I shared a glance. Our feigned misdirection had worked more effectively than we could have hoped—we'd even managed to confuse ourselves. "Know what?" she asked.

"That I was looking for Paul. That's why I came here before you distracted me with your . . ." He gestured in my general direction. "*You*-ness."

"Thank you."

"Not a compliment."

"Speak for yourself."

"I . . . You know what? Never mind. Have you seen Paul? The Buzzy Boys told me to come ask you."

"They're not at the forge?"

"No. I just came from there."

"Ahhhh. They must still be *there*, then."

Barry blinked. "Where is *there*?"

"Where all children yearn to go, mate."

He rubbed his eyes. "It's too late for riddles, Fischer. Where do all children yearn to go?"

"The mines, obviously."

". . . The *mines*?"

I barely managed to keep my face straight when confronted with the incredulity on his. "Yeah. Paul and the squad hit the old mine. Not to worry, though—they suited up first."

"Ruby and Steven made them suits?"

"What? No. They suited up in armor."

"Where the frack did they get the armor?"

"The smithy, of course."

"They *made* it?"

"Don't be ridiculous, Barry. That'd be way too dangerous. They got their armor and weapons from Danny."

"*Weapons?*"

"Well, yeah. One can hardly indulge their yearning for the mines without proper protection."

A vein protruded from Barry's neck, and I realized I might have gone too far. "Okay, mate, relax. I promise they're not in danger."

"That's not the issue, Fischer. I don't like that they have weapons, but I know they're safe. You wouldn't have let them go otherwise."

"Oh. Good. Wait, then what's the problem?"

"The *mines*!"

"What about them?"

"The—the yearning! That is absolutely *not* a thing here."

"Sure it is."

"Name a single time!"

"Ahhhh, your son and his new friends?" I checked the moon's position in the sky above. "Like . . . eight hours ago. It was literally today, mate."

"Right. And you didn't put them up to it?"

"Nope."

His frown drifted from confused and landed on suspicious. "You had someone else do it."

"Barry, mate, I'll swear an oath if it's what you want. Tell him, Snips."

She was dozing off in my arms, but she nodded slightly, blowing bubbles that confirmed the children did, in fact, yearn for the mines of their own accord. Claws chirped her agreement, and the top half of RPM rose from Claws's pocket to roll his eyes and chitter mockingly, implying everyone knew that. Barry's jaw started chewing again.

"You should drop it," Maria suggested. "You know better than to engage with Fischer when he's in this kind of mood. Besides, he's telling the truth."

"You swear as well?"

"Oh yeah. All the time."

"No—I don't—I mean you'd swear an oath! That it's the truth!"

Maria frowned in thought. "I don't know if I feel comfortable taking an oath on something so stupid."

"Aha! So you also think it's stupid?"

"Yes, Barry, I *do* think it's stupid . . ." If he wasn't so incensed, the muscleman would have seen it coming. "For you to have lived so long and not yet learned that all children yearn for the mines."

CHAPTER TWENTY-FIVE

Work and Play

Paul tried his best to hold it in, but the sneeze came rocketing out anyway, the sound amplified by the rocky tunnel they found themselves in.

"Bless youuu," Theresa sang from up ahead.

"Bless you," Toby echoed distractedly.

"Thanks!" Unlike Paul, the others didn't have enhanced hearing, so he mixed a bit of power into his voice—a little too much. The siblings flinched, hands covering their ears. "Sorry," he added.

Neither cared much. They had tasks to be about.

Theresa's curls draped down as she hunched and grabbed a vaguely rectangular stone. She made it do a flip, her arms rising in celebration when it stuck the landing. She had been playing with the rocks for literally *hours*. If not for her enthrallment, they'd have left long ago.

By comparison, Toby was a vision of maturity as he inspected the remains of a boulder. "Was this a part of it, too?" he asked. "The one that contained silver?"

Their Buzzy Boy chaperones, the first resting on Toby's shoulder, the other hovering near the mine entrance, made vibrations so affirmative even the unawakened teen could decipher their meaning. "Thought so . . ."

"How could you tell?" Paul walked over to join him. His cavernous armor clanked wonderfully with each step.

"See the slight difference in color?" Toby picked up the chunk and pointed at different parts of it. "This section is so gray it's almost black. It would have been the outside of the boulder. And this part here? It's much lighter."

"I think I see what you mean . . ." He didn't. They both looked like rocks. *Best to encourage my new friend, though . . .*

"If it wasn't part of that boulder, and was instead like the rest of the iron ore, it would be a reddish brown . . . Where's a good example?" Toby searched for a moment before snatching up a jagged lump. "This piece."

Paul squinted at both. "Ohhhh! I see!" And this time, he was only half lying. "I remember Ellis saying something about stone with high metal content turning rust colored. What was it called again?" He tilted his head to the side, tried his best to remember the proper term, then decided it wasn't at all that important.

Being a half ascendant was annoying at times. Like waking up from a dream, remembering that the already-faded memory felt significant but not being able to recall *why*. It was like that with so many things: words, knowledge, and . . . more words. Okay, it was *mostly* just words, but that didn't make it any less bothersome. "The words we use are important," as his mom loved to say. She'd said so only two days ago, when he'd referred to Sturgill's pastries as "fracking delicious," which hadn't been Paul's fault. They *were* delicious, and "frack" was a great . . . mollified adjective? Or was it *modified*?

He shook his head, deciding to let it go and focus on the positives. *Like my sweet armor,* he thought, twisting his gauntlet so it reflected the nearby torch's light. *And my ability to appreciate just how dang* cool *it is.*

But other annoyances drifted to the forefront of his mind.

Earlier today, while Theresa played with rocks and Toby examined . . . other rocks, Paul had finally felt safe enough to assess the knots that kept forming in his stomach. Paul's brain was . . . different. Even before ascending, he had always been responsible—except for when pies were involved, but that didn't count. Baked goods and bad choices went hand in hand.

His mouth started to water, and he used the sensation to launch himself back toward the positives. He had a perspective unique to any other, one foot in the mind of a child, the other in the brain of a responsible adult. Half kid, half cultivator.

It was a blessing. Something nobody else had experienced for who knew how long. So why did his stomach keep twisting over itself, causing that terrible feeling? He'd thought spending the day with people closer to his age would fix him, or at least help him find the answer, but it hadn't done either.

Even now, the feeling lingered in his abdomen, always there, like a winged insect that had dive-bombed and ruined an otherwise delicious slice of pie. You could fish it out, sure. Eat your dessert and pretend it hadn't happened. But a part of you knew.

"Uhhh," Toby said, waving one hand. "I know they're cool, but I didn't think you found them that interesting."

Paul, realizing he'd been just staring at the two lumps of rock with a blank look on his face, pressed his lips into a line. "Sorry. Got lost in thought."

"It's fine. I understand completely. They're mesmerizing, aren't they?"

Paul didn't deny it, letting Toby run with the assumption. He gazed up at the mine's ceiling—or tried to, but his oversized visor blocked most of it. He slid it out of the way, stared up toward the heavens, and sent out a silent prayer, asking to one day be as strong and sure of himself as Fischer.

Maybe without all the god-king responsibility, though. That seems like a lot . . .

"Okay!" Theresa announced, hair bouncing as she stood up. "I'm done! Can we go explore the other area?"

The two boys—who were actually young men, if you really thought about it— shared an amused glance at how fast she'd gone from engrossed to bored.

Paul gave her an apologetic look. "Sorry, but it's too late. We gotta head back."

"You said we were going to the beach as well!"

"That was before you played here for hours, sis . . ."

Theresa added a pout to the peevish disposition she was showing her brother. "Then you should have told me!"

"Uhhh, Paul tried to. Five different times. We've been waiting for you."

Amazingly, her visage got even more severe, brows lowering, eyes forming a slit. "Oh." All at once, her frown disappeared, replaced by a wide-mouthed yawn and mumbled words that sounded almost like, "I forgot."

"Even if it wasn't too late, you're clearly tired."

"No, I'm not," she retorted, which was immediately undermined by another yawn. "I could stay up alllll night if I wanted."

"I bet." Paul strode toward the front of the mine. "But then we'd have to delay tomorrow's adventure." He raised one hand, pressed his fingers between his lips, and let out a sharp whistle. The sound flew out into the darkness, barely audible—to humans, anyway.

There was a soft cracking sound, and a purple portal tore into existence. Two beasts leaped through it. Borks was all wags, his back legs struggling to find purchase on loose stones with how happy he was to have been summoned. Teddy landed with more grace than a bear his size should have, softly nuzzling the boys on his way past them to Theresa.

"Baby bear!" she yelled, wrapping her arms around his neck and squeezing him tight, his savage-looking spikes soft and malleable to her touch. "Where have you been? I thought—" This yawn was the largest yet, her knees bending as she released it. "—you'd forgotten about me."

He grunted an apology and dropped to the floor, inviting her to climb his shoulder—which she accepted immediately, of course, her sleepiness momentarily fleeing.

Borks, who'd taken a seat on his still-wagging haunches, cocked his head at Paul and whined, tongue lolling out the side of his mouth.

"Yep! We finished collecting ore a few hours ago, actually. We've just been playing."

The hellhound shaped like what Fischer called a golden retriever leaped toward the collection of unsmelted ore, nudging it with his nose when he got there.

"Nope," Toby answered. "If we're going to do it from start to finish, we should load it up ourselves, right, Paul?"

Paul's chest grew a little lighter at that. They'd spent most of the day here, gathering an amount of ore that Fergus or Duncan could have collected in a few strikes. The knots in his stomach had been twisting when he thought about how long they'd been here, but Toby's words relieved the tension—not a single second had been wasted.

"Yep! Let's do it!"

Ruff! agreed Borks, his tail once more sweeping back and forth as he opened a portal and watched the boys—who were basically men—carry large chunks of iron ore into his storage space.

CHAPTER TWENTY-SIX

Burning Daylight

The following morning, as with all days I got to wake up in Tropica, was a wonderful affair. I woke to the beautiful aroma of coffee and croissants, carried by an even more beautiful female.

Sergeant Snips.

"Has there ever been a more enticing sight?" I asked, rubbing my eyes as Snips scuttled closer, balancing the tray of goodies above her head. "If I was a crab, Snips, I'd challenge Rocky to a tussle for the slightest chance of earning your affec— Ow! *Ow!* It was a joke!"

Maria shook her raised hand, threatening another whack on my upper arm.

"Master courts death," hissed Snips, deftly hopping up onto the bed, not spilling a single drop.

I rubbed the top of her carapace, kissed my wife on the cheek in apology, and took a moment to stretch my arms skyward. "What do you say we take brekkie down to the shore and watch what's left of the sunrise?"

Less than a minute later, I sipped from my coffee as we crested a dune and couldn't help but smile as I caught sight of the spot Barry's family often greeted the coming day from. There were even more pals than I'd hoped to find.

The newly renamed Dodge and his kids were also there, Toby and Theresa standing in the shallows with Paul. Teddy and Borks lounged on the far side, the former sitting up, the latter closing the distance, all wagging tail and scrambling legs.

"Mornin', buddy," I said, grabbing Maria's brekkie so she could give him a good scritching for both of us.

As we sat down to the right of Barry and Helen, I took another bite of croissant, letting its buttery layers melt in my mouth before chasing it with a swig of Sue's wondrous coffee, its nutty and slightly bitter profile flawlessly offsetting the pastry's savory notes. "I'm guessing the kids were out late?" I asked. "Doing what they do best?"

Barry gave me some side-eye. "Yes, Fischer."

Helen smiled over his shoulder. "Not that you'd know it by how much energy they have."

They were twisting their feet in the wet sand, seeing who could dig themselves deeper. Paul was winning, of course, but he was showing just enough restraint to keep his adversaries interested.

"So," Maria said, the morning sun highlighting the emerald notes of her irises, "what's on the agenda for us today?"

"Sorry, can you repeat the question? I was a little distracted by the prettiest woman I've ever seen."

"You've already wooed me, Fischer. Now you're just being a suck-up." The curve of her lips betrayed the joy I could feel through our connection. "Or are you going to pretend you were talking about Snips again?"

"Don't be silly. Snips is the prettiest *being* I've ever seen. You're absolutely the prettiest woman, though."

"Aaaand there it is. If you're gonna insult me, can you at least answer my question?"

"Hmmmm. They *do* say the secret to a happy marriage is compromise. I *guess* I can meet you in the middle. But what are you bringing? What do I get out of it?"

"You're a better wife than I am, Maria," Helen said, eyes closed, head leaning against Barry's dummy-thick arms. "If I had your strength and my husband had half Fischer's cheek, I would have thrown him at the sun."

"I've never even considered it. I'm definitely not just waiting for the perfect opportunity to catch him off guard and fling him from the face of Kallis—not that I'd ever admit as much if that were my plan, of course."

Sharon nodded along. "Of course."

I cleared my throat. "Now that I think about it, I would absolutely *love* to share today's plans with my patient and beautiful and wise wife, who's definitely not planning to yeet me into the sun."

"Go on, then."

Theresa lunged forward suddenly and attempted to tackle Toby into the ocean. Her impromptu battle cry cut off as he sidestepped, and she plunged face-first into a low wave.

The girl that reemerged looked half drowned, her curls flat and plastered to her head, neck, and shoulders. "Ugh! Not fair! You're too fast!"

"Unfair? *You* attacked *me!*"

Torn between entertained and mildly disappointed, Dodge—still a cool name— shook his head, giving us a look that screamed, *What are you gonna do?*

"At least she has her health," Helen offered. "She's clearly feeling better."

"She was always like this. Her returned health just lets her do it more often."

Barry snorted. "Not surprising, considering her actions when she found a bear in the forest."

Teddy, who was sitting on the other side of Dodge, beamed with adoration, not tearing his gaze from the playing children for one moment. The sun's rays were nothing compared to the brilliance of his feelings for them.

It was a wonderful vision to end on, so I stood, rolled my shoulders, and lowered a hand to Maria. "Coming?"

Her answered stare was limper than Theresa's waterlogged ringlets. "That's all you have to say?"

"Uh-huh. I don't have to tell you what we're doing. I'm gonna show you. Come on. We're burning daylight."

"Really? You're not even gonna tell me where we're going?"

"Nope. I'm—"

"I'm gonna show you," Maria mocked, voicing the words before I could.

I glanced to the left. "I don't sound like that, do I, Barry?"

"Not at all."

"Thank the go—"

"You're worse," he interrupted. "*Much* worse."

"Oh, *ha-ha*, you muscly idiot."

Maria accepted my help to her feet, and she looped an arm through mine. "Let's get this over with."

Snips, who had shrunk down to sit in my pocket, apparently had places to be. She leaped down to the sand, blew parting bubbles, and scuttled off into the water, pausing only to wave goodbye to the children before slipping beneath the waves and out of sight. Off to rejoin her familiars in the depths, no doubt.

"What are we waiting for, dear?" Maria patted my bicep with her free hand and threw my words back at me. "We're burning daylight."

A half hour later, the scents of lacquer and sawdust were all around. The workshop fell silent as those within noticed our arrival. Maria had led the charge, having worked out what my plan was the second she saw the building.

"Greaaaat," Brad drawled, elbowing Greg to get his attention. "Look who's back. Come to distract our apprentices again?"

Greg, whose mind was still clearly on the wood he'd been in the middle of measuring, gave us a wide grin. "Welcome!" He bent and resumed marking periodically along his tape. "Make yourself at home!"

Brad frowned down, and by the set of his jaw, I guessed he was considering bumping Greg's elbow in retaliation. Instead, he chose peace. "Can we pretend my brother and I both riffed back and forth for a minute or two at your expense?"

"Done and done, mate. How cutting were the remarks?"

"Oh, *very*. One of us took it too far, saying something *so* terrible you considered smiting him."

I nodded seriously. "That *must* have been cutting. I'm usually so calm and composed. Which of you was it?"

"Greg, of course."

"Huh?" Greg's head shot up. "You say summin'?"

Brad sighed and spread his arms. "See what I mean? He means well, he just can't read the room."

Greg snorted, still measuring and marking. "Throwing stones from a glass house there, brother. You didn't learn to read until you were almost a teen. Ma was worried you— *Hey!*" He shot a withering glare up at Brad, who'd chosen violence after all and bumped his brother's elbow.

They stared at each other for a long moment, neither making the first move, then both surging forward at once. Brad threw a haymaker. Greg unleashed an uppercut. I'd seen it coming and gathered my chi in advance. Light exploded as I repositioned them outside, where twin thumps landed, followed by pulses of chi, good-natured laughs, and the off-tempo smacks of a daylight brawl.

Maria looked at a young woman on my other side, who appeared to be in the early stages of shaping a reel. "Is this a common occurrence?"

"They used to do it on the hour, but they've been a little more conservative lately."

An older gentleman, who I recognized as one of Gormona's former cultivators, laughed. "Which means they only do it a few times a day."

I smiled along with him. "Poor Greg just wanted to do some measuring."

"Don't feel bad for him. He starts it as often as Brad does."

"More often, actually," the young woman corrected. "Don't let them trick you into thinking your presence is a detriment. Your crafting might be a little distracting, but it's at least instructive—something that can't be said for our, uhhh . . ."

"Energetic?" I offered, earning a smirk.

"Exactly. Our *energetic* teachers aren't always so informative with their diversions."

That comment made a flicker of pride flare to life in my chest, joined by a twin flame of gratitude. With those conjoined sources of heat warming me, I moved around the room, selecting materials. It didn't take long. I set the single block of wood and a few bearings down on a workbench. The rest I'd brought with me, and I unloaded them all from a shoulder bag.

Maria perused my collection. "So, the eyelets, handle, and brackets make complete sense . . ."

"But?"

"Do I really need to say it?"

"Indulge me."

She sighed and faced me. "What's up with the sand? The other powders? The glob of . . . *is that tree sap?*"

"Secret."

"Right, you shit, I'm gonna—"

"Whoa, whoa!" I held my hands up in placation. "Don't hit me! It's for the rod!"

Glass, I said in her mind, not wanting to ruin the surprise for the many apprentices pretending not to watch us closely.

Glass . . . ?

You'll see in a moment, but first . . .

I'd not done any woodworking since earning the god-king mark. I'd worried it would be a slow process now that most of my power was being absorbed by the tunnels below—I was wrong.

Even to my enhanced awareness, it seemed too swift, the notoriously difficult ironbark wood peeling off like fruit rind beneath the endless carving of my chisel. I had only intended to carve out concave indents on either side of the block before swapping to a jigsaw and cutting out the circular shape. Instead, I covered the tool's edge with a thin layer of chi and sculpted away. So precise and measured were my movements that I didn't bother with a file. Using my second partition of will, I infused the wooden fibers with intention. My brow creased as I used every available strand of essence. The beginning of a headache pulsed behind my right eye.

Suddenly, the universe's essence began bubbling up from the ground.

No, I thought. *Not yet.*

Before I could issue the command and force it away, Maria did it for me. Her core was more than up to the task. She didn't even sever her connection to the network below. No one in the room had noticed, but Slimes let out an awed burble in the back of her mind.

After I'd popped a bearing into the finished reel, attached its bracket and set it down, I paused, smiling to myself. I hadn't even realized I'd not used a vise. It'd just felt more natural to chip away at my creation while holding it in one hand.

In that bare moment of stillness, whispers erupted in the room, each word washing over me. The best were from Brad and Greg, who swore with distinct-yet-equally-offensive words, neither bearing repeating and both related to a different god's mother.

I didn't let my amusement linger too long.

It was time.

"Back on Earth," I said aloud for the benefit of all present, "we had something called fiberglass. Before you question it, yes, it's exactly what it sounds like—glass made so thin as to be thinner than most wooden fibers."

"That . . ." Greg trailed off, pouting.

"Sounds useless," finished Brad. "What good is a material so fragile? Wouldn't it—"

"*There you are, you bastard!*" screamed the crazed woman charging into the work-shop. Bonnie's eyes were wild as they fixed on me. Her hair wasn't much better, tangled from her rushed journey. "*How dare you!*"

". . . How dare I what?"

"*Do this without me!*"

"Uhhh, do what?"

She took a deep breath, did her best to smooth her hair—which wasn't all that effective, if I was being honest—and peered into my soul. "I don't know. Whatever it is you're doing here. I could feel it all the way from the smithy."

"That's only next doo—"

"I could *feel it*!" she repeated. "Stop playing coy and stop changing the subject!"

"I would have shown you if it works, which I don't know it will. Pick a worksta-tion to wat—"

She blurred forward, evidently choosing *my* station to watch from.

"Uhhh, perhaps another one? I need a bit of space to—"

She blurred again, moving to the next one over, which was already occupied. Bonnie showed a little restraint, at least, going behind the young woman instead of in front of her. But that was as far as her consideration for others extended. She peered over my neighbor's shoulder, quite literally breathing down her neck.

"Anyway . . . as I was saying, we have fiberglass back on Earth—yes, Bonnie, it's exactly what it sounds like. I'd be lying if I said I knew how it worked, but I have a general idea. You asked how something so fragile was useful, Brad, and the answer is that it is combined with another compound. Some kind of resin, I imagine, which results in an incredibly strong and flexible material. It's what many modern fishing rods were made of. Or I think so, at least."

"*Bastard*," Bonnie hissed. "*Keeping such secrets.*"

I laughed quietly, shaking my head. "I wasn't sure it would work. I'm still not. I know a lot, but even with a mostly perfect memory, I never learned how the fibers were formed, nor what compound to use. That said, I think it's now possible because of the title my adorable yet dastardly followers gifted me, along with a lesson Ruby gave me on our trip out to sea."

I knew countless questions would stem from that statement. Especially from Bonnie, whose only reason for not voicing them was that they all appeared to be trying to leave her mouth at once. Before any made it out, I raised my hands to either side of the sand and sent my pure essence flowing out.

I'd been slowly getting used to the delay imposed by the tunnels below. I still missed the control I had before, but having to wait a few seconds before reshaping existence itself was about as first world as problems got. This time, it took far more than a few seconds. Slowly, effortfully, I scooped up every last grain of sand. By the time I added the comparatively small mounds of soda ash and lime, stopping only when my instincts told me to, minutes had passed. I estimated there to be a good three or four kilograms of material in the translucent bowl before me.

I ran a hand over my brow, actually wiping away drops of sweat.

Haven't experienced that in a while . . .

"I'm guessing most of you know how glass is made." No verbal responses came, but heads nodded, Bonnie's most vigorously of all. "And I'm also guessing you've noticed my lack of a furnace. If you assumed I was going to transport one here . . . well, you were wrong. Please watch the door for any non-cultivators, Brad and Greg."

I started gathering power in my second partition.

"Wouldn't want to blind anyone once this gets going . . ."

CHAPTER TWENTY-SEVEN

Poseidon's Salty What?

I poured out a single, condensed pillar of chi. It shone into the bowl and melted the sand in an instant, blistering enough to blacken and harden the molten glass. I couldn't let it. I drew back some of my power, stabilizing the temperature.

"Next, we separate the strands."

I flooded more will from my soul, ordering it to be so. When it found the liquid glass, it faltered, finding issue with the impossible number of distinct fibers I was imagining.

"Remember how I mentioned inspiration?" I asked Maria. "That was my reason for making Snips's eyepatch here."

She nodded.

"I wasn't talking about inspiration for her garment." I allowed myself a smile. "I wanted inspiration for *this*."

Just like I'd done with the bamboo's grain, I forced my chi to split into as many tendrils as possible. The tunnels below complained. I ignored them. Each tendril of essence latched on to the glass, and I sharpened my will, knowing it would need to make up for my diminished power. My intent became not a suggestion but a command. A god-king's decree.

It still wasn't enough.

A sudden urge struck me, but I pushed it away. Now wasn't the time for experimentation. Putting so much effort into my will made my brain foggy. My thoughts oozed like molasses. It took longer than I'd like to admit for me to realize my mistake. What was I doing? *Not the time for experimentation?* Of course it was. I listened to the impulse.

I raised both hands before me, one palm up, one palm down, facing each other. My fingers formed a grasping cage that I then stretched apart. It was like trying to pull apart solid metal, but the molten compound obeyed. Hundreds of thousands of hair-thin glass filaments followed my movement, separating from one another, shining brilliantly as a strand of chi attached to each.

So little power. So much control. I was close to my limit.

I could have asked for Maria's help. Unlike me, she could stop feeding the tunnels without consequences. She was primed and waiting, her essence sitting at the edge of our connection, ready for me to grab and bend to my will. So, too, did the mark on my soul beckon, urging me to use it. I thanked Maria's offer and shoved away the mark's, not giving it an inch lest it take a mile and "help" of its own accord.

I focused back on the task. One partition held the countless strands in place. I withdrew my will from the other, no longer needing the bowl I'd used to melt the materials. With a deep breath, I refilled this partition with intent—and almost bloody fainted. Maria grabbed my arms and helped steady me, letting go when she sensed I was okay.

Though I was now physically stable, doubt shook my confidence. Almost failing had made me realize just how much I needed to succeed. We had plenty of fishing rods, but none of them were mine. With my strength as it was now, some of the sport and challenge had been missing every time I went for a fish. It didn't have to be a battle every time, but I wanted the possibility. No, I *needed* the possibility. I was ravenous for it.

Which only fueled my doubt. I second-guessed whether sap was the right ingredient. A spool of monofilament fishing line might have been better. It certainly seemed closer to epoxy or whatever plastic compound was used to bind fiberglass on Earth. The molasses seeping through my brain stopped me from reaching a decision.

Suddenly, a sweet voice came to caress me.

Your instincts have gotten you this far, Maria said in my mind. *They're the one thing that, time and time again, haven't let you down. Other than me, of course*, she added with a waggle of her brows.

She was right. And beautiful. And all mine. But now wasn't the time for the last two.

I sent her my love and returned to the task at hand, applying will to the intent in my second partition. Maria grabbed the tree sap and lobbed it underhand. I caught and spread the malleable substance over the molten glass fibers. A surprising portion of my intent went toward stopping it from overheating and bursting alight.

It was in that position, hands stretched before me and all the pieces in place, that I reached my limit. Every ounce of chi I possessed was locked, frozen by the task of keeping everything stable. I could shape the rod. It was ready to come together. But all my available essence was in use, leaving none available for the last step of any creation, picturing what purpose it needed to fill.

The sap started hardening. If it solidified, I would fail.

Again, Maria offered her power. Again, my god-king mark implored. And again, I turned them both away.

But Maria called out once more, a hint of realization coloring her thoughts. She wanted me to . . . *use the mark?*

I shook my head. She was only trying to help, but she was correct when she'd said to trust my instincts. My entire being screamed that I had to do this alone. I couldn't articulate it, but so what? Listening to my hunches had gotten me this far.

I pushed at the limits of my core, but the partitions couldn't handle it. Each of them amplified my will, letting me focus on two tasks at once. They could do more than that, but not with the trickle of essence I currently wielded. I needed more power.

The sap grew harder still.

I snarled at my lack of agency, my soul feeling the vast torrents of chi pouring down into the tunnels, my body unable to harness it. Over and over I tried, asking, *begging* the network to relent just a little, to give back a tiny bit of what I was feeding it. Silence was the only answer that came.

Maria nudged me. Her chi was still there, ready to be harnessed, but that wasn't why she nudged my side. She wanted me to use the mark. It made sense to listen to her. She was my wife. She bore a mark on her soul mirroring my own, and I trusted her implicitly.

So why, then, did my instincts continue screaming to do this alone?

My perception of time slipped away. I measured its passage through the hardening tree sap, whose consistency slowly shifted, getting less pliable. It was a race against the clock, and I was losing.

The sap started changing color, a crust forming on its surface. My brain felt similar. How much longer could I do this? At least it wouldn't be long until I failed.

If I haven't already . . .

I latched on to each thought that came, desperately trying to follow them. Maria no longer called out, not wanting to interrupt. The god-king mark, though, wouldn't shut the frack up. It kept screaming for me to use it, getting more insistent—and distracting—as time dragged on.

As I considered ways to ignore it, the sap lost its luster, turning matte and lifeless. Just like that, it had finished curing. I had failed.

Yet the mark was still screaming, not giving me a moment's peace. My blood boiled with frustration, skin itching, lungs burning, throat constricting. I might have succeeded if it hadn't pestered me the entire time.

I bit my cheek to center myself. There was no point blaming things outside of my control. This was my fault; I had agreed to the limitations. Would I go back in time and make a fishing rod before I started powering the tunnels? Absolutely not. As annoying as it was to feel out of control, for every second the expanded underground network remained empty, my friends were in potential danger.

Besides, I could try again. Even if it took weeks to comb through this experience and devise a new plan, I'd get there eventually. I let go of my will, but before it could leave the molten glass and now-black sap, the mark called out again, bellowing so loudly that it vibrated against my core.

Frustration threatened to boil over again. I rolled my eyes and brought its instructions to the edge of my awareness, hoping it would stop throwing a tantrum if I acknowledged it. I blinked, my brow furrowing as the mark seared a suggestion into my mind.

It hadn't been offering power at all. It'd been trying to give me direction. In my desire to do this myself, I'd incorrectly assumed it was trying to take over.

It can't be that simple, can it? I wondered, considering the suggestion. *I guess it can't hurt to try . . .*

Instead of wielding my excess will like a mallet, I grabbed hold of a sliver, formed it into a thin-bladed chisel, and smacked it against the conceptual borders between my two partitions.

Pop!

The god-king mark rushed in to create a third partition, empty and unused, ready and waiting. All it had taken was a whisper of my intent . . .

You have got to be fracking kidding me.

It really was that simple. I felt like an absolute moron for not listening sooner. I pressed again into the space between borders, and there was a second *pop*, the mark rushing in to create a fourth container. My eyes flew wide.

How many can I make . . . ?

Could I handle dozens? Hundreds? I re-formed the imaginary chisel, pressed its edge between my three containers, and smacked—

I reeled, vision going white, head pounding. I groaned.

Four. I can handle four.

Gray matter still thumping, I gathered my will beside one of the empty vessels and paused to gather my thoughts. I wouldn't have a spare millisecond once I started. Despite the pain, my mouth curled up into a smile. I would need a hand, but this wasn't over yet.

I slammed my will into the partition. In tandem, two souls answered my call, their full might bearing down on the blackened sap. Maria and Slimes made not a sound as their pink essence surrounded the ruined substance. They weren't assisting in the creation, but reverting the sticky compound to what it once was. It would take every ounce of their concentration, and I didn't doubt them for a second.

Resplendent heat poured from my newly harnessed partition. The mass of cracked sap surrounding my still-molten fibers of glass shimmered, moisture flowing in from the air, its malleability returning.

I apologized to my future self for what I was about to do, then split half of my will from that last vessel and into the only other empty one. Before I could register how much worse I'd just made my headache, I used that fourth container to picture what I desired, demanding the System make it so.

Maria cackled, partially *at* me for not listening to her and the mark earlier, but mostly *with* me, elated that my ambitious plan was going to work.

And work it did. Countless glass threads condensed, combining with the sap surrounding them. They formed a glowing pole that tapered at the end, a luster beaming from them that shone not from me, but the System. The reel flickered, wavered, and flashed across the bench to join the condensing fibers. At least I think it did. I couldn't really see, what with my vision pulsing each time my head thumped. I closed my eyes, letting my partitions handle the rest.

Euphoria flooded my body. It was complete.

I squinted out, my splitting headache temporarily banished by endorphins.

Fiberglass Rod of the Composite Fisher
[Authorization error: protected asset in lower realm]

I cleared the messages to find the world spinning. A strong pair of arms grabbed hold of me, and the surrounding room grew blessedly still.

"Fair maiden," my savior purred, "are you well?"

"No." I clutched my head. The rhythmic pounding had already returned. "I feel like I just kicked myself in the skull."

"You kinda did. That would have gone a lot smoother if you trusted me or the god-king mark earlier."

I grunted. "To make matters worse, my oldest nemesis taunted me, giving me an error message instead of telling me what my sweet new rod does. And worst of all . . ." I paused to take a breath. ". . . My wife is currently carrying me like I'm her bride, in front of dozens of my followers."

Maria nodded. "That *is* a rather troubling series of events, especially the last one. How emasculating."

"Does that mean you'll set me down?"

"And leave you on your own, bereft of senses and dressed so brazenly? I daresay that could lead to scandal." She raised her chin and stared into the middle distance. "Nay, fair maiden! You are now under my protection. If your honor were to be impugned, so, too, would mine!"

I turned my neck, braving the pain to look at Brad and Greg. "Help."

They didn't so much as blink. Judging by the looks on their faces, they hadn't since the rod finished transforming. The entire room was the same, eyes cycling between vacant when inspecting the description, and wide like saucers when gazing upon the physical item.

"They're not even listening, Maria. You may as well set me down."

Her hero's facade vanished, and her beautiful smile was almost enough to make me forget about the two dozen monkeys that had snuck into my noggin and started smacking my cerebellum like bongos. "You can't joke your way out of this one, my love. I know how hard you just pushed yourself." She scooped up the rod and deposited it in my lap. "Sorry, everyone, but our god-king needs to recover. Good day."

This finally snapped the woodworking brothers from their stupor. "Wait!" they both called, stepping forward and bumping into the many benches separating us.

I cast a petulant gaze over Maria's shoulder, my arms looped around her neck as she carried me off. "Oh, *now* you wanna talk?" I held on to Maria with one hand, using the other to give them a decidedly rude gesture. "Frack y'all. I'm already feeling better, but I'll be keeping this to myself until after I've caught a few fish with its magnificent—"

The room, and the faces of my friends, vanished. My core flared with heat, but I barely registered it. More words had appeared. It wasn't the contents of the message itself that stunned me, but the golden, almost brocade border around them.

Then I actually read the sentences, and the border didn't seem that important after all.

"What in Poseidon's salty conch does *that* mean?"

CHAPTER TWENTY-EIGHT

Seer

Within Phostheia's throne room, high above the Kingdom of Light, the sun beamed down through a mosaic glass roof, casting a dazzling rainbow of colors across the vast sea of marble below. Floors, walls, ornate pillars. Even the furniture, bar one seat, was made of the white stone, boasting of the capital's wealth and the ingenuity of the mages who'd mined and transported so much of the exotic material.

The god-empress could see it all from where she sat, wearing the same rigid posture and indifferent gaze of countless leaders before her. It'd been beaten into her—sometimes literally, if her old tutor's thin switch counted—since she was a girl. She used to loathe those lessons.

The throne at her back was much the same. She'd hated it, too. The coldness of its touch. Its complete lack of padding. Even the way it glinted, reflecting the sun into her eyes. *Which daft fool,* she had often wondered, *thought a throne of solid gold was a good idea?*

She now knew better. As with her lessons from childhood, she understood the importance of such things. She gazed down at her seat, triggering its description.

Golden Throne of the Divine
[Authorization error: protected asset in lower realm]

So long had it existed in Phostheia that its creator was unknown, any record of them or the item's origin lost to time.

"Time . . . So fickle. So demanding." Her eyes snapped up, focusing on one of the five figures of the Prime Cadre before her. "Tell me, Evan, how go the boats?"

Her head mage bowed at the waist. "They are progressing as well as can be expected, God-Empress."

"No further damage has been discovered?"

"Not beyond those already listed in the ledgers, God-Empress. The prime vessel *Theoris's* hull, and the mast of her sister galleon, *Elegos,* are both being restored by the Twenty—" Evan cleared his throat. "By the Forty Hands, Your Holiness," he corrected. "The same is happening with the rear vessels of the fleet, whose decks are in various stages of decay."

There was something he wasn't saying. It shone through his concealment, sure as the sun's rays slipped through the colored glass high above. "Hesitance is unbecoming, Evan—especially on a mage of the Prime Cadre."

He dropped to the floor and pressed his forehead to the marble in one swift movement. Well, relatively swift—to her senses, it was as if he trudged through mud. "Forgive me, God-Empress! I wished not to bother you with trifles. I am but a bug compared to your mighty flame."

No, you're not, came Aletheia's quiet complaint in the back of her mind. *You're my trusted advisor. My voice of reason. My friend.* That word—*friend*—made an image of Eustace resurface. The blank look the seer had given when hiding her emotions resonated with the quiet voice, giving it power.

The God-Empress snatched those sentiments and crushed them in her fist. "Tell me, Evan."

"At once! The restoration efforts have been going slightly slower than expected . . ."

She didn't realize she was shining with fury until Evan trailed off and stole a glance, his eyes reflecting her brilliance. Again, the quiet voice protested. This time, the god-empress let her anger fade, hoping acquiescence would shut the voice up.

Evan continued. "The fleet appeared to have lingered on the ocean before being moved to the dry docks. Ancient sea life clings to the hulls, and despite their lifelessness, these hardened shells defy the Forty Hands' holy chi. It should not delay the overall timeline, though!" he added in a rush. "Which is the only reason I didn't tell you, God-Empress! We called for the citizens' help in physically removing them, and they rushed to assist! Even now, they form lines in the industrial quarter, vying for a chance to help Your Holiness!"

"They understand your greatness, God-Empress!" yelled Grace, prostrate on the marble.

"Just so! Even those lacking experience! If anything, we are projected to finish slightly ahead of time!"

Aletheia Veritus, God-Empress of the Kingdom of Light, sat back on her throne, anger abated. "Good. Without illumination, one might accidentally stride into shadow. Tell me such things in the future. And that goes for all of you." *Please*, added the quiet voice, thinking what it couldn't say aloud. The god-empress forced it down.

"Yes, God-Empress!" chorused the mages, as did the two dozen honor guards fanning around the throne room, their golden armor glittering in the rainbow light.

Just like so many rulers before her, she showed not a hint of approval at their assent. Their obeyance was not to be rewarded. It was expected. She was the divine bridge, and they—

Something tugged at her soul, at the holy brand marking her as heaven's chosen. Eyes wide, she moved. White marble, gray hallways, and myriad stairs passed by in an instant, the world only ceasing its endless blur when she gazed down at a screen moments later. The words she found there were a direct challenge to her dominion.

A new Maker has risen!
Hail God-King Fischer, Maker of Kallis!

Where her surroundings had sped by a moment ago, now it was time that flew, racing past as she internalized the messages and considered their implications. The old her, who'd been an empress in name only, would have trembled. In fact, the former version of herself *was* trembling, whimpering deep in the pits of her awareness, causing their left hand to shake. Lip curling, the God-Empress slammed a lid of iron overtop the pit, sealing those pathetic sounds in.

Evan came barreling into the room. The rest of the Prime Cadre followed a moment later. All five of them joined their ruler at a respectful distance, shock washing from their cores as they read the screen. Evan's eyes, wide and panicked, flicked down toward her hand. "Are you well, God-Empress?"

Her skin creaked like leather, so hard did she clench her fist. "Why would I not be? I am divine."

He took a step forward, expression softening. "Aletheia, you don't—"

"Do not call me that!" Her radiant fury shone out once more, stronger than earlier, walls shaking, a spiderweb of cracks spreading across the stones beneath her. She inhaled a steadying breath and drew back her ire. "Do not presume to refer to me by name. Was it not you who warned me about letting decorum slip?"

"As you say, Your Holiness." All five of them were prostrate again. Evan pressed his face into the cracked stones. "Forgive me, God-Empress. I forget myself."

It was well-meaning. She knew that. But it didn't excuse his behavior.

"Do not make a habit of it. Now, rise. We must talk and alter our plans accordingly."

They rushed to obey, all attention on her as they stood and awaited instructions. The look on Evan's features gave her pause. It made no sense. Hadn't she become who he'd always wanted her to be?

Why, then, does he seem so sad? asked the voice in the darkness, lifting the lid just enough for the question to escape.

A third blast of rage for the morning was the god-empress's only answer. She slammed the opening closed and focused her anger upon it, melting the iron door's edges until it was welded shut, nary a gap remaining for the old her to whine through.

Evan had looked up once more, and when the light faded, he was gazing directly at her. "I will not ask again, God-Empress, but are you well?"

She stared back impassively. "As before, head mage, how could I not be? I am the divine bridge between Kallis and the heavens. I am she whose arrival was foretold by the Holy Seers. My victory is inevitable."

"As you say, God-Empress."

"As you say, God-Empress!" the others echoed.

Within, Aletheia's fists pounded on the seamless metal door. No one answered.

Eustice was just leaving her terrace when the third flash of incandescent anger came from the castle. The aged woman turned toward it, shielding her eyes with a hand as she stared up at the holy beams. Much like Eustace—or a fine wine—the grief caused by her former friend's affliction had matured, alchemizing into something wonderful.

A *quest*. Though she had invented it herself, it was no less important to her than one assigned by the System.

Above, the god-empress's fury faded. Eustace snorted. "And they call me dramatic."

"They're right, hag!"

"Kick rocks, Anius, you old toad!" Inwardly, she welcomed the duel. Outwardly, she leveled a withering glare at the bastard sitting on her favorite bench, the one that stayed shaded year-round. "Hurry up and die already!"

"And stink up the garden? You'd curse my poor soul before I made it to the afterlife."

"That's a good point. I don't want to—terribly bothersome work, you see—but if you stank up the garden . . ." She crossed her arms and sniffed. "I'm leaving. Want anything from the markets on my way back?"

Anius cooled himself with his paper fan. "An anvil dropped from a great height, if it pleases? Right on top of my head."

"That so?"

"Please. My hag of a neighbor snores something fierce. I've not slept well in days, and I crave the eternal release."

"Doesn't work for me, I'm afraid."

"Oh?"

"You'd stink up the garden, and I'd be forced to curse your soul. Swiftly, you understand—before you made it to the afterlife."

"Hmmm. That *does* sound bothersome . . ."

They shared a grin, then Eustace looked away, feigning annoyance as she inspected the nails on one wrinkled hand. "Anything else I can get you from the market?"

"That same anvil, dropped from the same height, but on a different head?"

"On mine?"

"Ah, but it's nice talking to another seer. Nobody gets me like you do. Shame you'll die soon."

"Via anvil to the cranium?"

"Just so."

Eustace flashed him a smile and marched out the gate. "See you shortly, *Anus*."

"Not if an anvil sees you first, Eust-*ass!*" Anius called from *her* bench, grinning at his parting shot.

She wasn't sure who'd won that joust, but then, did it really matter? They'd stopped tallying the score decades ago. Or was it centuries now? Their barbed insults had long since reverted to those of schoolyard children. Like a tiles player going over the notes of past games, Eustace mentally traced all possible branches of the conversation as she went, seeking the perfect childish retort for next time.

Another part of her mind dared to hope that Anius would join her cause, but his actions thus far had suggested otherwise. She sighed. The time would come to invite him. Until then, his allegiance wasn't worth consider—

A sharp gasp interrupted her thoughts.

"Seer!" the girl hissed.

"Seer?" asked another.

"Where?"

"Seer!" droned the flock, its sheep stealing what glances they dared as Eustace flowed down the street, her long robe and modest steps presenting a picture of piety.

Along the main avenue, around the market—*no need to brave that cesspit of humanity twice in one day*—Eustace strode. She ducked into a lane and donned a beggar's blanket, hunching her back for good measure as she exited the other side, now within the industrial district. Here could be found the laborers and their places of work, along with the usual vices that kept peasantry pliable and obedient the world over: drinking establishments, betting houses, and brothels.

Has our god-empress's ascension affected their business, I wonder?

She didn't have to go down the red alley to know the answer; simply peering down its length was enough to see a pack of particularly repulsive men stumble from a public house and into the open arms of a gaggle of floozies.

She judged neither party. Well, except for the men's visible lack of hygiene, which reaffirmed her long-running hypothesis that courtesans and their commoner ilk were the hardest workers of any kingdom. But the thought swiftly vanished. She, after all, was on a quest.

Deeper she went into the northern district. Soon the dry docks rose up, their size only truly appreciable from up close. A line of men, and even a few muscular women, stretched along its front, waiting to be admitted by a crisply mustachioed dockman.

Behind them stood what might be the largest damned doors ever built, and in the gap where they had been slid back, could be seen what were *definitely* the largest damned ships ever built. The Prime Vessel *Theoris*, and her sister galleon, *Elegos*. They'd struck her dumb when she first saw them, but that had been a lifetime ago. Multiple lives, really. She'd encountered them many times since then, these relics of ancient eras and forgotten wars, but never had their grandiosity truly faded.

She had expected to be stopped at the entrance, but the dockman spotted her from a mile away.

Sharp, this one.

"Hold there, beggar!" he called. "You've heard true. We're recruiting all able bodies, but you need to be cleared by the healers first. I won't have you spreading a pox around—"

Like a beautiful yet decrepit butterfly, she emerged from her cocoon, casting aside the rough-spun blanket.

"Seer Eustace!" The man dropped to the ground so fast she worried for the rigidity of his waxed moustache. "Holy Seer! Forgive me! My eyes were blind to your radiance!"

She ducked her head to hide her disappointment. *Perhaps not so sharp after all.* "No need, no need, dockman. I come to inspect the ships and, if possible, impart good fortune for their future passage." The rest of the line were kneeling now, radiating deference and piety to a one. She paused beside the man who may or may not still have a crisp moustache, patted him on the shoulder, and immediately regretted it when a shiver ran through him.

"Holy Seer Eustace, I am not worthy of your touch!" His hands met before him in prayer. "I will never forget this kindness! Would the Holy Seer like an escort to—"

"Absolutely not!" she snapped, then remembered herself. "Uh, I need quiet and solitude. Lest the flock's wonderful thoughts affect my own." *By making me sick*, she didn't add.

He shot to his feet so fast that she almost reflexively kicked him, but his facial hair, now markedly floppier after all, distracted her just long enough to still her muscles. "Runners!" he called, re-twirling his semi-flaccid strands.

A squad of adolescents, who'd been doing a terrible job of keeping their spying a secret, dashed from behind one giant door.

"Alert the docks! If I hear of anyone bothering Holy Seer Eustace, they'll be out on their ass—" He gasped at himself. "They will be fired, I mean! Apologies, Holy Seer! This humble worker . . . *Holy Seer?*"

Eustace was already inside, and she shook her head as she marched toward a ramp leading down into the giant pit. Sycophants and zealots, the lot of them. And those working the ship weren't any better. Those damned children, with their spry legs and youthful exuberance, had rushed ahead. One of them was ten meters down, descending scaffolding like a rodent escaping a flood. She tore her gaze from the young woman. The workers being forewarned of her arrival hadn't been planned, but perhaps it was to her quest's advantage.

She peered into the eyes of every worker she passed. Or tried to, anyway. The bastards kept bowing and scraping, looking away. Each was assessed, and each was found wanting. Halfway down *Theoris's* mighty hull, she had her first taste of hope. A man with impressive girth neither looked away nor bent an inch, staring directly at her as he scratched his belly button—on a quest of his own, in search of lint. He reeked of booze, and when he didn't respond to her raised brow, she waved in front of his face.

He made a sound that was half drowning, half gargle, which took her longer than it should have to identify as a snore. The bastard was asleep, eyes open, body erect, finger scratching away.

"Damned impressive . . ." she said, and she meant it. What magnificent skill. But not the kind she was looking for. "The working girls certainly earn their money with this one . . ." She stepped past and grabbed the scaffolding for support, drew back her foot, then kicked him square in the ass.

He made a wonderful series of sounds as he fell, woke, and continued tumbling farther down the sloping ramp, his girth causing the structure to shake. He went farther than she'd expected. Thankfully, she didn't have to save him—that would have ruined the whole point. A support beam brought the fleshy avalanche to an abrupt end, one final grunt capping off his a cappella performance as the air was knocked from his lungs.

The deeper she went, the more workers she saw. These laborers were awake, which was welcome at first but swiftly grated on her.

Too subservient by far. This is the problem with societies built upon the existence of gods. When one actually comes along, everyone soils their underclothes over it.

Her only consolation was the prize she sought. They were down here somewhere. She was sure of it. Never before had a vision been so clear.

With each incompatible soul she passed, however, doubt crept in. What if they weren't here, after all? Had the vision shown her a different time, her treasure either long deceased or yet to be born? Or had it just been a regular dream, one which her grief had latched on to, a lifeline to pull her from the grips of despair?

She frowned as she stepped down onto the lower levels. The bottom of the ship's great hull blocked out the sun from above. The unawakened workers relied on lanterns of divine chi to navigate the space, and as that golden light illuminated her unimpressed visage, their bowing and scraping got worse.

Not him. Not him.

. . . Definitely not him.

There wasn't a solid pair of rocks between them. Her hopes flared upon seeing a look other than subjugation on one man, but then she noticed his quickening pulse. She had been a beautiful woman in her youth, all those centuries ago, so she knew that expression well. She could be his great-grandmother . . .

Disgusting. She would have kicked him over the side, but paused after gathering essence in her leg, wondering if he'd derive sick pleasure from that. Then she kicked him anyway, right between the legs, lifting him into the air, only for him to crash bonelessly to the floor, bereft of consciousness. Just as she'd thought. Nary a solid set of rocks to be found.

"Impure!" she accused in afterthought, realizing she probably shouldn't have used such violence in public.

As she continued on, her displeasure was alleviated by the ashen faces of the men who rushed in to help her downed foe. Anything was better than their former meekness. Even those who didn't go to his side seemed to feel some of his pain, their gazes lingering on the limp fellow who'd been kicked in his limp member.

Funny, that. She'd noticed long ago that no matter how self-serving the man, they could empathize with another being struck in the jewels. She had once suggested it be used as a method for teaching violent criminals compassion, but it had been called "cruel and unusual" by the previous Veritus girl. Perhaps she should broach it with Aletheia now that she—

Oh? What's this?

A sense of joy washed over Eustace, coming from the abdomen of another. Someone else had enjoyed seeing the lecherous bastard struck down. She gazed over at him—only to find it wasn't a him at all. Narrow shoulders, slim fingers hidden by cloth and wrapped around a chisel, and decidedly feminine features, no matter how much grime she had tried to hide them beneath.

"Was he the reason for your disguise?"

The woman jumped. And Eustace felt a pang of frustration, fully expecting deference to replace shock when the laborer realized who was before her. Instead, the worker's pupils darted back and forth, thoughts clearly racing as she tugged her hood down.

"One of," she grunted, then raised her chisel to the hull, set its tip against the shell of some ancient sea creature, and smacked it with a hammer. "I would appreciate you lowering your voice, Seer. If it pleases you, I mean."

It didn't please her, but the woman's flippancy did. "Unnecessary, dear. See for yourself."

Eustace's loud tone made her freeze like a cornered rabbit. She dropped her tools and gazed at the seer, her eyes . . . furious? *Not a rabbit, then. More a pup ready to nip, for all the good it will do her.*

When the cloaked stranger noticed the bubble of golden light around them, she turned pensive. Almost curious. "This . . ."

"Protection, dear. Neither eyes nor ears can penetrate it."

"Which means that people and objects can?"

Eustace gave her an appraising look. *Clever girl.* "You've discovered my limitations. It's as you say, but I wouldn't worry about that. Anyone stupid enough to enter will find that my body is similarly unimpede . . . oh, speak of the devil." She lashed out, felt the ball of her foot collide with a hip, then felt the floor shake as the idiot crashed into the scaffolding beyond. "I imagine that should be adequate deterrence for the rest, don't you?"

The woman nodded but didn't elaborate.

"My name is Eustace."

"I know."

She waited for her to continue, then laughed at the brazen disrespect when she didn't. "Might I ask yours?"

The grimy woman pondered that for a moment. "Fern."

"Why are you working down here, Fern?" She gestured at the sharp shells covering the section hull within the bubble. "Hardly a job I'd be signing up for . . ."

"The diligent *men*—" She spat that last word. "—who help clear the lower level have more chances of being chosen."

"Being chosen . . . ?"

"For the expedition. Anyone working up top gets one entrance per day, while anyone down here gets two, so long as they fill a bucket by nightfall."

"A lottery, then?"

"So they say . . ." The healthy amount of scorn in Fern's voice told of her faith—or lack thereof—in the integrity of such a system.

"How many spots have they offered?" Eustace asked, imagining the hundreds of people she saw working just on her way down. There had been dozens on the lower deck.

"Ten."

"*Ten* . . . ?" the seer repeated. That was only a quarter of a person per rear vessel. They must have been behind schedule, so the Prime Cadre—likely Evan—had hatched a scheme to increase productivity. And hidden it from the Veritus girl, no doubt. Eustace smiled as she imagined the head mage trying to navigate *that* conversation.

She peered down at Fern's hands. Unlike those of the women she had seen in line, Fern's weren't accustomed to hard labor. What she had assumed to be camouflage were actually bandages. All this, for only a chance to join the voyage. A slim one, considering how many names would find their way onto the list before any were actually drawn.

Noticing the seer's attention on them, Fern tried to hide her hands.

Eustace shook her head. "Show me."

Fern scowled, hesitated, then unlooped the linen wrapping her left wrist. She tensed her jaw as the bandage stuck to her palm, unable to hide her discomfort. What skin wasn't blistered looked supple and soft, telling of work that involved oils rather than laboring with tools. Eustace's respect for the girl grew. The hardest workers in any kingdom indeed. Each layer of cloth that came away revealed more wounds, unhealed and yet to callus.

"That's enough. I can see the extent of your injuries."

As she returned the wrappings, pain seemed to steel Fern's temper. "Can I help you with anything else, Seer? The longer we talk, the less I can remove, and the more scrutiny I'll be under when you leave."

"Let's make this swift then, shall we? I have two more questions. First, why didn't my arrival scare you? You're no fool—bowing and scraping like the rest would have gotten you further, no?"

"You might not remember, but we've met before. You came to my orphanage when I was little and, uh . . ."

"You'll find my memory is terribly accurate, dear. I didn't have to visit very many orphanages, thankfully. You were a resident of the Divine Guidance Institute?"

"I was." A hint of a smile. "You showed us your true self, Seer. Unless *this* is the mask . . . ?"

"Hmm. It's possible I was a little too furious to keep up appearances at that time, considering my reason for visiting. How is that old bastard of a headmaster? Is he well?"

"Uhhhh . . . he's very dead, Seer. You killed him. Kicked him through a wall and into the base of the old tower."

"Ahhh!" She clapped her hands as if just remembering. "So I did. And he wasn't revived?"

"They tried, Seer, but no."

"Wonderful. Happy to hear he's no longer plaguing the kingdom."

Fern didn't respond, but the look on her face confirmed that she, too, was glad of it.

"On to my second question, then—why do you want to join the expedition?"

Again, she did a good job of hiding it, only flashes of her true feelings showing on her features. But the terror screaming from her core was unmissable. "I wish to aid the god-empress in destroying the forces of evil."

A lie, of course. "Truly? You took on this backbreaking task, despite never having done physical labor before, merely for a chance to sail into battle against a foreign power who, by our god-empress's accounts, wields corrupting chi? You've not even experienced your first awakening, child. You would willingly brave annihilation?"

"Yes," Fern growled, attempting to disguise her panic as righteous anger.

"Ahhh. That's a shame. Yes, yes, no need to voice your confusion. I meant what I said. It's a damned shame. See, I came down here to find someone like me."

"Like—" Fern's voice failed. She cleared her throat. "Like you, Seer?"

"Just so. A person of upstanding character who, like me, is bored with this pointless drudgery. Bridge this, divine that, holy champion—*blah, blah, blah.* You think you're sick of it after what, twenty-five years of life? Imagine how I feel after centuries of waiting for this blasted 'chosen one' to arrive."

Fern's terror was no longer concealed, skin flushed white beneath the layers of grime, eyes darting toward where she thought the castle was—it was actually in the complete opposite direction, but Eustace supposed now wasn't the time to point that out, amusing as it might be.

"Oh, stop moving your mouth like a fish, dear."

Fern closed it with no small amount of reluctance.

"Divine shield, remember? Our words are our own. You knew I could sense your lie, right? I can't know the exact truth, but based on your actions, I'm guessing you mean to run? To flee once we reach the foreign shores?"

Fern once more resembled an aquatic creature.

"Can I tell you a secret?" Eustace leaned in. So did Fern, forcibly sealing her lips again. Eustace gave her a sly smile. "I was planning the exact. Same. Thing."

With that, the Seer dismissed her protective bubble, letting the weave of golden essence shine in all directions. As the divine was wont to do, it cleansed every impurity it touched, removing dirt, minor ailments, and even the rank odor of a few men who didn't bathe nearly as much as they should.

Fern was in shock, a slew of emotions coming from her core. Fear. Terror. *Hope.* Before she could realize just how exposed she was, her face now free of the meticulously applied layers of concealing grime, Eustace released a pulse of chi, drawing all attention. Including that of the god-empress, whose awareness weighed heavy on the platform.

"Look upon my new apprentice! Gaze upon the fair maiden that has been working amongst you!" The men openly gawked, still reeling from the divine energy. "Fern has been hiding among you, donning a disguise and toiling harder than some of you lifelong laborers. Why, I can see you wanting to ask."

She made her brow twitch, her upper lip quiver.

"For the same reason you should all be doing it! For the glory of Phostheia! For the glory of the Kingdom of Light! For the glory of the god-empress!" Eustace dropped her voice to a near whisper. "She, a young woman with nary a hint of divine power in her core, does all this so she might be chosen to join God-Empress Aletheia in her holy war against the void! Ah, yes, I see the question. It's true—working on the lower platform only grants one additional entry in the lottery per day."

The seer grabbed Fern's hand. She didn't need to fake the look of apology as she unlooped the first length of bandage. Thankfully, the divine chi had cleansed the blood and purulent discharge from the ruptured blisters, making it come away easier than before. The sores still remained. They looked terribly painful.

"Gaze upon the fruits of her labor! The reward her sacrifice reaped! She knew not that I would appear and claim her as my follower, yet I can say with complete certainty that Fern would have continued striking shells from the prime vessel *Theoris*'s hull until her wounds festered and poisoned her blood!"

It was true, if a little—or extremely—misleading. The veracity of that carefully worded statement caught the god-empress's attention. Just as planned. Eustace opened herself, letting her true feelings leak out between the gaps of her circulating chi. At the same time, she leaned on Fern's shoulder for support.

"Citizens of Phostheia!" Eustace called, casting her voice across the capital.

A tear rolled down her cheek as she remembered her young friend and confidant, whose body was now inhabited by another deluded Veritus. Dismay flowed toward the castle. Only Fern knew its source, their contact letting her see Eustace's thoughts.

"As you know," she continued, addressing the city. "Of the seers, only Anius and I remain. My dear colleague has remained steadfast in his beliefs, all these centuries. But I, Holy Seer Eustace, have strayed far from the sun's divine light!"

She imagined all the future events that Aletheia's sickness of the mind had stolen away. Feasts. Conversations. A wedding, Aletheia as the bride, Eustace walking her down the aisle. Regret streamed toward the god-empress, its cause concealed. Fern stiffened.

"Though I am one who helps guide the will of the heavens, I am imperfect. The weight of my task was too much. I lived longer than I ever hoped to, and with each generation that passed, a darkness spread through me . . ."

In her mind's eye, she imagined the kind and curious and sweet face of Aletheia, then replaced it with the burning gaze of the god-empress, and her regret turned into a sense of deepest loss. A sob wracked her. She had to take a shuddering breath before continuing. Fern took one too.

"I lost my way. I lost my faith. Worst of all, I lost sight of my mission—to be a shining pillar of virtue that keeps the darkness at bay. In that, I have failed this city, this kingdom, and humanity. I have failed you all."

Now for the coup de grâce . . .

Eustace imagined Aletheia again. She remembered all the wonderful memories they had made together. The young princess confiding in the seer, admitting she didn't believe in the Church—not in the way it was presented. Eustace staring back, only to guffaw and freely admit that she didn't either. Them sneaking up onto the castle's roof at least once a week to watch the sunset, where they'd have what a young Aletheia had called "secret meetings." The years passing by as the conversations took on a serious nature, shifting toward changing the kingdom for the better.

Almost too late, Eustace realized she had gotten lost in the memories. The intended joy and gratitude were there, but they were tinged with melancholy. She focused on the woman beside her. Tears streamed down Fern's face, her eyes puffy and red. Eustace imagined a new future. One where they escaped, fled the corrupt mire the Kingdom of Light had become. What wonders, what adventures, would they find beyond its borders?

All that the god-empress felt was pure elation as Holy Seer Eustace lifted her face toward the heavens.

"Despite my many failings, I am glad to have lived long enough for the divine bridge to arrive. I am human, as are you. It is in our nature to step from the path of righteousness. But the god-empress? She isn't of the divine—she *is* the divine. She is the bridge who will connect this fallen realm with the heavens. For that, I rejoice, as should we all."

Eustace smiled at her apprentice, who was still too distraught to speak. An orb of purest gold flashed across both Fern's hands. Aletheia. It was the god-empress's chi. Even to Eustace's enhanced awareness, it was astoundingly quick. Just like that, the open sores disappeared, healed as if they'd never been, and Aletheia withdrew.

The seer openly sent her satisfaction and gratitude up toward the castle, not needing to obscure the emotions. Her mummer's farce had worked even better than expected.

Fern stared dumbly at her hands, at Eustace, then at her hands once more.

"Come, apprentice. We have much to do. And all of you!" She cast a withering glare over the men, each of whom were suitably stupefied. "Look no longer upon my novice, lest you want me to kick you from the platform!" She squinted at the formerly unconscious man, who had been awake for the last half of her farce. "Except for you, deviant. If *you* so much as glance at Fern's feet, I'll turn your rocks into skipping stones."

His eyes darted around in search of anything else to look at. Eventually, he decided it was best to cover his face with his hands.

The first smart thing that moron has done since I arrived . . .

Eustace gave Fern's now-healed hand a quick squeeze, looped an arm through hers, and moved with the nun-like poise all expected of a seer, raising her hood and lowering her head so none saw the wide grin. Her quest was complete.

This is going to be fun.

CHAPTER TWENTY-NINE

Higher Realm Things

This is gonna be fun," I said, lifting my new rod before me and inspecting its form in the sunlight.

To anyone else, it might seem entirely out of place. This world, as wonderful as it was, hadn't yet achieved a fraction of Earth's scientific advancement—which wasn't really all that surprising, considering the existence of a System, awakened beings, and a formerly oppressive ruling class in Gormona.

My mind drifted outward, wondering if there were any other societies on this planet that had advanced further than the post-medieval setting I'd found myself in. Then I snorted at myself.

Who bloody cares? I've got a new fishing rod!

It sparkled with a silvery sheen under the direct light of the sun, easily grounding me in the present. Beneath those reflective specks, it was carbon-fiber gray, its eyelets midnight black and aesthetically pleasing. The reel was the only recognizable part, looking like every other Alvey variation, but stained the same color as the pole. And within, it had a new function that I couldn't wait to try: an adjustable drag.

Maria cleared her throat and cocked her head to the side, leaning over so her concerned expression could be seen beyond my new toy. "It's certainly lovely to look at, but—"

"I know you are, but what am I?"

Her face went flatter than a recon crab's stealthy shell. "*You* are a man trying to change the subject. I need you to be serious for a second. Are you sure you're fine?"

"I am. I promise. Besides, you can feel it, right? Through our bond?"

"It wouldn't be the first time you've hidden your worries from me, and of all the things you've read, I thought that last message might have sent you spiraling."

"The last message?"

"Uhhhh, yes? From the System?"

I sipped from my second coffee of the day, feigning ignorance. "You mean the one that said I reached level 112 in Fishing? It was cool, for sure, but—"

She groaned at the sky. "Fischer!"

"Ohhhhh! You meant the message about me becoming a Maker? And encouraging the entire world to hail me?"

"Yes, you big goof. Stop being silly." She grabbed me by the chin, slight yet inhumanly strong fingers tilting my head so she was all I could see. "Promise me you're not deflecting."

I set one hand on my heart and raised the other. "I swear on our love, our marriage, and my many animal pals that I am playing dumb for sport, and not because I'm genuinely worried and trying to hide it."

"Okay. Good."

"Besides, if I was gonna worry about anything, it would be the fact that someone else has been tinkering around in the tunnels Ellis carved with our love."

". . . What? You're serious?"

"Yup. They've been adding essence and something else. I wasn't positive at first, but I am now. The fluctuations have been too severe."

She arched one brow at me. "And you're not worried about it?"

"Nah. Pretty sure I know who it is. No clue why they're being all sneaky, but I'm sure they have their reasons."

"Okay . . ." She leaned closer, studying my face. "And you're not hiding doubts?"

"Nope! All my doubts are out in the open, like Ellis demanding I let my friends endanger themselves, or Ellis taking Roger off to a secret island I'm forbidden from visiting, or Ellis warning of an incoming threat and refusing to elaborate, or . . ." I tapped my chin. "I'll save us some time and just summarize my doubts as 'Ellis.'"

"Good," Maria said, then smacked me on the butt, which might have felt nice if her open palm hadn't swung down with the force of a comet. The sound would've deafened any unascended nearby, and a circle of sand flew out, the slap creating a shock wave.

"Uhh, ow? What was that for?"

"For keeping secrets."

"All right, I'll give you that one. I—"

She smacked me again. I glowered; she smiled sweetly.

"And that was for using me for sport by playing dumb. Now, are you gonna sit there rubbing your butt all day and pretending those little taps hurt, or are we gonna go fishing?"

I smirked at her. "Ohhh, so *now* you want to try out my rod?"

"Of course I do. Whip it out."

I'd taken a sip of my coffee after dropping my innuendo, and hers made me choke. Coffee sprayed out over the sand as I coughed and sputtered. She guffawed.

"Wasted caffeine is no laughing matter, Maria."

"Is that so? Then why is the corner of your lip trying to tug up into a smile?"

"It isn't," I lied. "It's a sneer, see? I'm just so *angry*."

"Riiight. Angry. Would it make you feel better if we go play with your rod?"

I froze.

She gave me a coy look, grabbed my newest creation, and strode down to the water. "What are you waiting for?"

"You are *evil*."

A breeze blew past her, washing the intoxicating scent of her across my awareness as she stopped at the shore. "You coming? I know you are dying to have a fish."

"Super *evil*. Like Corporal-Claws-with-a-pocket-full-of-sand evil."

"I will make it up to you later." She sent me the flash of an image that almost made my knees buckle. "The day's just getting started."

"Deal, but if you ever show me that again, you'll be responsible for whatever happens afterward."

"I'll keep that in mind."

I joined her down by the shore, and as her floral scent threatened to overwhelm me, I focused on my newest creation, hoping the description would distract me.

I immediately cleared my vision, eyes going wide. "What the fuck!"

Maria quirked a brow, her cheeky smile replaced by confusion. I used our connection to show her what I'd seen.

"What the frack!" she agreed, if a little more politely.

It started off with the same two lines:

Fiberglass Rod of the Composite Fisher
[Authorization error: protected asset in lower realm]
But then it changed.
[Protection overridden—Maker detected]
Rarity: Maker
Description: This fishing rod was created by a Maker, God-King, Traveler, whose composite identity lingers within its many fibers. Creatures hooked on this rod will be as difficult to catch as the wielder desires.
Such creations are whispered of within the heavens, but no reputable accounts have ever been recorded—until now, should you choose to share.
Effects: +50 Fishing, +10 Luck, +50% Fishing (inclusive of other boosts), +100% mutability
Duration: null

I didn't even know where to begin. Scratch that—I did know where to begin.

"I absolutely do *not* want to share!" I yelled at the heavens. Staring up, I waited, half expecting a response.

"Oh no," Maria said. "Were the effects so wonderful they broke your mind? I can try healing you if you like."

"Appreciate the offer, but I'm good." I deepened my scowl, still gazing up at the clear sky as I sent the description across our connection. "That last line, 'Until now, should you choose to share.' The System has *never* said anything like that. I don't know if it's even possible, but the last thing I want is it doing some of its System frackery and adding that item—or worse, our *location*—to some kind of metaphysical library of the gods."

"I guess it doesn't hurt to be safe. Now that you have been, though . . ."

I turned to peer sidelong at her, only to find the same expression already leveled my way. We held the stare for as long as we could, and both cracked at the same time.

"Inclusive of other boosts!" we yelled.

Her eyes grew hungry. "Including its own?"

"Yup!"

"So its base increase is seventy-five?"

"Yuuup!

"And that's only if someone had literally *zero* Fishing?"

"Yuuuuup!"

"Holy frack!"

"Holy *frack*..." I agreed. "And the 'mutability' is even better. It's *exactly* what I wanted."

"I know it is." She rubbed my back. "I'm happy for you, even if you had to become a Maker—whatever that is—to do it."

"About that . . . should we tell someone? The animal pals connected to me all felt it, but nobody else knows."

There was a moment of tension, both of us casting gazes up and down the empty shore.

Maria sighed. "I'm conditioned to expect Ellis to fly out of nowhere whenever you pull off something crazy. I guess he's not close enough to have felt it."

"I could let him know, but he *did* warn me about spying on his precious isle." My expression turned conspiratorial.

So did hers. "It'd be downright *rude* to go against his wishes, wouldn't it?"

"A real betrayal of his trust. Guess we should just keep this to ourselves for now. Wouldn't want someone else feeling the need to go interrupt his seclusion, you know? Keeping this secret is only prudent."

"Prudent. Yes. Quite."

"Agreeeed!" burbled Slimes, wobbling out from my wife's shoulder.

"Maria!" I gasped in mock affront, raising a hand to my chest as I stared at Slimes. "You invited him? To the inaugural fishing of my new rod? When I didn't even tell a *single* crustacean? How could you?"

She frowned at my shenanigans. "What are you . . . *Ohhhh.* I see what you're doing. You could have just invited her, you know. She's more than welcome."

"I have no idea what you're talking about."

"Really? You weren't feigning offense as a pretext to invite a certain—"

"Hey! What's that?" I pointed at the horizon, where a gout of water was shooting up from the ocean, so large it could be seen by unawakened eyes. "Who or what could possibly displace so much seawater?"

Maria laughed when she spotted it. "You already told her?"

"Told who what? Wait, you think I would go behind your back and invite someone? Without consulting you? Now I'm doubly offended. Possibly enough to confide in another. Someone of reliable character and rigid carapace."

"Let me guess, when you confide in another and recount my actions—"

"Crimes."

"What?"

"When I recount your *crimes*. Or egregious actions. Your choice."

"When you recount my *egregious actions*, you'll then be obligated to invite them to come fishing, right?"

"Obviously. It'd be terribly rude not to." I let out a great sigh. "If only there were a crab of such repute nearby . . . *Hang on a second! Beneath that spout! Is that who I think it is?*"

Sergeant Snips, reliable of character and rigid of carapace, launched herself from the bay, skimming across its surface on jets of blue chi.

"Snips! It *is* you! What impeccable timing—I have actions most egregious to report!"

It was nearing on twenty minutes later that I finally crouched down to set up my new rod. It had only taken a few seconds to show Snips my new rod, but the rest of the time had been spent running, dodging a crystalline slime, and otherwise escaping the grips of domestic violence.

"Don't even joke about that," Maria said, planting a kiss on my back before sitting in the sand.

I grabbed the line—gods, was it thin—and fed it through the first metal eyelet. "I didn't say anything."

She gave me a look that said, *You were thinking it,* to which I replied by kissing her on the forehead. My deft fingers wove the line and rod together, and when it was time to attach my tackle, I gave the length of line a good tug. Just as I'd sensed, it was incredibly strong, stronger even than regular string enhanced with my chi.

I cut off a section of the string, added a swivel between two knots, and completed the most basic of setups: a free-running sinker with a hook at the end. Before I could get to the bait, a crab scuttled forward with a strip of eel and slid it onto my hook.

"Thanks, Snips."

As I peered at her slick eyepatch, a sudden thought hit me. I'd been so overwhelmed by everything else today that I'd forgotten all about the eyepatch I'd made her. When I'd tried to inspect it after creating it, I saw the error message about protected assets and lower realms for the first time.

I focused on it again, letting its blackened leather and hidden spikes draw my eyes in.

Transformative Eyepatch of the Traveling Fisher
[Protection overridden—Maker detected]
Rarity: Artifact
Description: This eyepatch was created by a Traveler God-King on the path to becoming a Maker. Their affection lingers within the eyepatch, offering protection to the subordinate it was created for (Sergeant Snips of Tropica). This garment, and the spikes concealed beneath its surface, can be altered at will when worn by the intended subordinate (Sergeant Snips of Tropica).
Such creations are whispered of within the heavens, but no reputable accounts have ever been recorded—until now, should you choose to share.
Effects: +100 Bonding, +5 Luck, Bound (Sergeant Snips of Tropica).
Duration: null

"Damn . . ." I said, shaking my head and banishing the words. I relayed the information across my bonds to Snips and Maria as I considered what I'd learned.

I had wondered about the light shining from my abdomen when I crafted Snips's eyepatch. Now, I knew what it was: my first step on the path to becoming a Maker.

Maria frowned after she'd read and reread the description a few times. "The boost to bonding . . . is it talking about every bond or just the one between you and Fischer?"

"I assume the latter, or it would have been specific. Have you felt any difference in your bonds with your crustacean army, Snips?"

"I did!" hissed Snips. Her visible eye glittered, as did the bubbles steaming from her mouth. "Our connection grew stronger over the days following its creation. I thought it was related to the eyepatch, but there was no way to be sure."

Maria sat down on the sand, and Snips scuttled to rest in her lap. They slipped into a comfortable silence.

I stood to my full height. My rod was baited and ready to go. I drew it back and flicked open the reel, which made a solid *thunk* as it clicked into place. There I paused, breathing deep of the ocean air, soaking up the midmorning sun that beamed down upon me. More than my awakening as a Maker or a God-King or even my status as a Traveler, this moment—new creation in hand and on the precipice of being put to use—filled my heart with anticipation. I cast it out into the bay.

A sharp *swish*, followed by the hiss of dozens of meters of line, punctuated with the soft *plop* of sinker and bait plunging down into the small waves far from the shore. *Thunk* went the reel as I flicked it back into place. I wound the handle, stopping only when the drag clicked, and set my finger against the monofilament, waiting for what would come.

"Hey, Maria?"

"Hmm?" She glanced up at me from where she lounged on the shore, eyes half lidded, face painted by a soft smile. Gods, she was beautiful. "What's up?"

"I've decided."

"Oh? What have you decided?"

"That we've waited long enough." I returned her smile, my love for this woman filling my chest with warmth. "Let's go on our honeymoon."

CHAPTER THIRTY

Presents

Two weeks later, on a shore far south of Tropica, my reel made its customary thunk as it slid into place. I recalled the first time using this rod, the sense of novelty, the feeling of anticipation. The novelty might have faded, but my anticipation sure hadn't. Neither had my love for the woman beside me.

Maria and I stood on an unexplored section of coast. Behind us, the forest stretched almost all the way to the beach, only a thin strip of sand dividing tropical palms from the softly lapping waves. The sun set above the greenery, coursing inexorably down toward the western mountains.

Maria caught me stealing another look. Her face lit up. "This honeymoon was a wonderful idea, Fischer."

"Couldn't have said it better myself."

Borks agreed with a playful groan. He flopped to his back and wiggled side to side in the sand. I crouched to pat his fluffy belly but froze when the line against my finger twitched.

Bump.

I braced myself, ready to strike.

Bump.

Bump. Bump.

They were the testing bites of something small, likely not big enough to justify keeping for dinner, but that didn't discourage me. The fish ate the bait, and the fight began. I set the hook gently, heart fluttering despite the relative triviality of the fish, just as it had every time I'd used my new rod.

I was yet to hook anything massive, but even the humble fish on the end of my line was difficult to catch. I felt every shake of its head through my line, and when it turned to the left, the rod's tip was dragged with it. Two enriching minutes later, I brought it to shore.

"Thanks, fishy," I said, freeing it from my line and lowering it into the water. With a few rapid kicks of its tail, it vanished from view. I attached a fresh strip of eel to my hook, flicked the reel forward with a heavy *thunk*, and cast it out once more, the tackle landing with a tiny splash out past the waves. "We should have done this sooner."

Maria rested her head against my arm, her eyes closed and forefinger resting on her line. "I think the timing was perfect. You wouldn't have enjoyed it so much without your new rod. Besides, you can hardly be blamed for putting it off. Neither of us can. We had a lot going on."

"We still do," I replied, sensing my chi pouring down into the ground. The network of tunnels was almost half full. The secretive third party had increased their output over the past two weeks, which had really added up over time.

Maria leaned her head against my shoulder. "With any luck, it'll be finished by the time we get back."

"You think it'll last that long?"

"Our honeymoon?"

"I was gonna say the peace, but that, too. I'm surprised we've gone so long without something coming up."

"Oh. Right."

Something in the tone of her voice made me peer down at her. "What's wrong?"

"It's just . . . I can feel how much these last couple of weeks have helped you. I mean, I can *literally* feel it." She reached up and squeezed my traps. "You were so tense before we left. Ever since you started powering the tunnels, it's like someone wound you a little tighter every day. Since we left on this trip, though, it's the opposite. A little bit of tension leaves you each morning." She leaned closer and waggled her eyebrows. "And each night. Wonder why that is?"

I barked a laugh, and she continued.

"I don't think you're ready to go back yet. I'm not saying this only because I want you all to myself—which I very much do—but I think we should spend as long as possible out here. We shouldn't head back unless you're actually needed. I'm talking a life-or-death situation."

"What if we run out of coffee?"

"Obviously. I said we could go back for a life-or-death scenario, and coffee is the bare minimum for survival."

We smiled at each other, and I pulled her into a side hug, my fishing rod preventing me from giving her the affection she deserved. "You're right. I know you are. I feel like myself again, but I can't help but feel a little—" *Crack!* "—guilty."

We both glanced at the bolts of lightning rapidly fading in the northwestern sky.

"What do you think she's up to?" I asked.

"Something borderline treasonous, no doubt."

I barked a laugh. "If not her, then RPM for sure. I wonder which of them is worse?"

"Impossible to say. It's hard to tell where Claws's degeneracy ends and the raccoon's begins."

My eyes drifted toward the orange-to-blue gradient painting the western horizon. "Two weeks without checking up on everyone . . . that has to be a record for me."

"It is." Again, her tone told me something was wrong, but this time it was playful. She smirked back at me, rolling her eyes. "Go on, then."

"What?"

She sighed, leaned her head against me, and rubbed my back. "You're allowed to check up on them, Fischer."

"But—"

"*But it's our honeymoon,*" she interrupted, putting on a gruff, vaguely insulting voice. "*And I should be focused on you, my beautiful, flawless, and humble wife, who is better than me at fishing and tells way funnier jokes than I do.*" She laughed and continued normally. "You've been present this whole time. Go on. Treat yourself to a little peek."

I opened my mouth, but she held up a hand to forestall my objection.

"Let's skip the back-and-forth. You'll ask, *Are you sure?* I'll say yes. Then you'll be all, *But you just said I needed more time,* and I'll say, well, yeah, but maybe you checking up on everyone will reassure you that they don't need your help right now, and you should instead focus on your honeymoon with your gorgeous, tanned, and always-correct wife. Besides . . ." She met my gaze with a smug grin. "Claws is always most passionate *immediately* after failing or succeeding at something. If you wait any longer to check what that lightning was about, you might miss the show entirely."

"*Frack me,*" I swore. Maria really was always right. I reached out sluggishly with tendrils of essence that sped up the longer I controlled them.

"Brittle! Weak! *Useless!*" screeched Claws a moment later. "Stupid rock! Stupid rock! *Stupid rock!*" Each proclamation was accompanied by the sound of . . . shattering glass?

She started to say more but paused. She'd sensed my attention, my lack of power making me clumsy. I fled from the irate otter, dissipating that tendril and shooting along another to the northwest.

"Are . . . are you sure?" hissed Shelly, sounding nervous.

"Do it," replied Pistachio.

"I—I don't know if I'm ready."

Pistachio paused stoically. "You can take it."

My eyes flew wide, and I fled that scene even faster than the previous. It was probably less intimate than it sounded, but I wasn't hanging around to find out. Maria giggled softly in my mind.

The next location was kilometers to the east, deep beneath the waves. I found my trusty guard crab right where I'd expected. Though I had a rough idea of what I would find so far underwater, the imagery still brought me up short. All of her bonded crustaceans—rock crabs and shrimps and the humans who'd attained carcinization—meditated in a circle around her, their snippers limp and swaying in the ocean currents of a cavernous ravine. Like Claws, Snips sensed my awareness, so I departed before I could disturb her.

The next location was within Tropica. Cal and Fathom. The two cephalopods had been sketchy as anything since the meeting with Ellis. Every time I had tried to contact them before leaving for my honeymoon, they'd pushed me away, so I gave them some distance, not wanting to be found out. But then I felt the others there with them and couldn't help but drift closer.

Interesting. The lava elemental? George and Geraldine, too. Wait, is that—

"**Leeeave!**" boomed Fathom, not inviting rebuttal.

I obliged, withdrawing my awareness—though only after blowing the requisite raspberry in his mind.

I checked up on a certain underground structure next, where I found the children guarded by a bear and once more doing what they yearned for.

"Hang on!" Paul yelled, crouching down and peering intently at a lump of reddish stone. "I'll come play soon! I'm trying to guess the iron content of this rock!"

"Boooo!" Toby droned.

"Boooooo!" his sister agreed.

My eyebrows rose at the look on Paul's face. He had his back to his friends, mouth pressed into a thin line, eyes closed as he took a deep breath, trying not to let his frustration morph into anger.

"Come onnnn!" Toby called. We've been working all day! Let's explore for a bit before the sun sets!"

"Yeah! Come onnnn!" Theresa had climbed onto Teddy's back and was rocking back and forth with impatience. "We can't see in the dark! You *promised* we could explore!"

Paul's cheek twitched. He gave a half snarl, then took another breath, sighed it out, and stood, letting go of his emotions. "You're right. Sorry."

"Yayyyy!" Theresa clapped, wiggled a happy little dance atop Teddy, and started chanting. "*'Ven-tur-ing! 'Ven-tur-ing! 'Ven-tur-ing!*"

I frowned at the expression I'd seen on Paul. I lacked the strength to probe his emotions without him knowing, so my mind whirled with different possibilities. Had asking him to help the other children been too much . . . ?

"Stop that." Maria squeezed my arm. "Teddy's with them constantly now. You should focus on the positives—Toby is pressuring Paul to play. It's almost as if he's remembered he's a kid."

Just like the boy I was worrying about, I let my misgiving go with a sigh. She was right, of course. "Though I bet he'd revert to being a 'cool teen' instantly if he heard you call him a 'kid.'"

"Or if he knew we were watching."

Content to leave it for now, I checked on another . . . but Lemon wasn't in her grove. I cocked my head to the side, using an entire partition to scan Tropica, then using another to scan the surrounding lands when I didn't find her in the village. Where was she . . . ? With panic prickling my chest, I used a third partition to scan my surroundings.

It was a desperate move—why would she be near me, so far south of Tropica?—so when I found her only hundreds of meters away, I whirled toward the forest separating us, a line creasing my brow.

Ruff!

My best bud's bark was loud in the waking world, and even louder in my mind, sweeping aside my thoughts. I shook my head and turned toward him. His tail was wagging so hard that the rest of his body had joined in, his back legs sliding side to side in the sand.

"A secret . . . ?" I asked.

Ruff! he confirmed.

"And you're in cahoots with Lemon . . . ?"

He ran circles around us, barking nonstop, limbs a blur.

"How am I supposed to focus on anything else now that I know there's a conspiracy going on just a few hundred meters—"

Bump.

I cut off, head whirling around, conspiracies forgotten. The tip of my rod moved with the next bump, confirming the first hadn't just been wishful thinking.

"Take it . . ." I whispered.

Bump, bump. Bump!

That last one had some weight to it. The stillness that followed seemed to last forever.

"Bite it, fishy. You want free food, don't you? Doesn't that strip of eel smell delicious?"

"Looks like he already forgot about the secret, Borks." I could hear the smile in Maria's voice. "You're in the clear."

Borks wagged his tail, just happy to be included, as usual.

"Come on . . ." I felt the urge to wind the line in and check the bait. If the fish had stolen the last strip from the hook, leaving my tackle out there would be a mistake. But if it hadn't, and it was instead biding its time, reeling it in would scare it away. "You're hungry, fishy. You're *starving*."

Another span of seconds passed, and still nothing. I let out a hissed breath. "Damn." I drew the line in slowly at first, but when no bite came, I started retrieving at full—

"Fish on!" I yelled, scrambling to my feet, holding the pole high to set the hook. And what a fish. The thing's head thrashed, its powerful tail thumping as it tried to escape. "Massive frackin' fish on!"

I had caught so many things over the last two weeks that I'd lost count. Combined, my numerous catches had granted intimate knowledge of my new rod and its rigid length—*Oh, grow up, Maria. You know I meant my fishing pole.* She chortled in my mind.

A mature shore fish had been the largest thing I'd landed so far. Whatever this was, it was way, *way* bigger. It tore a path from land to horizon, its immense headshakes sweeping my rod from side to side. I'd assumed size was unimportant when fishing with this rod—it made every catch a challenge—but as I strained against the creature on the end of my line, I realized just how wrong I'd been.

Size was important after all.

"Yeah it is!" Maria choked out.

"*Stop!*" I laughed, failing to hide my amusement. "I need to— *Whoa!*"

The massive creature swam down, making my reel's drag scream. Then it raced to the surface at speed and leaped from the ocean. Time seemed to freeze as it kicked in the air, gigantic tail thrashing back and forth, flinging arcs of water in every direction.

It was the color of mottled sand, its fins so dark they were almost black. The creature's head was a full third of its length, but the rest was pure muscle, two hulking fillets lining each side of its frame. Though the shape reminded me of the shovelnose rays we had occasionally caught, it was undeniably unique. I'd never seen one of its kind on Kallis.

I locked in, as did Maria, the echoes of her mirth vanishing from our connection.

The fish crashed back down with a heavy *slap*, and it was once more tearing away, my line cutting the ocean from left to right as the unidentified beast raced off in that direction. After seeing its body, I finally understood the massive sweeps of its head, but still they seemed too strong, too wide. It slowed a touch. I considered tightening the drag and winding it in. An impulse stayed my hand—and thank the gods it did.

It reached deep into its reserves and sped off again, its defiance clear, moving the swiftest it had yet. I stared down at the dwindling line on my reel. I faced an impasse—tighten the drag and risk it snapping my line or have it spool me and snap off anyway. Gritting my teeth, I clicked the drag three times, making it expend more energy. The line raced away, and on an impulse, I loosened the drag one click. With that, the stage was set, and my vision shrank. I saw nothing beyond my line, the ocean, and the creature beneath.

We took turns, both of us stealing line when we could. I couldn't say how many rounds we went for. I couldn't say how long it took. Five to ten minutes, maybe. The rest of the world slowly returned to my awareness as its defiant runs grew weaker and shorter, but the fish was always the center of my world.

Before I realized it, I was knee-deep in the small waves. Twin swirls of water announced the fish's presence only meters away, and with a few more winds, its head came into view, sweeping to the left, the ancient creature taking one last stand.

I strode up to it and lowered an arm, grabbing it under the gills. Maria appeared at my side and relieved me of the rod, freeing my other hand to lift the animal by its thick belly.

"Frack me . . ." Maria and I both said, too awed to say anything else.

Ancient Sand Flathead
Rare
Found along the ocean shores of the Kallis Realm, this fish is . . .

The words disappeared without fanfare, almost immediately succeeded by others.

[Error: inaccuracy limit exceeded.]
Recalculating . . .

They, too, were dragged away, replaced by a series of blinking ellipses, which were also subsequently banished.

Species re-identification bonus: +10 to Fishing! Congratulations!

Then returned the description. It had changed.

Ancient Sand Flathead
Mythic
Found along the ocean shores of the Kallis Realm, this fish was once a staple source of food. Their numbers sharply declined following the gods' departure, which killed all but the hardiest of them. Those that survived did so via hibernation.
They are one of few creatures possessing the innate ability to incorporate the world's chi into themselves, making the venomous spines on the sides of their gill plates potentially deadly to the awakened, and fatal to the unawakened. These spines, along with the venom within, are a prized alchemical ingredient.

Acutely aware of my hand's proximity to its gills, I covered my left arm in a barrier of essence and carefully thumbed the twin barbs on one side of its head, finding them just as sharp as expected, but not enough to pierce my skin, even if it wasn't protected.

As the fish kicked feebly, my mind raced, drawing what conclusions I could from the various System messages. With power returning to our little pocket of the world, it seemed this fish's hibernation was no longer necessary. An entire species, once functionally extinct, had been revived.

Maria swallowed audibly, her mouth dry. "The alchemists would kill for this . . ."

"They would."

"What are you gonna do with it?"

I shook my head, attempting to slow the information whirling in my mind. "I'd be lying if I said I don't want to take it back to our camp and cook up a feast. Look at the meat on this thing. And it was a staple food source, despite being deadly. That means it has to taste godsdamned delicious."

Maria nodded. "My mouth is watering just thinking about it."

Borks leaned forward and gave it some rapid-fire sniffs, his tail raised high, the yellow fur on his lower body drifting languidly in the water.

I abruptly smiled at the ancient beast I held and started moving it back and forth underwater to run oxygen through its gills. "There's no way I'm gonna end its life. Even if there isn't a mate nearby for it to breed with, I couldn't in good conscience turn it into a feast after who knows how many centuries of hibernation."

"Can you imagine? Talk about bad luck. Most of your species dies off, you fall asleep for hundreds, maybe thousands of years, only to wake up and be eaten." Maria softly squeezed the nape of my neck. "Lucky for you, fishy, my husband is a good bloke."

"I *am* a good bloke, aren't I?"

Ruff! agreed Borks, his tail thwapping back and forth atop the ocean's surface, flinging salt water every which way.

The fish was much less impressed with my morality. It suddenly thrashed its head to the side, the two venomous barbs on its left gill plate raking along my forearm.

"Oi! That would have hurt if I wasn't overpowered!"

It tried to stick me again, this time on the right.

"Okay, you cheeky bastard. You're clearly fine." I pushed it away, and the fish weaved off beneath the waves, giving us a glimpse of the sweeping shakes of its head I'd felt through the rod earlier. "You can apologize by making an infinite amount of babies!" I called after it.

"Won't its babies be able to take out non-cultivators?" Maria asked. "Maybe you shouldn't tempt fate by asking for a never-ending number of them . . ."

"You know what? That's a good point." I cupped my hands to my mouth. "Scratch that—you can apologize by making a *reasonable* amount of babies! And don't expect me to go easy again! Next time, you might be dinner!"

No response came, of course. It was just a fish, magical murder barbs or not.

When we got back to the shore, I took a deep breath, soaking in the present. But now that the flathead was gone, my mind kept returning to those damned System messages and all their implications. I was used to being on the receiving end of errors, but never before had they corrected themselves like that. The System had said: "Inaccuracy limit exceeded." So the limit for inaccuracies was two? The rarity had changed from Rare to Mythic, and the first sentence of the description had changed from present to past tense.

Was this going to happen more often? Would every fish be "rediscovered" in the coming months? The last two weeks had been wonderfully relaxing, and I'd needed it more than I thought, but maybe it was time to get back to reality. If creatures were reawakening, we'd been granted an opportunity to farm them for experience, just as I'd thought of when first discovering the mudminnows and alligator gar. Was that not what a good leader would do? Ensure his followers were the ones to benefit from the rediscovery of countless species? I—

Ruff!

I blinked, glancing down at Borks. "What?"

He barked again, sitting in the sand, his entire body wagging.

The message his two *ruffs* conveyed was as clear as it was confusing.

"Present . . . ? You want me to stay present?"

He whined in the negative, then in the affirmative, head darting to the northwest before returning to me, ears alert.

"Mate, I gotta be honest, I don't really get—"

"The surprise!" Maria interrupted. "It's a *present*!"

The canine stood and spun on the spot, whirling with so much vigor that a hole started forming, sand flying in all directions.

"Borks . . . are you sure? I appreciate it. Really, I do. More than you know. But you don't have to reveal it early for my sake. There's no guarantee whatever scheme you and Lemon have cooked up will distract me from—"

He tore a portal in space, unleashed a barrage of licks across both Maria's and my hands, then leaped through, his fuzzy little tooshie vanishing from sight. My wife and I shrugged, shared a grin, and followed.

It had been a while since I'd found myself disoriented by teleportation. The feeling was made more bewildering as I glanced up at the thin trunks that towered all around me, their tips sprouting a crown of fronds.

"Borks . . ." I said. "And Lemon. You both . . . *wow.*"

My pals shook with glee, one with the body of a golden retriever, the other with an entire grove of palm trees.

I pointed up at the light-green fruits. Or were they seeds? Nuts? I shook my head, centering my thoughts. "Are those what I think they are?"

Lemon answered first. Her voice was usually like a soft breeze through leaves, but with how fast she spoke, she sounded more like a hurricane tearing through a building. "*Yes they are master are you happy with them I'm sorry they're not grown but Borks said now was a good time to let you know and I really just want you to be happy and you too Mistress it's been so hard to stay away but now that you're here how has the honeymoon been and how do you like the grove and I hope you're not mad we used the one fruit you had to make some more!*"

"Ruff!" answered Borks at the same time, Lemon managing to say so many words in the span it took him to bark but once.

"Guys . . ." Maria walked up and rested her hand on the trunk of a fibrous tree. "Fischer is a little stunned right now—" It was true. My mouth was moving inaudibly. "—so let me answer for him. This is *amazing.* How did you do it from a single seed?"

Lemon was so delighted she made the entire grove swish. "Magic! I approach a breakthrough! And my brother helped me."

I followed her mental direction, finding the unnamed spirit far below, hoping to remain unnoticed. "Brother . . . ?"

"Yes!"

"Huh. Neat."

Maria barked a laugh. "That's all you have to say? They grew a whole forest of something you desperately wanted, and Lemon has started calling our helpful-but-shy tree-spirit friend her brother, meaning there's a nonzero chance you get to think of another silly name in the near future."

I knew all of that, of course. It was present in my mind, a great wall of knowledge pressing up against the immovable implications of the System's earlier messages. They fought for dominion, each teetering, threatening to fall and crush the other.

Lemon snorted—which was damn impressive, given she did so by blowing wind past her various trunks. "Do not be silly, mistress. My brother's name is also Lemon."

And just like that, the great wall of knowledge won, the apparent fact that there were now two Lieutenant Colonel Lemony Thickets enough to sway the tides of battle. It tickled me pink.

I strode forward, scooped up Borks and Maria, then wrapped one of Lemon's trunks in a hug. "Thank you, Borks. Thank you, Lemon. And you too, second Lemon."

All but the latter returned my embrace, Maria with her arms, Lemon with a thick root grown from beneath us, and Borks . . . Okay, he didn't so much hug me as he did wiggle around as a very licky Dachshund, but the intent was the same.

When I finally let them go, I stepped back and gazed up at the canopy, its fronds painted with the red and orange hues of sunset. "This is exactly what I needed to see." I reached out and squeezed Maria's hand. "You were right. Let's extend the honeymoon as long as we can."

She played it cool, by which I mean she only danced and pumped her fists a little.

Another two weeks passed by in bliss. Our friends sporadically showed up alone or a few at a time, joining us for feasts, delivering coffees and sweet treats, or just rocking up for a yarn. The only ones I didn't see were Snips, Cal, and Fathom. Cinnamon and the pelicans came sparsely, my martial bunny having taken up patrolling the skies atop Pelly and Bill. Claws visited even less, only materializing when food was involved—or mischief to be had, according to Barry and the endless piles of sand he kept finding.

If left to our own devices, Maria and I might have continued living that leisurely life indefinitely. The tunnels below filled more with each passing day, easing the nagging voice that worried about some impending attack. As soon as they were full, I'd have full control of my chi again—along with four partitions with which to exert my will on the world.

Unfortunately, it couldn't last forever. And, as was often the case, everything seemed to happen at once.

CHAPTER THIRTY-ONE

Rude Gestures

I was walking through the forest in search of wild berries when a panicked scream shattered my peace of mind.

"Fischer!" It was raspy, as if bellowed on an inhalation. "Healer! I need a heal—"

The seconds it took to seize control of my power felt like an eternity. Maria and I arrived in the northern district of Tropica, both riddled with anxiety and surrounded by light that obscured the bedroom we stood within. I drew the brilliance back into my core before it could disperse, not wanting to cause any further stress.

"It's time! It's happening! It's here! What do I do?" Steven's eyes looked ready to bulge right out of his head. "*What do I do?*" he repeated, hysterical. "*What do I—*"

Ruby cut him off with a noise that was half hiss, half growl. "Would you . . ." She paused to grunt. "Please calm down?"

Steven spoke again, trying to reply to his wife at the same time as he addressed me, his two different sentences taking turns at controlling his tongue. It was just as illegible as it sounded.

Ruby blinked, then cackled with laughter. "What was that?"

I reached out with my senses to feel her aura, and what I found made the heat return to my extremities. "Frack me, Steven. You about gave me a heart attack, mate."

Maria swept forward to Ruby's side, her clouds of pink chi flowing out, engulfing the room.

Steven was far from reassured. "She's pregnant!"

I laughed at that, unable to help myself, and I clapped him on the shoulder. "She *is*? Since when?"

"She's! I mean she's—"

"In labor. I know. We could tell just by looking at her. No offense, Rubes."

"None taken." Sweat ran down her bunched brow. "However I look, I feel worse." She grunted. "I forgot what pain felt like."

As her essence assessed Ruby, Maria's eyes went wide, but her smile was tinged with awe. "It should be too early, but your baby is in perfect health. The pain is coming from your core. It's . . . it's giving some of itself—some of *you*—to your unborn child."

Steven took a step forward, his terror returning in full. I bathed him in calming essence. Or tried to. "Normal, mate."

He whirled on me. "How do you know that?"

"Maria can tell. I know yours is the first child a cultivator has had, but her purpose doesn't lie."

My wife nodded, both hands resting on Ruby's abdomen. "Everything is going well. It's . . . it's almost time. Not much longer."

"Anything I can get you, Rubes?"

"Helen and Sharon. Please. They know what I . . ." She winced, whole body clenching. "*Dionysus's effeminate cock! Why does it hurt so much?*"

"His effeminate *wha*—"

"Helen and Sharon!" she bellowed.

I dashed from the room before Ruby could launch an attack my way, reaching out to forewarn the two women. I waited a few seconds for their mental approval, then brought them to me. Neither said a word as they ran past me, arms laden with all manner of things. A jug of lemonade, assorted herbs . . . *a stitched blanket radiating power?*

Before I could inspect the latter, they closed the door behind them, and I withdrew my senses. Others mentally checked in with me, detecting the happenings and asking if their presence was needed, but at my reassurance, they reluctantly went about their day. A few couldn't help themselves, however, and they soon arrived outside. I went to meet them.

Barry, Bonnie, and I talked quietly on the stoop of the lavish, System-made home. We'd only just started to broach the subject of cultivator-born children when a sanity-splitting scream tore out into the village. Before it could come again, I used all of my will to raise walls of chi, containing what should be the private noises of a soon-to-be mother. But instead of another scream, an anomalous rush of chi came next.

"No way . . ." I said.

Barry had shot to his feet, his heart thumping, a grin forming on his face. "Add one more item to the list of benefits being a cultivator brings."

"No kidding," Bonnie replied, curiosity flooding from her core. "How long was that?"

"Not even ten minutes," I answered, fighting off the urge to either run back in or send tendrils of awareness in my stead.

Fischer! Maria's voice in my mind was sweet like honey. *Come in! All of you! Ruby says it's fine!*

I dropped my shielding and almost fell to my knees when the various sensations hit me, but Barry caught my arm, and we rushed inside as swiftly as seemed appropriate. Which, in retrospect, was probably still a little too fast. It wasn't an everyday occurrence that one of your best friends gave birth.

Helen held the door to their room open, and I slowed just enough that I could stop without skidding across the hardwood floor. Ruby was weeping, as was Steven, lines of tears streaming down their faces. Their daughter rested on her mother's chest, the newborn's tiny face moving only slightly. Her lip quivered, parted, and released the mightiest cry her little lungs could manage. It would have come close to rupturing a normal human's eardrums.

"Yep!" I said as she drew another breath. "Definitely a cultivator!" Just like with

Paul, the System had stepped in to limit her strength, the restrictions on her grape-sized core even more thorough. I strode forward without realizing it, my hand moving to rest on her tiny back. I caught myself just in time. "Oh. Uh. Is it okay if—"

"Of course," Steven interrupted, shifting aside.

I took another step, fingers extended, palm lowering, and froze again, this pause for a very different reason. Her tiny nexus of power drew in hungrily, and the newborn changed. Amniotic fluid, remnant vernix, and a thin line of chi I suspected was the umbilical cord all disappeared with a wet slurp, sinking into her core. Her small lil' noggin, slightly cone-shaped from passing through the birth canal, formed together, skull plates fusing. It shouldn't have taken place for months, if not years, based on what little knowledge of human development I possessed.

Stunned gasps cut through the tension, each coming from one of the women. The men, however—myself included—all shared a glance. Even Steven looked vaguely horrified, his eyes darting to check if Barry and I had just seen and heard what he had. We nodded in silent agreement, knowing that acknowledging how disconcerting that was might result in violent expulsion from the house—likely via one or more of the walls.

"That's amazing!" Maria said, entranced.

"Y-Yeah!" I fibbed, my stutter earning me an accusatory glare from Maria. "It reminds me of . . . of . . . *uhhh* . . ."

"A seed!" Helen helpfully yelled. "Like a seed absorbing the surrounding fruit, using it as fuel with which to sprout!"

"That's what *I* was going to say!" Barry lied. "It's . . . what's the word?"

"Poetic!" Sharon's eyes were filled with cultish fervor. "It's *poetic*."

Steven, his chest shaking, wiped a remnant tear from his cheek. The bastard was feigning speechlessness. I wished I'd thought of it.

Blessedly, it was too positive an experience for those negative emotions to linger, and Maria's stare drifted away, landing on a far more adorable target. Absorbing the various sources of her mother's essence had apparently tuckered out the newborn, causing her to drift off to sleep.

As I stared down at her miniature form, I felt the need to reach out again and rest my palm against her back and shoulders. There would be plenty of time for that, though. For now, I stepped back, giving them space. Steven engulfed his wife and newborn daughter in a hug. Maria wrapped her arms around me and squeezed me tight, her love for me pouring out, the room slipping into silence.

The quiet was abruptly shattered by twin hisses, far away yet deafening in my mind. Maria and I jolted. They'd called to her, too. We shared a glance, nodded, and I lingered just long enough to gather my chi.

"Love you guys," I said in a rush, "but we gotta go."

"We'll be back soon," Maria added, clinging tight to my arm. "We're needed elsewhere."

"And don't worry." I shot Ruby a wink. "I'll have a name by the time we retur— *Shit!*"

I had to teleport us away before I could finish my sentence, lest Ruby's thrown jug of lemonade smash against my forehead.

The scene we arrived in was entirely divorced from our last visit here. Where the moon's haunting light had cast an ethereal glow over the murky lake, the sun now beaming down from above made its waters shine emerald green. A soft breeze brushed past, a cool respite from the humid air already clinging to my skin. All around, insects chirped, competing to be heard above the twittering of tiny birds who flitted about the surrounding forest. The lake looked almost inviting, if not for my knowledge of the spirit beast who dwelled in its depths.

Just beside us, two lobsters screamed overtop one another, using both words and memories to communicate what they needed from . . . us? Nope. Only Maria.

I pouted and folded my arms. "Am I just a convenient—and classically handsome—taxi service to you people? Today's gonna give me some kinda complex."

"They're not people, dear. They're lobsters." Maria patted my arm. "And try not to blame yourself. It's not your fault I'm so talented."

"That's a good point. Lucky I'm—"

Shelly raced forward with foam streaming from her mouth, having no patience for our jokes. We'd known she wouldn't, which was exactly why we had tried to inject a little whimsy into the situation. What neither of us guessed, however, was that Pistachio would have even less patience for our shenanigans. He squealed in outrage, letting out a high-pitched noise I'd never heard from the stoic lobster.

Maria and I shared some side-eye, and I wisely chose to shut my mouth and get out of the way. Maria swept forth, clouds of pink chi preceding her, already flowing out over the placid lake.

The colossal fish within sensed Maria's approach. It had withdrawn its power from the surroundings and suffused the lake, explaining the emerald tint I'd misattributed to the sun. The thing bristled beneath the surface, broadcasting its intent, fins flaring out, the deadly spines protruding.

A pal with spikes of his own felt the threat. Teddy growled in my mind, but I reassured him, telling him not to worr—

"Fischer!" chided Maria, her thoughts cutting through mine. "Kinda busy! Stop yapping!"

Teddy's whine was the bear equivalent of *oh shit, she mad.*

"And stop misinterpreting Teddy on purpose!" Maria added for his sake, but he had already fled.

The fish let out a rumbling grunt that shook the world, vibrating my every cell. Maria's awareness had encroached on the surface layer of the lake, making the impact even more visceral for her. She had to stop feeding power to the network below, but she and Slimes didn't relent. They eased in toward the aggrieved spirit beast with care, constantly radiating their good intentions. Like the cornered animal it was, the creature dug itself into the mud, its savagely spiked fins puffed out in warning.

"*Now,*" hissed Shelly.

Despite my focus being on Maria's senses, the ideal forming in Sergeant Shell's core drew me once more back to my body. It was warm, then cold. Solid, then shifting. Insistent, then passive. Ever it changed. Altered.

"Yes," confirmed Shelly, her will slamming down into Maria's pink haze. "Alter." The air buzzed with it. "Change." Time slowed. Sound retreated. All went still. "*Transform.*"

Maria gasped. Slimes cooed. The fish attacked.

It lashed out, anger and confusion and terrible fear demanding action, its fins raising, retracting . . . *shooting?* I tried to raise a dome of solid light, intent on catching the dozens of barbs that shot into the sky, but I wasn't ready. It took me too long to gather my essence. The last thing I wanted was for one of the spears to come back down on the other side of the continent and turn some poor farmer into a shish kebab, so I used all four of my partitions to create giant rectangular shields high above, pushing my will and weakened essence to the brink.

When the barbs hit my shields, they made a sound like hail on a tin roof, shafts of bone exploding, the splinters raining harmlessly down. A small part of me was curious how long the spines would take to regrow, but the creature wasn't given a chance to try. Maria's essence engulfed it, the clouds of chi assisted by Slimes and guided by Shelly.

The transformation began. The fish could only witness while its core was altered. Great craters, barely half filled by the last attempt at healing, shone brilliantly. Shelly was there, down on the metaphysical surface, her soul screaming her intent.

Change.

In her view, it was the basis of existence. To be without it was to be stagnant. Dead. To her, it transcended all else. There was no such thing as a perfect soul. Even among those who called themselves "good," morality was subjective. People and things changed from moment to moment and from situation to situation. All one could do was take another step forward, learning from the past as they went.

That resonated with the fish. It—no, *she* was far more aware than I'd given her credit for. I spiraled down, drawn into her memories. I braced myself. What secrets would be revealed? My vision faded, my expectations soared . . . and I was spat back out with force, the fishy spirit beast sending me a pulse of chi akin to old Rocky's aggressively passionate gestures.

Maria laughed so hard she almost lost control of her essence. Shelly, however, wouldn't allow it. The time for change was nigh, and each of the now-countless translucent crustaceans slammed shut their ephemeral clackers.

The spirit beast's core flashed, accepted Shelly's influence, and was made whole— a perfect sphere. Just like that, it was done. No discovered ideal, no breakthrough, no personality adjustment. For the fish, that is. Shelly was a different story.

Fwoooom!

Air rushed into her, as did the countless bubbles of pure chi that had been building all around. Her desire for change flooded out, creating an explosion I let bloom, my curiosity too great to smother it. Shelly's transformative aspect consumed the nearby trees, completely changing their layouts, each plant taking on a unique shape.

One was all twisty, like a bonsai manipulated over hundreds of years to grow in spirals. Another seemed inverted, its branches and leaves reminding me of moss-covered roots. The rest were too abstract to describe in the moment.

I wanted to inspect them up close. I got as far as taking a single step forward before I was blasted with a thick pillar of water. Soaked, I wiped the lake from my eyes and stared at my assailant. "Do you feel good about yourself?"

The fish stared back, showing no remorse.

"Maria?"

"Yes, Fischer?"

"She knows I could kick her into space if I wanted to, right?"

"Yes," hissed Shelly, nodding.

The colossal fish spun to face Shelly, gave her what could vaguely be perceived as a thankful nod, then sank back down to the depths, one fin lingering to give me the same rude gesture as earlier, but physically this time.

I looked down at my clothes, shrugged, and cleansed the muck and moisture away with a pulse of light. "I'd hoped letting her hit me with that would help lower her guard. Turns out she's just an asshole."

"Yes," hissed Shelly again.

"Forget that!" Maria dashed forward, ducked down to Shelly's height, and released an absolute onslaught of words. "You did it! This is where you two have been? I can't believe it! Your purpose might not be healing, but it's kinda similar! No matter how much I tried, I couldn't have done what you just did! What *did* you even do? You fixed it, but the fish is clearly still a bit of a prick."

Shelly shrugged.

"She is a prick, isn't she?" I asked. "Sassy as hell for a big fish in a small pond. I'm of half a mind to bomb-dive into her lake and say wassup. Maybe give her a piece of my—"

All four of us, two humans and two lobsters, went rigid as a pulse of essence struck us, so strong that we felt it all the way out here.

I started gathering my chi, swept forward, and hastily patted Shelly's carapace. In the same movement, I crouched to fist bump one of Pistachio's massive snippers, but straightened as a guttural roar came flooding into my mind.

I grasped Maria's outstretched hand, pictured where the harsh call had come from, and prayed that we would get there in time.

CHAPTER THIRTY-TWO

Cracks

One hour earlier, southern Tropica

Paul gazed down at the pile of failures heaped against his workshop's wall. Each tiny vessel was handmade from start to finish, all the materials gathered, processed, and shaped by his crew. And not one of them had been a success. The knots in his stomach squeezed so tight that the sensation rose into his chest. He couldn't breathe. He had to get out of here. Needed to—

"Are you sure about this?" another asked, stepping up beside him. "I kinda feel like trying again. What if we craft for a few more hours, then play until dark?"

Paul whirled on the speaker. He knew just how insidious a single dissenting voice could become. His memories demanded he snuff it out. Best to go too far than not far enough in response.

Better to be feared than loved, if one cannot be both, his mind quoted from somewhere deep within.

Paul frowned, coming back to himself. His hand had drifted to the pommel of his sword, where it now rested in obvious threat. Whose voice had that been? What had he been about to do?

Toby blinked. A smile curled his lip as his gaze drifted from Paul's expression to his sword. "Forgive me, my liege!"

Teddy had lifted his head. He watched from his spot beside the heaped vessels, ears alert, eyes penetrating.

As Paul floundered for a response, Theresa came to the rescue. She withdrew her wooden blade and pressed its splintered edge into an insubordinate neck. "Shall I remove his head, sire?"

They'd both assumed Paul was joking. He ran with it. "Hmmm. I say we let him live this time. Consider this your last warning!"

Toby gulped. "I yield! Please don't give me any splinters!"

Theresa sniffed and slipped her training sword back into the cloth belt she used as a sheath. "Count yourself lucky, low-blood! Next time, it's off with your noggin!"

"You know we have the same blood, right? You're literally my sister."

She rested a hand on her lacquered pommel. "He's getting lippy again, sire . . ."

Toby raised his hands in mock surrender, forcing his eyes wide, and Teddy lowered his head. Paul focused on how grateful he was for his friends, the adolescent part of his mind taking over. The knots in his torso relaxed.

The last few weeks had brought so much fun.

Toby had been above playing with them at first, too embarrassed to join in. Paul and Theresa played tag for like three whole hours one time while the teen carved a spear, pretending he didn't want to join. The adult part of Paul had found that ironic. Caring what others thought was far more immature than just doing whatever you found enjoyable, childish or not. Paul hadn't pointed that out. Doing so would have pushed Toby further away.

Instead, he'd continually made bids for connection, subtly inviting Toby to play. It had taken all of four days for the older boy to join.

Paul stepped forward and lowered Theresa's wooden sword, which had once more found its way to the side of her brother's neck. "I'm absolutely certain about our quest. We need new materials, and I think I know where we can find them." He started leading them from the workshop. "I know you've taken to crafting, Toby. If we find what we need this morning, you can be creating something with them by this afternoon."

"But you won't tell us what they are?"

"And ruin the surprise? Is that really what you want?"

Toby considered that for a moment. "Okay," he finally said, shrugging to himself. "I trust your judgment. You haven't led us wrong yet."

Paul jarred to a stop, his eyes going wide. Those words had made his semi-suppressed core ripple something fierce. His adult self took over. Rather than grow tight, the knots in his stomach loosened further, his abdomen tingling with possibility.

With a shake of his head, he returned to the present. Toby wore an expression that mirrored how Paul felt. The teen's peepers were unblinking as they drifted down to stare at his own abdomen.

"You . . ." Paul swallowed. "You felt that, too?"

"Yeah . . ."

Their surprise lingered a moment, then morphed into excitement as they charged out of the workshop. Paul felt like someone had injected some of his mother's famous berry pie directly into his veins.

"Felt what?" Theresa asked, scrambling after them. "What did you feel? Hello? What did you feel? I'm seriously gonna start swinging this sword if one of you doesn't—"

"Our cores," Paul said in a rush, coming to a stop on the street. "Well, my core. Toby doesn't have one yet, but if he sensed it, too . . ."

"I might be close to awakening."

Theresa pouted in thought, inspected her weapon, then smacked the flat of its wooden blade against her stomach. "What the *heck*, core?" She turned her displeasure on Paul, as if it were his fault. "Why didn't mine do anything?"

"Dunno. Age? Compatibility?"

"Combati-what-now?"

"Don't worry about it. Point is, you'll get there eventually."

She scrunched her nose, then gave an easy shrug. "You're probably right. Like my stinky brother said, you've been good at choosing what we do so far. And besides, it's been fun—"

Paul wasn't sure if she'd actually cut off or if the drumbeats thumping in his core had drowned out her words, but by the time he came back to himself, he didn't much care to find the answer. Flashes of pure white swirled across his awareness, like currents of air winding around himself and his two friends, seeming to push and pull them toward his center. Both returned his stare, just as stunned as he was.

No words were needed. All three of them, young as they might be, understood the implication. Their futures, and their very purposes, were linked.

A giant head shoved its way between them, projecting a red aura that flooded Paul with energy. Paul wrapped Teddy's neck in a hug, his adolescent half unable to resist. The bear's blood-colored mane of thorns turned softer than silk at his touch and easily parted. "We're okay, Teddy! Better than okay! They're close to awakening, and our future ideals are aligned!"

Teddy suppressed a low growl as he lumbered along behind Paul, the armored and clanging forms of Toby and Theresa riding on his back. He wasn't so sure about his cubs being okay. His spiked hackles agreed, refusing to fully retract, no matter how much he willed it to happen.

Paul's outbursts were getting worse. Teddy had been watching the children closely since his breakthrough, his ideal demanding the young be protected. He'd noticed the changes in Paul almost immediately; he could smell the scent of iron and leather when the "older" version of Paul took over. Thankfully, as the intensity of the outbursts grew, so did the time between them. Which was the only reason he hadn't yet informed his master.

"Woooo!" Theresa yelled, giggling and raising her arms as Teddy leaped over a ditch.

He let out an amused huff despite himself, her exuberant nature infectious. This was but a trot to him, but Paul was sprinting ahead, going as fast—and as loud—as his armored and partially awakened body could go. Theresa was a normal human child. She should have been far too stressed to let go of his fur, no matter how much he'd reassured her. He wondered if Toby felt the same.

Toby did *not* feel the same.

Teddy immediately slowed when he saw the white pallor on the boy's face, and let out a soft whine to get Paul's attention.

"Oh! Sorry! Was that too fast?"

"No," Toby lied bravely.

"We should walk from here, anyway! We're almost there!"

Teddy had been so lost in thought he'd not realized just how far they'd traveled. Over the sand flats, past the first line of mountains, and deep into the range had Paul led them, conquering a staggering distance of ground. No wonder Toby was so afflicted. A breeze blew through the forest—coming from the east, if its oceanic scents and the rising sun could be believed. He recognized this place. Or the general area, at least. He'd seen glimpses of it through his connection to Fischer. This was one of the places the master and mistress had camped over the past month.

Why had Paul come here? He seemed playful like a cub but smelled of leather and iron, hinting that the older version of the boy was in charge. Teddy didn't like it. Something felt wrong. He let out a questioning growl.

Paul flashed his impish smile, so similar to Theresa's. "You'll see. You'll all see! I reckon we'll find just the thing we've been missing! Relax, Teddy!"

He didn't. But he followed along without complaint regardless, eyes and senses peeled for the first hint of danger. All around them, birds flew between branches, chirping with nary a care in the world. The wind came and went, as did the sun peeking down through gaps in the canopy, its rays nowhere near warm enough to melt the icy gaze he gave the surrounding trees.

He paused, lifting his nose after catching a scent. It was faint. Barely noticeable amongst the aromas of the nearby shore. Yet there all the same. He lowered his ears in relief. There were two friends nearby. Friends that would arrive in an instant if anything were to go wrong. Maybe he should call out now and—

Crack! Cr-Cr-Cr-Crack!

The air split with a sound like dozens, then hundreds of snapping twigs. The black lines of a portal tore into space in front of them, tinged with purple, glowing with ominous intent. Teddy transformed and charged forward, placing himself in front of the children, his claws, teeth, and clusters of spikes glowing red.

The portal finished forming. A nightmarish bramble of thorns and writhing limbs flew out of it, skidding to a stop on the forest floor. A shape most foul leaped through next, teeth bared, lips pulled back, a declaration of violent intent grating from its tiny throat. It skidded to a stop beside the bramble, lowering its head and letting out a pathetic *blehhhh*.

Teddy scowled at the two idiots. He expected such trickery from the tree spirit pretending to be an evil bush, but he'd thought better of the hellhound who'd adopted the demonic form of a chi-wow-wow. Borks let out another *blehhhh*, his rapidly wagging tail giving away his true feelings. Lemon shimmied in delight, her breezy laughter hissing through the surrounding trees, replacing the cacophony of snapping twigs she'd been emitting.

Both tree spirit and hellhound abruptly froze, Lemon turning into a regular shrub, Borks becoming a golden retriever as they stared past Teddy in horror. He spun, raising his deadly forepaw, ready to cut down whatever threatened his cubs.

When he saw it, he froze.

Theresa and Toby were staring down at their abdomens, where their cores were forming. Paul's stomach shone, too. Instead of beaming out in every direction, the light of his breakthrough swirled out in ribbons. They were beautiful, powerful, and . . . flowing into his friends.

Teddy unleashed a great pulse of chi to alert everyone. His aura flowed out, empowering his cubs. Paul harnessed the strength and bent it to his will, which let Teddy know what he was doing to the siblings. Teddy's blood turned to ice, and every one of his crimson spikes twitched.

Paul's ideal wasn't aligned with Toby and Theresa—it was trying to subjugate them.

Teddy roared across every connection he had.

CHAPTER THIRTY-THREE

Chains

Surrounded by peaks, wrapped in swirls of his own essence, and cast in a red light befitting this victorious moment, Paul experienced ecstasy on par with the divine. Never had he felt so sure. So right. So in control.

All because Borks and Lemon, pretending to be nightmarish spirit beasts, had tried to prank them.

The tree spirit's and hellhound's arrivals had made terror wash through Paul's core. That split second of alarm had triggered not only Paul's breakthrough, but Toby's and Theresa's, too. Lemon and Borks obviously weren't a threat . . . But what if it *had* been two beasts capable of annihilating them who'd leaped at Paul and his accomplices? In their current state, they wouldn't have stood a chance.

And now that the possibility for advancement was here, Paul wouldn't let it go so easily.

He latched on to Teddy's projected power, bending its offensive boost to his will.

His real, "adult" self was free, his adolescent tendencies shoved to the back of his mind. He assessed his abdomen and beamed when he found no knots there. He was in complete alignment with himself.

Now that the System's iron grip was absent, he finally comprehended how stifling it had been. Its existence made objective sense, of course. It was to the benefit of society and the world at large if the young and inexperienced were prevented from wielding too much power. Even a simpleton could foresee the resulting disasters.

Fischer had warned him of the outcomes. Despite the Traveler's strength, he couldn't see into the hearts of others, nor could he predict the future. Thus, he'd presented Paul with the carrot and the stick—be a positive influence for other children and be rewarded, or step out of line and be imprisoned. Most would chafe at that, seeing such obvious manipulation as an insult.

Paul, however, saw it for what it was.

He wasn't a mere member of the masses. He wasn't one to be offended by Fischer's good leadership. And he wasn't in need of safeguarding by some faceless protocol. Paul could be trusted with his agency. He would only do what was best for Fischer, Tropica, and the world at large. Which was exactly why he was assimilating his two followers.

The moronic and emotional civilians would never understand. What did they know of genuine sacrifice? The vast majority would hesitate before giving their life to save their beloved, their body seizing up in that critical moment, the voice in the back of their mind urging self-preservation. His followers, though? Toby and Theresa understood. They were complicit. Both could stop the subjugation of their potential with the faintest thought. Yet neither did.

And he thanked them for it—praised them for the wherewithal to make the choices others would shy away from. Almost all of their individuality had been scouted now. He circled them, assimilating as he went. Perhaps a fifth of their souls were conquered already. He could feel their influence, their thoughts, just as they felt his. Never again would he be alone in this world, nor the heavens beyond.

Fischer would understand. He might be upset at first—the man was emotional for a leader—but he would come around. He prized agency above all else, after all, and this was what all three of them wanted. The god-king was here now. His weakened tendrils of essence encircled the clearing, stopping others from interfering. This made Paul smile.

A good leader, was Fischer. He wouldn't stand in the way of progress.

"The frack I wouldn't, mate."

The voice was conversational. Amused. Paul buckled as if struck by a wedge of mounted spearmen. What was Fischer's purpose with those words? A clear threat, but presented with humor . . . ? Was the point humiliation? A lesson? Setting the precedent that to go against his wishes was to invoke his wra—

"Nahhh," Fischer drawled back in his thick accent. "It's not that deep. I find this whole situation funny. Sorry if it came off as condescending."

Paul's lip and eye twitched. This was his moment of victory. A good leader would heap praise upon their general, not cheapen it with misdirection and inane chatter. Toby's and Theresa's reactions were just as visceral. They raged at Fischer's hypocrisy, incensed by the disrespect he was showing their sacrifice.

"Okay, okay. My bad." An image of Fischer appeared in Paul's mind. "In my defense, I only meant for Maria to hear that first message. I'm not as deft as I used to be. It's those damned tunnels sapping my power and making me weak. Sorry about that."

Paul had to fight down his fury. That his god-king had intended on speaking it behind his back was hardly any better. Such whisperings could easily lead to the downfall of a general, no matter their prowess or—

Maria cut his thoughts off with a muffled laugh. "There are no secrets between a man and his wife, Paul. I'm kind of surprised this 'adult' version of you didn't know that. Don't be offended."

"You mock me in my moment of victory." Paul hated how petulant his voice sounded. Damn his adolescent body. "Yet you claim no offense should be taken?"

"Mate. You've got it all wrong! She wasn't laughing at you. She was laughing *with* you."

"What is so funny, then? What do you find so humorous that you would undermine me so publicly?"

"That you reckon you're gonna subjugate Toby and Theresa."

And there it was. Fischer's hypocrisy laid bare. Paul had been a fool for believing in this man. "You speak of agency, *god-king*!" he spat. "Yet you would step in here? And how would you stop us? Imprisonment? Collaring? Will you cleanse us for having the audacity to find our purpose and follow through?"

A terse silence followed the questions. Paul's words had held up a mirror, and they were clearly flummoxed by what they saw in the reflection. He allowed himself a satisfied smile, knowing he had successfully talked his way through.

Fischer cackled. Actually *cackled*! Maria joined in, both leaning on each other in shared amusement. Paul's fury boiled over. Rational thought left him. Such a grave insult could only be answered with steel and blood. He reached for the souls of his friends, and though their assimilation was still in progress, they agreed with him—Fischer was no leader worth following. Destroying him would be a service to all his faithful.

With that thought in mind, Paul grasped at the last vestiges of chi tying Toby and Theresa to their mortal forms.

"Not laughing at you, mate. Neither am I stopping you."

Paul heard, but he didn't listen. Words were wind.

"Wanna know why?" Fischer continued. "Because *you're* gonna stop you. I don't have to do a thing."

Paul snarled. So did Toby and Theresa, lips curling, teeth clenched. They gathered up their autonomy and made the last decision they would ever make, choosing to cede their free will to Paul. Ribbons of essence flowing out to seal the pact.

But when something slammed into Paul, it wasn't the pact. It was the suppressed part of himself, the child that he'd forced to the back of his mind.

Subjugate his friends? Absorb their will into his own? *Yeah fracking right.*

"No!" Paul declared, no longer embarrassed by the tone of his adolescent voice.

"No!" Toby and Theresa agreed. The System obeyed. It had been lurking nearby, and with their denial, it collected their chi and wove it back into their cores. Their hearts beat in tandem, the rhythmic thumps reminiscent of the drums of war, each pulse urging action.

The limitations of earlier, the muting of his power by the System, returned. Paul watched as they laced his body, rested on his skin, and sank down toward the invisible channels running through him. Before they locked in place, the thumping tempo of his two friends' hearts became deafening. His joined in, matching their pace.

Someone spoke, but it was drowned out by the sound of scraping metal, creaking wood, and the thousands of armored feet marching, the tumult coming from within the three children.

"See?" I asked Teddy as light shone from the children he saw as cubs. "Told you! Paul was never going to— *Poseidon's pickled pecker on a platter, what the frack is that?*"

Great chains of chi wound out from Paul, thicker than my arm, stopping just short of the other two. Toby's and Theresa's now-awakened cores responded in kind, their own metallic links scraping out, each length wrapping around the others. From scraping to grating to a booming roar, the chains kept coming, and the three friends were encased in seconds by a metal sphere. It contracted, squeezed, condensed, then vanished in a flash of ephemeral silver.

The trio stood atop the cleared ground like nothing had happened. Their appearances were unchanged, but the same couldn't be said of their cores. Paul's breakthrough wasn't complete, but it *had* progressed. Rather than exploding out, the additional essence had been absorbed by his friends, Toby and Theresa drinking it in.

When I felt their conjoined ideal, I lowered my head into my hands. The groan started down in my chest, slowly growing louder as it crawled its way up my throat and out into the world. I hadn't been imagining it when Paul completed the first stage of his breakthrough back when making Bob the boat. His ideal hadn't been related to design at all; it was about strategy. Their souls had literally broadcast the sounds of a marching column.

"Your fathers are going to kill me . . ."

"Yep!" "Definitely!" "Ya-huh!" Paul and Toby and Theresa agreed, the children-turned-tacticians deeming it likely.

Maria rubbed a reassuring circle on my back. "Look on the bright side—the System limited their power."

"Greaaat. I'm sure that'll make Barry and Dodge forgive me for letting their kids awaken as child soldiers." I held up a hand to forestall their objection. "I know you're more like commanders. I'm only matching the hyperbole your fathers are gonna hit me with."

I felt and heard a muted *boom*. Another groan escaped me. "Speak of the devils . . ."

Barry sailed into view a moment later with Dodge clinging to his back. The former's powerful legs had sent them flying a little too high, but they'd arrive soon enough.

"Guess it's better we get it over with . . ." I said.

"Whoa!" Paul yelled, his comrades letting out sharp gasps when they saw what Paul had. "I knew it! They're perfect!"

They were pointing at the new grove of fruit trees, which was apparently the reason Paul had brought the others out here. Borks and Lemon—who had both been standing to the side looking extremely guilty for their role in triggering the breakthrough—perked up slightly.

"It's not your fault, you two. Who'd have known that jump-scaring them would lead to all that? I'm surprised you joined in though, Borks."

Reverting to the demonic form of a Chihuahua, he flopped onto his back in submission. I scratched his tummy. "I'm not angry, buddy. Just surprised. You've clearly been spending too much time around Lemon."

The bush she currently occupied nodded in agreement.

I gazed over at the three tacticians. They had run into the grove and were staring up at . . . "What the frack? How are the coconuts fully grown already?"

Lemon and Borks wiggled in delight. I took a step forward, wanting to crack one open and have a taste, but then a stern voice slammed into me.

"Fischer!" Barry had sailed into hearing range. His jaw was as annoyingly handsome as usual. "What have you done?"

I cupped my hands to my mouth. "Would you believe me if I said it wasn't my fault?"

Suddenly, the entire sky to the northwest flashed blue and yellow, not an inch of the horizon spared from the countless barbs of jagged lightning consuming it. I blinked in confusion, then grabbed Maria by the elbow, started gathering my essence, and gave Barry a shit-eating grin.

"Don't you dare!" he roared. "You need to answer—"

"Sorry, mate!" I yelled. "Gotta go! Bring some coconuts back for me, though, yeah? I really wanna give them a try!"

We left in a flash of light. We technically arrived in one, too. It was far less noticeable on the other side, though, given the mammal that clutched onto me and hit my core with at least a dozen bolts of lightning.

CHAPTER THIRTY-FOUR

A Good Zappin'

14.37 seconds earlier, the grounds formerly known as New Tropica

Corporal Claws, fuzziest and most patient of all Fischer's animal pals, was getting reeeal sick of this shit.

For over a month, she had hidden away in the clearing that had once been New Tropica. All manner of experiments had been conducted. More days had passed than she had digits on all of her dexterous paws. And yet there was nothing to show for it.

Was she not Fischer's strongest follower? Could she not have thousands of thoughts in the time it would take a regular being to consider scratching its butt? Why, then, hadn't she succeeded in reforging the beautiful and frustrating object before her?

"Stupid vulgarite," growled Claws. "No wonder they called you that. You *are* vulgar. *And* stupid."

"Fulgurite, mistress," chittered RPM.

"What?"

"It's called fulgurite."

The old Claws would have head-butted her familiar for interrupting her while she was busy insulting an inanimate object. The current Claws would, too—and did, in fact—but with only a fraction of her power.

"Very gracious, mistress." RPM wobbled his way back into her pocket. "I thank you for your . . . *restraint.*"

Ignoring him, Claws peered up at the many-pointed sculpture she'd been working on, trying to see it from a different perspective. But it looked the same as always: an upside-down lightning storm, three meters tall and composed of glass, growing thicker at the base. She'd created it following her ascension as an elemental, when she'd slammed her master into the sand and hit him with everything she had. That made her think of Fischer, but she banished him from her mind just as swiftly, worried she might accidentally lure him in. She narrowed her eyes at this "fulgurite," doing her best to scowl it into submission.

What was up with this stupid rock? It contained her chi. She'd been the one to make it. The damned thing was even shaped like lightning. So why wouldn't it obey? She kicked it for good measure, resulting in the same as usual: a tinkling chime that resonated in her core. She swiftly withdrew RPM, who robbed the sound from the air before Fischer could sense it.

Again, she thought of Master. Her eyes flicked to the southeast for the barest moment. He was down there. Close by. She had a desire to zap over and receive a good scritching. She'd been intentionally avoiding him for the entire month, her resolve only breaking when food was involved. Perhaps that was why she, the otherwise unflappable corporal, felt so abbreviated.

"Agitated, mistre—"

"I said what I said!" screamed Claws, once more head-butting her sniggering familiar down into her soul.

Fischer had been teleporting to and fro all morning, routinely interrupting her concentration. He was extra busy right now, most of his awareness flooding out, focusing on something she couldn't be bothered to identify. This wasn't like her. Never before had she felt so . . . Claws fumbled for the word, then cast a mental glare at the still-amused raccoon attached to her soul.

"Dejected, mistress," suggested RPM.

"Yes. Never have I ever felt so dejected."

Despite her uncharacteristically morose mood, the upside-down tree of glass taunted her with its beauty, each branch reflecting the stunning oranges and reds of the rising sun. Her master would love how it shone. Perhaps it was risky thinking about him again, but something had to change, so she considered him long enough to curse him out.

Stupid Master. Stupid rock. Stupid raccoon.

"Hey!" hissed RPM. "What did I do?"

But he knew what he'd done. The manic mammal descended into a fit of giggles. Claws rolled her eyes and considered her master again, finding comfort in the thought of him. What would he do in this situation? After a month of wasted time, in which no progress had been made? She'd tried everything to break some of the fulgurite off. She had even attempted making more by channeling vast currents of electricity into the sand. It created fulgurite all right, but it was nothing like the giant tree of glass before her, neither in scope nor power. None came close to replicating what she'd accidentally produced by slamming her master with everything she . . .

Her musings trailed off, jaw falling open as something moronically simple occurred to her. Her master. He had been there. She'd spent the entire month pushing away any thought of Fischer, so the possibility hadn't crossed her mind. Half hoping it was the answer, half hoping it wasn't, she pressed one paw to the fulgurite and sent a pulse of essence into it. This time, she let it ring out, picturing her master as it resonated with her core—and there it was. An echo of his chi within the fulgurite, so pure she hadn't sensed it. Fischer was the missing link.

Claws head-butted the ground once, twice, and a third time for good measure. "Stupid master! Stupid rock! Stupid *otter!*" She flopped onto her back and rolled around, screaming the frustration and regret out. An entire month wasted. All those hours spent failing, when she could have been eating oysters, hunting shellfish, or hiding even more piles of sand in Barry's belongings.

Then, faster than lightning, Claws sprang to her feet, her needlelike teeth crawling with electricity as she let her emotions pass.

Ready? she thought at her familiar, sending him the devious thoughts she was having.

"Yes, mistress," chittered RPM. His grin matched hers as he zapped from her pocket.

Together, they reached for their power. It used to take minutes for her to summon natural lightning down from the skies. No longer.

Roiling clouds formed. Her fur rose as the static built. And Corporal Claws cackled, forearms high, calling down a distraction so large, so brilliant, that Fischer couldn't ignore it.

At the same exact moment I arrived next to Claws, her rat of a familiar latched on to me, his core stealing from the world around us. He yoinked nothing from me, which was a pleasant surprise. But his lack of larceny was overshadowed by an entire sky's worth of lightning being redirected into me.

It wasn't painful so much as it was annoying, like a mild version of a static shock delivered to my abdomen. That didn't mean I'd let it continue, however. I grabbed the little bastard by the scruff of his neck, drew him back, and prepared to launch him clear over the western mountains—perhaps all the way to Theogonia—but froze when the furry bastard yoinked something from me in that moment of distraction.

RPM laughed no more. His body had gone limp, eyes unseeing, cute lil' chompers clenched with effort. He'd taken . . . I didn't even know how to describe it. It was more akin to pirating than stealing; the little prick had done the fantasy-world equivalent of torrenting my chi.

Claws snatched it, went to shoot me a grin—let out a choking noise when my copied essence hit her—and swiftly pressed her stolen goods into a sculpture. It was exactly what I'd suspected she was working on, and as I saw it for the first time, I couldn't help but appreciate its beauty. Like a tree made of glass and lightning, it shone with the colorless brilliance of my chi, which swirled within its forms in wisps. Then Claws flooded lightning into it.

Her blue electricity crackled around my wisps, refusing to touch them at first, then combining with them as our distinct aspects became one. I shielded my eyes with my arm, as did Maria and Claws, the light so hot it started to melt the nearby sand.

RPM, in a remarkable display of ambition or stupidity—probably both—stared directly at it, his forepaws wide, trying to steal some of whatever was taking place.

He succeeded, too, though I'm sure the outcome wasn't what he'd expected. The raccoon, a being whose body was made of elements beyond my comprehension, spontaneously combusted, only managing to take a fraction of the heat before succumbing to its energy.

"*EEEEEEEEEEEEEEEE!*" his mind screeched, so loud it traveled from him to Claws, then from Claws into me.

His master released a screech of her own and drew him into her core even as disappointment flowed out of it, joining the smell of burned hair that lingered. The light slowly faded. I lowered my arm and stared at the sculpture.

The fulgurite's glass and lightning branches were incandescent, yellow and blue and white flares flickering into and out of existence, each making a sound like a soft intake of breath. They shrank in size, reduced in frequency, and then stopped altogether, leaving behind a feeling of dormancy, reminding me of the needful moment before a lover's touch.

It was a sculpture no longer. Through whatever Claws had done, she'd created the impossible—another artifact.

Maria squeezed my arm. "Is—is this what you felt from the other artifacts? I haven't sensed them since my last breakthrough . . ."

"Yeah . . . Exactly like that, but this one's a little weaker." I winced, shooting a look at Claws, expecting her to take offense and deliver me a good zappin'.

She hadn't even heard me. She took a slow step, followed by a swift one, then swarmed forward all at once, head low and eyes wide. She climbed the artifact's trunk, skittered along a branch and grabbed its tip, applied pressure—

Clink!

It snapped off cleanly. She held it up, gazing at the tri-colored pattern that flared and faded, going dormant again. She tucked it into one pocket with a shaking paw, more grave than I'd ever seen her. RPM, completely restored but still bearing a slight musk of scorched raccoon, popped his head from the other pocket and stared at Claws, the situation demanding even his respect.

Claws's eyes met mine, and I cleared my throat. "You can't tell anyone."

"You can't tell anyone," she croaked at the same time. Well, she made a sound like a dying frog, but the meaning was the same.

I smiled at her with a slight shake of my head. "Come here, you little rascal."

When she landed in my arms, it was like holding an entirely different otter. The expected pridefulness and boasting were nowhere to be seen, and trembles wracked her in waves, shaking their way across her slight form. Maria patted her head, and I joined in as my eyes drifted back up toward her creation.

I could hardly believe it, but my senses weren't lying. She'd really produced a mini version of the ancient- and naturally occurring artifacts we had already collected. Though its potency was reduced, its aura was just as strong, echoes of its luminescent flares radiating out.

"Are you okay, Claws?" Maria asked.

The elemental of lightning and chaos nodded, but another tremble struck her at the same time.

"Actually, Claws, I might need to tell someone else. Is that okay?"

She nodded, so I reached for my power. Before I could grasp it, Borks tore a portal open before me, his excited form skidding to a stop on the sands. He peered up at the tree with unbridled excitement, his head darting back and forth between us, eyes wide and tongue lolling.

"It's exactly what you think it is, mate. Our troublesome otter seems to have created a weak version of the natural artifact. Would you mind stor—"

"*Weak?*" screeched Claws, standing upright on my arms, her face close enough to touch mine, forepaws squeezing my cheeks together. "Weak, master? *Weak?* You *dare?*"

Maria giggled into a closed fist. "There she is. Welcome back, Corporal."

Claws folded her arms and sniffed haughtily as she shot me some audacious side-eye. RPM's paw exited her pocket to give me an undignified gesture.

"Yeah, yeah. My bad. Let me rephrase." I cleared my throat. "Corporal Claws, our one-of-a-kind wielder of lightning and tamer of treacherous beasts—" RPM tried to protest via the offensive gesticulation of a forepaw, but Claws stuffed it back into her pocket and nodded for me to continue. "—has done the impossible by creating a natural artifact."

Her pride rolled across her shoulders, then wiggled across the rest of her.

"Glad you approve. Would you mind storing it for her, Borks? I don't wanna lure any more terrors of the deep to Tropica. The two we have are plenty enough."

He barked and tore another portal open, but before we could put anything into it, hundreds of green fruits came tumbling out.

"Mate . . ." I gestured at the mountain of coconuts. "We were gone for like a minute. How did you collect so many?"

He wagged his entire body.

"Do you have space in your secondary storage? I don't want those tactician kids plotting against me for leaving their coconuts all the way out here."

With a proud bark, he ripped his other portal open, its surface a different shade of purple. And again, before we could put anything in, something came flying out. Power. *Unbelievable* power. The combined aura of eleven other artifacts—ten crystalline trunks and the thankfully unspoiled bill of an ancient fish—put the potency of Claws's fulgurite tree to shame. Not that I'd tell her that.

Borks flexed his will, spread the portal wide, and we eased the dormant tree of glass and lightning within. Claws instructed like an overprotective foreman, donning a hardhat that was really a shell, and blowing on a whistle that was in truth . . . No, it actually was a wooden whistle.

"Where the frack did you get that?"

She shrugged in response, accompanied by a taunting waggle of her brows.

"All right. Keep your secrets. Can you at least tell me what you're going to make with the bit of fulgurite you broke off and put in your . . ." I trailed off, seeing the truth on her fuzzy little face. "You're not gonna tell me shit, are you?"

Her grin spread wider still. She patted me on the shoulder, leaped down to the sand, paused to give Borks a chirp that landed somewhere between thanks and a warning, then tore off through the sky, smiling as the lines of her body shimmered and became lightning.

When any trace of her passage was gone, I pursed my lips and glanced around. A faint sense of unease washed over me, growing stronger by the second.

"That's it?" Maria asked, also peering in all directions, waiting for the next insane event to occur. Seconds passed. "Huh. Maybe that's it? I can't help but feel that—"

Chi slammed into my body and mind, the first rushing in from the east, the second coming in through one of my connections. "I fracking knew it!" I reached for my chi and turned to Maria, both of us sensing that the call was for me and me alone. "I'll be back soon. I love you."

"I bloody knew it," she said, squeezing my arm as I finally got control of my essence. "Say hello for me."

I disappeared in a flash of light and was greeted by crushing pressure, freezing water, and the languorous shifting of *thousands* of crustaceans.

CHAPTER THIRTY-FIVE

Crabbing

Sergeant Snips hated that she'd missed the honeymoon camping trip, along with all the relaxation, fun, and delicious food no doubt involved. But as she peered out at her many followers, seeing their bodies drifting this way and that in the tumultuous current, her disappointment was all but forgotten.

They were at the bottom of a vast ravine between two seas, its walls sheer and smooth, worn down by the ocean's currents over millennia. Once, it had likely been a tiny crack. A barely visible fault created by tectonic movement or the attack of some long-dead being. Over the years, the clashing tides had done their worst.

As if summoned, another torrent arrived, forceful enough to obliterate all but the mightiest of crustaceans. She and her bonded familiars were safe, of course. Water flowed around the flattened bodies of the recon crabs, met its match against the stack of boulder-sized rock crabs that were the Church of Carcinization, and passed over the meditative cloud of assault shrimp.

Considering the crushing pressure, there shouldn't be any animals down here, save for those with hard shells: snails, limpets, and the deep-sea mussels attached to the ocean floor. The latter were what had drawn an opportunistic scout down into this channel, the crab having spotted them from afar and wondered what they tasted like. What said scout hadn't expected, however, were the tiny creatures she'd discovered clinging to the shellfish.

Crabs. So small they resembled ants, the hardy crustaceans had somehow found a way to live in these harsh conditions. Snips had assumed the secret to their survival was their size, allowing them to hunker down and hide in gaps barely larger than themselves.

She'd never been so happy to be wrong.

Snips reveled as thousands of tiny crabs let go and flew past her, tumbling chaotically, limbs tucked into their bodies, their eyestalks flattened sideways in specialized grooves, making them look pleased by the involuntary travel.

Suddenly, a second blast of water came from the right. She'd been here an entire month, and never had she seen the opposing forces meet in the middle. She had wanted to keep this a secret until at least one of her groups of followers had experienced a breakthrough. With the arrival of this rare event, however, things changed.

She exerted her will, using every ounce of intent she had to hold two oceans at bay, and hissed an invitation across her strongest connection.

* * *

I had known that it was Snips calling to me. I had known she was far beneath the ocean. And I had known, beyond a shadow of a doubt, that the rest of her bonded crabs were there, too. Rather than a cry for help, she had sent a call to action, promising that if I came to her, I wouldn't regret it.

I'd never been so happy for Snips to be right.

The moment my light faded, Snips let go of two opposing forces, both with the power of an ocean behind them. The one pouring into the ravine from the left arrived first, sending me whirling sideways, limbs splayed, body cartwheeling at incredible speed. I nodded at the tiny little crabs spinning with me, whose expressions made them seem overtly pleased with our current predicament.

"Fellas," I burbled. "How are we this morn—"

The second ocean cut me off, its force pouring in from my right. Or what used to be the right. My cartwheel of immaculate form turned omniangular, water blasting me from—and in—all directions. So, too, did the crabs fly. If I didn't know any better, I'd think they were looking even more pleased.

Some of the poor buggers sailed up into my nose, so I blew them out, returning them to their brethren as our passage finally slowed. All of us—Snips, her bonded crustaceans, thousands of those little crabs, and me—all swirled to a stop hundreds of meters above the ravine.

We slowly drifted back down, flitting through the lingering currents like leaves in the wind. I grinned all the while, closing my mouth whenever one of the happy little crabs flew too close. The last thing I wanted was to eat one by accident.

"Snips," I said across our connection. "You've outdone yourself. Thank you. A thousand times, thank you, once for each of our crabby little frien . . . *Huh?*"

I focused on one of the tiny creatures. The cheeky little git had landed on the tip of my nose and tried to grab hold with a claw. Its pincer would fail, of course. An unawakened crab couldn't hope to find purchase on my enhanced body.

Except it *did* find purchase. And instead of holding on, the little bastard *ate* me. A part of me, anyway. That first claw, smaller than the head of a needle, removed a cluster of dead skin cells and chucked it into its mouth. Its second claw followed suit, but I used the chi I was still holding to raise a barrier. I breathed a sigh of relief when its snipper bounced off. Being eaten alive by a swarm of gnat-sized crabs was *not* on my to-do list.

The ambitious crustacean tumbled away, having accidentally launched itself off my shielding. I raised more walls around it, watching it close, my senses flooding out. I'd only meant to ensure it didn't absorb my chi. Instead, words flooded my vision.

Deep-Fathom Cleaner Crab
Uncommon
Found . . .

This time, I knew what to expect, and I waited for the updated description to arrive.

Species re-identification bonus: +10 to Fishing! Congratulations!
Deep-Fathom Cleaner Crab
Rare
Once found within the pots of crabbers and believed to have lived on the ocean floor, this crab was a good-luck charm and source of wealth. Their initial discovery revolutionized the crabbing industry, unlocked the final wave of naval classes, and eventually led to the first, second, and fourth Deep-Fathom Wars. They survived the gods' departure via hibernation.
Cleaner crabs are one of few creatures possessing the innate ability to incorporate the world's chi into themselves, making them deadly to awakened- and non-awakened beings alike. Their potential for harm is mitigated by the spontaneous disassembly they undergo when lifted from the ocean floor. Only their claws survive this process, which are a treasured crafting ingredient.

I shook my head to clear my vision and smiled at the information. Being hit with so many implications would usually bring me grief. But this . . . ? Almost all of it was fishing and crabbing related!

These are the kinds of revelations I can get behind!

I had so many questions. Crabbing industry? Naval classes? And if these snippy little things caused the first, second, and fourth Deep-Fathom Wars . . . what the frack caused the third one?

Before I could find any answers, I had to make sure that crab hadn't consumed any of my power. The description had only said they could incorporate the world's chi, but I wasn't taking any chances. I narrowed my eyes at the cleaner crab, ready to call all of Tropica's forces here if needed.

Its mouthparts undulated, chewed thoughtfully, and . . . spat my dead skin out. It ate underwater carrion for a living, but my cells weren't good enough? What was up with that? I'd be lying if I said my feelings weren't hurt.

There was a blur of blue, and my reliable guard crab appeared before me, metal-spiked eyepatch giving her a severe visage, claw cocked open and ready to slam closed. "Shall I destroy it, Master?" hissed Snips.

"For hurting my feelings or because it might have taken some of my chi?"

"Yes."

Laughter bubbled from me. "Nahhhh. It's all good." I caught the cleaner in question on my palm. It tried to pinch my skin again, so I flicked it away. I focused on its clackers as it drifted down toward the seafloor. "Did you know about the chi in its claws, Snips?"

"I was not aware, Master. They did not try to eat us. An evolutionary advantage, perhaps, to not eat other crustaceans."

"I didn't sense it, either. Something about the essence used by unawakened creatures makes it hard to notice, maybe? Which reminds me . . ."

I sent her the memory of the flathead. A stream of contemplative bubbles rose from her, and she drifted down to wrap her limbs around my arm, clinging to me as implications unfurled in her pretty little carapace.

But she was ripped back into the present moment later when hundreds of crustaceans—every single recon crab, Church of Carcinization member, and assault shrimp—started to glow. The world's chi responded. It flowed in from all around with the undeniable weight and strength of an ocean. Swirling, it went over and under them, through rock and stone, and pooled at the bottom of the ravine.

One of the cleaner crabs, its body bereft of chi and movement, likely already dispatched by the collision of two oceans, drifted down into the gathered essence and . . . *popped*? I got my first look at "spontaneous disassembly." There one second, a small cloud of matter the next. As stated by the System, only its claws remained. The wisps of substance streaming from them reminded me of the smoking boots of an otherwise-exploded cartoon character.

Frack me. That was a bit much.

If my shock was a surge, the shock of Snips and her bonded souls was a tsunami. They hissed in unison at the dispersing cloud of atomized crab, clearly disturbed. I raised a layer of solid chi, stopping any more of the unawakened creatures from making contact, but the damage was already done.

The light of their impending advancement flickered, dimmed, and vanished, as did the pool of essence below, only a small portion flooding into the now-dull beings. Something changed within Joel, Jess, and the rest of the Church of Carcinization, but the same couldn't be said of the others.

Silence settled in the ravine, then faded with a series of quiet pops as more cleaner crabs suffered spontaneous disassembly, having perished from the earlier clash of water. It was only a dozen or so, but each *pop* made the awakened crustaceans cringe. I smiled, rueful. Such was life for the average unawakened animal.

After such movement and violence, the stillness was unnerving. The fact it was raining tiny crabs made me feel a little better. I tried to catch them like snowflakes, but they no longer saw me as a potential snack, avoiding my outstretched hand with their rear swimmers. As they hit the bottom of the ravine, they flattened their bodies and went still, just as disquieted by their exploding brethren as Snips and the others. It was amazing how swiftly they blended into the environment. Not wanting to bother them any further, I crossed my legs and floated above the bottom of the ravine on wisps of chi, overwhelmed by all that had occurred over the last . . . what even was it? An hour?

Ruby had given birth to an awakened newborn. An absolute prick of a fish had been healed. Shelly had discovered her ideal. Three kids had become strategists. Claws had created a natural artifact. And now all this . . .

A faint needle of anxiety poked my side, but it swiftly vanished. I instinctively knew there were no more major events about to occur. The world felt still. Balanced. I breathed a sigh of relief that formed into bubbles and raced away, charting a path to the ocean's surface.

A soft hiss drew my attention, and I glanced down to see Snips looking amused. She nodded at the object beside her. I floated closer. Not an object at all. A cluster of creatures, whose long brown shells I'd never seen before.

Species identification bonus: +10 to Fishing! Congratulations!
Deep-Fathom Mussel
Common
These mussels evolved from another species following the departure of the gods.

I blinked, half expecting more information, but none came. Snips's visible eye cleared at the same time and met mine. Despite our ability to speak directly into each other's heads, it wasn't necessary for us to communicate our feelings. I reached out, grabbed a mussel, and prepared to pull it away but was stopped by a swift clack of Snips's claws. Communication *was* necessary, apparently. I cocked my head in question, and she answered by ushering over the Church of Carcinization.

Honestly, they were kinda terrifying as they scuttled over like giant underwater spiders covered in armor. Their long forelimbs reached down, their snippers going toward patches of the just-discovered shellfish. Before they removed any, however, unknown powers rushed from their cores and into their bodies.

I watched with bated breath, wishing more than ever that my senses weren't reduced by how much essence I was feeding into the tunnels below. I'd have detected their new ability already if I were at full strength. What would this new ability be? The fact that a crabbing industry and nautical classes existed in this world at some point had made me think about gathering skills. Was that why Snips had stopped me? Could they collect them more efficiently? The heavens were the limit when it came to System frackery.

But then the transformation happened, their rigid claws shifting, changing into a new form that could much better grasp the massive mollusks. They paused just long enough to give me respectful nods, then raced around the ocean floor, collecting the mussels at incredible speed.

They looked ridiculous. I probably should have laughed until I choked. Instead, I rubbed my chin, a plan forming in the back of my mind. I . . . I could use this transformation. It was the perfect counter to the two belligerent fathers who were waiting for me back in Tropica. A trump card I could whip out if my other preparations failed.

A grin spread over my face and broadened as the newly transformed crabfolk swam along the ravine, plucking mussels from the stones.

CHAPTER THIRTY-SIX

A Period of Calm

Barry moved as carefully as he could, yet the ground shook with each stride, his anger bleeding out into the surrounding world. His ideal had been challenged. His purpose for living had been harmed. And his core, his very soul, demanded action.

Beside him, another advanced with similar intent, weaker but just as seething.

Normally, Barry would have glanced over at Dodge, curious about the man's apparent invulnerability—Barry's muscular legs created miniature earthquakes each time they met the ground—yet Dodge remained unaffected, his core resonating with purpose and manifesting the beginning of a breakthrough. Dodge's ideal seemed related to stability, letting him glide overtop each disturbance. Such was the weight of his fury.

But Barry didn't look the other man's way. Nor did he delight in Dodge's approaching advancement. And he certainly didn't consider the implications. All he could do was focus on himself, lest his tempestuous anger tear the ground beneath Tropica asunder.

He could hear voices coming from the headland. Even from here, his acutely sensitive ears picked up joyous conversations between villagers, spirit beasts, and elementals. He didn't begrudge them their mirth, but neither did he revel in it. What did the storm in his mind care for the squalls of seagulls?

As he rounded the outcropping of rock that marked Fischer's home, Barry caught sight of them. The deepest part of his subconscious counted them all out: dozens of members of the congregation, almost every animal pal Fischer had tamed, and a twisted trunk that could only be Lemon. Their friendly faces, all spread around a campfire with a large cooking pot at its center, usually would have spiked his endorphins.

Again, the storm felt nothing.

Barry balled his fists until they creaked, the folds of his enhanced skin complaining like taut rope. And there was his target. Fischer stood tall and relaxed, caressing a small bundle. Barry heard something crack. He belatedly realized it was his neck, the surrounding muscles growing so tense that the joints within popped.

"Ruby." His voice sounded far away. As if it echoed down a long hallway. He pointed at the bundle his foe held. "Collect your child from Fischer."

"Uhhhh," said the object of his ire. "Bit rude, mate. She literally gave birth like three hours ago. She's physically healed, but her core is still pretty tender. Besides." Fischer tilted his body to show off the bundled infant. "Look how damned *cute* she is!"

Barry tore his eyes from Fischer, and they settled on another. "You do realize that this coward is wielding your child as a shield, don't you?"

Content lounging on the sand, Ruby just shrugged.

Beside her, Steven snorted. "Realize? It was Ruby's idea."

"Yup!" Ruby beamed as she glanced up at her baby girl. "The safest place for my little Fiona is in Fischer's arms, given that it was only a matter of time before you and Dodge came tromping over here with your ideals, demanding revenge or recompense or whatever."

"Yeah!" Fischer said, patting the infant's back. "It was *Ruby's* idea for me to hide behind her newborn baby like a coward! We— *Wait!*" Fisher's head blurred back and forth at dizzying speed. "Hold the fu . . . er, fra . . . errr, phone. Hold the phone. Did you just call her Fiona? *You gave her a name?*"

"We did," Steven replied. "Care to tell him the associated nickname, darling?"

"*Oh-my-god-there's-a-nickname!*" Fischer whisper-yelled. "Share! Quick! I can't handle the anticipation!"

Ruby's eyes sparked in the firelight like her namesake gem as she dragged the moment out. "Fifi was—"

"Fifi!" Fischer interrupted. "It's beauti—"

Ruby's left shoe bounced off the top of his head, interrupting him right back. "Let me finish! Fifi was our initial impulse, but we have another option. We figure we won't know which one suits her best until everyone tries them out."

"What . . . what is it?"

Ruby let the silence hang, and the air grew thick with suspense.

Barry considered dashing forward and punching his enthralled leader in the mouth. But he wasn't like Fischer. He wouldn't endanger children.

Finally, Ruby spoke, dispelling the tension. "The second option—that we think you'll love, Fischer—is *Fin*."

The god-king's eyes went wide, then lost focus. "Fin," he said, his voice soft yet rumbling, laden with power. "I choose *Fin*."

That final word seemed to squeeze the air within Barry's lungs—and everyone else's, judging by their reactions. The sensation disappeared a moment later, only for another sensation to arise. Euphoria. Curls of golden light poured from the base of Fischer's throat and wound around the newborn, never touching, but changing her all the same.

Echoes of it came from her tiny core as the illumination ebbed then vanished altogether. Fischer wobbled, almost fell, but caught himself.

Nobody moved. Neither did the world. Everything froze for the span of three heartbeats.

When the wind and the waves returned, and the clouds above resumed their crawl across the sky, so, too, did Barry shift. His legs strode of their own accord, muscles bulging, entire body tensing up. "What did you do?"

* * *

I looked from the raging Barry and Dodge to the bemused Ruby and Steven, and finally, down at Fin. She was sleeping peacefully, her tiny little mouth pursed. How was anything able to be so damned cute? The ground shook, reminding me I was in danger.

"Uhhhh, if I can be real with you for a second, Barry . . . I have no idea what I just did."

This made Ruby and Steven snort. Which was nice, considering the effect it had on Barry and Dodge. The muscleman started vibrating so hard that the edges of his body blurred. And Dodge, well, dodged it. I couldn't say how, but his feet just . . . refused to acknowledge that the bloke beside him was casting tremors strong enough to threaten my house's structural integrity.

After everything else that had happened today, I wasn't at all surprised when bubbles of chi rose from the ground, foreshadowing an ascension. They slammed into Dodge's core. I reached for my chi, already knowing I wouldn't grasp it before the explosion went off. Teddy's growl reverberated in my chest, and his crimson aura surrounded everyone. The explosion passed harmlessly over us.

Cold as ice, Barry didn't acknowledge any of it. He took another step forward.

Well, I thought, staring at the now-prone man beside him, who'd been knocked unconscious by his own advancement. *At least it's only one irate father I'll have to talk dow—*

Dodge rose from the dead like a fracking vampire, arms held out, body rigid, skin pale. He started sliding forward across the ground like a godsdamned nightmare. I kept losing track of him for some reason, my brain forgetting he was there, only for me to remember him an instant later and get jump-scared all over again.

Damn. This was bad. Fin's presence was supposed to nullify their definitely unjustified and not-at-all-deserved resentment, but I'd made it worse by accidentally doing . . . something. I still had no idea what.

"I—I didn't mean for your kids to awaken as warlords! It . . . It wasn't my fault!"

"It kind of was, though," someone taunted from behind me, sounding suspiciously like my wife if she deepened her voice. "They'd just be regular farmers right now if you'd never come to Kallis."

"Not helping, Maria!" I took a step back, holding Fin tight. "Fellas. *Fellas.* Your kids discovered their ideal. It's a good thing! Give it some time, and you'll, uhhh . . ." I glanced to the side. "*Now! Crab scrambled egg! Go-go-go!*"

A part of me had hoped the carefully chosen phrase would be unexpected enough to disarm Barry and Dodge. No such luck. They didn't so much as flinch, ever approaching, one with booming steps, the other sliding across the sand like a flattened cardboard box—but, like, upright.

I'd think of a better analogy later. I had more important things to do. Such as watching the events my spoken phrase had set into motion.

The Church of Carcinization flew from Snips's core in their crab forms, creating a tower in seconds—only for the entire structure to tumble back down like a puppet with its strings cut. Even though I knew what was going to happen, I couldn't help but be mesmerized by the falling avalanche of shelled friends as they transformed into beings far more fleshy.

Barry and Dodge froze. They blinked at the church members, who stood tall on two legs, adopting bodies they had left behind in pursuit of the perfect form.

"Ta-daaah!" sang Joel and Jess, sprinkling in a liberal amount of jazz hands. "Long time no talk!" The rest of them fanned out to either side, crouching down like crabs, entirely naked save for their carapace-covered privates. Joel looked up at Dodge. "And nice to meet you! We've heard so much!"

"Uhhhh," Dodge said, torn between holding on to his anger and being rude. "Likewise . . ."

Thus, my trump card was spent. Not missing a beat, the next act came marching in, their metal suits making an absolute racket. Paul, Toby, and Theresa were fully armored, with real weapons strapped to their waists. If Barry and Dodge were allowed to think about it too long, it might piss them off all over again—which was exactly why we weren't going to give them that chance.

The three children wrapped their fathers in energetic hugs.

"I love you, Dad," Paul said, hugging Barry so tight that the joints of his basic armor bent and buckled. "I'm still the same person. I'll always be your little boy." Barry's fury melted away like butter on an uneven skillet.

Toby and Theresa echoed similar sentiments, which had an even stronger impact on Dodge—and thank the gods for that; the way he slid about on unmoving legs made my skin crawl.

I gave Helen the slightest of nods.

Told you, she mouthed back, a hint of amusement bunching around her eyes.

The script had been her doing. I'd initially planned for Paul to say he loved Barry, then follow up with an insult. I stood by my version being funnier, but I couldn't argue with Helen's results. I gave the Church of Carcinization a thumbs-up. They returned it, their awkward movements making it painfully obvious they'd spent the last couple of months as crabs.

"Well," I said, looking pointedly down at the steaming pot and the absolute mountain of shellfish beside it. "With that settled, I think we can—"

Barry interrupted me. "Nothing is settled, Fischer."

"Sure it is! My senses are cooked because of the whole feeding-the-tunnel thing my soul has going on, but even I can feel how happy your children are. They're . . . I don't even know if there's a word to describe how closely they're linked. 'Colleagues' doesn't do it justice. Those three would walk through the fires of Hades together."

His scowl deepened, and I held up my hands.

"Yeah, good point. Forget that last bit. They will absolutely not be walking through, or around, any fires of Hades's making. No offense, Borks."

Ruff! Remaining seated, his tail swished across the sand.

Barry wasn't swayed by Borks's cuteness. "You should have told us. You should have *brought* us. We had to feel it all from afar. Can you imagine how terrifying that was?"

"Dad . . ." Paul said. He tried to grab his dad by the arms, but his bent armor was in the way, so he ripped it off—*sick move*—revealing an outfit Steven had whipped up less than an hour ago. The shorts were white, as was the sleeveless top, whose red-banded collar extended up to the base of Paul's neck.

Theresa and Toby repeated the same to their own suits of armor, showing off their new uniform. It looked surprisingly sharp on the three kids, given that shorts and a singlet would bar you from some pubs back on Earth.

Paul rested a hand on his father's shoulder. "Fischer did exactly what we needed. I love you, but if it had been you there instead, things might have gone much, *much* worse. He let me run with my mistake without correcting me. I had to do it myself. If you had felt me trying to make my friends subservient"—he turned to Dodge—"or if you had felt me trying to subjugate them, would you really have been able to stop yourself from interfering?"

I winced, unsure if bringing that was the right move, but I shouldn't have doubted the tactician. Both Barry and Dodge's expressions softened.

"Fischer did exactly what Ellis told him to," Paul continued.

"I did?"

He smirked at me as if I was joking. I wasn't. I'd been so overwhelmed by the sequence of events, and the constant need to harness my defiant chi, that I'd not considered it. Now that I did, I realized he was right.

Barry's face told me he'd realized it too.

Paul nodded. "He let us place ourselves in danger. If he'd stepped in to stop us, who knows what would have happened? At worst, that version of me might have doubled down and actually absorbed Toby's and Theresa's wills." He smiled at his friends. "I, for one, am extremely glad he let us work it out for ourselves."

Barry sighed as his fury faded. "I guess it is settled. I'm still worried about your ideal, but that's my problem to deal with."

Dodge had also calmed, but now confusion creased his brow. "Fischer . . ."

"Yeah?"

"The thing you yelled to call out the Church of Carcinization—crab scrambled eggs."

"What about it?"

"What kind of code phrase is—"

"Don't!" Barry tried, but it was too late. My trap had been sprung.

"Pretty straightforward. There were crabs, they scrambled, and the eggs . . ." I pointed at the kids. "When a daddy and a mommy love each other very, very much—"

Barry cut me off with a heavy sigh, squeezing the bridge of his nose. "You really are the worst at naming things."

It was no easy feat keeping the smile from my face. "You're one to talk. You named your son *Paul*. Talk about a terrible name. Absolute dogshi—"

"Fischer!" Ruby yelled, pointing at her newborn, who was still sleeping soundly in my arms.

"Hey!" Paul added. "What did I do?"

I raised my hands. "My bad. Took that one too far. I'm sorry."

Barry frowned at me for a long while before wisely choosing to disengage. With Ruby's blessing, I passed Fin to him, letting him and Helen fawn over the cute little . . . whatever it was I'd accidentally made her.

As Paul marched over to chat with Toby and Theresa, I covered my mouth and whispered into his mind with a tendril of essence, ignoring the headache caused by embracing my essence far too many times today. "Hey. Mate. Don't look this way, or they'll know I'm talking to you. Wanna know a secret?"

He paused for the barest of moments, then nodded and resumed walking.

"Good lad. Here's the thing—I lied. I'm not sorry. I was *absolutely* going to call your name dogshit, and I'd do it again."

Paul missed a step.

"Actually, I probably would have said even worse, had I not been rudely interrupted. I never know where my mouth is gonna take me once I open it."

He stood stock-still, and his head slowly turned to stare at me, face confused and a little hurt.

"Relax. I didn't mean it, obviously, but I would have claimed as much. Verbal warfare is the best way to get your old man flustered."

Paul blinked rapidly, thoughts running through his tactical mind at a million miles an hour. "Why are you telling me this . . . ?"

"Because you're one of the big boys now. I know you're still young, but you've proven time and time again just how mature and reliable you are. Don't get me wrong, I'm not gonna start riling you up the way I do your dad, but as far as I'm concerned, you're wise enough to be fair game. Don't expect me to go easy on you with the smack talk."

A grin had slowly spread over his face with each word. He closed his eyes, tensed his jaw in concentration, and created his own tendril of chi.

"That goes both ways, Fischer," he whispered, the syllables a little muddy from inexperience.

Still, it served its purpose. No one else heard him, his partially suppressed core manipulating sound to an impressive extent.

I barked a laugh as he turned and marched away. "Cheeky little bugger . . ."

Someone appeared by my side, and Maria's fingers laced themselves through mine. "That was sweet of you."

"Perhaps a little *too* sweet. Might have bitten off more than I can chew by challenging that little demon in the making . . ."

"If it makes you feel any better, little actions of kindness like that are part of the reason I love you so much."

"I love you, too." I pulled her into a hug and kissed her on the forehead. "Maybe even more than seafood."

"Only maybe . . . ?"

"Yeah. I haven't had a chance to try the deep-fathom mussels Peter just added to the pot. The jury's out until I sample them."

"Let's go get you some, then. I'd like to get to the bottom of this."

Hand in hand with my wife, I smiled at all my friends as we strode back to the campfire. Now that the chaos of the day was finally over, a wave of exhaustion washed over me. Everything related to the tunnels was still a major source of stress, especially the third entity that kept tinkering with the vast stores of energy. That was okay, though.

The tunnels were almost full. I would soon regain complete control of my chi. And above all else, I had a strong feeling that Tropica was about to go through a period of calm.

CHAPTER THIRTY-SEVEN

Never Mind

War was coming. Seer Eustace could feel it in every single one of her wizened bones. There would be death and destruction. Misery and pain and heartbreak. More heartbreak than most could fathom.

So why did she feel so calm?

Wind whipped past as she stood at the prow of *Elegos*, sister galleon to the prime vessel. *Theoris* was the only preceding ship in the Divine Fleet, and they sailed behind and to the side of its wake, carving a graceful line through the deep blue.

Theoris was lined by metallic constructs. Those on its stern and starboard sides glittered like gems under the rising sun, almost as brilliantly as the divine chi stored within and slowly pouring out into the water below. Eustace turned to the left, gazing at the twenty ships fanning out to that side—one wing of the giant V carving a path toward Gormona.

The same relics covered their hulls, just as they did *Elegos*'s, creating a giant dead zone that would annihilate any cultivators or spirit beasts wielding essence of a different aspect.

Perhaps that was the reason for Eustace's calm . . .

Someone swore behind her. A sailor had lost hold of a rope. When it hit the water, it immediately started to smoke, the water seeming to boil around it as it melted, the section exposed to air catching flame before sinking into the depths. The sailor stared at it with wide eyes. So did Eustace. Curious, she leaned down, picked up an empty crate, and tossed it into the sea.

It, too, caught flames. Eustace frowned. The divine chi wouldn't only destroy enemy cultivators, as Aletheia had claimed; it would also destroy inanimate materials. Eustace grimaced as she imagined the effects. Would the constructs dissolve reefs and other hiding places, leaving the creatures inside exposed to predation? Such was the fate of the weak.

She had long ago cast aside the inherent guilt that came with power. Strength, to anyone with even half a brain, meant responsibility. If one could annihilate evildoers, was it not objectively immoral to not? She'd thought so, once. The first few decades following her awakening, she had worn herself thin doling out justice and righting wrongs.

It had almost killed her. So she had stopped.

Call it selfish. Call it a coping mechanism. Hells, call her a monster. Far worse names had been flung her way over the centuries, more often than not coming from fellow seers. And where were they now? Departed, one and all. Their divine wicks had caught flame, flared bright, then burned away. The kingdom's faithful saw them as martyrs. They'd slurped down the Crown's propaganda like pigs at a trough. Eustace couldn't hate the citizens for believing those lies—who would want to believe the terrible truth that each seer died by their own hand?

She didn't hate the fallen seers either. She respected their choice, even if she didn't understand it. Unlike them, Eustace took a more measured approach. Rather than rail against every perceived injustice, she only eliminated the foulest of offenders. She had preserved her own sanity. If they had all followed her example like Anius, there would still be dozens of seers alive. It broke her heart to think of all the good they could have done over the centuries, if only they had rejected some of the guilt and responsibility.

Realizing that her thoughts were souring the fresh air, Eustace turned to the woman beside her.

Fern was hardly recognizable. Gone were the wounds, tattered clothes, and layers of muck she'd used to hide her identity back within the dry dock, replaced by the simple robe of a seer. She held on to the railing and leaned into the wind, her dark hair swept back to reveal beautiful features enhanced by the telltale flawlessness of a cultivator. Newfound confidence radiated from her, seen in the soft smile gracing her lips, the looseness of her unburdened shoulders, and the genuine enjoyment of life that shone from her core for all to see.

In this woman stood the proof of Eustace's resolve. If the seer had burned herself away like all those fallen comrades, who would have led the charge for little girls to be schooled alongside little boys? Who would have opened up and secured funds for Phostheia's orphanages? And, more importantly, who would have eliminated that disgusting pig of a headmaster who had been content exploiting the capital's most vulnerable?

Without Eustace's denial of responsibility and guilt, there might be no Fern on this voyage. For that, Eustace experienced a rare glimpse of divine euphoria, a genuine smile of her own arriving on her face as she stared out at the ocean they sailed across. She lost herself in that moment, the sun a pleasant counterpoint to the gusts of wind sporadically blowing over the deck.

"Should I be worried?"

The question snapped Eustace out of her reverie. She raised a brow and cracked an eye to peek over at Fern. "Why . . . ?"

"Because you actually looked happy for once. Besides, it's been a good fifteen minutes since you last insulted someone. I was starting to think you'd fallen asleep."

"Perhaps I did. I was dreaming of the most wonderful scene . . ."

"Oh?"

Eustace nodded and let out a satisfied sigh. "Picture this: I've just thrown my toad of a neighbor overboard. He is bobbing along beside the ship, his voice and prodigious size getting farther and farther away by the second. Ahhh, if only it were true."

The only other person near the prow snorted. Anius was fanning himself as he lounged on a certain bench, which had once sat in the shade of a tree but currently sat atop a warship sailing to a far-off continent.

"I'll never forgive you for bringing that along, bastard."

Anius's gaze flicked to Fern. "See how I dominate your master's every thought? I daresay she would be lost without me, a ship with torn sails in the middle of a becalmed sea."

It was closer to the truth than either seer would care to admit. Eustace didn't know if she would have made it through some of the darker times without the genuine spite that had, over time, turned into friendship. They had told each other as much in rare moments of openness, but it had been a long while. Perhaps now was the perfect occasion? She planned on deserting the kingdom at the first opportunity. She might not get another chance . . .

A sudden wave of sadness crashed down upon her. Would he attempt to stop their desertion, or would he watch them go? She hoped he would come, but after his recent actions, she wasn't sure he would risk running.

Before the emotion could overwhelm her, she raised two middle fingers at her old friend and used an almost-extinct language to level an insult so severe, so offensive, that their god-empress might execute Eustace on the spot if only she understood the words.

Sven—who still claimed he was a "honey merchant" and definitely *not* a spy— was the only other person by the prow. Judging by his expression, he understood the sentiment.

Even Anius was taken aback, eyes wide and brows high. Then laughter erupted from his throat, his stomach shaking as he struggled to breathe. "By the divines, Eustace! When was the last time you said something like that to me?"

"Probably back when we actually wished for each other's demise."

"Wait . . ." He leaned forward, face going serious. "You ceased wishing for my death? If I'd known, I would have stopped prodding this sympathetic charm years ago." The bastard produced a small doll resembling her from his robe, then withdrew a needle from its arm and stabbed it back in, watching her as if waiting for a reaction. But he couldn't keep it up for long. His laughter returned just as loud and violent as before.

Eustace shook her head. "How long have you had that prop for?"

"I had it prepared specifically for this trip. I didn't think I'd use it so soon . . ." Suddenly inquisitive, he raised the doll, stared at it, then at her, then at it again. With a thoughtful expression, he lobbed it over the side of the ship, watching her closely. When she didn't also sail over the railing, he threw up his hands and let out an exaggerated sigh. "Guess I'm stuck with you. For now."

Fern's frown had been progressively deepening in confusion, and she finally reached her limit. "You two are . . ."

"Weird?" Eustace asked.

"Attractive?" Anius suggested at the same time, which made Fern's frown turn into a glare.

Eustace patted her apprentice on the shoulder. "I still have many lessons to teach you, so many that you'll likely forget half of them, but *never* forget this one, dear. Seers live long lives. If you wish to keep your sanity, find at least one friend that keeps you on your toes and makes you laugh." She gestured across the deck at her companion of countless years. "I obviously failed to find such a friend, but he was the next best thing." Sadness tugged at her again.

"You can talk, hag," Anius replied, unaware of her conflicted thoughts. "At least you had some choice. I was your subordinate back then, so I *had* to let you stay by my side at first. And later, no matter how many times I cut you off, you just grew right back. Like a recurring wart. Or—"

Golden light shone over everything. Burning agony followed. Someone screamed. Fern. More voices joined in as the rest of the ship's crew were blasted with power they couldn't hope to handle. Anius leaped to his feet, casting aside his visage of indifference. The seers both reached for their essence, and they slammed a divine shield into place.

The reprieve was immediate. The sailors on the main deck gasped in relief, many from the wooden boards they'd collapsed to. Eustace grabbed Fern to stop her from suffering the same fall. Her apprentice's knuckles turned white as she strained to keep hold of the seer's arm, the rest of her skin pink and tender. Anius grabbed Sven and pulled him into the bubble, bolstering the man's comparatively weak level of cultivation. Behind them, veteran mages of the Forty Hands dashed to their surrounding ships, checking on the vessels manned by the newly awakened.

Another pulse of gold came, originating from the galleon and washing over the entire fleet. This time, it was restorative, healing the destruction wrought by their god-empress's lack of control. Fern blinked and stared down at her repaired hands, still shaking all over from the memory of Aletheia's touch.

That momentary exposure must have been torturous, and as Eustace looked toward the leading warship, she felt an old, *old* anger flare to life in her chest. She leaned forward, expression contorting, vision pulsing.

Anius's shielding pressed down on her. "Peace, Eustace," he said, resting a hand on her shoulder. "It is not worth it."

She wanted to spit in his face. Wanted to scratch and flail and escape his grasp. But he was right. She took a slow breath, and he let her go.

"Thank you. Old toad."

"Any time, hag. Shall we go check in with the god-empress?"

Before Eustace could answer, their ruler spoke. "Come."

Eustace gestured for Fern to stay, and both Seers leaped across the divide to find a confusing scene. The moment they landed, they prostrated themselves, emulating the Prime Cadre's submissive posture.

"Stand, seers," God-Empress Aletheia commanded.

They obeyed, bowing at the waist, awaiting further instruction.

"My apologies for the damage done to your apprentice, Eustace. I will compensate her upon returning to the Kingdom of Light."

You can compensate us all by flying into the sun, was what she wanted to say. Instead, she bowed lower. "That is fair of you, God-Empress."

"No." The word slammed down onto Eustace, making her legs shake. "It is *just*. There is a difference. But that is not why I summoned you. Tell me . . . what do you think of this message?"

Eustace looked up, gazing at the artifact in the center of *Theoris*'s deck. She read the words. A chill ran down her entire body. As she read them again, the blood drained from her face. She licked her lips, trying and failing to alleviate their sudden dryness.

Well, those were the reactions she emulated, anyway. Anius did the same. Neither of them would have survived the previous monarchs if they hadn't mastered the control of such things. Internally, she rejoiced, seeing nothing but opportunity in the messages.

She read the words for a third time, and it took everything she had to stop her true feelings from leaking past her careful circulation of essence.

God-King Fischer has marked a Chosen Champion!
Long live Fin, Chosen Champion of Tropica!

CHAPTER THIRTY-EIGHT

Fetch the Pans

The following morning, I seethed. No matter how much I had twisted and turned, or cuddled Maria, or rubbed Borks's fluffy belly, I hadn't been able to get more than an hour's sleep. The tunnels below had been shifting and warping all night, influenced by the third party feeding power—and only the gods knew what else—into them.

So, with the sun shining down overtop the buildings of Tropica, and the flavors of croissant and double-strength coffee lingering on my tongue, I challenged my problems directly. I knocked on the door as hard as I could without breaking it.

"Let me in, you treasonous bastards! If I can't have any rest, neither can you!"

The response I got was unexpected.

"Leave," ordered Fathom. It was more of a suggestion, really, considering how tired the too-many-tentacled prick sounded.

I peered down at the good boy beside me. "Fetch the pans, Borks."

He cocked his head and made a questioning whine. I was forced to pat him behind the ear; he was too cute to resist.

"Yes, I'm sure. Their crimes demand it."

That was all he needed to know. His tongue lolled and tail swished as he tore a portal open and leaped in. He returned carrying two of the biggest bloody cooking pans Tropica had to offer.

"Thank you, Borks. Whosagoodboy? *Whosagoodboy?* You! Yes you are!" When I finished fussing him all over, I picked up the instruments of my vengeance and cleared my throat. "Last chance! Open the door or I'm playing you the song of my people! And in case you were wondering, my people *suck! At! Music!*" The last three words were punctuated with so many clangs of the pans.

Please, Fischer, came Fathom's mental voice. *Now is not the time.*

"Ohhhhh, *now* I get hit with the 'please,' huh? You think I don't know what you've been up to in there? I'm connected to those damn tunnels! What the frack were you even doing to them last night? It felt like you were pouring in pure acid!" No response came, so I yodeled at the top of my lungs, played the pans like they owed me money, and changed tack. "We had a feast last night to celebrate all the breakthroughs! *Everyone* I invited came along, except for all of you! Even Ruby was there, with her newborn! You rude pricks missed—"

The door exploded out as if struck by a freight train, the chunks of wood shattering against me.

"Oh, and now you're *littering*! Great! I'm gonna have to start charging . . . you . . . uhhh . . ." I trailed off, my mind going blank as the splinters cleared and I tried to reconcile the scene before me.

It wasn't a freight train that had struck the door. It was Geraldine. Her cheeks were gaunt, her skin ashen, made all the more noticeable by the panicked look on her face. Usually, seeing her abject fatigue would have immediately drawn all my attention.

But I found my gaze drifting over her shoulder, into the blackened depths of the alchemical workshop. Everyone within squinted against the morning brightness, as shocked to see me as I was to see them. They didn't hold my attention for long, though. The floor in the center of the building was gone, replaced by a swirling, three-meter-wide funnel of abyssal chi. Fathom was slumped against the desks, which had all been pushed to the back of the room. George was beside him, arms extended, holding the vortex open. Cal floated above it, his elemental chi tumbling down into it like a landslide, fueling the tunnels. And the two alchemists, both staring at me with wide eyes, were in the middle of pouring the green contents of a cauldron into the spiraling void.

"I fracking knew it!" I yelled. "You *are* pouring acid in!"

"It's not—" Solomon started, but then George came back to himself.

He dashed for the doorway, bringing a table with him, using it to block both me and the sunlight from peering into the building as he joined us outside. Fathom took control of the void, letting faint echoes of their task pulse over me. I tried to sense it—tried to glean exactly what they were doing, other than adding power—but I was too slow, too tired, and too weak.

"Soooo," I said, looking from George, to his wife, to the table-turned-door. "What you guys doin'?"

"Nothing! Just . . ." George rubbed the dark rings around his eyes. "Just, erm—"

"A surprise!" Geraldine finished, trying to give me a reassuring smile that looked more like a sneer, her eyes squinting against the light of day.

"That so? I *am* pretty surprised, because it looks to me like you're trying to create some kind of portal to the underworld."

Geraldine scrubbed her hands over her face. "I can't believe Ruby had her baby . . ."

George did his best to both reassure his wife and compose himself before turning to me. "Fischer, this really is bad timing. I'm sorry. We have to get back inside. You need to trust us."

"I want to trust you. I really do, but *mate* . . ."

"I know it looks bad, Fischer. Please. There's a reason we can't tell you."

"Bad? It doesn't look bad. It looks *evil*."

"I know. I know. But I can't explain myself."

"Where is the first sister?" I asked. "I felt her in there a couple weeks ago."

George licked his lips. "Are you sure . . . ?"

"Yes, I'm bloody sure, you peanut. Do you think I got her confused with one of the other lava elementals we have?"

He pressed his palms into his eyes. "Fischer, *please*. You *need* to stop asking questions. I am begging you. I cannot stress how important this is."

"Is . . ." Geraldine let out an involuntary whimper. If she weren't so dehydrated, she'd probably be crying. "Is she okay? Is the baby healthy?"

My exhaustion was stopping me from thinking clearly. Assuming my friends weren't being the baddies, I was being rude to Geraldine, if not cruel. I took a deep breath, forced the damn nightmare scene I'd just witnessed from my mind, and gathered my chi. I fired off two mental requests into the village, and with the respective people's consent, I brought them to my side.

"Geraldine," I said, grimacing as my vision pulsed. "Meet Fin. Ruby birthed her, but I named her."

"You did not, Fischer, you lying bast—"

"Not right now, Rubes! Time is of the essence!"

She looked like she was going to retort. Or throw a shoe at my head. Possibly both shoes. Thankfully, Geraldine stumbled forward with tears in her eyes, getting Ruby's attention before I could suffer violence.

I turned to the other person whose consent I'd gotten. "I need you to verify some truths, Theo."

He covered a yawn. "It couldn't wait . . . ?"

"You tell me." I still held my chi, so I sent him to the other side of the table currently serving as a door.

There was a second of silence, followed by a muffled, "By the hounds of Hades!"

"**Leeeeeeave!**" boomed Fathom, pissed enough to find some reserves of energy with which to yell.

I retrieved Theo with a minor flex of will, and I couldn't help but laugh at the look on his face as he reappeared beside me. "Feeling awake yet, mate? Reckon it could have waited?"

"What the *frack* was that?"

"A surprise, apparently."

"I swear," George said, rushing forward and grabbing Theo by the shoulders, "what we are doing is for the good of everyone in Tropica. We have reasons for not telling Fischer. And if we don't get back in there, months of work will all be for naught."

Theo nodded. "All true."

"Okay," I said. "Last question. Was this Ellis's idea?"

"It—we . . . Stop asking questions!"

"That's clearly a yes." I raised a hand before he could reply. "Relax. I won't ask again. Look, seeing as I've already discovered you're up to some bullshit, is it okay if Maria comes and heals you? You look half dead."

"She can't. Her chi . . . Godsdammit this is annoying! I can't tell you, okay, but no. We can't have anyone else—"

A pulse of darkness flew from the workshop, slamming into us with the power of three elementals and whatever concoction the two alchemists were pouring into the tunnel-lookin' thing. George's and Geraldine's eyes flew wide with panic.

"Go on." I shooed them away with one of my giant pans. "Get back in there, you scoundrels."

George didn't even say a word. He just sprinted for the building.

Geraldine, at least, had some manners. "Nice to meet you, Fin. And congratulations again, Ruby. She's adorable!" She passed the infant back and followed George, who closed the door behind her. Well, it was a table, but that felt unimportant compared to everything else going on with the workshop.

"And thank you, Fischer!" came Geraldine's muffled yell.

"You're welcome, but don't think this is over!" I called. "You all owe me a full explanation when you finish . . . whatever the hell you're doing!" I blew air from my lips. "And you. What do you have to say for yourself?"

Theo frowned at my question. "Uhhh, nothing?"

"Really? Because I'm pretty sure you used Borks as a swear word earlier. By the hounds of Hades? Look at him—he's distraught."

Borks, ever happy to be included, wagged his tail vigorously as he stared up at us.

"Sorry, Borks. I didn't mean it." Theo bent to scratch his head but ended up rubbing him all over, unable to resist.

"Looks like he forgives you," said a feminine voice.

Theo started, looking around the empty street before his eyes landed on me. "Did you just hear Maria?"

"Maria . . . ?" I scanned our surroundings. "Are you feeling okay, mate?"

"Maybe not. I could have sworn I just— *What the!*"

Tropica's newest broken-through cultivator released his ability, making himself, Maria, Barry, and three children appear on the street.

"Did you just . . ." Theo frowned at them, then turned toward Dodge. "You can make *everyone* invisible?"

The man grinned, one hand resting on Theresa's and Toby's heads. "It's not so much going invisible as it is making your vision slide right over me. I didn't know I could extend it either, but my little tacticians thought of it."

"So?" I asked. "Do you forgive me yet?"

"Hmmm." Barry rubbed his stupidly muscular chin. "I don't know . . ."

"Oh, c'mon! I could have just come here by myself. Tell me that wasn't fun to watch?"

"Okay, it *was* fun, but any goodwill was mostly undone when I saw . . . whatever they're doing in there."

"Seriously." Maria glanced at the door. Er, table. "What *are* they doing?"

"Other than feeding power into the tunnel? No clue. I'm even more confused than before." I sighed. "And I still haven't earned the forgiveness of two of my homies? This was a *disaster*."

Barry narrowed his eyes at me. "If that's the case . . . why are you grinning like that?"

"I don't think I am."

"Yes you are. And now you're waggling your eyebrows."

"Am not."

"You know, Barry," Maria said, "I think you're onto something. They do appear to be waggling."

"Okay, okay. You got me." I grinned even wider as I raised the two massive pans I still held. "I knew you'd play hard to get, Barry. There's another way I can earn your forgiveness, and after this, there's no way you can still resent me." I gestured for everyone to come closer. "Bring it in, especially my three brilliant, well-rested tacticians. Here's the plan . . ."

CHAPTER THIRTY-NINE

Clang!

Corporal Claws—sharp of tooth, capable of violence, humble of heart—truly was a once-in-a-millennium talent. She took a deep breath of the forest air, so overwhelmed by her innumerable successes that a tear of lightning rolled down one furry cheek.

As she exhaled, she opened her eyes and gazed at the creation she'd nestled in this clearing. Bricks of clay, perfectly spaced. Mortar made of volcanic stone, covering the inside wall and impervious to heat. A tall metal chimney, requisitioned from the coffee roaster, that she would return when she was done here. Probably. All in all, the miniature forge appeared expertly built.

She chuckled to herself. Her master liked keeping her in the dark, did he? Two could play that game. She knew he was hiding something. Something important. Fischer thought he was sooo clever, withholding such electable secrets.

"Delectable, mistress," chittered RPM, one larcenous little paw drifting up to steal her electric teardrop. "Is what you meant to—"

Claws yanked him from her pocket and flung him forward. "Make yourself useful, cretin!"

He giggled, curled into a ball, and readily accepted the trajectory she had set him upon. His spherical form rocketed into the open mouth of the forge, where he became a blur. He rolled around within at blistering speed. The entire structure glowed with their combined power. The blue of his lightning body leaked into the outside world as he got even quicker, the nexus of the brick shining so bright it eclipsed the sun's brilliance. The sound, too, was all-encompassing, her familiar's soft "*EEEeeeEEEeeeEEEeeeEEEeee*" mixing with the loud hum of their elemental power.

But now wasn't the time to consider such things. Something was forming within the electrified furnace. She slipped forward and stared into it, having to squint against the heat and potency radiating out. This abnormality, this source of mysterious power, was entirely unexpected. They'd only sought to create an area of high temperature, but for such an aberration to appear . . .

Claws flashed a vicious smile. It might be just what they needed.

She reached into her pocket, her digits closing around an object smooth and somehow cold. In a single blur of movement, she cast it into the forge—and almost immediately regretted doing so. The two powers collided, the light flickering like 10,000 candles as the forces clashed.

The chain of tiny explosions was so potent that she initially assumed RPM had done something shifty in a misguided attempt to steal the chunk of lightning-infused fulgurite. But with every incremental clash of essence, she sensed the raccoon's growing fear. Each burst was more unstable. Harder and harder to comprehend. They should stop the experiment here and now—only a fool would tussle with two mysterious powers at once.

She locked eyes with RPM on one of his rotations past the furnace's glowing maw. His pupils shone with more panic and power than she'd ever seen. There was no time to exchange mental words, yet the terror plastered across his face was communication enough; he recognized the madness of wrestling two incomprehensible concepts at the same time.

She reached out with all the essence she had, just as she'd done so many times before when calling RPM back into her abdomen. His eyes flashed with relief. Claws winked. His brow creased in confusion, then rose in realization. She yanked herself forward and leaped into the furnace, a grinning cannonball of chaos and schadenfreude.

They bounced across the internal wall like shellfish over slick rocks. Whenever they strayed too close to the exit, the clashing powers drew them in with a gravitational pull that affected their very souls.

RPM's acceptance came hard and fast. As strong as his horror was at being forced onto the battlefield of two unknown powers, his curiosity swept it aside with ease, followed soon after by the same elation radiating throughout Corporal Claws.

Soft chitters of laughter built within their chests, then tumbled out like a stack of opalescent rocks piled a little too high. They must have sounded absolutely unhinged if anyone was nearby—it certainly sounded so from within—but neither of them cared nor extinguished their formidable mirth.

RPM was the first to act. Once more rolling around the chamber in chaotic yet graceful arcs, he reached out with his will and stole what waves of force he could handle. Despite his larcenistic capabilities, most evaded his call, instead choosing to fight the other mysterious force. The fulgurite was particularly resistant, so he sent Claws a silent question, seeking her permission to focus on the energy of the furnace.

RPM had . . . sought permission? Claws had to stop a tear of lightning from forming in her eye, lest her familiar get distracted when he inevitably tried to steal it. She tucked herself into a ball, did her best to emulate the raccoon's masterful movement, and let out an affirmative chirp.

The moment RPM focused on absorbing only the forge's waves of power, things changed dramatically. Where before they were opposing forces, like two colorful fish fighting over a single anemone, now the forge fell into line, occupying the spaces between the fulgurite's pulses of power. So, too, did Claws and RPM coexist, both intersecting each other's paths without colliding.

Corporal Claws pounced, sinking into herself and pouring her will out. It slammed into the branch of fulgurite, whose form was starting to glow under the intense heat, its previously dormant tongues of electricity dancing like hungry flames. With a grin, she obliged. Her intention struck like a hammer, seeking to feed them. They rebuffed her with such admonishment that she almost faltered.

The rejection felt physical, and she barely stopped herself from hitting her familiar when next their paths crossed. Worse, the feeling lingered, a sense of pointlessness suffusing her. Why had it hit so viscerally?

With her enhanced awareness, and using her curiosity as fuel, she assessed her emotional state. She had given her own mind and purpose much thought over the past months. She'd exaggerated her chaotic nature in the weeks leading up to the arrival of Fathom and Cal, intent on making Fischer believe she was capable of hurting others if that was what her identity as an aspect of chaos demanded. It was an easy lie because it was so close to the truth.

Given other circumstances, it was precisely who she might have been. Her relationship with Fischer had led to her forming bonds with others. Humans and animals both lived in harmony where possible, but the slightest deviation could lead to despair. And it was made worse when either awakened. With knowledge and power came responsibility. Had she never interacted so closely with such a variety of sapient beings, perhaps she would be content with enacting chaos on whomever or whatever she could.

But she could never be that otter. Not now. Though her nature yearned for it, she refused to willingly hurt others. Greatly, anyway. She'd never stop leaving sand in Barry's belongings. Even thinking of the pranks he'd yet to find brought her great joy. Like the clump of manure she had hidden beneath the ointment he liked to moisturize his face with.

Claws shook her head. Now wasn't the time.

She had a nature demanding chaos, but her relationships stopped her from indulging in it. This internal conflict, if left untended, would surely cause problems down the line. Which was exactly why this creation was so pivotal. The ability to make items from artifacts that shouldn't exist . . . it would scratch the chaotic itch in the depths of her soul. Even one weapon would be a source of infinite mayhem, and unlike her usual pranks, they could be used as a force for good in service of Tropica.

Claws scoffed at herself. No wonder the fulgurite's refusal had hurt her otherwise unflappable sensibilities. It was a rejection of not only her, but her purpose, too. She wanted this to work. *Needed* this fulgurite to accede to her demands. She gritted her teeth, closed her eyes, and allowed herself a small smile.

Rebuff her attempts at creation, would it? Let it try denying the full weight of her desires.

She gathered them deep within, envisioning the future she craved and letting it swirl around her abdomen. It flowed in an infinite loop, growing wider, gathering more potential with every lap of her mind and body. The fulgurite must have felt the impending strike—it, too, collected its essence. The pulses of chi coming from it got stronger.

The harmony between the two mysterious powers started to fall apart. RPM's devious little forepaws lashed out, physically grasping the excess waves. He failed at first. But that only further ignited his ideal. Lightning fast, he pulled them into himself and contained them with his will before they could escape.

Claws wanted to grab the tricksy bastard by the cheeks and kiss him—platonically and consensually—right on the mouth. But she had her own role to play.

RPM's "*EEEeeeEEEeeeEEEeeeEEEeee*" came even faster now, his body forming circular lines of light. Claws moved just as swiftly, the river of intent flowing around and around her core, sending her rocketing forward.

In her mind's eye, another hammer formed, just as strong as the one she'd struck with earlier. Another appeared at its side. And two more beside them. On and on, they stretched, an armory's worth of blunt-force weapons forming a great circle around the fulgurite. The handles grew longer, allowing more leverage.

As one, they descended.

The first was denied, as were the second and third. The fourth and fifth bounced off, too, but only after landing glancing blows. The tenth—or perhaps it was the eleventh—landed true, the natural artifact overwhelmed by the flurry. And the rest, hundreds upon hundreds of sledgehammers, all struck with terrible accuracy, reshaping the fulgurite in the image of her will. Sparks flew. The sound was deafening. Heat greater than an active volcano came from the forge.

Claws relented not. The first hammer swung down again, as did all those that followed. She'd envisioned a certain shape, but as the forge's light shone over her creation's imperfect faces, she was struck by their beauty, altering her design on the fly. Rather than smooth and uniform, she let the hammer strikes leave facets in their wake.

When the object started to blur, her stomach sank, then was driven lower by the fear of failure. But then she realized what was happening. The System. It had come to aid its transformation. Just as she'd heard and felt her master do so many times before, Claws imagined the outcome she desired, imperfections and all.

The universe obeyed. All at once, the blurry outline snapped into place, gleaming, brilliant, perfect despite its "flaws." RPM came to a stop beside her in the bottom of the forge, and they stared at the weapon together. So immense was RPM's awe that he didn't try to steal it. Not immediately, anyway. He did attempt to yoink it a moment later, but Claws easily held him at bay with one paw.

She clutched her creation and slunk out into the clearing with great care, her body shivering from overexertion and disbelief. She lifted the physical manifestation of her chaotic nature high. Sunlight filtered down through the canopy, and as it reflected off the blade's multifaceted surface, it finally hit her. She had succeeded. Claws, a mere elemental, had used a resource that shouldn't be to create something impossible, all without anyone discover—

She sensed a fluctuation in the nearby chi.

Claws cast about, scanning the trees in search of interlopers. When she found none, she extended her already fatigued will. Who dared sneak up on the queen of trickery? Still she found no one. She must have imagined it. Suddenly, the laughter came. It burst from her throat in breathless chitters. RPM joined in, and together they let the sounds of their complete victory roll out. Her familiar tried to steal the weapon one more time but gave up when she threatened to stab him with it.

All the while, the System had tugged at her mind, demanding she inspect the newly formed item. Claws took a deep breath. The air smelled sweeter, and unlike before, it wasn't just her imagination.

Still grinning, she finally gave in, letting her eyes drift up toward—

Clanggg!

CHAPTER FORTY

Betrayer

I winced at the sound of two gigantic pans colliding. Barry had clanged them with such vigor that they'd flattened against one another and now looked more like abstract art than functional cookware. Claws wobbled on the spot, her upright-yet-catatonic state starkly contrasted by Barry's booming laughter.

Her furry familiar chose that moment to strike. RPM recovered from his dazedness by . . . stealing it from himself? It didn't make sense, but when did he ever? He rocketed forward, eyes twinkling, grin malicious. I could have easily stopped him, but I found myself entirely distracted by the item his dexterous digits were even now reaching for.

The gleaming weapon drew my vision in.

Multifaceted Dagger of the Maker's Apprentice
[Protection overridden—Maker detected]
Rarity: Artifact
Description: This dagger was created by a Maker's apprentice, whose chaotic nature echoes within the blade. Chi channeled through it will be concentrated, amplified, and have a moderate chance of striking a random enemy.
Effects: 100% concentration, +20% amplification, 25% random enemy targeting.
Duration: null

I understood the words, but the full depth of their meaning was yet to hit me. I scarcely had the chance to wonder what the distinction between "concentration" and "amplification" was before RPM reached his target. With speed only possible due to his nature and ideal, he swiped the dagger right out of his master's paws and released a villainous little squeal as he turned for the tree line.

Before RPM got there, Barry slapped Dodge on the shoulder, flinging him forward. Dodge slid across the grass, his feet somehow dodging friction. He easily outpaced the lightning-fueled raccoon. Rather than collecting RPM by the scruff, he grabbed the blade of the dagger in the raccoon's closed fist and yanked it away.

Sans prize, RPM whirled, body aglow with anger as electricity shot from him, changing his trajectory. The momentary delay had allowed another to recover from her shock. Corporal Claws head-butted him with everything she had. His elemental body lost its form for a fraction of a second as it wrapped around her noggin, then he rocketed away, somehow flickering through trunks and branches rather than obliterating them.

Claws turned to glare at me, her fury seeking a new outlet now that she'd already hit her familiar hard enough to defy physics. Chi arced from her eyes as she took a step forward. Another step, her face contorting into a snarl. All at once, her anger disappeared.

"Master!" cried Claws, zapping into my arms and staring up at me with a quivering lower lip. "*How could you conspire against me?*"

"Don't give me that." I reached out to scratch behind her ear. She retreated from it, but only for a moment. My fingers soon found their mark on her fuzzy neck. "This was fair game after the sheer amount of pranks you've subjected Barry to."

She leaned back to meet my eyes again, some of the heat returning to her gaze. "Really? This was for Barry's sake? You didn't rob me of my satisfaction in exchange for winning his forgiveness?"

"Oh, I absolutely did, but only because I know you love a well-executed ruse. Even if you're on the receiving end of it."

She gave a haughty sniff, crossed her arms, and twisted away from me—but not enough to stop the slow scritching I was still delivering to the back of her head.

"I'm sorry if it went too far. We might have gotten a bit carried away once the kids got involved—they helped us pick the perfect moment for maximum impact. But that just shows your genius, Claws." I stroked from the top of her head to the base of her tail. "It took an entire party of cultivators to sneak up on you. Even then, it wouldn't have been possible without Dodge's new ability."

Mentioning the man made Claws's predatory stare flick over toward him. Knowing better than to antagonize her any further, he offered the multifaceted dagger on his open palm. She snatched it, retreated to the top of the closest tree, and cast one more warning glare everyone's way before looking directly at her creation.

Her eyes went distant, and I fought to suppress my smile. Because of its rarity, the System would give her a redacted version of its description. Only my status as a Maker allowed a complete inspection of its stats. The seconds stretched. I blinked and cocked my head. What was taking so long?

Power pulsed high above, then echoed within Claws. Realization had only just started worming its way into my consciousness when the words arrived in my field of view.

An apprentice Maker has risen!
Hail Corporal Claws, apprentice of God-King Fischer, Maker of Kallis!

Banishing the notification, I stared up at Claws; she stared back.

The message was almost identical to the private one I'd received from the System upon my ascension as a Maker. Based on the others' reactions, only she and I had seen it. Even Maria had been left out, the System doing something to suppress our connection.

Confusion swam across all present, but its currents were strongest in Claws, threatening to overwhelm her fatigued mind. Her bewilderment was suddenly swept aside by the return of fury.

"Betrayer!" she screeched down at me, her dagger leveled in accusation.

I raised my hands in supplication, my diminished chi failing to untangle what aggrieved her so. "I'm sorry I snuck up on you, Claws. I really thought you would appreciate a good . . . Why are you frowning?"

"I don't care about that! Stop trying to change the subject!"

It was my turn to be confused. "Uhhhh. I'm not. I don't—"

"Master is cruel!" interrupted Claws. "Master is selfish!" She suddenly sagged and folded backwards, her spine draped over the trunk with the dramatic flair only an elemental otter can wield. "He understands me not."

I blinked as my chi obeyed my command and I tried to read her aura, but she'd shut me out completely. She started muttering. All I caught was: "dagger," "description," and a string of hissed expletives.

Realization struck me. "Oh! I inspected it before you!"

"So you *do* know what you did!" Her fury returned, re-inflating her body. She leaped to her feet and leveled the dagger at me once more, chi roiling. It danced through her, arcing across her limbs, and . . . *down into the dagger?* Its faceted blade shone with the blue-white brilliance of her element, begging to be released.

"I'm sorry, okay? It was instinctive. I didn't mean to. It just sorta happened."

My apology made some of the fury leave her. Or at least I thought it did, but then she poured more chi into the weapon, a devious smirk forming on her face.

"Uhhhhh, Claws?"

"Master is cruel," whispered Claws. The shining dagger illuminated her face from below, making her look even more malevolent than usual. "Master deserves *punishment.*"

I gathered the essence I still held. "Punishment, sure, but that's starting to feel a little deadly. I don't have all that much power to defend myself with. Why don't you put it down so we can talk—"

An inhuman scream tore through my awareness. Like a banshee's wail, the high-pitched screech was filled with hatred. It seeped into my body, etched itself into my bones, threatened to boil my marrow with each second the howl dragged on.

When it abruptly ended, I gasped for breath. Claws's dagger thudded against the forest floor. Nobody said a word. The scream had come from the far edge of my Domain. It'd been unleashed by a divine being, and they sought the destruction of any who would stand in its way.

They were coming to Tropica.

They were coming for *us.*

CHAPTER FORTY-ONE

Thoughts and Prayers

Eustace hit *Theoris*'s mast at terrible speed. She had accepted her death the moment she'd launched the attack. To strike out at a fledgling deity could bear no other outcome. Despite her acceptance—and that her foolish action had stopped her apprentice from being burned alive by the sonic waves of the god-empress's wail—she couldn't help but despair at her life coming to an end when she was so close to earning her freedom.

The pain was excruciating. Her lower body was blessedly numb, but her shoulders and spine felt like they'd been shattered. They probably had been. If she'd hit the mast of a normal ship, it would have exploded under such a forceful blow.

There's something to look forward to, at least. The anguish will soon vanish . . .

When it didn't, she blinked, her vision slowly returning. A dreadful sight greeted her: the underside of Anius's jowls. He was holding her upright. He had saved her. Cushioned the impact with his power. It was the only explanation.

"You look . . ." The wet wheezing of her lungs confirmed just how much damage she'd sustained. "Terrible from this angle."

Her old friend ignored her. "I beg your forgiveness, God-Empress! Seer Eustace had no other option!"

"Explain!" A wave of authority came with the command. It would have scoured Eustace's skin, perhaps even killed her, if not for Anius's divine shield. Panicked, she reached for her essence. Fern was unprotected. But no matter the weight of Eustace's resolve, her body was too damaged, her spirit too broken.

Anius held her down. Though he averted his gaze, he remained facing their leader. "Your power is too great, God-Empress. If Seer Eustace had not interrupted your war cry, the unascended crew would have been annihilated. The only reason those aboard the sister galleon *Elegos* survived is because of the Prime Cadre's swift intervention."

Eustace probably should have felt relief at learning Fern was shielded. All she felt was pain.

Their holy leader's face remained a mask of indifference.

"Even Sven would have passed, Your Holiness, and I know how important he is to you . . ."

That brought a flicker of the old Aletheia to the god-empress's face, but it was replaced by fury a moment later, as if that glimpse of humanity shamed her. "Weakness should be burned away, should it not, Seer?"

He faltered for a fraction of a second, then changed course. "Yes, God-Empress, but we believe our enemies have embraced the abyssal. The death of a divine cultivator might have alerted them of our approach."

"I see." With the casual flick of the god-empress's wrist, a giant cone of divine energy blasted across both wings of the fleet. It healed Eustace's spine. Awareness of her broken lower body roared into her mind, and then the agony vanished altogether. She and the rest of Phostheia's forces were healed so aggressively that the Prime Cadre tried to shield against it, assuming the wave to be another attack. The golden light evaporated their attempted protection like thin fog under a rising sun.

"I apologize, everyone. I will compensate you upon our victorious return to Phostheia." That was it. That was all their magnanimous leader had to say, her uncaring mask firmly back in place.

Eustace would have liked to claim she had to fight down her fury. Would have taken great pride in needing to beat down raging columns of indignant light with her soul. But all she felt was joy and relief that her pain had been lifted from her.

The anger didn't arrive until she landed back on *Elegos's* deck, having lingered only long enough on *Theoris* to see the message that'd triggered Aletheia's outburst—another Maker had arrived, an apprentice with the dread-inducing moniker of "Corporal Claws." That, too, should have been a cause for celebration, but now that she saw the fear and numbness lingering on Fern's face, all Eustace cared about was comforting the woman. She marched toward her. She had brought Fern on this trip. This was all her fault—

A firm hand gripped her shoulder, stopping her in her tracks. She turned to find Anius glaring. "You should have tried a less-direct method of interrupting our god-empress, Eustace." His expression grew severe, the lines of his face sharpening. "I only just saved you in time. Next time, I might not get there."

The words were carefully selected. Their insane leader wouldn't understand the true meaning. Eustace, however, grasped the subtext. He would not intervene on her behalf again.

"Understood, Anius." She slipped on an indifferent mask of her own. "I'm sorry you had to save me. I felt compelled to action by our shared purpose. Do not worry yourself—I won't expect you to step in again."

A part of her had hoped he'd join her and Fern when they fled. She now understood how foolish that was. He would never risk himself. Only one question remained: would he stop her, or would he let them slip away?

She turned away and faced the mages of the Prime Cadre. "Thank you for protecting the unawakened. Their lives matter to Her Holiness."

Evan nodded, doing his best to emulate Aletheia's stoicism, then leaped back toward *Theoris.* The other four followed him.

Eustace focused on Fern, whose expression remained fearful. She hated seeing her apprentice—this proud and strong woman—wracked by such emotion. Like a puppy kicked by its owner, Fern had just learned the brutal truth of pain's effectiveness at guiding behavior. Hardly surprising, considering part of her skin and most of her hair had been burned away by a temper tantrum.

"Come, child," Eustace said, holding out a hand. "Let us find some privacy. We must get you new robes and even out your hair, lest your appearance impugn the kingdom's presence."

Fern accepted the offered hand. Anger flashed in her eyes, and before it could leak out, she circulated chi the way Eustace had taught. Good. She hadn't forgotten her true enemy.

Eustace led her down to the lower decks, hoping—praying—that someone in Tropica had heard the god-empress's scream.

CHAPTER FORTY-TWO

Circulation

Of course we fracking heard that." Sharon looked at me like I'd just asked if water was wet. "That scream sounded like Hades's own hounds were howling in my . . . *Oh*. Sorry, Borks. I didn't mean—"

He cut her off with a loud bark, his entire back half wagging.

The rest of Tropica were arrayed before me. All had gathered in the amphitheater at record speed, and they'd nodded along with Sharon's words. Borks's joy at being included usually would have brought me endless joy. Today, I felt nothing. My core was simmering, at the very brink of boiling over. If not for how close it was to being completed, I would have severed my connection to the network the instant that strange wail had afflicted everyone bearing even a drop of essence. That made me think of our youngest cultivator.

"Is Fin okay, Ruby?" I asked, gathering my chi in case she wasn't. "The scream didn't hurt her?"

"She's totally fine." Ruby smiled down at her daughter, who wore an expression of supreme concentration as she reached for a wooden-bead necklace that dangled from her mother's neck. "She had a moment's fright but returned to her happy self immediately after."

"Her eyes did glow white for a bit, though," Steven added.

"They *what?*" I asked.

Ruby just shrugged. "Probably something to do with the mark you put on her. Nothing to worry about."

"Rubes . . ." I paused to consider my words. "I don't wanna tell you how to parent, but I feel like you should be *at least* ten percent less chill. Even I'm freaked out, and I'm the one who put the mark there. Glowing eyes? How glowing are we talking . . . ?"

The corner of Steven's mouth formed a line, and I thought I might have broken through to them. Ruby just gave me a reassuring smile. "We're connected, Fischer."

"Yeah, I know. I can feel the tendril of chi between you. It makes me nervous."

"Yeah, well, it shouldn't. Everything is okay. I'm sure of it. She is happy and healthy and *adorable*." Ruby beamed as Fin caught the necklace, shoved the beads into her mouth, and started gumming them ferociously. Ruby hugged her daughter tight.

"A mother knows best, Fischer," Sharon said, nodding to herself as if that explained everything.

I could feel skepticism trying to cross my face, but I kept it at bay. Some of my roiling core was spilling over, coloring my emotions. I had to trust in Ruby. Besides, there was no way to counter Sharon's claim without pissing off at least a third of the gathering. If an attack was coming, I needed morale to be high.

I gazed at the crowd lining the amphitheater's tiered seating. Despite the objectively cute mauling of wooden jewelry happening before their eyes, a trepidatious murmur came from Tropica's citizens. Even without those worried conversations, I could see their anxiety reflected in their shuffling feet, creased brows, and hunched backs.

I wanted to assuage their concerns, but I had to assuage mine first. I closed my eyes and sent a tendril of essence out toward the east. It was something I had been practicing over the past month, knowing such an event might take place. I closed my eyes and clenched my fists, using everything I had to extend the finger-wide rope farther and farther out to sea. My head started to ache. The muscles in my neck grew tense. When I could go no more, I reached for my fourth partition—the only one currently unused—and used it to send soft pulses from the end of my tendril.

At least one of the three idiots I was calling for sensed my broadcast, because he latched on to the thick rope of chi and bent it to his will, his power solidifying the foundation I'd laid.

"Hello, Fischer," Roger said, his voice broadcasting from my chest for all to hear. His speech had steadied. He sounded a little more . . .

I sighed. He sounded cooler than before. More sure of himself. *Damn that island.*

"Hi, Roger. Are you okay? Want us to come get you?"

"No. We are fine, but your concern is appreciated. I assume you heard that scream?"

My eyebrow twitched at his eloquence.

"Nahhhh," I drawled. "I'm just reaching out for shits and giggles. Definitely didn't hear any screeches sounding like they came from the ill-fated pairing of a kaiju and an eldritch horror."

"That . . ." A spike of irritation came along my temporary connection. "Do you understand the threat? Now is *not* the time for jokes, you foolish, fish-headed son of a dehorned goat—" He cut himself off with a grunt then hissed out a breath. "I apologize. I was slightly overwhelmed by your sarcasm, Fischer, and someone on my side is pestering me. One moment. Ellis needs to say something."

"Hello, God-King!" came the archivist's cheery voice. "Just warning you that I'm about to take some of your power, okay?"

"Uhhh, I don't know what kind of holiday you've been having mate, but I'm still powering the network below. It's almost done, but until it is, I don't really have power to spa—" I cut off as most of the chi I'd flooded into the tendril was ripped away, suddenly used by Ellis to facilitate gods knew what. Everything went fuzzy. It felt like a small crab had materialized in the middle of my brain and was now snipping out in the general direction of my prefrontal cortex. Maria's healing essence splashed over me, fighting back the imaginary crustacean.

"Can you still hear me, Fischer?" Roger's voice sounded quiet now. It slowly grew louder as my senses returned. "Is my voice still being broadcast?"

"Yeah, mate." I pinched my nose, barely remaining upright. "We can hear you. What's up?"

"Is Sharon there? Can *she* hear my wo—"

"I'm here!" His wife leaped from the seats and onto the stage. She grabbed my shoulders, staring at the spot on my chest his voice was coming from. "It's so good to hear you! How is everything going? I've missed you!"

He paused for a moment that was, in my estimate, roughly the time it took to take a hit from a wooden pipe. His tone was sonorous when he continued. "My dear, my only, I miss you like the grass beneath an eternal night misses the sun. I yearn for you more with each minute we spend apart. And though my training must continue for now, know that I dream of your touch." He sighed longingly. "There are flowers local to this small island that mere words cannot describe. Their beauty and fragrance are stunning, unmatched by any other, yet even their distinctive allure is nothing before the memory of you." A long pause. "I will return soon, my love. Wait for me."

"And Fischer . . ." he continued. "Keep my girls safe."

With that, he let go of my chi, leaving us in silence.

Sharon's face had gotten redder by the second. She remembered herself suddenly, eyes going wide. "S-sorry!" She withdrew from me like I'd burned her, and instead of running out of the meeting, she leaped clean over the eastern wall of the amphitheater, every inch of her skin flushing crimson under the morning sun.

I shared a look with Maria. Her face was similarly colored by embarrassment. Hushed conversation and pockets of laughter came from the crowd, who all welcomed the distraction from their worried thoughts. I leaned into the absurdity, hoping it would do the same for me.

Any hope of that was smothered when a vessel sailed into view high above the eastern horizon.

"He didn't . . ." I said.

Maria's forehead furrowed, her gaze drifting up to scan the clouds. When she spotted the vessel rocketing through them, she half cackled, half choked. It was Bob. Bob the boat. Trapped within a bubble of stolen chi, his sails were completely still. And right behind him, pressed to the wall of that same shielding, were a bearded thief and his carapaced co-conspirator.

Noises of shock or amusement or both came from the crowd when they spotted them. I rubbed the bridge of my nose. "Pelly, Bill, would you and the squad mind intervening? If I use my power to stop him, the strain might knock me out."

They honked their assent, and a loud peep came from the masses as Cinnamon rocketed up and latched on to her adopted daughter. The pelicans took flight. Barely a minute later—after an excessive expenditure of wind chi and a few well-placed martial strikes—Bob the boat was lowered to the stage. Despite his time at sea, his hull was spotless. Unfortunately, so was his thief.

"Hello, everyone." Ellis leaped down to the stage, shirt unbuttoned, tanned torso glistening in the sun. "So lovely to see you all. How have you been? Actually, don't answer that. Forgive my brusqueness. I have much to reveal and even more to do. You heard the scream. So did we. It—"

"Ellis," I interrupted. I'd gathered my chi, and I used it to appear between him and everyone. "I'm glad you're chill, but I'm not." I pointed toward the east. "Don't beat around the bush—is this the threat you were talking about?"

He thought for a moment, his eyes going distant as he rubbed his beard.

"Mate, you gotta give me something here. If you don't tell me, I'm gonna cut myself off from the network right now, consequences be damned. I can't have them arriving and laying waste to Tropica in the seconds it takes my chi to obey."

His eyes snapped back to mine. Was I imagining the slight smile that crossed his face? "Very well," he said. "No. They are not the impending threat I spoke of before leaving."

I exhaled as an immense weight fell from my shoulders. "Okay. That's good news. Who are they?"

"I cannot say." His lip tugged up again. I wasn't imagining it.

Fury roiled through me, and I grabbed him by each unbuttoned half of his shirt. "Now is *not* the time. Stop fracking around, Ellis."

He tried to smooth his features, but whispers of his amusement remained. "And what will you do if I do not tell you?"

I clenched my fists.

"Ellis!" Maria said. "Stop being such a dick!"

A black crab covered in red lines scuttled down from Bob's deck. Rocky took a drag of his cigarette, gave me a respectful nod, and leaped to crack Ellis softly on the noggin with a mighty claw. He landed on the stage. "What would our teachers say?" hissed the explosive crab.

Ellis grimaced. "You know my smile was not at their expense!"

Another hiss. "They do not."

Ellis refocused on me, rubbing the back of his head. "My question is sincere, Fischer. What will you do if I cannot tell you?"

"That's easy. I'll sever my connection to the network so I can scout our enemies myself."

Ellis didn't smile again, but I could tell he wanted to. He gave me a measured nod. "I believe it is a foreign kingdom. As I am sure everyone sensed, the leader wields divine chi. It is likely they all do."

"They come via ship?"

"Yes."

"How many?" I asked.

"I cannot say." I tightened my grip on his shirt, and he gave me a flat stare. "I do not know, Fischer. At least one."

"How long until they arrive?"

"At their current speed, I estimate they will arrive in a week."

"And what if they double their speed? What if they teleport the rest of the way here? Why shouldn't I stop filling the tunnels now? It's still gonna take me and your squad of goons in the alchemical workshop a few days to finish filling the network."

His head rocked back. "When did you learn they were helping . . . ?"

"When they started pouring concoctions into it. Don't change the subject."

He stroked the ends of his beard. "It is a risk to share, but if you will sever your connection unless I tell you . . ."

"I will."

Again, I got the sense he was suppressing a smile. "You need not worry about an early arrival. If it would take a few days for you and your helpers to finish, the enemy might get here before its completion. It will not take a few days. Your estimate is . . . misguided."

"Is he telling the truth, Theo?"

"Yuuuup!" he called.

I sighed, the surface of my core finally calming enough for me to let go of Ellis. I took a step back. "How long exactly will it take to finish?"

"Now that, I cannot tell you, no matter what you threaten. I apologize, Fische—" A faint wave of abyssal chi pulsed over us. Even to my muted senses, it was unmissable, holding a sense of urgency.

Ellis smoothed his shirt and leaped from the stage. He landed on the stairs and marched for the exit. "I am needed elsewhere." He glanced back, but his legs kept moving. "We can speak again soon."

I looked from him to Bob the boat and back again. My core might have calmed, but I still wanted to throw a crab at Ellis's head. The only nearby crab was Rocky, though, and he'd done nothing to deserve a good yeeting. I felt words swelling in my chest, a combination of syllables and vowels and consonants to inflict maximum emotional turmoil on the annoying archivist. I bit them back. Now wasn't the time for pettiness.

But then Ellis paused on the top step. His beard swayed in the breeze as he turned back, met my eyes, and gave me a broad grin. He winked.

My petty words came flying out. "Do you know what a Maker is, Ellis?"

His entire body went rigid, one leg freezing as he turned to leave. He whirled around with none of the careful control he'd possessed a moment ago. "How do you know that title, Fischer?"

"How do you think?"

"Are—are you claiming to have become a Maker?"

"Yep. Shame you don't have more time to stay and talk about it."

He gave a shrug that was a little too stiff. "You becoming a Maker changes nothing. I—"

"Lie," Theo interrupted, beaming at Ellis before shooting me a wink.

The archivist gave Theo a warning glare, then resumed his departure, his emotional state sealed off so I couldn't assess it.

"Let me know when you're free, mate! Claws and I are terribly curious to hear more about it!"

He froze again. "Claws . . . ? You *and* Claws?"

"That's right. She became a Maker, too."

"You lie . . ." His eyes glittered hungrily in spite of the accusation.

"You think I would tell you porkies? I'm offended, mate. She awakened after turning a natural artifact into a dagger."

Ellis snorted and crossed his arms. "Now I know you're lying. That's impossible, even for *you* . . ." He trailed off as Claws stood atop Fergus's head and channeled her chi. Up it jolted. Through her body, along her fur, and directly into the silvery dagger held between her needle-sharp teeth. Its blade shone with blue-white brilliance as echoes of its nature flew out into the amphitheater.

"Huh," Theo said, glancing between me, Claws, and her weapon. "*Truth.*"

Ellis fell to his knees. His arms hung motionless at his side as he stared wide-eyed at my wonderfully devious otter. She spat the dagger out, shoved it into her pocket, and gave Ellis a two-digit salute before slinking down from Fergus's head and retreating into the crowd.

"W-w-wait!" He shot to his feet. "I can delay a short while! Please, Claws! If I could just see that dagger for a second, I can properly advise you!"

"What's the matter, mate? You don't like it when people withhold information?"

His eyes were desperate when they met mine. "Fischer . . . *please.* I have good reason for intentionally leaving you in the dark. I—I cannot tell you. You know this." He took a step forward. "I promise I'll tell you *everything* as soon as possible. If you could just make Claws show me that dagger for a moment . . ."

"Make her? Mate, have you *met* her? You'd have better luck making a kraken yell." Before anyone could question my nonsensical analogy, I sent a tendril of essence two streets over and used it to open a certain door. Er, table. They still hadn't replaced it.

"**Hurry!**" boomed Fathom. I'd meant it as a distraction for Claws to slap Ellis or something, but the waves of abyssal power that flew out into the world through the now-open doorway were even more intense than expected. Fathom was on the brink of finishing his current task. He and everyone else in the alchemical workshop needed help, lest they fail.

I grinned up at Ellis. "You'd better run along. Say hello for me, will ya?"

Ellis's mouth puckered like I'd made him swallow poison as he turned and fled. Before he made it three steps, Claws exploited his distraction, slapping him across the face with the electrified rump of a trash panda. Claws returned the chittering RPM to her pocket and kicked off Ellis's back. He rocketed out of the amphitheater, and she sailed down to the stage.

I caught Claws and skidded backward, coming to a stop against Bob the boat. All eyes were on us, and I gave Claws a good scritching as I took in the smiling faces of Tropica. Seeing Ellis smacked upside the head with a larcenously inclined raccoon had done wonders for their moods. They must have seen something in my expression, because hints of anticipation joined their smile lines.

I nodded. "I have a plan for how to best deal with those sailing toward our shores, while also growing Tropica's strength." I swallowed, relying on Claws's soft fur beneath my fingers to keep me present. "The thing is, though, I'll need your consent . . ."

CHAPTER FORTY-THREE

Vessels, Part 1

Two mornings later, I sat on the shore at dawn. It'd been just over a month since the god-king mark on my soul had started channeling my chi into the tunnels below. Late last night, my work with the network had finished. The tunnels were full. I was once more in control of my chi and senses.

So as the sun peeked over the distant horizon, I wondered, why didn't it seem any brighter?

Its pastel colors painted the sky, from yellow to red to purple to blue and everything in between. I leaned back and lay in the sand, gazing at the thin clouds above, whose textures enhanced the sweeping hues. They were beautiful. Stunning, really. Yet they did nothing to soothe my racing mind.

I had assumed that the network's completion would bring an end to my woes, and I had been wrong.

The moment the tunnels were full, I'd jerked awake. Maria had stirred beside me, but I'd reined in my essence and slammed our connection closed, then remained still until her breathing steadied. There'd been nobody else home—our animal pals were busy advancing before the enemy force arrived—so I had slipped out into the night and wandered down to sit by the shore.

Back when I'd presented my plan to Tropica, it had seemed so logical. The right thing to do. But now that I had full agency over my power again, it all felt too real. Like a crab escaping boiling water, I had leaped from the pot and into the campfire.

Even if it was the pragmatic choice, even if it was objectively correct, and even if my friends consented . . . could I do it?

I had told—ordered—everyone not to answer immediately. I wanted them to mull it over, to consider it for as long as possible. Had that been a mistake? Would it have been better to encourage them? Whip them into a frenzy about defending Tropica? Some had grown fervent without my encouragement. Especially Paul, Theresa, and Toby, who had bounced from foot to foot, beyond excited by my words.

Remembering their childlike exuberance made me feel a little better. So did the woman I sensed waking up nearby, but even her pulses of affection didn't completely alleviate my anxiety. Rather than teleport to me, she took her time to leave our home and stroll across the sand, soaking up the scenery and radiating her impression of its beauty into my mind.

"Thank you," I said when she was only a few strides away. "That was helpful."

"Good. That makes me feel better about having to do *this*." With that last word, she teleported beside me and flicked me in the center of the forehead.

Before I could so much as make a sound, she crashed down into me and wrapped her arms around my abdomen, squeezing me tight. Her head rested on my chest and a swift breeze blew past, which tousled her hair, tickling my neck.

"What was that for?" I asked.

"For not waking me up." She squeezed me tighter. "And for working yourself into a tizzy."

"What makes you think I've been working myself into a tizzy?"

"I'm your wife. You can seal our connection all you want—I can still read you like a book. How long have you been out here?"

"Too long," I answered honestly. "Sorry. I didn't want to interrupt your beauty sleep."

"Are you saying that I need beauty sleep, and you don't?"

"Errr . . ."

"My poor husband has been robbed of his charm." She nuzzled in closer. "Whatever will we do?"

I didn't reply. I was too busy focusing on the sensations of her body against mine. I wrapped my arms around her, one hand stroking her hair.

"I have a crazy idea," Maria said. "Maybe we can start by, I dunno, opening the magical connection we have to one another?"

"You're sure . . . ?"

"I insist. I'm not just going to let you sit and wallow by yourself."

She meant it, too. She let her resolve slam against the solid wall I'd placed between us. My hand drifted down to cup the side of her neck, and I opened our connection. Slowly at first, then all at once, my every thought became known.

"You're serious?" She lifted her head and stared into my eyes, a line forming between her brows. "That's all?"

"What do you mean, *that's all*—"

I gasped as her potent feelings flooded into me at full strength. It made heat flush through my chest. I hadn't felt this warm since we'd started feeding chi into the tunnels. When I grew a little accustomed to the overwhelming sensations, she sent her thoughts my way.

"Wait, what? You thought I was gonna go fight the boats by myself?"

"Yes, you handsome idiot! Why do you think I didn't teleport to you the second I woke up? I was worried you'd disappear before I could talk you out of it."

"You really think I'd do that . . . ?"

She arched an eyebrow. "Do I think you would leap on an explosion in order to save your friends? You *literally* told me yesterday that you were tempted to do exactly that."

"You've got a point, but I was being hyperbolic."

She arched her brow even higher.

"Okay, I was being *mostly* hyperbolic. Still, what makes you think I would just run off and do it without telling anyone?"

"No offense, my love, but you can be impulsive. I woke up to find the tunnels full, your power returned, and our connection closed. What was I supposed to think? You were out here having a ponder?"

I grimaced. Maria had a point.

"I do," she agreed.

"Sorry. I didn't mean to alarm you. I hoped that if I considered it long enough, I'd find a way out."

"Find a way out . . . ?" she repeated, then got up and knelt in the sand, rubbing her temples. "You can't think your way out of this one, because you can't change anything. It's out of your control. You need distractions, not more rumination."

"That . . . Huh." I sat up. "Yeah, that actually makes sense."

She laughed as she felt my mentality shift, that obvious truth and our restored connection doing wonders for both our moods.

"Is that how you would have spent the week? Overthinking things you can't change?"

"If I said no, would you believe me?"

Before she could reply, we both turned toward the west. Three grinning children crested the closest dune, lifted into view by the bear they rode atop.

"Good morning!" Paul said. Theresa and Toby echoed the same, if a little less exuberantly. The siblings looked as tired as I felt. Teddy gave us a polite nod and trundled closer.

"What are you all doing here?" I asked. "Weren't you up late with the smiths and woodwork—"

"How'd you know about that?" Theresa snapped, leaning past Paul to give me a fierce scowl.

"Uhhh. Your dads told me. Don't worry. I didn't poke around."

"That so?" She leaped down from Teddy and crossed her arms, her expression turning dubious. "Are you gonna poke around now that you're back at full strength?"

"Not at all. You're welcome to keep secre— *Wait.* I've been suppressing my power. How did you know I finished filling the network?"

Toby rested a hand on Theresa's shoulder. "We have more important things to discuss, sis." He turned his attention toward me. "Our cores are still weakened by the System, so we couldn't sense that you'd finished . . . but there were signs." He pointed over his shoulder.

I quirked a brow, seeing Barry's head and stupidly muscular neck coming over the dune behind them. When I saw the object he was pushing—and the bloke within it—I understood what Toby had meant.

Ellis's limbs were hanging from the wheelbarrow Barry pushed. The archivist looked half dead, his skin withered, his eyes sunken. It reminded me of how George and Geraldine had looked when I confronted them a few days ago, except worse. If I couldn't sense the vitality whirling around his core, I might have assumed he was actually dying.

"You with us, Ellis?" I asked.

He groaned, slightly tilting one hand in a so-so gesture.

"Why in Apollo's taunting lyre are you here? Your secret plan worked. You won. Why aren't you sleeping it off?"

"Because he wanted to be here to watch," Paul answered, grinning up with the mouthful of adult teeth he'd eventually grow into.

"To watch what . . . ?"

"Your reaction!" Theresa blurted. She absentmindedly clutched the fur of Teddy's right shoulder. "When we tell you everyone wants to do it!"

A thrill ran through me, making my stomach flutter. "You mean . . . ?"

Paul nodded. "Yep. *Everyone* agreed to your plan."

"But there's still time. Don't you wanna take a few more days? What if you all change your—"

"Told you," Paul interrupted, raising a hand toward his dad. Barry rolled his eyes, reached into his pocket, then placed a single copper coin on his son's open palm.

"We decided almost immediately after you told us what it was," Paul continued. "We thought we should wait until you got your power back, so you could tell we meant it."

Maria giggled and flicked my arm. "Looks like I'm not the only one who can read you like a book . . ."

I didn't respond to her. Paul's words lingered in my mind, making my hope flare and butterflies take flight in my abdomen. "When you said I'd be able to tell everyone meant it . . ."

All three child strategists grinned, Paul widest of all. "See for yourself."

My chi hesitated, but this time, it had nothing to do with the network below. I feared what I'd find when I reached out toward them. Maria leaned against my side, but gave me not even a hint of a mental push. This was entirely my decision to make.

With a slow breath out, I ordered my essence to do my will. Countless tendrils flooded across the sand and into Tropica. When I got there, my breath rushed back in. Paul hadn't been exaggerating. It really was all of them. And they were ready for me.

The entirety of Tropica said two words. Some were groggy with sleep, others were already caffeinated, yet one and all spoke with absolute certainty.

"We consent."

Even Ellis joined in with a mutter. He skipped a few syllables, but the intent was the same.

I stumbled beneath the weight of their resolve. There could be no denying them, nor would they change their minds. All had agreed, knowing it was the best course of action. I smiled until my cheeks hurt, sending my tendrils of essence whirling around Tropica, checking in on the workshops, curious what they were all working on—

"I knew it!" Theresa screamed. "I *knew* you were gonna poke around!"

"Sorry! Sorry!" I raised my hands in surrender as I withdrew my chi. "Honest accident. Got a bit excited."

Her fierce scowl returned. "Do it again and I'll have you mauled by Little Bear."

"Grrrr," agreed her not-so-little bear.

Teddy's eyes were alight with joy, making my smile reform. "Please. Anything but that. I won't look again."

"Good." Theresa gave a haughty sniff and averted her face to hide her own amusement. "See that you don't. Let's go." She leaped back up onto Teddy, who gave a polite nod of his massive head and turned to lumber away.

"Don't you want to hear my orders . . . ?" I asked.

All three kids sat bolt upright and whipped their heads around in tandem, their ideals churning at the prospect of a command.

"You, my three strategists, will be pivotal in the upcoming battle. I'll need to focus on my own task, after all." I squared my shoulders and straightened my back as I stared at them. "I order you to take charge of Tropica's forces and lead us to victory."

CHAPTER FORTY-FOUR

Vessels, Part 2

An hour later, Paul caught himself still grinning as he watched the wall of the smithy disassemble itself. The stone bricks folded down over themselves, then slipped into the ground in large lines, vanishing from view. When just over half of the bricks were gone, he caught sight of Toby and Theresa within the neighboring building, whose closest wall was coming apart at the same rate.

"Oh, hey!" Paul said. "Fancy seeing you two here!"

Toby rolled his eyes good-naturedly, and Theresa tapped her chin in thought. "I say, these workshops appear to be faulty! Their walls just fell apart!"

Paul nodded along as the two workshops became one, some of the bricks folding up to join them together. "Thanks, Tropica."

He wasn't exactly sure that it *was* Tropica who'd granted his request, but it felt like the right thing to say. The formless soul below sent a pulse of chi in return, then sank from his perception.

Beside his massive forge, Fergus shook his head with a grunt from the smithy side of the room. "We can change it back later, right?"

"I hope so." Duncan huffed beside him. "I don't want to catch whatever illness of the mind woodworking seems to afflict on those who practice it . . ."

"That 'illness' is called oxygen, smith," Brad said from the other side of the room. "You should leave your forge and try it sometime. It'll do wonders for your intelligence."

"Or lack thereof," Greg muttered, not looking up from the block of wood he was planing.

Despite their feigned animosity, all four men bore similarly pleased expressions, as did the dozens of apprentices scattered around the now-singular building. Slowly, they all turned toward Paul and his two friends.

"So. Our young masterminds . . ." Fergus said, watching them. "What now?"

The three tacticians shared a look, their grins remaining. As one, their purpose flowed up from their cores, filling their minds and bodies. Paul strode toward the new section of wall before turning and addressing all present. He spoke with the air of what he believed a leader should be. "Thank you, everyone, for your willingness to work together. Though Fischer was the one to leave us in charge of the defense, it isn't lost on us that you've put aside your preconceived notions of age and maturity."

Someone raised a hand.

"Yes, Bonnie?"

"Uhhh, yeah, I think I can speak for everyone when I say we trust your leadership after you just marched in here and ordered *buildings* to change shape for you."

He tilted his head side to side. "It was more of a request that I made of the village, but I understand. Do the rest of you feel the same?" He already knew they did; he wouldn't have asked otherwise. Their answering cheers still made his heart sing. Who knew leading could feel so rewarding?

"In that case, I'll say thanks once more. We appreciate your trust. As for the actual work . . . I think you'll all greatly enjoy it. You especially, Bonnie."

"What . . ." She leaned forward, her desire for adventure radiating from her core. "What are we making?"

He let just the right amount of silence lapse, the tension in the room building. "We're going to finish a group project that Theresa, Toby, and I started over a month ago. Back then, we believed it was something that Tropica was missing. Now? It could be the very thing needed to sway the winds of battle." That was based on information from Ellis, but they'd promised not to share it.

Paul whistled, and Borks charged into the room, then opened a portal. Hundreds of coconuts flew out, tumbling against the wall opposite Paul. As Borks retreated from the room—pausing only to accept an aggressive scritching from Theresa—Paul spoke a single word. Combined with the pile of coconuts, that single word made understanding resonate from the crafters' cores, the joined excitement of so many cultivators making the ground shake.

Back within her clearing, Corporal Claws shot a withering glare toward Tropica. She couldn't say what so many cores were agreeing on, but that was irreverent—all that mattered was that it would possibly overshadow her own malfeasance.

"*Irrelevant*, mistress," corrected RPM, unhelpful as ever. "And *magnificence*."

Rather than launch him for his insubordination, she sighed. "Yes. Now get in the forge."

He took a few milliseconds too long, so she launched him anyway. He chittered maniacally as he struck the inside wall and rolled around, flooding the structure with chi. Before following suit, she gazed back at the pile of materials she'd gathered. Dozens upon dozens of fulgurite branches, each filled with the dancing tongues of lightning essence. Would it be easier to create weapons from them now that she had become an apprentice Maker? It had certainly made it easier to break the pieces off the giant tree of glass.

A villainous laugh started down in her abdomen, building as it climbed free of her needle-sharp teeth. There was only one way to find out what becoming a Maker had changed. She chucked a small stick of fulgurite at her gyrating familiar, then leaped in after it. As she and RPM traveled in loops around the inner wall of the forge, their giggles rose, their efforts in sync.

They lost themselves to the process. Only the coming and going of the sun and moon told of time's passage.

Three days later, with the sun's light just cresting the horizon, they finished the project they were working on. Claws went to retrieve another artifact and froze when she felt power swelling within Tropica. It was something she recognized well: the System, coming to aid in the completion of something vast. She glared toward it. It was the dozens of cultivators again, those who'd made the ground shake. They had succeeded.

RPM landed by her side, scowling fiercely—well, trying to. He wobbled on the spot, dizzy from spinning for three straight days. Claws steadied him with one paw so he could cast the requisite scowl toward their rival crafters in Tropica. She nodded to him, and he nodded back. They knew what had to be done.

The pair gazed back at the pile of unprocessed fulgurite. It had diminished greatly, many of the lengths turned into multifaceted daggers by their efforts. The biggest piece in the unprocessed pile glinted at them, its elongated form poking out, begging to be used. Claws gingerly extricated it from the others and held it out before herself as she inspected its form. She'd not thought they would need to use it, but with the others threatening to overshadow her . . .

She let out a deafening whistle, and Borks answered her call a moment later, stepping through a portal in the center of the clearing. She patted the top of his head, then gestured toward the pile of completed daggers. He wagged his entire body as he placed them inside a pocket dimension. After giving the side of her fuzzy cheek a swift lick, he disappeared, his portal closing behind him.

Claws scream-chirped her gratitude. With his help, their contribution to the battle was guaranteed. A small voice in the back of her mind wondered what those dozens of cultivators had succeeded in making back in Tropica, but she covered her curiosity with a heap of imaginary stones. It didn't matter. She was going to create something far grander.

She grabbed RPM under one arm, tucked the big length of fulgurite under the other, and launched all three of them into the forge.

Paul bathed in the euphoria. Though the light shining inside the joined building felt amazing, its touch flooding his body and making his skin tingle, that was nothing compared to the feeling of rightness coming from within.

He, Toby, and Theresa had been working on this for *weeks* without success. They'd tried countless materials, methodologies, and even professions. None of them had worked until now. The relief was indescribable. As the lines of their many creations solidified, the System's transformation coming to an end, he took a shaky breath. It was fortunate that his last breakthrough had only been partial—he'd likely have passed out from overstimulation otherwise.

For three whole days they'd toiled, only pausing for brief breaks to eat, sleep, and use the bathroom. He reached down to pat the unconscious bear on his right. Teddy had been instrumental in the success of this group project, his ability to empower them staving off exhaustion. They owed him. Big time.

As the light faded from the room, Paul tore his eyes from the now-dozing bear to find a sea of stunned faces, all staring down at the pile of transformed items in the center of the room. His body moved forward of its own accord. Toby and Theresa stepped up beside him, and together, they gazed down at their spoils.

As the description filled his vision, there wasn't a single sound in the room. He read it again, and again, and again, the truth of the words slowly sinking into him. He shook his head and returned to the present. Everyone had gathered around the stack of transformed items, their eyes clearing one by one.

The coconuts had been husked, and the shells within cut in half. Plates of metal lined the outsides, and the insides were filled with perfectly carved sections of soft wood, increasing their buoyancy. They each had a leather strip attached. The ends of the leather had been nailed in place on opposite sides of the soft-wood inserts, but the System's transformation had melded them into each coconut seamlessly. Paul leaned down and channeled chi into one of the leather straps, resizing it with a faint effort of will.

He couldn't say for sure who laughed first, but Bonnie was the loudest, her exultation drowning out even the booming laughs of Fergus and Duncan. Conversation slowly rose as people animatedly discussed the experience. Paul and his fellow tacticians soaked in each word just as they had the euphoric light, reveling in the merriment of those they'd been tasked with leading.

"How many are there . . . ?" Theresa asked, slumping to the ground to rest against the sleeping form of Teddy.

"Hundreds," Paul answered. A sudden smirk split his face. "More importantly, what will our enemies think when they see them . . . ?"

CHAPTER FORTY-FIVE

Vessels, Part 3

The god-empress choked on her anger. She read the screen again, and again, and again, but the message remained the same. She raised a hand, forestalling the attack she herself had ordered to take place should she lose her temper again. The seers skidded to a stop on the deck, one of them holding their gathered power, refusing to let it go.

The god-empress's mask cracked for but a moment as she sneered at Eustace and the divine power glowing in her fist. "Do not test me, Seer. Force me to strike now, and it will be your head that flies."

Eustace dismissed her gathered chi, so the god-empress dismissed her in turn, loathing that her emotions had cracked through the mask again. She appeared at the front of her galleon in a flash, teeth gritted, hands clutching the ornate balustrade. She'd been so sure this enemy force was sent to challenge her, placed in her path to facilitate growth. For that reason, she'd taken her time crossing the ocean, knowing that any advancements her adversary achieved in the meantime would only prove her righteousness when she eventually prevailed.

Had it been a mistake . . . ?

Though she couldn't hear them, she could sense the complaints of the old her—Aletheia—as the girl she'd locked in the depths of her soul seized the moment of doubt. The balustrade groaned within her grasp, and she let go of it before the wood cracked. She couldn't think straight. She could scarcely control her body, let alone her mind.

Desperate, the god-empress reached for her ideal. Aletheia Victus, the girl she'd once been, pounded at the metal door of her prison. But the mask knew what to do. This doubt served neither her nor humanity.

Burn it away.

No! the vexatious girl screamed from within, the mask's doubt granting her strength. People could die!

It was the exact wrong thing to say. The mask already knew the answer.

Kill the few, save the many.

Silence. Blessed silence descended upon the god-empress. A lesser woman would have wept in relief. The god-empress didn't. On the deck behind her, she heard her seers and the Prime Cadre discussing the messages on the screen.

"This can't be correct . . ."

"The artifact is divine! It is *always* correct."

"What does that error mean . . . ?"

"Alternative reward?"

"How large is their force if they can captain so many?"

The god-empress read it again.

Tropica has created their 100th vessel and earned the naval class: [error].
Naval class system offline. Calculating alternate reward . . .

What should she do? Should she rush there and attack them before a reward could be assigned? Or was it better to wait and see what the reward was, then react accordingly? Her thoughts were mired in shadow.

Before she could reach a decision, the screen flickered, rapidly powering off and on again. When it stopped, the lines had changed, their contents even more terrible.

Tropica has created their 100th vessel and earned the naval class: [error].
Tropica has created their 200th vessel and earned the naval class: [error].
Tropica has created their 300th vessel and earned the naval class: [error].
Naval class system offline. Alternate reward calculated.

Yet more messages arrived. They almost drove the god-empress to her knees.

Tropica has been granted a Prime Vessel!
Scanning fleet . . .
Prime Vessel identified.
Congratulations, Bob the boat!

Sensing the god-empress's shock, the foolish girl within chose that moment to strike. She rammed against the metal seal with all her might. Rather than earn her freedom, all it did was recenter the mask's purpose.

The god-empress hammered against the seal to send Aletheia hurtling away, then latched on to the horrible information revealed by the screen. It didn't matter what Tropica did. They were a threat to the Kingdom of Light, and humanity as a whole. No matter what, she would destroy them.

And she now knew where to strike the first blow.

"Gods above," Anius was saying. "They have a sentient boat!"

Eustace had turned white as a ghost.

"Empty heavens . . ." Evan swore, showing just how addled he was. Never before had the god-empress heard him utter such vile filth.

The rest of the Prime Cadre looked to her for an answer.

She ignored them all.

"Return to your ships." Her words were a command. "I will shield *Theoris*, *Elegos*, and the entire left wing of the fleet. It is your task to shield the others."

She didn't wait for their acknowledgment; they'd either do so or prove themselves unworthy of being brought along. If they failed to protect the right wing and all the souls aboard, so be it. She had to strike now, no matter the cost.

Kill the few, save the many.

The god-empress lifted her arms and drew from the vast stores of divine energy held within the containers covering each ship's hull. The seers and the Prime Cadre repeated the same across the rest of the fleet. She felt no joy that half of her forces would survive—she couldn't spare a single thought for anything other than the task at hand.

She grabbed hold of yet more condensed chi, then sent it racing ahead, charting a path across the ocean. All became a blur over the next few seconds. The ships sailed along as streaked lines of light, everyone on their decks shielded by her and her most powerful followers. The god-empress mark on her soul called out to her as she strained, begging to be used. She denied it. Now wasn't the time.

She gritted her teeth and focused her will, sending her awareness even farther forward, stopping only when she reached the heretical village named Tropica.

Geographically, it was almost identical to the map she'd found in the royal library.

The bay was the same, as were the headlands to the north and south. The layout of the village had grown, but still it seemed . . . insignificant. Barely a tenth the size of Phostheia. Its squat buildings were obviously System-made; they were composed of the same bricks as her castle. The wooden dock extending from Tropica's seawall was also constructed by the System, its dark wood unweathered despite the coastal elements.

She couldn't see any of her enemies, only the physical layout, as was expected when projecting one's awareness. Sensing no threat from the village proper, she returned to the bay. Her fleet, her forces, and her physical body would arrive there in a matter of seconds. Before they did, she would annihilate Tropica's greatest weapon against them.

All of her newly chosen mages had awakened by refilling the ancient containers with divine chi, but they were still weak. They would stand no chance against powerful spirit beasts in physical combat. Which was why she'd had them fill the containers in the first place. Those ancient relics once more lined the fleet's hulls, flooding the Kingdom of Light's divine essence out into the surrounding ocean. It was a death sentence for any being stupid enough to approach from underwater.

Her plan was to wage war from atop the bay, raining down holy judgment on their enemies while staying far from shore. Their attacking formation would be the same *V* they sailed in, with *Theoris* and *Elegos* at the tip, pointing toward Tropica. The two hundred mages of the Forty Hands might be weak—especially those who had recently awoken—but they were still incredibly dangerous. They could attack unimpeded from their arrayed ships, knowing both that none of Tropica's forces could reach them, and that she, the seers, and the Prime Cadre would protect them from above.

But only if Tropica didn't have boats of their own.

If the enemy vessels remained intact, their spirit beasts and cultivators could simply sail closer, surrounding them. If the leaders wielded abyssal chi as she feared they did, keeping distance was the key to victory. Even the royal library's books, whose pages were dedicated to the divine, repeatedly stressed the dangers of fighting in close quarters with an abyssal cultivator. Small wonder that spears and arrows were the hallmark weapons of the heavens.

She allowed her spirit a smile as she assessed the bay one last time. These heretics had no idea what was about to hit them. The Divine Fleet was less than a second away now, so she reached for her god-empress mark, which had been calling out to her this entire time, begging her to make use of it. Finally, she acquiesced. She'd not used a drop of her own chi in transporting her fleet here, so the mark latched on to all the essence suffusing her core, condensing it, sending it out beneath the waves.

She couldn't see Tropica's boats. They were invisible to her projected awareness. But if they were anywhere in the bay, they had no hope of escaping this strike. Her god-queen mark sent out a command along the thousands of divine lines drifting beneath the bay. Countless golden spears sprouted as one, rocketing skyward.

The Divine Fleet arrived, and the god-empress shot back into her body. She opened her eyes to a scene of holy devastation. Each golden spear was two stories tall and ended in a deadly tip, some of which protruded harmlessly through *Theoris's* deck, as she'd known they would. She glanced behind herself and saw the same happening to the rest of the Divine Fleet.

She paid it no mind. The spears would only hurt cultivators and spirit beasts without divine chi.

And boats belonging to an enemy fleet . . . she thought, gazing across the golden sea toward Tropica's seawall.

The System-made dock was no more. All that remained were splintered and broken sections of plank skewered atop the spears where it'd once been. Her god-queen mark had tripled the spear density there, knowing it was a likely spot for Bob the boat to be docked. Did some of the skewered wood belong to that prime vessel?

Her mark called out to her again, and she grinned. Unlike the last impulse it had sent her, she agreed to this one immediately. The mark drew hungrily from her core. She had only regenerated half of her essence since last time, so this strike would be weaker than the spears littering the bay. That wasn't the only difference between the last attack and this one, though—this one was aimed at the city. Non-cultivators might not be harmed by the spears themselves, but they would be harmed by the destroyed buildings that came tumbling down atop them.

Her strongest followers had rejoined her on the deck of *Theoris*. When they sensed her intent, spikes of horror came from some of them: Evan, Grace, Esmond, Seer Eustace, and Seer Anius. The god-empress pushed down her disgust at their weakness, lest it make her remove their heads. Everyone in this village was complicit. What did her seers and the Prime Cadre think would happen here? When abyssal chi was involved, not a soul could be left behind. The quest made it clear. Tropica, and those within, were to be *annihilated.*

She unleashed the attack. A hundred arrows of divine judgment fanned out as she loosed them at the village. Perhaps this would end the battle. She smirked as she watched the arcing shafts reach the village, imagining them passing through the System-made buildings like they were made of the same paper as Anius's fan.

But then the arrows all changed course. They curved up something barely visible—a shimmering ramp of light. Each projectile only just missed the first row of structures, and as they trailed off into the distance, they fell apart, dissipating into motes of light.

"Mate . . ." came the booming voice of a strangely accented man, his tone conversational and sickly sweet. "Do you frackin' mind?"

CHAPTER FORTY-SIX

Riddles

The god-empress couldn't see the speaker, so she ordered her divine spears to disperse. Most of their power returned to her core, and she readied it, preparing to launch another attack the moment she caught sight of . . . *them?*

"Bad Fischer!" a young woman said, slapping a man on the shoulder. He was wearing a weird suit. "You're supposed to let everyone else do it!"

"That didn't count. The battle hasn't started yet. And she destroyed our dock! Who does that?"

The god-empress took in the crowd of people on the shore in an instant. They stood on the sands just south of Tropica, a stone's throw away from the rock walkway separating the village from the ocean, and within firing range of the god-empress's Divine Fleet. There was a medium-sized tree behind them, its canopy swaying in the breeze.

There were three at the front of the crowd, positioned a step before everyone else. Odd, considering all three were children. They wore shorts and sleeveless, buttonless tops with a red-banded collar that extended up the bases of their necks. On the children's flank stood a frightful bear. It had terrible canines, and patches of needles that grew from its elbows and neck, all glowing an ominous crimson. A man and woman stood on the bear's other side. They ignored the Divine Fleet in favor of staring down at a bundle in the woman's arms.

Finally, there were the two that had been bickering. God-King Fischer and God-Queen Maria. Their marks were unique yet undoubtedly paired. They resonated with her own. The god-empress couldn't help but sneer as she considered the woman Fischer had chosen as his wife. Maria wasn't worthy of her title. She was a slight thing, with the build, complexion, and even the clothing of a peasant.

Drab as Maria's outfit was, it was leaps and bounds better than Fischer's. The god-king wore something resembling a suit, but his jacket was open, revealing a sleeveless top and short leg garments made of rich material. Possibly silk. If the sand-colored outfit didn't fit him so well, she'd have assumed he had plundered a set of pajamas and a suit jacket from a king's wardrobe. It was undoubtedly tailored to his body, though.

As she tried to make sense of it all, her Prime Cadre reached for their power, preparing a volley that would tear through their enemies. She raised one hand to stall them. Something was wrong here. She couldn't sense a single drop of abyssal chi from the forces before them, which was the only reason she hadn't yet launched her own attack. She needed more information.

"Detection formation," she said, not taking her eyes off of the enemy god-king.

The Prime Cadre rushed to obey. Evan remained on *Theoris* while the others scattered along the wings of the Divine Fleet. All five started scanning for threats.

"Checking out the threads, huh?" Fischer asked. The man waggled his eyebrows infuriatingly, and the god-empress considered striking him down after all. "Can't say I blame you. This was what I wore to my wedding. My two pals here are our tailors." He nodded toward the well-dressed man and woman at his side. "They made it for me and hid a secret effect in the jacket, the scoundrels."

"We worried you'd think it was controlling," the man replied.

"I mean, yeah. The description makes it sound absolutely cooked, Steven. I . . . *Steven?*"

"Yes?"

Fischer pointed down. "Why are your hands orange?"

"Oh. I was doing some painting. The pigment seems to have stained my skin."

Fischer nodded sagely. "Was it fun?"

"The painting?"

"Yeah."

Steven smirked. "It will be, God-King."

"I see."

"You do?"

"Nope. Not even a little, but I do like the cut of your jib—"

"Silence, heretics!" Evan's body shook with fury, and his voice was firm, filled with every ounce of divine energy he could muster. "You will properly address God-Empress Aletheia Victus, rightful heir to the throne of Phostheia, Chosen of Heaven, who rides atop the Prime Vessel *Theoris*, divine galleon of—"

"Yeah, yeah." Fischer's thunderous voice made Evan's throat seize, interrupting him back. "Breaker of chains. Mother of dragons. Whatever, homie. She just tried to level my village. I don't give a frack what you want me to call her."

The god-empress didn't know what to say. Normally, she would have been incensed, but this man didn't seem stable. Nor did he possess abyssal chi.

"Anyway," Fischer continued. "We were talking about my jacket. Lovely results, despite how dark the System made it sound. I assumed you could manipulate the effect, but you can't. It really does only show true feelings." Fischer glanced up at the god-empress. "I can show you. Here. You should be able to see it for yourself with your level of cultivation."

She no longer saw him as a threat, so the god-empress indulged her curiosity and let her eyes get drawn in.

Matrimonial Suit of the God-King
Mythic
Created for a god-king, on the day of his marriage, by his nation's leading

tailors. The god-king's followers have imbued threads of gratitude and love into this suit. So long as their faith holds true, the only thing capable of damaging it is a blow possessing even greater faith.
Hidden effect revealed by Maker Fisher: This suit's jacket allows the intended wearer (Fischer of Tropica) to broadcast his feelings about those nearby, and sense their feelings about him in return.

She dismissed the words. When she saw the smirk on Fischer's face, she realized she'd made a mistake.

"You knew, then?" he asked.

"Knew what?"

"That I'm a Maker. You didn't react at all." His smirk got sharper. "Have you been watching us? Is that what those two relics behind you are for . . . ?"

She took an involuntary step to the side, placing herself between him and the artifacts.

"Don't worry. I'm not after your goodies. What I'm after is *friendship*."

Aura pulsed out from him. She braced herself, ready to manifest a spear and cut any trickery to pieces, but none came. It was coming from his Matrimonial Suit of the God-King. If its description could be believed, it would broadcast his true feelings for her. His aura saw her as a potential friend. He really was looking for friendship. He didn't want to battle. If it came to violence, he would fight tooth and nail, but only if there were no other option.

His smirk turned into a frown as the artifact's secondary effect kicked in and he sensed her feelings in return. "Damn. You're kinda complicated, aren't you?"

"*I'm* complicated? You openly wear a jacket that claims to manipulate my feelings."

"Well, it sounds bad when you put it like that . . ."

"If you really want me to believe you, why don't you take it off?"

"Whoa. I'm married, lady."

The god-empress felt her jaw grow tense.

Fischer raised his hands to forestall her. "That was too far. My bad." He patted his chest. "But I can't take the jacket off. It holds my trump card."

"Your what?"

"Oh. Did that get lost in translation? A trump card is like a secret weapon. An ace up my sleeve, if you'll forgive the wordplay."

"Yet you showed me the description, giving away any secrecy?"

"Uhhh, yeah? That way, you know my feelings are genuine. Pretty straightforward."

She scoffed. "Do you take me for a fool, heretic? You are amusing, but don't think for a second I believe you, or that anything you've said has come across as *straightforwa*—"

"Told you, Fischer," the ruby-haired woman beside Fischer interrupted. "Steven and I are good, but not *that* good."

"Don't sell yourself short, Rubes." Fischer pointed at his loose-fitting leg garments. "Speaking of shorts, these are a testament to your brilliance. They don't leave much to the imagination, but there's nothing better on a summer's day. You should feel the breeze up here! It's like having Mother Nature's nourishing fingers reach into your jocks to tickle your b—"

"Fischer!" Maria slapped him on his bare shoulder. "I don't care how evil that lady is. I am *not* okay with you telling her about you ba—"

The one called Rubes dashed over and slapped them both with her free hand, the god-king on the back of his head, then the god-queen on her shoulder. "Language!"

When Rubes had dashed, the bundle shifted in her arms, letting the god-empress catch sight of a small face. Was that a baby? They'd brought an infant to a battlefield . . . ?

"Hey!" Fischer rubbed his head. "I was gonna say bits!"

"That's not any better! And don't call me Rubes when I'm angry with you!"

"Okay. Sorry. My bad, Ruby. Can you stop giving me that look? I'm not used to having Fin around yet, and there's, like, *a lot* going on."

"No! I *won't* stop giving you that look! You need to watch your mouth around her! Who knows how impressionable her little brain . . ."

They continued bickering, yammering incessantly as they had been the entire time. The god-empress tuned them out.

Fin . . . Chosen Champion of Fischer . . .

The god-empress's mind raced to absorb it all. He had chosen an infant as his champion? Why? Why was he conversing casually despite his impending annihilation? For that matter, why hadn't she attacked him yet? Was it the jacket's influence? Or was it the strangeness and novelty of these enemies delaying her hand?

How had they subjugated the ursine spirit beast without abyssal chi? And where were the rest of the spirit beasts? Had the intimidating bear somehow defeated the others? It didn't look *that* strong. She reached out toward it, finding that it—he—was at the third tier of cultivation. His ideal was related to . . . aggressive protection? The bear glowered back and shifted closer to the three children, his head lowering, his spikes bristling.

Fischer was blissfully unaware. He was busy being berated by an irate mother. Even if he wasn't as powerful as the god-empress had feared, he was still a god-king, yet he stayed silent as Ruby chastised him. A god-king, someone closer to the heavens than the lower realm, was letting a lowly cultivator dictate how he conducted himself.

They were insane. All of them.

Had the god-empress come all this way, gathered all this power, only to face a complete madman and his equally insane posse? She knew not how they'd survived her initial volley, but that didn't matter now. This upstart god-king would soon fall.

"Where are the rest of the spirit beasts?" she demanded.

Fischer paused in the middle of his fifth apology to Ruby, then turned toward the god-empress and gave her a quizzical look.

"Do not play dumb with me, God-King. You have a single bear by your side. We know Gormona was attacked by a cadre of different creatures. Where are the birds? Where is the beetle? Where is the rat who shoots lightning?"

Fischer choked back a laugh. "Lady, you are *so* lucky 'the rat who shoots lightning' isn't here."

"So they're gone? You killed the other spirit beasts? Or are you claiming you drove them away? You really expect me to believe you have that kind of power?"

His quizzical look returned as he considered how to respond.

She pushed her advantage. "Where is your fleet? Where is Bob the boat?"

"Wait, how do you know about Bob?" He leaned closer, his brow furrowing. "Just how long have you been monitoring us . . . ?"

"Your Holiness," Evan said. He was kneeling at her side, his gaze locked on their enemies.

She stared death at him. He was supposed to be scanning their surroundings. Her ideal stirred from within, reminding her of her purpose. If his words weren't of vital importance, she would end him. "Speak."

"The tree, Your Holiness. I believe a spirit beast dwells within. It's hiding by flooding the world's chi from the leaves above, making it difficult to sense."

She focused on the tree behind Tropica's forces, and her eyes went wide. Evan was correct. There *was* a spirit beast concealing itself within—

"Wrooong," Fischer drawled, interrupting her train of thought. Anger coursed through her.

"I can sense it, fool! Or are you so daft that you didn't realize?"

He blew air through his lips like a petulant child. "I know Lieutenant Colonel Lemony Thicket is a *tree* spirit. Not a spirit *beast*. Put some respect on her name. Tell 'em, Lemon!"

The tree grew another limb and waved hello.

Tree spirits were rarely mentioned in Phostheia's royal library. They hadn't been seen for thousands of years before the gods' departure. Even when they *had* still lived, they weren't creatures to be ordered around. It had to be a trick. Her theory was confirmed when the "tree spirit" extended a root from the ground and smacked Fischer on the behind. Tree spirits were benevolent beings. Allies of the divine. On the rare occasions they turned on cultivators, it was because the cultivators deserved it. And the punishments tree spirits doled out were far more . . . *final* than a soft smack on the rump. To earn their ire was to earn death.

The god-empress made a disgusted noise, unable to hide her contempt for such a blatant lie. It was one thing for this "god-king" to debase himself. It was another thing entirely for him to besmirch the memory of those majestic spirits.

In response to her disgust, however, the branch started radiating power. It was ancient. Pure. And undercut by a scent like decaying leaves, the aroma banishing any hint of the ocean they sailed on. Her divine essence responded to it, telling her the truth. This was no ruse. A tree spirit had allied itself with Tropica.

"How . . . ?" she asked, genuinely curious.

Fischer shrugged. "The power of friendship, obviously. You should try it sometime. I have all manner of weird and wacky pals. Check this one out." He pressed his fingers between his lips and let out a deafening whistle.

Cracks formed in the air beside him. Within moments, a purple portal had formed, and a spirit beast leaped from it.

"Borks!" Fischer knelt down to its height. "How did you go? Gather 'em all?"

The dog barked at him, its blond tail wagging violently.

"I knew you could do it. Who's-a-good-boy?" He started fussing the dog all over. "Who's-a-good-boy? You are! Yes, you are!"

The god-empress narrowed her eyes as waves of contented chi radiated from the creature. Much of it was indiscernible, just as Fischer's was, but a hint of something familiar dwelled under the surface. Had she experienced it before . . . ?

Beneath her direct gaze—and under the scratching fingers of its insane master—the beast transformed into something long and lithe and covered in midnight fur. Savage canines glinted as it rolled on its back, a tail wagging that wasn't a tail at all, but a serpent.

Suddenly, the chi's familiarity made sense. She'd read about it when researching enemies of the divine. The book had described the essence of this realm as dark, sulfuric, but not unpleasant. There'd even been an illustration of the beast before her. This fell creature belonged to Hades.

"Hellhound!" The word tore from her throat of its own accord. "To me!"

She flung her arm forward and summoned a golden spear that flashed through the air toward the spirit beast. Except it didn't. She glanced down at her hand, wondering why it hadn't loosed the spear. What was going on?

Fischer had rocketed to his feet, as had the hellhound, both watching her with glowing eyes of shimmering white and hellfire red, respectively.

The Seers and the Prime Cadre appeared at her side, all gathering their power. Her thoughts cut off immediately when she saw the other pair of glowing irises on the shore. For the first time since she'd donned the mask of a ruler, true fear washed through the god-empress. Fin, still bundled in her mother's arms, stared into Aletheia's soul with eyes the same shimmering white as Fischer's.

Fin, Chosen of Fischer, was a cultivator. She had to have been born as such; the System wouldn't awaken children, even partially, before their fifth birthday.

"Ne . . ." The god-empress licked her lips, willing her throat to cease constricting. "Ne—"

"*Nephilim?*" Eustace asked from her side. "They have a *Nephilim?*" Laughter oozed from her, the sound anathema to the horrified faces of Anius and the Prime Cadre. "Now *that's* something you don't see every day."

"Nephilim?" Fischer repeated, expression dubious.

"Nephilim is the title of children born awakened, their bodies enhanced in the womb. They are abhorred by the heavens, and all records suggest they should be kill—"

"Enough." Fischer's command slammed into them with force rivaling a god's, cutting Eustace off and redoubling Aletheia's fear. "What is your name?"

Eustace croaked. "Seer Eustace, Your Holi . . . uhhhh."

Fischer's expression softened, but his will didn't. "Sorry, Eustace. I don't wanna hurt you, so don't use any violent language if you're talking about Fin. My bond with her *really* didn't like that. It told me to throw you into the sun."

Eustace smiled at that, but Aletheia hardly noticed. As Fischer's will had pressed down upon her, his eyes swimming with pearlescent light, Aletheia had finally understood why she hadn't been able to sense his aspect. The god-king didn't have one.

Impossible.

Anyone attempting to wield pure essence shouldn't have survived past their first breakthrough, let alone become a god-king. The records told of pure-chi cultivators destroying entire cities when they lost control . . . and those were base-level cultivators. Just how much destruction would the man before her cause if he were to implode? He had to be eliminated. *Now.* No wonder the System had sent her after him.

So why couldn't she attack?

Her entire arm shook, her ideal warring with Fischer's will. Her divine chi could tear his bindings apart, yet she didn't move, something within telling her not to. She furrowed her brow, seeking the answer.

Her internal state had been slipping since she got here. Was it his jacket after all? If that were it, he wouldn't have shown it to her. Come to think of it, why had she agreed to inspect it? She'd stopped seeing him as a threat at some point—clearly a mistake, given all she now knew.

He had allied with spirit beasts. He had won over a tree spirit. He had chosen a *Nephilim* as his *champion*, for heaven's sake. On top of all that, he channeled an impossible power, which was strong enough to divert her volley of golden arrows.

In response, she had let him talk. She had watched as he spoke of useless things with his followers, all the while having a quest to *annihilate* them. Then he'd done the same with *her* followers. Eustace had shown incredible insubordination by talking to the man, and for some reason, that hadn't bothered Aletheia.

The god-empress's eyes flew wide. *Aletheia?* When had she started referring to herself as Aletheia agai—

Her unseen enemy chose that moment to strike. It all happened in an instant.

The spirit of Aletheia slammed into the god-empress, seeking to burn away the mask she wore. The young woman had escaped the internal pit and slowly retaken parts of the god-empress's body, seeking to eject her.

"Fool!" the god-empress screamed. She unleashed only a fraction of the chi from her core, forming a golden column that raced down from the mask and slammed into the girl she used to be. Her ideal empowered it, and Aletheia let out a wordless scream as she was blistered, burned, and forced back down toward the pit.

The god-empress didn't spare the metal seal; it clearly didn't work. She wouldn't need it after this anyway.

Aletheia, propelled by the column of divine light, struck the seal. It melted, fusing to Aletheia's form as the princess careened down into the bottom of the pit, never to rise again.

The god-empress opened her eyes. Her body was once more her own, and she summoned a second golden spear, drawing back the one in her right hand, aiming for Fischer.

"Damn," the god-king said, wincing. "I was hoping the other you won tha—"

"Enough!" It was her turn to enforce her will. *"Prostrate yourselves!"*

Fischer stumbled, as did Maria. Ruby, Steven, and the infant Fin remained upright, protected by Fischer's shimmering essence. He had shielded them, but not himself. Everyone else on the shore had fallen to their knees, but the bear's red aura surrounded them, letting the children hold themselves upright.

She didn't let that anger her. What did she care? So what if the insects momentarily defied the heavens? But then she noticed the hellhound, who had subverted her order by rolling onto his back. He grinned up at Fischer. His tail was wagging. That made her blood boil.

She drew her right arm farther back and doubled the golden chi filling the spear. "If you have any last words, speak them now."

Fischer forced himself to smile. "Gladly." His eyes flicked to her left, examining *Elegos* for a second before returning to her. "Looks like we've wasted enough time."

She didn't fall for the obvious ploy.

"My last words are a question," God-King Fischer continued, then paused. "Well, they're more of a riddle, really. But what's the diff—"

"Speak!"

"Sheesh, lady. I was getting to it." He stood upright, rolling his shoulders and stretching his neck, somehow defying her command. When his eyes met hers, his smile was no longer forced. "What has an exoskeleton, very-pinchy claws, and rhymes with tarnation?"

A young girl screamed from behind and to her left.

CHAPTER FORTY-SEVEN

Ephemeral Art

I cackled as the well-intentioned woman aboard the closest ship to the god-empress finally realized her mistake. It had taken everything in me not to burst into laughter at least three different times during the last minute, and I was glad I'd managed it. The timing of her scream couldn't have been any better.

The woman—apparently named Fern—was extremely perceptive. She had been the first person to notice the crustaceans boarding the *Elegos*, despite them not making a sound. I had left Paul, Toby, and Theresa completely in charge of this battle. All I knew was that they wanted me to waste time until *something* happened—this, clearly—so I'd been even more surprised by the crustaceans' arrival than she was.

If I was surprised, though, the bloke beside Fern was flabbergasted.

The moment Sven had spotted the half dozen recon crabs and assault shrimp clinging to the side of the *Elegos*, he tried to raise the alarm, but Fern covered his mouth with her hands. Just in time, too, because Rocky ambled up onto the deck a moment later, his black-and-red carapace obscured by multiple coats of orange paint. He looked . . . kinda normal, actually. Steven had done a wonderful job. I wouldn't have known Rocky was any different from a regular rock crab if not for his impressive size.

Before Sven could try to raise the alarm again, Fern had rushed to explain herself. These were *obviously* regular creatures. If they were spirit beasts, they would have been burned away. Surprisingly, that explanation swayed him.

Until Rocky's fresh coat of paint started to blister.

"Spiri—" Sven started, only to get shushed again by the compassionate woman beside him.

"Don't you see?" Fern hissed. "I told you! You heard the god-empress! Any spirit beasts or cultivators will be cleansed in an instant. This is like the rope that fell overboard. The poor thing is being burned over time."

She had a great imagination. The truth was Rocky couldn't suppress both his chi and ambient heat at the same time. If he suppressed his heat, the god-empress would detect his essence. Unfortunately for Steven, that meant his artwork was ephemeral—it would burn away before long.

Though Fern was entirely incorrect, she'd convinced Sven. I recognized the fervor in his eyes. He saw his god-empress's word as law, so he couldn't imagine a world where she was wrong and our forces could travel through the ocean. How *had* they done that? I'd have to ask Paul about it later. The chi flooding from those artifacts posed a serious threat if any of them actually touched it.

"We should put it out of its misery," Sven said.

The look Fern gave him in response could have melted steel beams.

"It's heretical!" Sven tried.

She proceeded to fetch a spare patch of sail from a nearby crate, which she folded in half, then placed overtop Rocky, hiding him lest he be discovered by another. All the while, she gave him a passionate recounting of her childhood. Before her parents had passed—poor girl—she had grown up by the sea. Church doctrine be damned, she'd loved spending time in the nearby rock pools, observing the sea life that could be found there. Rocky, though massive, looked just like the baby crabs who used to peer out at her from their hidey-holes. And who knew, maybe he was one of the small crabs she'd seen back then? Maybe the table scraps she'd stolen from the trash and thrown into the shallows had helped him grow big and strong enough to travel all this way.

She finished by patting Rocky's covered head. "Don't worry, little one. I've been burned by the god-empress, too. You'll feel better soon."

That explained it. She was an animal lover, crabs and fish included. My kind of person.

Sven actually teared up. "You're a better person than I am, Fern. Maybe I need to be more open-minded about— *Heavens above!*"

The material lovingly placed over Rocky had burst into flames.

Fern whipped it off him and threw it overboard. Her eyes were wide with terror and regret as she realized it wasn't just the sail that was on fire, but the crab, too. It was really just Steven's art going up in flames, but she didn't know that.

Both Sven and Fern shielded their eyes against the immense heat, only daring to lower their hands when the flames were gone. How must Rocky have looked to them in that moment? He stood atop a charred circle of wood that darkened the closer it was to his pitch-black carapace. The red cracks lining his body flared bright as he withdrew a cigarette from nowhere, lit it against his shell, and took a mighty drag.

Nobody made a sound for a long moment. Well, those three hadn't. I'd hit the god-empress with my riddle about something very-pinchy that rhymes with tarnation.

Finally, Rocky exhaled and gave a respectful nod of his carapace, which broke the spell.

Fern realized her mistake and took a step back. Sven stumbled past her, squealing like a girl. The god-empress whirled toward Sven's scream and caught sight of Rocky. She pivoted, redirecting the divine spear she'd intended for me.

My enhanced cognition flared, and time crawled to a stop. I was once more in control of every drop of my power. With her back exposed to me, my instincts screamed that I could end her. I'd need only a single partition of pure chi to do it. Maybe two. She was strong, but I was on another level.

I wasn't going to attack, though. I didn't want to end her, and this wasn't my fight. Not directly, anyway. I knew what had to be done. As I gathered the resolve to do it, I smiled at the scenes unfolding across the battlefield.

The enemy fleet was arrayed in a *V*, with each wing consisting of twenty ships spread out over a hundred meters or so total. *Theoris*, flanked by *Elegos*, was at the tip. I suspected they'd chosen this formation so every attacker had line of sight, letting them shoot us with their overpowered, hard-to-block chi. But that meant I could also see them, along with the groups of crustaceans that had scuttled up onto each ship's deck.

The assault shrimps were clustered together, and the recon crabs flanked them in a clearly practiced formation. There appeared to be a vast spectrum of capability among the enemy mages. Some had no idea they'd been boarded, others were already preparing attacks. I imagined those divine strikes crashing into Snips's bonded crustaceans and breaching their defenses.

I grimaced and closed my eyes. Looking at the battlefield had been a mistake.

How would I handle it if anyone were injured, or worse, killed? It was a very real possibility. Could I really do this? Could I hand over my power again and leave everything up to my friends . . . ?

One of my friends nudged me. Teddy. His awareness wrapped around me, a bear hug that told me everything was going to be okay. Another pal whapped me playfully and whispered in my mind, the sound like a soft breeze passing through her canopy. Lemon's message was clear: *It is time.*

They couldn't complete their task without me. And I couldn't complete mine without them.

I opened my eyes. The god-empress was halfway through launching her spear at Rocky. Most of the assault shrimp had sprouted their giant claws and were gathering power there. Some of the enemy mages had divine essence glowing around their hands, ready to be unleashed at any second.

I leaned against Teddy's awareness, opened myself up to the soothing rustle of Lemon's voice, and made my decision.

I surrendered my power to my friends.

Teddy and Lemon drank half each. They both roared, Teddy like a bear protecting his cubs, Lemon like a hurricane ripping through a forest. I might have joined them. It was hard to tell. I felt nothing. Saw nothing. Heard only the deafening roar. When I came back to myself, Maria was holding me upright. I was so, so weak. She held my chin with one hand, helping me see the battlefield. What I found there brought a tired smile to my face.

My ideal had merged with Teddy's, my desire for Tropica to prosper boosting his offensive aura multiplicatively, making red waves of power bloom from all of Tropica's forces. And that wasn't all. Lemon had absorbed the other half of my chi, which she'd merged with the world's pure essence. She flooded this potent combination out over the bay, and it surrounded the red waves of Teddy's aura, wrapping them in a shimmering layer of chi that contained and stabilized Teddy's aura.

Time's passage had resumed. The god-empress's two-meter-long golden spear was screaming toward Rocky. Smaller versions were flying from the hands of experienced enemy mages, rocketing for the clusters of crustaceans aboard their respective ships.

The sound of hundreds of claws clacking together was thunderous as the assault shrimps, recon crabs, and Rocky all launched their counterattacks. When the hundreds of strikes collided with the divine spears, it was deafening.

I witnessed only a fraction of it. All I saw before the world was consumed by light were golden streaks, blue arcs of chi wrapped in Teddy's aura, and twin red explosions from Rocky that were so large they engulfed the god-empress's spear and knocked her backward.

Maria sent what had happened across our connection. My smile widened.

It had worked.

Despite divine chi being a higher tier of essence, we had successfully nullified every single one of the spears without needing to use abyssal chi. Each had resulted in the magical equivalent of a flashbang. The enemy invaders were stunned. Fern had fainted. Even the god-empress stared in shock, gazing up at what remained of the galleon *Elegos*'s sails, which had been shredded and singed by Rocky's explosion. Her shock was made worse when over a dozen of her lesser fleet's masts tottered and fell, having been felled by crustaceans on any boats whose mages had been too slow or too inexperienced to attack.

Her strongest followers—the two seers and the five mages she called the Prime Cadre—all stood beside her on *Theoris*'s deck, frozen like statues of ice. None of them had lifted a finger. They'd seen their god-empress gathering her power, and had likely assumed that meant it was all over.

Paul, Toby, and Theresa were the first to speak.

"Hold!" Paul and Toby yelled.

"Atta—" Theresa had started, which she turned into an awkward cough. She studiously examined the sky as the other two gave her a pointed look.

The clusters of crustaceans on each deck hunkered down, the assault shrimp forming a tight group that the recon crabs surrounded. Not that any of the terrified mages were attacking them.

Rocky, however, advanced. He hopped from *Elegos* to the deck of *Theoris*, landing opposite the god-empress and her most faithful. The suave crab raised a claw to his mouth, took one last drag of his cigarette, then chucked the still-burning stub into his mouth.

"Do you surrender, Your Holiness? As you can see, you are outmatched. We use but a fraction of our might, yet you cannot hope to defeat us. We welcome any challenge, but would prefer to avoid bloodshed."

The god-empress clearly had something funky going on with her mind. I had sensed a second presence within, who'd almost succeeded in taking over. I hoped that seeing her attacks so easily nullified would help that other, kinder personality seize control.

No such luck.

She snarled like a cornered wolf, and lines of golden light swirled across her irises. She still held a spear in her left hand, which she passed to her right and flooded with power. Then she drew her arm back, the spear glowing with power.

Nonplussed, Rocky unhinged his clackers. The red cracks lining them glowed brilliant under Teddy's aura. He exhaled a cloud of smoke—don't ask me how he'd spoken without releasing any—and it billowed across the deck toward her like fog.

Eustace sprinted forward. I raised both eyebrows, wondering if she was daft enough to take Rocky head-on after he'd so easily matched her leader's spear. But she ran right past him, his smoke swirling behind her as she leaped diagonally from *Theoris* onto the deck of *Elegos*. She sprinted toward the unconscious form of Fern. Sven tried to get in her way, so she kicked him two meters in the air with a savage punt to the knackers. Then she collected Fern, threw the woman over her shoulder, and leaped off the side of the ship. Just before she hit the water, a golden platform appeared under her. She landed on it and sprinted northward, still carrying the unconscious Fern like a sack of potatoes. Was this an abduction? Should we intervene?

Perhaps wondering the same thing, the other seer dashed to *Theoris*'s railing, eyes wide as he yelled, "Eustace! Don't!"

She didn't so much as glance back, so he clutched at open air, which made a giant hand of light materialize over the bay. His hand shot forward, and so did its golden copy, fingers closing around the two women. Fern, who had been flopping around lifelessly until this point, lifted her head, flashed an impish smirk, and shot a thick arrow from each upraised palm.

This was no abduction.

This was an escape.

Both arrows struck the golden hand. Fern was clearly one of the newly awakened. She'd poured everything she had into the projectiles, and it only succeeded in slowing the hand for a moment. Her eyes rolled back as she fell unconscious, pushed beyond her limit. It might not be enough.

The seer aboard *Theoris* clenched his fist, and its golden copy did the same. The fingers formed a cage around Eustace and Fern, but Eustace burst forward at the last second, breaking free. "I won't forget that, Anius, you old bastard!" she called over her shoulder, now fleeing unimpeded toward Tropica's northern headland.

The god-empress had been gathering power the entire time. The spear had repeatedly grown then condensed, and the essence now radiating from it was so potent that tremors pulsed across the surrounding ocean. Her followers, even those at the far end of her V-formation, kept stealing glances before looking back at the glowing clusters of crustaceans on their decks.

She launched her spear. This time, I didn't have the full weight of my chi at my disposal, so the world neither froze nor slowed. Her golden projectile warped the surrounding air as it elongated, stretching to resemble a giant needle. With how close she was to Rocky, it would have reached him in the blink of a cultivator's eye if she'd aimed it at him.

She hadn't.

The giant needle raced northward, its tip piercing through Fern and into the back of Seer Eustace.

CHAPTER FORTY-EIGHT

The Impossible

All I could do was watch as the god-empress unleashed her strike. I had given the vast majority of my power away, reserving just enough to protect Ruby, Steven, and Fin. I could use that reserve to teleport the pair of divine cultivators to safety, but I wouldn't. That would leave my friends and their newborn vulnerable.

The golden spear continued its violent path. Though the tip was needle thin, the rest of it wasn't. By the time it finished passing through them, Fern and Eustace would be left with savage wounds. No matter how much chi Maria poured into them, I doubted they could be saved. In less than a second, their fates would be sealed.

A suave crab had other plans.

His claws slammed together. Twin explosions rang out. And Rocky slammed into Fern's back, knocking both her and Eustace out of the way, leaving himself in the spear's path.

He'd used most of his chi on the explosions, which had been necessary to get him there in time, but now he had nothing left to defend himself with. Most of his momentum had been transferred into the two divine cultivators, so he remained in place, the spear's power forming cracks where it struck the center of his mighty shell.

He could use his claws as a shield. Or he could angle his body and try to escape. Instead, he produced a cigarette from nowhere, lit its tip against the burning spear of golden light, and brought it to his mouth.

I watched a coin-sized circle of Rocky's shell start to deteriorate, but he just took a deep drag of his cigarette, accepting his doom. A stabbing pain appeared in my chest. Beside me, Borks whined. Maria's hand squeezed mine like a vise. Paul, Toby, and Theresa yelled something, its meaning lost on me.

The sound of Rocky's carapace shattering made the stabbing pain pierce further into my chest, making its way toward my heart. I couldn't see the damage to his shell through the blinding spear of light, but I heard the dozens of cracks, all overlapping one another. He must be covered in them. Why wasn't anyone saving him? What could I do to—

The yellow-furred head of Borks appeared from behind Rocky. The good boy opened his mouth, bit down on Rocky's rear end, and pulled the crab to safety. I whirled around as I heard something hit the sand behind me.

Rocky.

Wisps of smoke rose from both the top of his head and the cigarette in his claw.

His shell was whole, and though cracks lined his shell, they were the red ones he always bore. As my panic turned to relief, I could finally think straight, and I realized what'd happened.

The cracking sounds hadn't come from Rocky's carapace. They'd come from Borks, who'd opened a portal to retrieve the suave crab. Maria made a word echo across our connection—the one that Paul, Toby, and Theresa had yelled: *Fetch.* No wonder Borks had whined earlier. He'd had to wait for permission, forced to watch Rocky get assaulted by the god-empress's divine spear.

Now that I knew Rocky was safe, the stabbing pain faded, and I rubbed the side of my chest through my suit jacket.

Borks closed his portal to open another, and a moment later, Eustace and Fern came sailing through it. He'd angled them toward an immovable object—Teddy—and their flight ended abruptly when they struck the giant bear's flank. Maria was at their side in an instant, her pink chi flowing out to heal them, which was the only task Paul and the others had given her for the battle.

The two women literally had holes in them, but they were safe now, so I faced the bay once more. I found the god-empress irate, her face locked in a half snarl, her hateful stare directed toward us. She took a shuddering step forward. Golden light poured into her from the silvery artifacts lining *Theoris's* hull.

Paul, Theresa, and Toby were once again the first to speak.

"Roundhouse!" Paul and Theresa yelled.

"Shields!" Toby yelled at the same time.

A few things happened at once.

Paul and Theresa's heads whipped around, giving Toby a questioning look. Toby's cheeks flushed red, and much like his sister had done earlier, he stared up at the sky, refusing to meet Paul or Theresa's eye. A hundred meters south, I spotted two silhouettes come into view as Deklan and Dom rocketed to their feet. They froze, looked at each other, then crouched back down, disappearing from sight.

My mind raced. Was that where everyone else was hiding? The twins had likely shot up in response to what Toby had yelled. If the code to summon them was "shields," "roundhouse" likely meant—

The god-empress exploded forward, another spear already forming in her clenched fist, drawn back to jab at the prone forms of Eustace and Fern. Before she made it more than a few meters, a deafening honk drew her attention, and her head shot to the northern sky above her, where she spied Pelly rocketing down from the stratosphere.

The roundhouse kick of immaculate form, however, came from the south.

Cinnamon squealed her victory. The high-pitched scream was undercut by a thumping *boom* as she kicked the god-empress in the back of the head, and a booming *thump* when the god-empress's body hit the front balustrade of *Theoris*.

I had thought "Prime Vessel" was just an empty title, but it seemed I was wrong. Cinnamon's Teddy-empowered attack would have sent the god-empress careening through every one of Tropica's buildings, but *Theoris's* ornate wooden railing hadn't moved an inch.

Cinnamon landed gracefully on the deck. She took a low stance, presented an upturned forepaw, and gestured for the stunned monarch to bring it. When the god-empress didn't respond, she gave the Prime Cadre and Seer Anius the same gesture, but they didn't respond either, simply staring at the martial bunny in unfettered shock. A barely noticeable smile played on the corner of Cinnamon's lips in response.

Though I felt like I should be grinning along with her, all I could focus on was the anxiety building in the pit of my stomach, made worse the longer I considered the situation. There was the damage done to Eustace and Fern, for one thing. For another, Rocky had almost been cracked open like a coconut. Yes, he'd played it cool. And yes, Borks had waited until the last minute to save him, only delaying until Paul, Toby, and Theresa gave the order.

But that was the crux of the issue.

We had thrown all of our eggs in that basket, and twice already they had given contradictory orders—once when Theresa ordered an attack while the others called to "hold," and again when Toby yelled "shields," the others calling for Cinnamon. They were small errors that hadn't resulted in disaster, yet they were errors all the same. What if there had been a miscommunication earlier, resulting in Rocky's rescue being delayed? A few seconds could pass like *that* in the heat of battle. No matter how cool Rocky had played it, he would have been seriously injured if he'd remained in the path of the god-empress's attack any longer.

Worse, all this had occurred when there was only a single battle taking place. The rest of the enemy forces were stunned, but I doubted they would remain so. The severity of any errors or miscommunications would increase exponentially if the rest of the invaders conquered their fear of the crustaceans clustered on each deck.

That doubt resonated against my chest, making some of the stabbing pain return.

My introspection ended when I noticed the conversation taking place behind me.

"Hiiii!" Slimes burbled. He was clinging to Eustace's back, his head stretched around to look into her eyes. "My mistress tells the truth! You are not in danger. In fact, this is likely the safest place in all of Tropica for you to rest and recover."

I turned to find dubious expressions on Eustace's and Fern's faces. Maria gave them a bemused smile in return.

"It is all true," hissed Rocky, still puffing on his second cigarette of the battle. "I thank you for your kindness earlier, Apprentice Fern. You thought I was an unawakened crab, yet you tried to hide me, even spoke in my defense when another suggested stomping on me. You did all this despite knowing you could be punished for it. Bravo, Fern. Your bravery warms my blood."

It was a touching speech, and would have gone a long way toward convincing them they weren't in danger, except they clearly had no clue what Rocky was saying. If anything—judging by the way both women recoiled from the sincere crustacean—they heard his hisses and bubbles as a threat. Slimes only made it worse by nodding along emphatically.

Maria laughed.

So did I, in spite of my doubts. I translated for him. "Rocky thanked you for not stomping on him, and for risking your own safety by trying to hide him. He finished off by praising you, and saying your bravery warmed his heart."

"Warmed my blood," corrected Rocky.

"Mate, I know you said they warmed your blood, but that's *way* creepier. They're not crabs. See? Look at their faces. One mention of blood and you almost lost them."

Rocky nodded to me in acknowledgment, then bowed to them in apology, his intention clear to anyone with eyes.

"And for what it's worth," I continued, "I completely agree with Rocky. You standing up for him and trying to protect him showed remarkable strength of character. I reckon you'd fit in here after all is said and done. Assuming you want to stay, of course. We aren't in the habit of forcing people to do anything."

Eustace frowned, and she gave me a curious look, like I was a particularly colorful beetle she'd stumbled upon whilst on a garden stroll. "You mean that, don't you?"

"Yep. As far as I'm concerned, you two saying 'frack that noise' and trying to run from your god-empress only makes me trust you even more. We can chat more about it later, after my mates beat the ever-living piss out of your god-empress."

I turned back to the battlefield just in time for the god-empress to get to her feet. A calm fury ran through her, so strong that even I felt it with my weakened senses. She exploded across the deck and jabbed a divine spear at Cinnamon's heart, who slipped to the side and whirled around, cracking the god-empress with a spinning heel kick to the ribs. She crashed into the starboard railing this time.

"Are you going to kill them?" Eustace asked.

Though I wasn't facing her, I didn't miss the sadness in her voice.

Ruby snorted. "I can only imagine what you think of us, given you were raised in a 'divine' kingdom, but we're not monsters. If Fischer's plan was to obliterate everyone, I wouldn't be standing here with my baby."

The conversation continued, but I tuned them out. Maria had stepped up beside me, leaving Slimes to finish healing Rocky's shell. She grabbed my hand and squeezed it softly.

"I was worried about you," she whispered softly so only I could hear. The god-empress got back to her feet and flew at Cinnamon again, only for a savage uppercut to catch her on the chin and send her reeling skyward. "I could feel your doubt," Maria continued. "I thought I'd have to come over here and slap some sense into you the moment I finished healing them."

I gave her a tight smile. "I'm still not feeling great about it all, but talking some smack did wonders for my attitude."

"You know, I'd think that was a personality flaw if it were anyone else."

"What makes you think it isn't a personality flaw for me?"

"Because I know for a fact you're not a cruel person." Maria grinned as Cinnamon turned tail and wiggled her tooshie, taunting the god-empress. "You revel in being absurd, but it's never at the expense of anyone who doesn't welcome it, or doesn't deserve it. Though you *did* take it a bit far earlier . . ."

"What? When?"

"What do you mean *when*? You accused the god-empress of trying to undress you, then alluded to Mother Nature caressing your . . . *bits*."

"Oh. That was nothing." The god-empress fell for Cinnamon's taunt and charged in, using streams of her golden essence to propel her forward. "I'll have you know I was using *all* my restraint. I didn't even unleash my best bit of confusing information, because it would have for sure pissed her off."

Cinnamon ducked the god-empress's charge and hit her with a double kick to the abdomen, sending the god-empress flying out toward the left wing of the Divine Fleet. Cinnamon hopped after her.

Maria cleared her throat, so I risked a glance her way. She was giving me a flat stare. "Go on."

"Whatever do you mean, my love?"

Her eye twitched. "You know I'm gonna ask, so just tell me."

"I need you to say it."

At the far end of the V-formation, Cinnamon was exchanging a flurry of blows with the god-empress, who was holding her ground by absorbing streams of divine chi from the containers lining her nearby ships.

Maria was watching me instead. She quirked a brow, tried to give me a serious expression, then ruined it with her beautiful laugh. "Gods, you're annoying sometimes. Fine. I'll say it. What was your best bit of confusing information?"

"I thought you'd never ask." I beamed at her. "Forty-two."

". . . What?"

"Forty-two. The meaning of life. It's from *The Hitchhiker's Guide to the Galaxy*, which was originally a radio sitcom but got adapted into novels, a text-based game, and a TV series. The adaptation everyone knows is the movie, though, which was when it really hit the mainstream. The movie was based on the novel, and some people *really* hated it, but—" I flinched as Cinnamon kicked the god-empress in the chest so hard that a shock wave ruffled my shorts, cooling my . . . legs. "—but I reckon the movie was actually really well done, considering the limitations of the medium. Besides, Adams changed the story *every* time he adapted it, so people shouldn't have expected a faithful retelling of the novel. You can't please everyone."

Though Maria had let me finish my rant, she didn't look happy about it. "What in Eris's winged strife are you talking about? What does *any* of this"—she gestured at the Divine Fleet—"have to do with the meaning of life?"

"Forty-two," I said. Before she could whap me on the back of the noggin, I repeated her gesture at the enemy fleet. "It's how many boats they have. Forty-two."

She opened her mouth to respond, then made the smart decision and closed it, shaking her head. "You're right. That absolutely would have pissed the god-empress off. I'm in love with you, but everything you just said made me want to head-butt you over the ocean."

"Thank you. It's nice having my art seen and appreciated."

Cinnamon and the god-empress exchanged another series of blows, and for the first time, Cinnamon lost the exchange. The shaft of the god-empress's spear caught my martial bunny on the side, and I felt my jaw clench as Cinnamon smashed down onto a nearby deck. The wooden planks splintered beneath her, almost breaking in half. The assault shrimp and recon crabs aboard scuttled to surround her, raising their open clackers toward the sky in threat, but Cinnamon got back to her feet. She hadn't been injured. My jaw remained tight.

"Wedge!" the god-empress screamed. Her voice was ragged, laced with divine chi and guttural tones. "Wedge formation! And *fight*!"

Half of the enemy forces obeyed instantly, and the other half followed suit a second later. Each ship had five mages, two of whom started flooding divine chi into the sails, repositioning the ships. Wedge. They were going to form a triangular flotilla. Each ship's remaining three mages immediately attacked their respective cluster of crustaceans. The assault shrimp and recon crabs counterattacked, but only enough to nullify the strikes coming their way.

In the air behind them, Cinnamon and the god-empress clashed head-on. Cinnamon lost this exchange as well, careening into and ripping through an unfurled sail before landing vertically on a mast. Her lip tugged up into a grin as she launched herself back at the enemy monarch.

No orders came from our three strategists, so I looked at them. They were staring back at me, and though I couldn't feel their emotions, I could see the stress and worry wrought on their faces. Except for Theresa. She was giving me a fierce scowl.

I suddenly realized how much of an idiot I had been. My senses might have been muted, but theirs weren't. Considering their ideals, they'd absolutely be able to sense my doubts. What kind of commanders wouldn't be able to tell when someone's morale bottomed out? I'd tasked them with leading this battle, then undermined them before the real fighting even began.

It was starting now. The divine forces were finally attacking. The god-empress was drawing from the chi within the ancient constructs lining her fleet, using the power held within to overpower Cinnamon, who had been kicking the crap out of her only minutes ago.

And our three commanders were too busy worrying about me to focus on the task at hand. They might be leading this battle, but I was the leader of Tropica. They looked up to me, and I was letting them down.

I had to do something.

Maria brushed my arm and took a step away, withdrawing. She understood exactly what I was thinking—her senses weren't dampened like mine—yet she wasn't going to offer me any assistance. I thanked her for giving me the space, and for knowing me better than anyone else. This was something I had to do on my own.

The first thing I did was call out to the tunnels below. They were absolutely *bristling* with power. The last time I'd filled the network with power, it had empowered my cultivation to a ridiculous extent. If I could just harness a fraction of the latent chi dwelling beneath me . . .

But no. It hadn't changed since the other day. The essence was down there, but it was occupied, seeming to be "maturing," for lack of a better word.

Now that I knew that wasn't a possibility, I changed tack, focusing on the only other thing I could do.

I had to conquer my doubts.

It was far easier said than done. If anything, the pressure to get over my worries only made them worse. I bit the inside of my lip as anxiety swelled in my stomach, making it churn. A wave of nausea washed over me. I bit down harder, focusing on the physical sensation, hoping it would help. It didn't.

What could I do? My mind raced through all the possibilities, but the harder I tried, the worse it got. I made myself slow down. Trying to force the answer to arrive wasn't working, so I let go of that need, focusing on my breathing instead. I fixated on the sensations. The air cooled my nostrils when I inhaled. As it filled my lungs, my chest expanded, making me feel powerful—in control. And when I exhaled, my breath was warm and humid between my pursed lips, leaving my entire body with a lingering sense of calm.

I let my mind wander, trusting myself enough to hand over control.

Trust, I mused. Had it ever led me astray?

The first thought that arrived was when the network—which would go on to become the basis for expanding both my Domain and my personal power—had told me to trust my friends back when King Augustus and the rest of Gormona had attacked Tropica. Because I had listened, multiple breakthroughs and advancements had occurred. My friends had gotten stronger, lifting Tropica's overall capability.

Though that was the most obvious example, it'd hardly been the first time trust had benefited me.

Not long after my arrival in Tropica, I had trusted Barry enough to ask him about the System, and to let him know about the awakening of Sergeant Snips. Both were enough to see me collared by the capital—and had given poor Barry an existential crisis at the time—but look at all the good that had come of it.

I had trusted everyone with the truth that I liked fishing and seafood, even after I discovered it was considered heretical. I had trusted all my animal pals not to go full murder hobo back when they first awakened—even Rocky, back when the lingering soul of an evil cultivator was making him batshit insane.

I had trusted Teddy to go off and discover his ideal, and I'd trusted him not to obliterate Dodge when the bear found him, Toby, and the sick Theresa in the forest.

I had trusted Paul to show Toby and Theresa the ropes around Tropica, and I'd trusted him not to subjugate them when the misguided part of himself had assumed that to be the pragmatic choice.

I had trusted Claws to do whatever she wanted with the tree of fulgurite, despite how rare and powerful natural artifacts were.

I had trusted Ellis, despite his secrets. And I'd trusted his abyssal co-conspirators, letting them create—and pour random concoctions into—what'd looked like a funnel to hell in the middle of Tropica.

I had trusted Snips by ceding my will to her when I created her eyepatch, fully believing she would use it to protect everyone from the subsequent explosion, which she had, of course. That'd felt like a leap of faith at the time, but it was *nothing* compared to what I had done today. I'd trusted Teddy and Lemon and the rest of Tropica with the vast majority of my power. Teddy and Lemon could have done anything with it. They literally could have used it to stab me, and everyone I loved, in the back. I'd not doubted them for a second.

I barked a laugh, letting it boom out over the battlefield. I was too overjoyed and relieved to care if it angered our enemy. Gods, I could be such an idiot sometimes. When I opened my eyes, I didn't have to force the smile that stretched from one side of my face to the other.

"My bad," I said, shooting Paul, Toby, and Theresa a wink. "Promise it won't happen again."

No longer did stress and worry line their faces. The three tacticians grinned, turned toward the bay and all of Tropica's forces, and yelled at the top of their lungs.

"Attack!"

CHAPTER FORTY-NINE

¿Por Qué No Los Dos?

Fischer's trust flooded through Paul. The doubt and despair coming from Tropica's god-king had made it hard to think. He'd barely been able to focus on the battle while Fischer's faith in him waned, let alone make any clear-headed decisions.

But now, Fischer had conquered his misgivings, and Paul felt lighter than air.

Yet his brow still furrowed as he spotted an imbalance in the battlefield. Paul reached out to Toby and Theresa, and they latched on to his tendrils of essence, joining their awarenesses together. The three of them assessed the situation.

The enemy force was about to mobilize. The assault shrimp and recon crabs were already in play, and they were a good match for the two hundred mages spread evenly across the Divine Fleet. Cinnamon was having to be cautious, but she was still a close match with the god-empress. What Tropica didn't currently have an answer for was the Prime Cadre and Seer Anius, who were already gathering divine chi in their limbs, preparing to wreak havoc.

The three tacticians had to find a way to nullify those powerful enemies, or else they'd have to initiate the next stage of the battle, which might swing it too far in Tropica's favor, robbing the defenders of potential breakthroughs.

They found a perfect solution almost immediately. It was playful enough to appease Theresa, and logically sound enough to keep Toby happy. Paul's sensibilities were smack dab in the middle of theirs; if they were content, so was he.

With their wills still joined, the three of them addressed different defenders.

"Pistachio! Shelly!" Toby called, facing the nearby dunes. "Suppressing fire!"

"Aerial forces!" Paul yelled at the sky through cupped hands. "Diversionary tactics!"

"Maria!" Theresa screamed so loud that Maria jumped a little. "Throw Slimes over there so he can slap! Them! *Silly!*"

Shelly and Pistachio's claws were already cocked open and trained on the closest ship as they crested the closest dune. The black, white, and brown forms of the pelicans exploded into view directly above, leaving holes in the clouds they'd shot through. Slimes appeared on Maria's palm, burbling and jiggling in anticipation.

Teddy's red offensive aura glowed around every single one of them.

The lobsters' snippers clacked together, releasing blasts of chi that were thicker than Pistachio. The pelicans honked at full volume, announcing their arrival and already diverting attention. And Slimes yelled "Hiiiii!" as Maria launched him for the dead center of Anius's torso.

Slimes got there first. Understanding that his purpose was to be a temporary distraction, his form was gelatinous, not crystalline, when he struck the seer. The sound of their collision was horrifying. Anius rocketed backward, and when his body hit *Theoris*'s mast, it made an only slightly less horrifying thud.

Paul knew the diversion would be a success, so he tore his eyes from the amusing spectacle and considered the rest of the battlefield.

He grinned as he watched hundreds of assault shrimps unleash attacks at their opposing mages. With the recon crabs guarding them, they didn't have to hold back. The blasts were devastating. Some of the less experienced mages failed to block or divert the attacks, resulting in direct hits.

Paul squinted and leaned closer when he saw gold essence flare around the bodies of those struck. He, Toby, and Theresa focused on one such cultivator, combining their forces to examine her core. The woman had been hit in the chest with two arcing blades of water essence, and her core had reacted, expending a large portion of its reserves to counter the strikes. A moment later, her reserves were restored. That same golden essence had flared from Anius when Slimes hit him, but they'd assumed it was due to the seer's higher level of cultivation. Slimes was clinging to *Theoris*'s mast and whipping himself around like a gelatinous flail. He caught Evan on the side of the head, and the same thing happened, though Evan hadn't needed to expend as much chi to defend himself.

"Fascinating," Toby said, his gaze flicking around the battlefield. "Their cores spent a bunch of their chi to defend against incoming attacks, and then the cores of those around them all pitched in to restore those who'd been drained."

Toby was right. Paul had seen the thin lines of divine essence flowing across the Divine Fleet, forming an intricate spiderweb.

"I wonder if it's because of the containers?" Toby continued. "Is it the god-empress's will? Or is it just the inherent nature of divine chi to defend then bolster anyone else using it?"

Theresa blew a loud, impressively wet raspberry. "Who cares, you nerd!"

"Who cares?" Toby repeated, confused. "We need to understand the enemy if we wish to beat them . . ."

Theresa rolled her eyes and shook her head.

The difference in their personalities made Paul remember the miscommunications that'd already happened between himself and the two siblings during the battle. But he was feeling too content to let that reminder bring him down. Of course they wouldn't agree on everything. They were three individual people. Their unique personalities were something to be celebrated—even if the possibility of conflicting orders made him a little nervous.

Though many of the assault shrimp's attacks had been devastating, the enemy forces recovered swiftly. Many of the ships had actually overcome the attacks, their divine spears eviscerating the arcing projectiles of water essence. Thankfully, the recon crabs had spared the shrimp from any harm, redirecting the golden spears with blasts of their own.

All across the bay, the Divine Fleet continued carrying out their god-empress's will. Two of the five mages on each lesser vessel were channeling their power up into their sails, making the enemy ships move with surprising alacrity. Some had been blown off course when the onboard mages had to defend themselves, but then the god-empress intervened, flooding out divine chi that pulled the flotilla back into shape.

Paul glanced up at the god-empress. She'd been drawing in more and more of the golden chi from nearby containers. Cinnamon had been forced to alter her fighting style. Even with the god-empress diverting some of her will and power toward the ships, Cinnamon had to rely on speed and timing, shifting from pure assault to calculated skirmishing.

The fleet resembled a diamond more than a *V* now. Those at the far ends of the wings fanned in as those toward the front of the formation drifted closer, forming the wedge.

Paul grinned. He could feel Toby and Theresa doing the same. It was time for the next stage. Paul opened his mouth, sending out tendrils of chi for his friends to latch on to, inviting them to join him. Toby latched on to it, his ideal in complete alignment. Theresa, however, clearly felt differently.

"Coconut crabs!" she screamed alone, her voice flying across the bay.

Paul's head whipped toward her, as did Toby's. It was what they would have yelled, too, but their ideals railed at her doing it without them. She had essentially seized control, putting herself above them.

When she realized what she'd done, her cheeks flushed red. Instead of gazing at the sky and pretending it hadn't happened, she stared down at her toes, her curls hanging to hide her embarrassed face.

"Sorry . . ." she said.

Guilt and shame roiled in Paul's core. She hadn't meant to do it. Sure, she'd gotten carried away, but his and Toby's visceral reaction hadn't helped. To make matters worse, Toby hadn't relented. He was leaning into his anger, clenching his jaw as he stared wordlessly at Theresa. Paul had to get control of this situation. They had to work together, lest it snowball into something as debilitating as Fischer's earlier doubts.

Thankfully, the perfect distraction was about to arrive.

"Coconut crabs?" Fischer asked. "If you befriended coconut crabs without me, I'm gonna be pissed. That . . ." He trailed off, staring at the open ocean to the southeast. "What the frack?"

"What are you—" Maria started, cutting off when she spotted what he'd seen. "Wait, is that . . . ?"

Two dozen lines carved their way toward the Divine Fleet. Maria reached out with her senses, frowning as she strained to force her way in. When she succeeded, she cackled with laughter.

"What?" Fischer asked, his head moving back and forth between Maria and the distant lines. "What is it? Is it coconut crabs?"

Maria ignored him, clearly trying to rile him up.

It was working.

"Oh, come on!" Fischer said. "Paul! I see you smirking! I order you to tell me who or what the frack that is!"

"No need. You can see it for yourself."

Just then, Dodge dropped his aura of invisibility, revealing the twelve beings sailing toward the Divine Fleet's southern flank. Paul stole a glance at Fischer and found the god-king's eyes glazed over. Paul smirked, recalling the description Fischer must now be seeing.

Tactical Coconut Boats of the Faithful
Mythical
Created through the multidisciplinary efforts of a god-king's faithful, these boats are suffused with the will of those who created them. When within their god-king's Domain, and so long as the creators' remain faithful, these boats are completely immune to foreign chi.
[Error: Naval systems offline.]

"Immune . . . ?" Maria asked.

"Naval systems offline?" Fischer added, his eyes clearing. "But no mention of insufficient power . . ."

Tropica's naval force approached in a V-formation of their own.

Dodge led the procession. He wobbled a little, still getting used to the half-shell "boat" strapped to each foot. Following in Dodge's wake, Barry flexed his muscles and spun on the spot, oiled body glimmering under the morning sun. His prideful ideal had somehow overcome the inherent instability—and insecurity—of someone so muscular skating around on coconuts. Composing the rest of the *V* was the Church of Carcinization, and their mostly human bodies had assumed the perfect form, with only sparse sections of carapace covering their privates. They clacked their claw hands threateningly.

It was enough for even the god-empress to pause a beat. Her irises glowed golden as she took in the oncoming fleet. The same happened across the entire bay, every battle momentarily pausing, their attention arrested.

"Forty-two!" Maria yelled for some reason.

Then, as if they'd all agreed to it beforehand, everyone moved at once. Every single enemy mage with a clear line of sight to Dodge, Barry, and the Church of Carcinization released a divine projectile at them.

Dodge sped toward a gap between ships in the middle of the enemy flotilla. At the last moment, he crested a small wave, veered to the right, and slammed against the hull of a lesser ship. He made himself go invisible as he bounced off and tried to regain balance.

Barry, either inspired by Dodge or trying to make it seem like his friend had struck the boat on purpose, slammed right into the same spot on the same ship.

Unlike Dodge, he didn't bounce off. His muscular head punched through the hull, followed by the rest of his oiled body, leaving a Barry-shaped hole in the ship. Water poured in after him, and before Paul had a chance to worry about his father, Barry's muscular form exploded through the upper deck, glistening like a Christmas ham.

"Forty-one!" Maria yelled as the boat started to sink.

The Church of Carcinization, who had been moving head-on, suddenly zigged and zagged to the left and right like scuttling crabs, avoiding the countless arrows, spears, and even a bucket someone had thrown overboard in panic. Not one projectile hit its mark. Back and forth and round and round the Church zipped, drawing everyone's attention toward the ocean.

It was absolute mayhem. Everyone on the shore watched—laughing, awe-struck, or both. Even Eustace and Fern were more amused than horrified.

It was too much for Theresa to handle.

Paul felt it swelling in her chest, a desire to once again act out of turn. He could have stopped her if he wanted. Indeed, his ideal railed against it, ordering him to enforce their equal hierarchy. If he did nothing, she would spend one of their strongest troops. He clenched his fists, grabbed hold of his own ideal, and shoved it aside momentarily.

He would give her this one. He had to. Better to compromise and remain as a unified front.

Paul expected Toby to be giving his sister a baleful glare like the last time she'd presumed to act, but when Paul looked at the older teen, Toby was instead staring his way. Calculating eyes stared at Paul from beneath a furrowed brow, and with a barely perceptible nod, Toby approved.

Rather than invite them to join his will, Paul offered to join hers. Toby followed suit a moment later. Theresa's head whipped around, and the look on her face alone was enough to tell Paul he'd made the right choice. She absolutely shone with both disbelief and unbridled excitement. She spun her entire body around, not facing the bay, but the nearby mountains. Paul and Toby did the same. Unified, they released their command.

"Zeusify!"

Lightning cracked behind the mountain range. Its blue-white brilliance was bright enough to outshine the morning sun. Or so Paul thought. He blinked, looking all around himself, gazing curiously at the bubbles of chi rising from the ground and coalescing in the air.

"*Oh . . .*" the three tacticians said together, then the chi slammed into them.

CHAPTER FIFTY

For the Love of Seafood

The reason for their breakthrough was as simple as it was contradictory. The longer Paul considered it, the more he wanted to laugh.

Being a commander or leader meant giving orders, but that didn't mean you were a dictator. No matter how much experience one had, it was still possible to make a mistake. Which was why it was important—*vital*, even—for a commander to take the opinions of others into account. It was even more vital in this case because Paul, Toby, and Theresa were three individuals of the same rank. If ever they disagreed, the only way for them to remain a unified front was through compromise.

Which was exactly what they had just done. *Compromise.* And somehow, that had been significant enough to trigger their breakthrough.

By pushing their ideal aside . . .

What kind of an ideal *wanted* you to defy it?

Looking back, it made a weird sort of sense to Paul. His partial breakthrough had also stemmed from defiance, when he'd denied the obtusely pragmatic part of himself that had wanted to subjugate Toby and Theresa. This time too, he had ignored his ideal, forcing it to the side so he could make what he believed was the right decision. Toby had done the same.

And Theresa had been ignoring her ideal the whole damn time, following her instincts to shove it aside and do what she thought was right. In holding on to their ideals, Toby and Paul had believed she was being immature—indulging her childlike tendencies despite the stakes at hand. Perhaps that *was* all she'd been doing, but it didn't matter now.

Their breakthrough had arrived.

Paul's entire body crawled with power. It pressed into his skin and flowed down into the channels his chi ran along. There, he felt it push against the System's influence. The System relented, removing the shackles that reduced his strength.

Paul bellowed, and so did Toby and Theresa.

My smile was so wide that my cheeks ached, the ascension before me even more enjoyable than the arrival of Barry, Dodge, and ten crab-people had been. The battlefield had frozen again. Even the god-empress and Cinnamon were unmoving, the god-empress floating above the ocean on a platform of golden light, my bunny pal perched atop the mast of a lesser ship.

The three little rascals had really done it. They'd finished their partial breakthrough from less than a week ago, and the System had removed the limits placed on their cores. Power flooded out into the world, announcing to the universe that they'd earned the System's approval.

Before I could consider the implications of that, Eustace asked a rather reasonable question.

"What is *wrong* with you people?"

I smiled over at the seer's baffled expression, her gaze locked on Paul, Toby, and Theresa.

Despite how close we were, and the fact a breakthrough of this caliber usually resulted in a massive explosion, I knew we had nothing to worry about. Our three tacticians wobbled on their feet, but their resolves were ironclad, and they ordered the explosive chi to flow out across the bay in an intentional web whose purpose was beyond me.

What wasn't beyond me was the part of that web that flowed into my body. I took an involuntary gasp of air as it refilled a third of my essence. No. That wasn't it. I frowned down at my abdomen. Whatever they'd done had increased the capacity of my core, letting it draw essence from my surroundings. I glanced up at the children, who had been caught by Teddy, but were now once more standing with their own strength. Then, I looked out at the bay. The brilliant red aura surrounding my friends glowed brighter. Just like mine, the capacity of their cores had increased.

Fern repeated Eustace's question. "What *is* wrong with you people . . . ?"

"Huh?" I asked, feeling much more jovial now that I had some spare chi. "The children back in your kingdom don't ascend as commanders?"

"We don't let children come to battles," Eustace said. "Let alone lead them."

"There's your problem! How are your younguns gonna learn if you don't let them get any experience? This Kingdom of Light of yours has it all backwards." I turned to grin at them. Besides, that was nothing. You'll find this next bit downright *shocking*."

Maria groaned at my pun, then yelled "Forty!" as Barry leaped onto a neighboring ship, grabbed some fella by the waist, and suplexed him. The entire vessel broke in half. Barry leaped onto the next boat, but before he could dole out any more sweet moves, *she* arrived.

Corporal Claws didn't so much streak through the sky as she just kinda . . . appeared. She floated a hundred meters or so above the ocean in her elemental form, her body blue and translucent. Held to the side was RPM, gripped by the scruff, limbs splayed wide as he let out a villainous chuckle. Protruding from her pocket, I could see the hilt of a . . . *Was that a sword?* She held a multifaceted dagger in her other forepaw, and as she angled it down toward the god-empress, she grinned, revealing her needle-sharp teeth.

The god-empress stared back in defiance, finally drawn from her stupor. She summoned a golden spear in her right hand and hefted it back, aiming it for Claws's glowing form.

"Slimes, aerial forces," Paul said. "Withdraw. You too, Pistachio and Shelly. Stop firing. Don't draw attention to the shore."

"Cinnamon," Toby said. "Stand by."

"Claws, RPM," Theresa whispered. "Strike once."

Corporal Claws obeyed. A trill screamed from her throat as she started gathering chi in her dagger, then launched RPM down toward *Theoris*. Spherical, the devious raccoon raced down toward the Prime Cadre and Seer Anius, who took up defensive stances as Slimes and the pelicans retreated.

Just before RPM struck, Claws's elemental chi exploded from the dagger. The bolt of lightning that left its blade was thicker than *Theoris*'s mast. It tore a jagged line down toward the god-empress, whose eyes went wide as the bolt approached, arced past her, then slammed into some poor bloke in the center of the flotilla.

The god-empress frowned down at her follower as he was sent flying over the decks of five different ships, everyone in his path leaping out of the way. At the sixth ship, a woman finally took pity on him, spreading her arms and standing in the path of his lifeless form—only for her to get flooded with the electricity still wreathing his body when she caught him. Both enemies collapsed on the spot, their cores emptied, rendering them unconscious.

"Interesting," Paul said, seemingly to himself.

"Thirty-nine!" Maria called. A ship at the back of the flotilla had succumbed to the crustaceans atop it, who'd then leaped across to the closest vessel.

What Paul said next was sent out to the whole battlefield. "If we deplete their cores with a single strike, their allies can't help them recover. Focus on powerful strikes that— *Claws! What are you doing? Theresa said to strike once!*"

"Yes, she did . . ." chittered Claws, her grin even wider than before. "My dagger's passive made me miss. It didn't—" Claws cut off as the god-empress's golden spear rocketed toward her heart.

My stomach dropped when I sensed the spear's power.

The god-empress had been drawing more and more chi from the surrounding containers, and the chi now condensed into the single projectile about to pierce Claws made every hair on the back of my neck rise. I wasn't sure *I* could take a direct hit, even if I hadn't surrendered most of my essence.

Claws scrambled to dodge, but the spear was too fast. It caught her in the side, and I took a step forward, reaching for my chi, but there was nothing I could do. I stared up in horror as Claws clutched her side, doubled over, and slowly, weakly, lifted her head.

Maria reached for her chi and summoned a pink cloud of essence. I offered my power to her, praying it would be enough. We both froze when we caught the look in Claws's eyes.

"It didn't count," she finished, flashing her sharp grin as she straightened and let go of her side, revealing a patch of fur that had been shaved off by the golden spear's deadly tip.

Before the god-empress could release another attack, Claws released hers. The bolt of lightning thundered down, looked poised to tear its way right through the enemy monarch, but again turned at the last second.

It struck somewhere else this time, but only because the mage it was targeting had recently been sent flying roughly six ships over. Claws howled with laughter as it cracked down toward the exact same bloke as before.

Two of the mages on that ship had gone to help the unconscious enemies. Claws's lightning wasn't like normal lightning. Rather than seeking the path of least resistance to the ground, it sought chi-filled cores. Thus, the pair of well-intentioned enemies trying to assist their fallen comrades were much more attractive targets than the two whose cores had already been drained.

The lightning forked and slammed into both of them, hammering them down into the deck.

"Thirty-eight . . ." Maria said somberly, biting the inside of her lip as the ship blew apart.

Like me, she knew how close we'd just been to losing a friend. If Claws could be destroyed by a direct hit from one of those spears, anyone could.

"That-one-didn't-count-either!" screeched Claws.

Paul, Toby, and Theresa ignored her, instead turning toward Borks, who was sitting by my side. "Daggers," they said.

Borks opened a portal and leaped through. I didn't see where the other side appeared.

Claws's third blast of lightning slammed directly into the god-empress's chest, causing Claws to look a little annoyed. Her disappointment didn't last long. She let out a victorious trill as the god-empress's smoking form crashed through the deck of a ship toward the front of the Divine Fleet, obliterating it. A plume of seawater fountained into the air, carrying with it the debris of the destroyed vessel.

"Thirty-seven!" chittered Claws, zipping in my direction.

Stunned as they were, two of the Prime Cadre were present enough to launch attacks at Claws as she shot by, Evan with a spear, and a woman with a volley of arrows. The tricksy otter easily dodged the projectiles. She retorted with small bolts of lightning shot from the tips of her dual-wielded finger guns. Both mages flared with golden light as their chi countered the relatively weak strikes.

I frowned. Where was RPM? Wasn't he supposed to be battling the six people aboard the *Theoris*? He was nowhere to be seen. Before I could even consider using some of my limited chi to find him, Claws slammed into my chest. I caught her, and she rested her rump on my arms as she grinned at Maria and me.

When she saw our expressions, her joy faltered, replaced by confusion, then understanding. She nuzzled my chin and stroked my face, consoling me the only way she knew how. "I'm fine, Master!" She flopped to her back and rolled onto her side. "See? The evil lady only hit my fur! Everything is *fine*!"

I wished I believed her. The sharp pain from earlier stabbed into my chest.

Though my doubt hadn't returned, I couldn't help but worry for the safety of my friends. I knew that letting them struggle was the best way to ensure Tropica thrived long term, but that didn't alleviate my anxiety. Any one of them could be struck down by the god-empress if she released another of those spears.

I finally spotted Borks. His right legs were standing on Pelly, his left legs on Bill. The rest of the pelicans trailed close behind. They were dropping weapons. Daggers. Dozens of them. The multifaceted blades rained down, each finding their way into one of the claws, hands, or paws of Tropica's forces.

An assault shrimp leveled its new weapon at an opposing mage. Water chi flowed from it and slammed into the woman. Golden light flared around her, then faded completely. She collapsed, her core emptied by the strike. The assault prawn's eyes twinkled as they stared at the weapon. He poured more chi into the dagger, then set the tip of its blade against the deck.

Thirty-six.

Seeing that ship blown apart, a recon crab redirected its dagger from an enemy mage to a neighboring vessel. The dagger's passive kicked in, making the blast do a 180 and obliterate the ship that the crab stood atop. Claws laughed so hard she almost choked.

Thirty-five.

Before the blast had changed course from the targeted vessel, a mage had panicked and leaped off its deck. He really should have checked the water first. He found himself directly in the path of Joel, who was racing sideways between the Divine Fleet, carrying five unconscious enemies back to shore.

Joel's arms were full, so he didn't have a dagger. Jess did, though.

She slid across the ocean in his wake, and the empowered blast of water shot from her blade slammed into the man before he made it halfway to the ocean. Joel plucked his unconscious body from the air and threw it over his shoulder. Claws's tittering got louder with each successful attack.

Thirty-four.

Even more of the assault shrimp and recon crabs had weapons now. Eight vessels were destroyed within moments of each other.

Twenty-six.

Still perched atop a mast, Cinnamon had been laying low, obeying her orders to "stand by." The moment she caught a dagger, that changed. She smiled deviously and unleashed a half dozen martial aura attacks in so many seconds. Each one resulted in the destruction of a vessel, the crustaceans atop it leaping to a nearby vessel and joining the cluster of assault shrimp and recon crabs already on that deck.

Claws had leaped down onto the sand. Her forepaws were weaving through the air, and she blew a merry tune on her wooden whistle as she pretended to conduct the battle.

The Divine Fleet was in shambles. It no longer seemed to hold any sort of formation. Though the Prime Vessel *Theoris* and its sister galleon *Elegos* remained in their original positions, what lesser vessels remained floated in a chaotic pattern, adrift between the flotsam of so many destroyed ships.

"Twenty," Maria said.

Cinnamon shot a sidelong glance at the three tacticians, expecting to be reprimanded. I hadn't heard from them in a while, so I looked at them, too.

Paul, Toby, and Theresa were obviously talking—I could see them doing it—but they weren't making a sound. Whatever conversations they were having, or orders they were giving, were taking all of their attention.

Anxiety flared in the pit of my stomach as I felt energy shifting within the ocean beneath the Divine Fleet. Great torrents of divine chi. They were flowing inward, being drawn toward a single point. The hair on the back of my neck stood on end again, and a chill ran down my spine.

A moment later, my fears were made manifest when the god-empress reemerged from the waves looking like a god of vengeance. Her entire body glowed with her holy power. It carved swirling lines through her skin, concentrating around her neck, chest, and hands.

"I am the divine bridge!" she shrieked. I winced and covered my ears. "You dare defy me?"

She extended an open hand toward one of her own ships, then closed her fist in the open air, yanking it toward her as if pulling up a crab pot. There was a terrible screeching sound as the artifacts lining the ship's hull were ripped open, freeing the clouds of condensed chi within. They flowed up toward her, and the golden swirls marking her skin flared, growing brighter as she consumed the chi.

No wonder my instincts were screaming to be wary of her. She had absorbed the chi from every sunken container.

And she'd just absorbed more.

Someone beside me let out a derisive snort. "*Divine bridge?*" Eustace called out into the bay. "Are you gonna tell her? Or shall I, Anius?"

Anius blanched, his expression caught somewhere between hatred and pleading.

"We made it up," Eustace continued. "You really thought *you* were the divine bridge? Our seer powers haven't worked in centuries. You were just the first Victus girl to come along who showed the vaguest hint of humanity."

Someone popped up from behind a nearby dune. "Truth!" Theo called, before he was pulled back down from either side by arms that looked like they belonged to Peter and Danny.

Eustace's mouth twisted in disgust, not taking her eyes from the god-empress. "So much for that. You're not as mad as all the Victus failures before you. You're worse, Aletheia. *Far* wors—"

"Do." The god-ripped open another ship's artifacts. "Not." Another. "Call." Two more. "Me." She spread her arms wide, the golden swirls covering her skin spreading to consume her. "*Aletheia!*"

Most of the power she'd absorbed came roaring back out in hundreds of thick and winding tendrils. They wound across the battlefield and connected to her followers, making the same patterns swirl across their skin. Each divine mage's eyes flew wide, their pupils, irises, and sclera consumed from within by liquid gold. Even the unconscious mages were affected as their cores were refilled with the light of their god-empress's will.

They floated into the air, pulled by unseen strings. They looked like an army of marionettes, each hovering a foot above the decks of the enemy fleet. Their expressions were all blank—including Anius, whose frustration with Eustace, and fear of his god-empress, had been replaced by mindless obedience.

As one, they attacked.

CHAPTER FIFTY-ONE

Coin Flip

Endgame!" Paul, Toby, and Theresa yelled, their voices reverberating along the threads of their ideal. It reminded me of the way I could communicate mentally with anyone bonded to me, except they had spoken to everyone in Tropica.

The only thing that stopped me from immediately using what little chi remained in my core was the confidence—the *excitement*—lacing their words. I focused on my trust in them and the rest of Tropica.

Pain prickled near my heart. I rubbed it through my suit jacket as I stepped to the side, putting myself between Ruby, Fin, Steven, and the horrifying scene.

We had a plan. We *had* to have a plan . . . right?

But the longer I stared at the bay and the hundreds of cultivators loosing blinding spears and volleys of arrows, the less sure I became. Thousands of projectiles screamed down toward the assault shrimp and recon crabs, who the enemy mages had all focused on, choosing to target the least mobile of our forces. The golden spears loosed by the Prime Cadre and Seer Anius were particularly horrifying, making an audible hum as they tore over the ocean, whipping up droplets in their wake.

Tropica intervened. Barry, Dodge, and the Church of Carcinization countered what few attacks they could. The pelicans unleashed blasts of wind, Bill and Pelly with a dagger held in their beaks, the rest of them without. Cinnamon unleashed multiple aura attacks, each slamming through at least one projectile before hitting its intended target.

Before me, Claws cackled on the shore, shooting off thunderbolts like an unhinged gunslinger. To my side, Teddy transformed, his aura flooding out, burning away his reserves of chi at incredible speed. As his claws, canines, and the spikes covering his body quadrupled in size, he unleashed a terrible roar that shook my bones. Even Rocky had rejoined the battle. He'd requisitioned one of the coconut boats, which he used to zoom across the bay, his clackers slamming closed with the rhythm of an early 2000's club banger, detonating scores of golden projectiles before they could reach their targets.

Together, my friends had managed to eliminate the spears of the Prime Cadre and Seer Anius. It wasn't nearly enough.

Maria took a step forward. "No," Toby whispered, stopping her in her tracks. "Not you."

Why? Why wouldn't they let her intervene? She could help. If this was the "end-game," shouldn't she . . . *Oh.*

The clusters of crustaceans, whom the vast majority of spears and arrows were still streaking toward, had paused just before unleashing counterattacks of their own.

They started to glow from within.

Maria squeezed my hand. A seed of hope sprouted in my stomach. The world's chi was bubbling up from the ocean, forming little pools of water essence all around the battlefield. Time slowed. The bubbles flowed down toward the crabs, sensing their need, responding to the direness of their situation. A breakthrough. It was a *breakthrough*. My hope blossomed, flooding me with relief.

The bubbles were fast, but compared to the divine projectiles of cultivators empowered by their god-empress, they were glacial. The spears and arrows not only sped past the bubbles, but destroyed them, banishing the breakthrough and leaving Snips's coned crustaceans defenseless.

The prickling pain stabbed into my chest. Paul cursed. Theresa cursed even louder.

Toby uttered a single syllable. Calmly, as if he had not a care in the world. "Shields."

An aura slammed into place around me. It was so strong that if not for its defensive ideal, it would have sent me sprawling. It wasn't just a regular aura. Like Teddy's, it had been empowered. Teddy hadn't been increasing his output when he transformed . . . He'd been lending my surrendered strength to another.

The assault shrimp and recon crabs shimmered with silvery light under Teddy's red aura, and as countless spears and arrows struck them from every direction, the projectiles were absorbed. Nullified completely.

I turned around. A second tree had sprouted beside Lemon—her brother, the *other* Lemon. There were two pairs of hands pressed palm-first into his trunk. Deklan and Dom grinned at me, both tried to give me a cheeky wink, and passed the frack out. Maria rushed to their side, Slimes flinging out ahead of her, already flooding pink chi into the twins.

I turned back to the bay.

Twelve.

Another eight boats had been destroyed in the onslaught. Some had fallen from friendly fire, a few had sunk after the god-empress tore open their artifacts, and the rest had become collateral damage when a dagger's passive kicked in, redirecting an empowered stream of chi into their hulls.

The enemy forces paid no mind to their dwindling fleet. They gathered more power, which was accelerated by the god-empress, who was gathering the divine chi from the just-sunken artifacts and pouring it into her followers.

"Retreat," said the three tacticians.

I frowned when those riding coconut boats—Barry, Dodge, Rocky, Joel, Jess, the rest of the Church of Carcinization—all turned in the opposite direction and sailed farther from shore. But their reason for doing so became clear a moment later. The assault shrimp and recon crabs leaped out into the air, where they were collected by Tropica's naval forces, not one of the crustaceans falling into the bay.

My eyes flicked from my friends, to the god-empress, then to the hundreds of enemy mages. The god-empress looked catatonic, immobilized by her own efforts. The enemy mages, however, were anything but. Their torsos swiveled, tracing the passage of the coconut boats, their arms raised toward my friends.

Any second, the next volley of spears and arrows would arrive.

"Teddy," said the three tacticians. "Now."

Teddy's eyes pressed together. He hunched his shoulders, and as a deep growl rumbled from his chest, he withdrew his ideal. All across the bay, the offensive red light surrounding Tropica's forces flickered. Faded completely. They were defenseless. I shot a look behind me. Deklan and Dom were still unconscious. Maria stared at me, her eyes wide with the same fear coursing through me. I whirled back around, clutching at my heart, the stabbing pain feeling like it would rupture my chest at any moment.

"Paul," I croaked. "What are you—"

He cut me off with a sharp gesture of his hand, his ideal radiating disapproval at me for speaking out of turn.

He turned to face me. So did Theresa and Toby. They were still radiating disapproval, and I expected to see it reflected in their expressions. Instead, they gave me shit-eating grins. All three of them extended a single finger, which they then pointed up at the sky.

When I spotted what they were pointing at, I frowned, then rubbed my eyes. When I gazed upward again, I confirmed it. There was, in fact, a boat descending from directly above. It looked like Bob the boat, except it couldn't be. This ship had the same gothic trim designed by Paul, but it also had five fracking cannons, two on either side of its hull, and a single, much larger one mounted at the very tip of the bow.

I could see people clinging beside the cannons, holding onto the chain-link railings so they didn't fly away. I frowned and rubbed my eyes again. They looked like . . . but it couldn't be. There was no way. Yet it *had* to be them. Teddy's red aura was surrounding them. How had they—

My oldest nemesis pounced, taking advantage of my confusion and forcing me to inspect the approaching vessel.

Name: Bob the boat
Rarity: Prime Vessel
Description: Now with more cannons!
[Error: Naval systems offline.]

I forced the description from my eyes. Another naval system error? Bob the boat had become a prime vessel? And what was up with the description?

"Okay," I yelled up at the fire cultivators clinging to Bob's railing, unable to keep a laugh from my voice. "How the *frack* did you guys—"

Boom! Boom! Boom! Boom! ***BOOOOOM!***

Every single one of the cannons fired as the cultivators channeled torrents of flame into them. The larger one on the prow was so loud that I felt it in my chest. Even if I hadn't seen it, the sounds were unmistakable. Defender and attacker alike all looked up into the sky as five cannonballs came thundering down toward the bay.

Except they weren't cannonballs at all. They were condensed balls of flame, each holding the potential of a wildfire while remaining the width of a coconut—except the one in the center, which had come from the lead cannon and was the width of a barrel.

The god-empress shrieked. Her followers redirected their focus, raising their arms toward the incoming fireballs. They unleashed a golden wall of projectiles. Six deadly spears—launched by Anius and the Prime Cadre—led the charge. Just as they'd drawn water droplets into their wake the last time they'd been released, those six spears drew the rest of the arrows and spears behind them. It looked like a fifty-meter-wide shield of golden chi, from which the six spears protruded like spiked studs. I shuddered as I imagined that wall of deadly points hitting me.

The fireballs, however, felt no such apprehension.

They met that golden shield of light a hundred meters above the bay, and I had to squeeze my eyes shut against the resulting detonation. I turned to wrap Ruby and Fin in a hug, pulling them close and covering them with my body just in case.

But I needn't have worried. The opposing forces of fire and divine chi had been evenly matched. I gazed up at Bob the boat, and the bloke clinging to the railing beside the main cannon. Such unbelievable power . . .

Trent's red hair was swept back by the wind of their descent. This gave me a good look at his face, which was manic with glee, mirroring the same smile I could feel on my own cheeks. Holding on to the railings beside the portside cannons were four of Gormona's former handlers. They were similar expressions to mine. Aisa—the fifth and final handler—and Keith held on for dear life to the farthest starboard cannon, while Tryphena, the former princess, held on to the closest one.

That left only Penelope, the former queen. She was guffawing as she held on to Bob's wheel, laughing so hard that tears streamed from her eyes and across her temples.

I sighed in relief.

Though I didn't yet know exactly what Bob the boat had become, it was clear that he and the fire cultivators hanging from him were an even match for the enemy forces. The god-empress had spread her power across the invading army, and with her will split evenly between our hundreds of enemies, she could no longer unleash another spear like the one that had almost annihilated Corporal Claws.

If she reached for more of the condensed chi within the containers attached to her fleet, she would only end up hurting herself. Her body was barely handling the power she already wielded.

It felt as though two giant boulders of worry rolled off of my back, and I relaxed my shoulders, letting the relief wash through me. The stabbing pain in my chest agreed, the sensation vanishing entirely for the first time since I'd regained my trust in Tropica's forces.

Someone cleared their throat. I glanced over to my left and found Maria with her arms crossed, giving me a pointed look. One of her eyebrows was raised so high that it threatened to merge with her sand-colored hair. Her gaze flicked down to my torso, then back up to my face. Her other eyebrow rose to join the first one.

I abruptly remembered that I'd used my body to shield Ruby and Fin. That was fine. What wasn't fine was that my arms were still wrapped around them, and I was tenderly stroking Ruby's back, my body subconsciously trying to comfort her and Fin. I sprang away like a startled cat.

"Oh—er—my bad."

"Your bad?" Steven somehow looked even less impressed than my wife. "You pushed me away! *Forcefully!* I only just managed to avoid slamming into Maria!"

Well, that sure explained the looks I was getting.

"I thought it was sweet," Ruby said, patting my shoulder. Her barely concealed smirk told me she was intentionally trying to make things worse.

"Uhhhh . . ."

"Fire!" Trent yelled, his voice echoing across Paul, Toby, and Theresa's ideal.

B-B-B-B-BOOOOOM!

Having closed half the distance to the bay, Bob the boat's guns were even louder this time, and I gazed up toward them.

"Whoa!" I yelled, perhaps a little too excitedly. "Another round of cannon—"

The god-empress screeched again, and her forces released the same studded wall of divine projectiles. I rushed to shield Ruby and Fin again, but this time, I made sure to bring Steven in as well. He elbowed me in the side, the cheeky prick, but there was no real force in it. I called for Maria to help me, and she did. She positioned herself so I couldn't avoid her questioning look, but just like Steven, she didn't really mean it. We grinned at each other as the divine- and fire-based projectiles collided, creating a red-and-gold plume only fifty meters above the bay.

When I turned back to see the aftermath—only after taking a good three steps away from Ruby and Fin—I realized I'd been wrong. The border of the explosion hadn't ended fifty meters above the bay.

I let out a soft whistle.

Most of the enemy mages were singed and smoking, as were the sails of a few of their ships. The god-empress was apoplectic. Though her body remained immobile where she floated above the deck of *Theoris*, her lip twitched, and her face seemed locked in a permanent snarl as she stared up at the incoming boat.

I grinned in response, matching the expressions of all those clinging to Bob the boat, who . . . *Wait.* I frowned at the bloke I spotted through the open door of Bob's cabin. He was puffing on a pipe that was longer than his torso. "Is that . . . ?"

"Dad?" Maria yelled, also spotting Roger.

As shocked as we were, Corporal Claws's reaction was even more visceral. She wiggled on the spot, her paws dancing a little tippy-tapped beat when she spotted the sword-chi cultivator. She raised one forepaw high, striking a grandiose pose, then shoved it down into her right pocket.

It emerged holding something silver, System-made, and much larger than the daggers she'd prepared for this battle. It had the same multifaceted blade as her other creations, but this was no dagger. It was a fracking two-handed *sword*. My eyes were drawn into it.

Multifaceted Bastard Sword of the Maker's Apprentice
[Protection overridden—Maker detected]
Rarity: Artifact
Description: This sword was created by a Maker's apprentice, whose chaotic nature echoes within the blade. Chi channeled through it will be concentrated, amplified, and have a [variable] chance of striking a random enemy.
Effects: 100% concentration, +50% amplification, 0% random enemy targeting.
Duration: null

I shook my head to clear my vision, already sending the description across to Maria. Before I could question the boosted amplification or the apparently variable chance of striking a random enemy, Claws hurled the sword through the air.

Roger raced forward like he'd been shot from a longbow. In one smooth and annoyingly cool movement, he ashed his pipe and slung it at his belt, then caught Claws's bastard sword. He channeled his chi into it.

Roger wasn't a Maker. If he inspected the sword, all he would see was its name and an error message. By the dangerous glint in his eye, however, I could tell his chi perfectly understood how powerful the blade was. He landed on the broken hull of a ship, somehow keeping his balance as it skidded along the ocean toward the Prime Vessel *Theoris* and the woman suspended above it.

He drew the sword back over his shoulder, and when he thrusted it forward a moment later, a column of blades carved its way through the air.

Directly toward the god-empress.

CHAPTER FIFTY-TWO

Chest Pains

Roger's column of chi blades raced overtop the bay. Despite the small amount of chi at my disposal, I could tell it was a battle-ending attack. When it struck the god-empress, even her monstrously vast core would be overwhelmed.

But then Claws did . . . something. She exerted a tiny fraction of will, which I only sensed because of our bond.

The sword flashed with blue power. Claws started snickering. And the column of blades, only a few meters away from the god-empress's torso, changed direction. The countless blades of silver chi slammed into some random mage above an entirely different ship. Roger's attack was so strong that all of the mage's chi rushed from his core at once, expending itself so his body wasn't sliced apart, rendering him unconscious. The second his core was empty of divine essence, the column of blades left him alone, instead cutting the ship beneath him into splinters.

"Eleven!" cackled Claws, rolling around and pounding her forepaws into the sand. She was laughing so hard that she accidentally broke her whistle, one paw shattering it apart. She glared at it for a moment, as if it was at fault for breaking, but then she just continued cackling. She was too amused to care.

Bob the boat crashed down onto the heads of four enemy cultivators, his curved hull knocking them out cold and sending them skipping across the bay in different directions. That was nothing compared to what Bob did to the ship beneath them, though. He flattened it like a pancake as most of his hull disappeared beneath the surface of the bay, his deck only a few inches from going underwater.

A few things happened at once.

Bob, well, *bobbed* back to the surface, his deck swiftly stabilizing. The fire cultivators on board scrambled for the cannons, readying their chi to unleash more fireballs. The god-empress poured even more chi into her followers, whose channels started to break down under the strain, especially those who had only recently awakened.

She screeched an order; her followers rushed to obey. They all leaped toward Bob, summoning spears of divine chi in their hands.

They weren't going to throw them. They were going to jab them into him and tear him apart. The faint stabbing pain in my chest returned.

The cannons wouldn't be enough.

Trent and the others were still gathering their fire essence, but even if they got their shots off, they couldn't hope to hit the entire circle of descending mages. At least half of them would make it through, and though Bob had apparently become a prime vessel, I held no disillusions that he'd escape this unscathed. My stomach churned as I imagined dozens of spears stabbing into his unprotected stern.

Unlike Tropica's fire-aspected cultivators, he wasn't surrounded by Teddy's aura. Even if Deklan and Dom were still conscious, I assumed their shielding couldn't extend to cover him. Before I'd had a chance to find out what Bob's transformation meant, he was about to be destroyed.

I stared in confusion as Teddy removed his empowered aura from Trent and the rest of the fire squad and sent it somewhere else. My gaze darted toward Roger, but the aura surrounding him hadn't grown stronger. Next I scanned the sky, and though I spotted Pelly, Bill, and the rest of the pelicans, none of them were wreathed in the red-and-white light of Teddy's empowered ideal.

But then I spotted the four-limbed good boy that was in free fall, having leaped from the backs of Bill and Pelly. Borks's entire body glowed. He opened a portal in the air before him, which he plunged through in the form of a golden retriever. When he exited the other side and landed silently on Bob the boat's deck, he was in his natural form—that of a red-eyed, serpent-tailed, midnight-furred hellhound.

Trent and the rest of the fire cultivators unleashed their burning torrents of chi, not into the cannons, but toward Borks. I leaned forward. What was their plan? Was Borks going to reflect it somehow? Create a firestorm like he had done on the same deck back when Cal was still an amalgamation of earth elementals? He created a firestorm, all right, but not by reflecting their flames.

Borks *ate* the billowing columns of fire.

His ideal flared, and he asked for more flames. He trusted the fire cultivators. They were members of his pack. Returning that trust, Trent and the rest of them opened their cores and offered up everything they had. Eight cultivators' worth of fire chi disappeared down Borks's gullet.

And then, throat glowing, eyes smoldering, tail wagging so fast he might take flight, Tropica's goodest boy unleashed hell.

A cone of crimson flames spewed from his mouth, and the dozens of enemy mages unfortunate enough to be in its path blanched as they sensed the wrath about to consume them. And when Borks started doing spinnies, casting his hellfire in all directions, the blood drained from the rest of the enemies' faces.

I wondered why. Roger—with the help of Claws's unreliable sword—wielded enough power to slap their god-empress silly, yet her followers had remained stoic in spite of his strength. How much could Borks really do to them on his own? Every enemy had readied a spear of divine chi. Were they not evenly matched?

My questions were answered when the Prime Cadre all launched their spears into the approaching flames.

Borks's firestorm didn't just look like hellfire.

It *was* hellfire.

The conflagration was of Hades's realm. Like the divine cultivators, Borks was controlling chi of a higher tier. That wasn't all.

The golden light and the bloodred fire seemed antithetical to one another. They each sought to extinguish the other. And unfortunately for the entire enemy force, their higher-tiered chi wasn't being enhanced by the combined aura of a bear, a god-king, and an ancient tree spirit.

Borks's hellfire surrounded them, consuming their chi, using each spear as fuel. Though his flames had also engulfed the fire cultivators and most of Bob the boat, they remained unharmed. The hellfire's heat only affected those Borks saw as enemies.

Seconds later, the good boy's spinnies came to an end, and almost two hundred unconscious mages splashed down into the sea, every drop of chi in their cores burned away. They yet lived, but they'd been gravely injured by divine chi on the inside, and by hellfire on the outside. Only the Prime Cadre and Seer Anius remained conscious.

The surrounding boats had fared about as well as Phostheia's mages.

"Two . . ." Maria whispered, staring wide-eyed at the scorched remnants of the Divine Fleet. Of the enemy ships, only *Theoris* and *Elegos* remained.

The god-empress's reaction was far more intense. She released a wordless scream, and potent tendrils of condensed golden chi shone from the ocean, coalescing above the bay before pouring into her. With another scream, she sent half of the chi flooding back out, six winding ropes that streamed into her six conscious followers.

"Roger!" Paul yelled, eyes locked on the Prime Cadre and Seer Anius as they were filled with twice as much chi as before. "Handle them!"

Handle them? I thought. *Why would Roger need to . . .*

Borks stumbled, teetered, and collapsed. The hellfire he'd released had only been a glimpse of the power he might one day wield. It'd been far too much for him to handle. He had exceeded his limits. So had Trent and the rest of the fire cultivators. They collapsed to the deck beside Borks, barely clinging to consciousness.

"Aerial forces!" Theresa called. "Fetch the fallen!"

The pelicans were already swooping down from above, angling toward the ocean.

"Maria," Toby calmly said. "Please heal them."

She gave a sharp nod. She'd have healed them even if ordered not to.

I looked up as Roger raced across the ocean. He'd procured coconut boats from somewhere, and he cut a direct path for the six mages. The god-empress hadn't stopped flooding them with power.

Their cores doubled in size, then doubled again, tears forming around the nexus of their power. They were my enemies, yet I winced all the same, knowing firsthand how it felt to rupture their cores like that. Divine essence leaked out into their bodies. It flooded them, burning them from within, consuming their channels as sure as Borks's hellfire would. Still, the god-empress forced more chi into them.

I felt the stabbing pain slowly return to my chest. Beside me, Teddy was trembling. He'd been enforcing his ideal this entire time—his limit was near. Out on the bay, Roger thrust his bastard blade forward, striking out with a column of blades. On the shore in front of me, Claws trilled nervously. She sent a pulse of will across the bay, setting the bastard blade's chance of attacking the wrong target to 0%.

Roger was now the sole recipient of Teddy's offensive aura. His column of sword-chi struck true, thousands of blades cutting, slicing at Anius's chest. But the Prime Cadre all moved to block it. Roger's strongest possible attack hit all of them . . . and only managed to remove just over a third of their combined chi.

Rubbing my chest, I stared at the god-empress. She was staring back, her face a mask of golden fury.

No longer having to split her absorbed power between hundreds of mages, her threat level had risen significantly. She was even more dangerous than before. Like her followers, she was burning herself away by holding on to so much chi, but that wasn't a good thing.

I didn't want her to die. I'd let it happen if it saved my friends, but only after exhausting all other options. If Ellis was right and a worse threat would eventually come Tropica's way, the Kingdom of Light could be an invaluable ally. I had to get through to the other part of her—I had to get through to Aletheia.

But *how*?

The stabbing pain got worse, and I rubbed my chest. It didn't help.

The god-empress tore her gaze from mine. Her hands and forearms had been replaced by razor-sharp blades of divine chi. Golden light streaked behind her as she flew closer, stopping when she was above the deck of *Elegos*. She raised her arms to either side, and with two deadly slices of the blades covering her hands, she cut the top off of the containers lining *Elegos*'s hull.

Paul, Theresa, and Toby opened their mouths to bark an order, but I beat them to the punch.

"Borks!" I yelled.

The goodest boy to ever grace Tropica's shores lifted his head, gave a single wag of his tail, and tore a portal open beside him.

As the element of those concealed within Borks's dimensional space came flooding out into the world, the god-empress went rigid, losing hold of the condensed chi she had already started absorbing from *Elegos*'s containers.

Three abyssal cultivators and an earth elemental came striding out at full power. As planned, they had rested for the entire battle, leaving them reinvigorated for when it truly mattered.

Or so I had hoped.

In truth, George and Geraldine stumbled out into the light, leaning on one another for support, cheeks gaunt, skin pale. Fathom slid out like an inky blob, dragging himself from the portal with lethargic tentacles. Cal wasn't much better, but he did manage to float above the deck, at least.

My heart sank. These four were one of our trump cards, and they looked like shit. I hoped they had recovered enough to succeed.

The god-empress released another furious screech. She was already too far gone for rational thought, but she'd clearly recognized their aspect. Fathom was an abyssal elemental. George and Geraldine were his bonded humans. And while Cal might not be able to summon abyssal chi by himself, his connection to Fathom let him manipulate it. Before they could strike, the god-empress resumed absorbing the divine essence from *Elegos*'s sundered containers.

George, Geraldine, and Fathom responded immediately. Despite their visible exhaustion, they reached for the abyss, attempting to open a void as close to *Elegos* as possible. It wouldn't be close enough. Cal joined his will to theirs, helping shove it nearer to the god-empress. Teddy let out a rumbling growl. He wanted to aid them. But Roger was still fighting the enemy mages, his sword and body a blur as he parried, countered, or dodged the six deadly spears that jabbed at him constantly. He needed every drop of Teddy's offensive aura.

The abyss opened up above the portside railing of *Elegos*, only meters away from the god-empress. It started as a midnight-colored pinprick in the air but swiftly expanded to the size of a basketball. I held my breath, hoping it continued to grow, praying my friends had enough essence to absorb all the divine chi remaining on the battlefield.

Though the black hole they'd opened didn't grow any larger, it started drawing in the golden light that the god-empress was trying to grasp. She shook with fury as those luminous strands started drifting away from her, curling toward and into the void. The god-empress tried to leave, but she couldn't move an inch, the abyss and the four wills controlling it keeping her locked in place.

I clutched at my aching chest. The best I could hope for was that they'd keep the void open long enough to drain all of the condensed chi from the containers lining *Elegos*. But even if they managed it, the artifacts lining *Theoris* were still full to the brim . . .

Realizing that I was worrying about the future, I reined my thoughts in. This moment was all that mattered. I focused on the battle before me, willing my friends to succeed.

They faltered almost immediately.

Only half of the divine chi had been absorbed, and they were already at their limit. All four of them barely remained upright atop Bob's deck, their spirits and cores still fatigued from their efforts with the tunnels below.

I looked at Maria. The enemy mages had been delivered to shore by the pelicans, and she and Slimes were already healing them. The damage to their channels was so severe that their cores had become unstable. If Maria or Slimes stopped healing them for even a second, the instability would spread. In the short term, they'd lose their ability to use chi. In the long term, they'd die. Maria couldn't help me.

I reached for my chi. I'd been holding on to it as long as possible, knowing that once it was spent, I'd be completely powerless. If I used it now, I could stop the god-empress from absorbing the rest of *Elegos*'s chi, but I'd have to attack her. And with the state her body was in . . .

If she absorbed more divine essence, she would die. If we attacked her to stop her from absorbing it, she would die.

Paul turned my way, his gaze demanding my attention. When my eyes met his, his ideal drew me in. With a series of shared thoughts, we went over the facts, seeking a way out.

We had to get her to use all of her chi somehow. If I didn't use any chi, and we got her to empty her core without burning herself away, I could enforce my will upon her and knock her out. It was the only way for everyone to survive, and it all hinged on the god-empress not being able to absorb a single drop of additional essence.

Rather than give me an order, Paul left it up to me, inviting me to choose our next course of action. I chewed on the possibilities for a long moment. We had all the pieces needed to defeat the god-empress. There was a path we could take that would let us win without spilling any blood, but only if we had an answer for the containers lining the hull of Prime Vessel *Theoris*. Those artifacts, and the condensed chi within, were the only things giving me pause. No matter how hard I tried, I couldn't find an answer.

I stared at Paul. How was he so confident? What did he know that I didn't?

Paul gave me nothing. He stared back unflinchingly, refusing to give me any reassurance. Yet I knew the answer he was looking for. He wanted me to trust. Not just him, but the entirety of Tropica.

"A trust fall, huh?" I asked.

"I don't know what that is, Fischer."

We continued staring at one another. Eventually, the corner of my lip tugged up into a wry smile. As I broke eye contact with Paul and returned to the present, I rubbed my chest. Now that I'd reached a decision, the stabbing pain had faded.

"Cal!" I yelled, cupping my hands to my mouth. "Cadet Calamari! This is your god-king speaking! It's now or never, mate!"

His slitted pupil focused on me, its surrounding iris flicking between brown and black.

"Yes, I'm sure! You'll just have to trust me!"

The speed with which he accepted that statement made me feel like a real prick—it had taken me ages to conquer my doubts today. No sooner had I finished the last word than he'd reached deep within, latching on to something he'd been slowly cultivating since my wedding.

Starting from his pupils, a black sheen washed over his entire body. It was like he'd slipped on a cloak of midnight.

With how fast my heart was beating, you'd think he was about to unlock some anime finishing move—like laser eyes, or laser tentacles, or laser anything, really—but he was doing something *way* cooler than that: the impossible.

As if shrugging off a torn shirt, he cast aside his earthen aspect, leaving it behind. The cloak of midnight took its place, settling on his skin and soaking into him, suffusing his entire body.

Fathom, George, and Geraldine went bolt upright. They turned away from the enemy monarch, their sunken eyes filled with life as they witnessed the ascension of another of their kind.

It felt like a cold wave crashed down over my chest.

Cadet Calamari, terror of the deep and newly awakened abyssal elemental, writhed with power.

He flooded it into the faltering void. The abyss flared back to life. That black orb of nothingness grew blurry at its edges as it consumed the surrounding light—divine chi included. The ripped-open containers were drained in the blink of an eye, leaving nothing for the god-empress to absorb.

The void collapsed, and so did Cal. His reawakening had filled him with power, but only temporarily. Barely remaining conscious, Fathom, Geraldine, and George caught him. They huddled around him atop Bob the boat, staring defiantly at the god-empress.

She paid them no mind. Instead, she flew onto *Theoris's* deck and raised both her bladed arms, gathering the chi she would use to tear the surrounding artifacts open.

I reached for my power. This was it—the moment I didn't have an answer for. I stared at Paul, Toby, and Theresa, but they ignored me, simply watching *Theoris* with passive gazes. Without realizing it, I gathered my chi, preparing to slam it into her.

If she absorbed so much condensed chi, she would die, but not immediately. Who knew how many attacks she could get off before she burned herself away. Wouldn't it be better for me to end her now?

I clenched my jaw, softly rubbed my chest, and let go of my chi, choosing to trust in my friends.

My heart leaped up into my throat as the god-empress's blades descended. They sheared through the metal artifacts. The screeching cacophony made my every hair stand on end. From within the containers came . . . nothing.

I frowned at them. "What the fra—"

The god-empress wailed. I felt it in the depths of my spirit, as if she was doing damage directly to my soul.

It had a similar effect on the two glorious idiots who had been hiding in plain sight.

A patch of air shimmered at the front of *Theoris's* deck, right by the bow. Before I could wonder what it was, Dodge lost hold of his invisibility, revealing both him and the portly mammal he was trying to push overboard.

Dodge's eyes went wide, and he took an involuntary step back from the god-empress. RPM, however, couldn't have taken a step back if his life depended on it. The rotund rascal had been busy. He'd grown to the size of a small shed, and his entire body was glowing gold, leaking strands of stolen essence. He belched, and a cloud of divine chi spurted out. He sucked it back in before the god-empress could get a hold of it.

He had not just stolen some of her chi. He'd stolen *all* of it.

"Roger!" Paul yelled. "Retreat!"

The god-empress wailed again, her face twisting in rage, the blade on her right hand extending until it was a spear. She drew it back and shot forward.

Dodge made like his name and got the frack out of there, leaping overboard and sailing away on his coconut boats. Claws tried to cackle, chitter, and chortle all at once, which resulted in her wheezing silently on the shore, doubled over with mirth. The god-empress ignored Dodge, her spear arm stabbing forward, seeking to pop RPM like a balloon and retrieve her chi.

"Master," gurgled RPM, his tiny little limbs flailing to no effect. "Hel—"

The god-empress's spear stabbed out, a full third of her chi contained in the weapon.

She found only empty air.

Claws had absorbed her familiar. She was already streaking over the western mountains on bolts of lightning, intermittently roaring with laughter and groaning in agony. RPM managed to extend one of his dexterous little grabbers from Claws's pocket. He gave the god-empress a single-digit salute as Claws zapped over the mountain range and disappeared from sight.

I wasn't sure the god-empress even noticed. The moment she struck empty air, she'd drawn her spear arm back, doubled the power flowing into it, then used the rest of her chi to leap from *Theoris*.

She wasn't going for RPM or Claws, though.

She was coming for me.

Her speed was terrible, as was the spear aimed for my heart. She closed the distance before I could hope to respond, her arm thrusting forward, its deadly tip hurtling toward my heart.

Maria shot to her feet. She launched Slimes toward me. He flew like he'd been launched from a trebuchet.

Too slow.

Roger had listened to Paul and started retreating. He'd left his six pursuers behind and was now fifty meters from shore. He thrust his bastard sword. A column of blades bore down on the god-empress.

Not fast enough.

Teddy knew those chi blades wouldn't get here in time. He withdrew his aura from Roger. He shook, trying to redirect it toward me. Hints of the red-white flow flickered around my torso, then faded. Teddy collapsed.

I was undefended.

I gave the world a sad smile. This was the problem with caring about others. If I'd been more selfish, this never would have happened. Still, I wouldn't change a thing. Since my arrival on Kallis, I had lived on my own terms. I could have guaranteed my own survival by squashing the god-empress like a bug the moment she arrived, but that wasn't who I was.

If following my heart and doing what felt right caused my downfall, so be it.

This battle had gained Tropica three tacticians, an abyssal elemental, and an entire fleet of ships. Even if I perished here, they would not only survive, but *thrive*. I had complete trust in them.

As the head of the divine spear got closer, I pressed my eyes together and thought of my time in Tropica. I had too many good memories to count. I cycled through them over and over, letting my enhanced memory pick their details apart.

I stole one last glance at the outside world. The god-empress was staring directly into my soul, her baleful gaze anathema to the memories running through my head. She was watching for my reaction. She wanted to see my defeat. Wanted to see my terror.

I wouldn't give her that. I countered her hateful stare with a shit-eating grin.

When the divine spear reached me, it didn't pierce my jacket. That was something. According to my jacket's description, it could only be damaged by "a blow possessing even greater faith" than my followers.

I'd still die, of course—instead of getting dispatched by a spear, I'd be dispatched by a spear wrapped in a nice jacket. But it made me feel all warm and fuzzy that my followers had more faith in me than she had in herself. It was a small win, and I'd take it.

As my demise arrived, there was only one soul on my mind. One might assume I was thinking of Maria, my funny, endlessly kind, whip-smart, and criminally attractive wife. But they'd be wrong.

It was Sergeant Snips who scuttled back and forth through my mind.

In my defense, it was hard to think of anybody else—her eyepatch had been stabbing my chest on and off for the last hour or so, the spikes extending every time she got nervous. It itched something fierce, and I'd considered pulling the jacket off at least three different times.

I was sure glad I hadn't.

"Pocket crab!" hissed Snips, a slew of bubbles trailing her as she burst through the front of my jacket.

CHAPTER FIFTY-THREE

Change

I had wanted to show the god-empress an expression of feigned indifference when I finally revealed Snips, the spiked and reliable ace up my sleeve. Instead of feigned indifference, I gaped in genuine amazement as Snips tore her way free of my jacket.

It shouldn't have been possible. The material had parted like tissue paper. The only way she could have done it—

"Is if I had more faith in you than everyone else combined," hissed Snips in my mind.

She was the actual target of Teddy's aura transfer earlier, and he'd clearly succeeded. His red-and-white power glowed from every inch of her carapace. Even without that visual proof, though, it was obvious his power surrounded her—Snips was neutralizing the tip of the god-empress's spear with a single claw.

Snips had absorbed her hundreds of bonded crustaceans into her core earlier. She'd timed it with Cal's reawakening, hiding it from the god-empress. The god-empress certainly knew they were in there now, though. Their power was unmistakable, even if it was being wielded by Snips.

If this were a movie, Snips and the god-empress would have had a back-and-forth battle, in which Snips only triumphed after someone—probably Rocky—sacrificed themself. If it was a movie by a particularly sadistic director, they might even have Snips win by sacrificing herself, turning the trauma of her death into a "flaw" the main character has to overcome in the next installment.

But this wasn't a movie. Nor was it that kind of story.

Snips's mighty clacker slammed together. The twin blades of foaming water that shot from her claws were two meters wide, thicker than a fantasy epic, and wreathed in Teddy's red-and-white aura. They sliced through the god-empress's divine spear like it was nothing, leaving only harmless light in their wake.

The god-empress herself would have been slapped ten ways to Sunday if the blades hit her, so I made sure I got there first. I separated my reduced chi between all four of my partitions and pressed down on the god-empress with all my might.

She flopped to the shore like a fish.

When Aletheia woke, she was on a sandy shore, the expansive ocean stretching out before her. She tugged on her limbs, but they didn't budge. Her wrists and ankles were bound by tendrils of pure-white chi. Someone spoke. A man. His words, quiet and excited, were unintelligible at first. Slowly, Aletheia grasped their meaning. She shifted, rising to her knees.

"Yeah! That's it!" the man was saying. "Now put your other hand here, see? That one on the reel, this one farther up the rod so you can rest your finger on the line. That way, if a fishy comes along to nibble your bait, you'll feel it."

"I see . . ." a woman replied, her tone suggesting that she absolutely didn't.

Eustace. It was *Eustace*.

That made Aletheia smile. The seer would surely help her out of this bind. A slew of fond memories flashed by. All the times Eustace had played with her as a child. All the secrets and laughs they'd shared atop the castle's roof. All the plans they'd made to improve the Kingdom of Light. But then reality beamed down, revealing the wicked truth.

"*Betrayer!*" hissed the mask in Aletheia's mind.

The moment it returned, the mask immediately vied for control. It shoved her down, plunging her back into that dark pit, flinging her into the deepest corners of . . . *what?* The pit was no more. It was riddled with holes and cavities large enough for Aletheia to stride through. Golden light streamed in, illuminating the abyss. The mask froze.

She remembered now. Wielded by the mask, Aletheia's own divine chi had perforated the prison and torn it apart. It had done the same to her body. She stared down at her arms—they were whole, though they shouldn't be.

Aletheia shouldn't even be alive.

She had tried to steal back control of her own mind and body, and when the mask discovered the attempt, it had tried to kill her. She shivered, remembering the agony of her own divine essence being turned against her. The mask had absorbed far too much power, and ripped her core to shreds. But as she inspected her abdomen, she found her core whole, held together by a thin membrane of pink chi.

"Mornin'!" came the voice of a strangely accented man.

The mask was shocked into action. It tried to cast Aletheia aside, but there was nowhere to put her. Every single corner of her soul was now illuminated by the light of the heavens.

Aletheia and the mask both looked up at the god-king on whose shores they sat.

"You've been out cold for most of the day. Your Forty Hands, or whatever you call them, will be out cold for a few days until my wife fixes the damage you did to their channels, but she already fixed the Prime Cadre and Anius. They healed up stupid quick. Crazy how much vitality you divine cultivators have." Fischer rubbed his neck with one hand. He wasn't wearing his jacket anymore. "Anius and the rest still have to take it easy, though. Lucky for you guys, Tropicans are *masters* of relaxation. I've been spreading my heretical ways by teaching them to fish." He nodded toward the coastline. "Evan is a natural."

"What's that?" Evan asked. He wore a relaxed smile that made Aletheia want to weep with joy.

When he saw her, though, his smile died.

The mixed look of fear and regret on his face made the mask want to tear his eyes out.

"*Betrayer!*" it screamed with her mouth.

They all looked her way. There was Sven. And the other mages of the Prime Cadre. Even Seer Anius, who sat on a familiar-looking bench with Eustace and Fern. Seeing them together made tears swell in Aletheia's eyes. It made the mask claw and scratch for control. How could Anius sit with those deserters? Worse, the three of them were *fishing*, as was everyone else on the shore.

Evan rushed forward, so lost in the enemy's spell that he didn't discard his fishing contraption. "Please. You have to hear them out, Aletheia. It's—"

"God-empress!" roared the mask. "I am your god-empress, *swine!*"

His expression shifted again, hopelessness and anger flashing across his face. It resonated within Aletheia, breaking her heart despite the mask's potent outrage.

"Damn, the evil you is still holding on, huh?" Fischer frowned and rubbed his chin. "Okay, time for plan B. Hit it, Claws!"

Lightning struck the shore. Aletheia flinched back, remembering its kiss all too well. It would hurt even more with her core so empty. Instead of wordless agony, however, all that hit Aletheia was a light spray of sand. It tickled her skin. She tentatively opened her eyes.

The creature, an elemental otter whose ideal was *chaos*, had struck the shore. It wiggled its butt at her and scooched backward, grinning encouragingly. Its familiar, that damned thieving raccoon, climbed out of a pocket and started rubbing its master's furry behind with both forelimbs, nodding for Aletheia to do the same.

She felt a line form between her eyebrows. Why weren't her enemies attacking? And why were her friends and followers being so jovial with God-King Fischer? These people weren't of the heavens.

"You have it all wrong, Aletheia," Fischer said. "Spirit beasts, the water gods, even the divine pantheon. Most of it was a lie. You sensed what Corporal Claws is, right?" Fischer bent to scratch the creature behind its ear. It cooed in delight. "Claws is a spirit beast and a cultivator. Her aspect is lightning and her ideal is *chaos*. If she can happily coexist with us, a whole damned village of humans, does that not prove how wrong you . . ." He rubbed the bridge of his nose. "Claws, *please*. You're *not* helping."

The otter was now aggressively shaking her rump at Aletheia, giving her a fierce scowl.

"You can't force people into butt scritches," Fischer continued, bending down to scoop the otter up and rub her all over before glancing down at Aletheia. "Do you really think Claws here is a threat to humanity?"

The little beast trilled and cooed in adoration. Small arcs of electricity crawled harmlessly over Fischer's hand as she leaned into his touch.

Aletheia had already started questioning the threat presented by spirit beasts. Every single one of the beasts had put themselves at risk for Fischer and the rest of Tropica's humans. They were far from the mindless, bloodthirsty creatures described in the royal library. Even the hellhound was quite cute sometimes. If not for the hellfire spewing from his mouth, that spinning move he did on Bob the boat would have been adorable.

But it wasn't Aletheia that needed convincing. The mask seethed, forcing her down, doing everything it could to take control. Aletheia shoved it away. She wouldn't let it take over. It couldn't make her surrender.

Or so she'd thought.

She gasped as it pulled a stream of divine chi from her core. It pierced the pink membrane and left a hole behind. Sensing her weakness, the mask repeated this a half dozen times. The ecstasy of divine chi warred with the agony of the damage being done. Both sensations weakened Aletheia's hold, letting the mask wrest more and more control.

"Plan C it is," Fischer said. His will pressed down on her, somehow forcing her essence back into her core.

Even through the pain, Aletheia questioned it. How was he using pure chi to suppress the divine? The mask remembered the feeling of Fischer exerting his will. He'd knocked her out cold in an instant at the end of the battle. No matter the strength of his willpower, he shouldn't be able to control her essence.

"Nothing?" Fischer asked. "How about this?"

Aletheia gasped as the full weight of his power pressed down on her soul, her damaged core barely rebuffing it. The mask shrank back, radiating fear.

"By the iron chains of Hephaestus . . ." Anius said. "I already forgot how oppressive that felt." He looked to the side. "If he'd done that at the beginning of the battle, I might have joined your flight, hag."

Eustace snorted. "I didn't know you could fly, you old toad."

"Why?" Aletheia asked. "Why show me this power? It changes nothing."

"Power . . . ?" Fischer asked. "Oh. You thought plan C was to swing my will around? Nah. I'm trying to share some memories with you, but your divine chi is making it hard. That was a fifth of my will . . . I think. It's kinda hard to tell—pretty sure I'm only back to like fifty percent capacity. It's taking a while to recover after the whole surrender-my-power-to-my-friends thing."

Aletheia's expression had gotten more and more dubious with each word. There was no way that weight pressing down on her was only a portion of his strength.

"Sorry about this, Aletheia," Fischer continued. "Have to be a bit heavy handed because we're running out of time."

Whatever Fischer did, it was instant. His will doubled in power and slammed into her core. He was going to kill her. She couldn't hope to withstand this. His intent formed a wedge, which parted her essence with ease, letting something flow in past her divine protections.

Memories. They were Fischer's, and they started with . . . *death on another world?*

"Traveler . . ." Aletheia croaked, stumbling, barely catching herself. This man was a Traveler? *How?*

More memories came. Fischer's arrival in Kallis, and discovery of Tropica. His small act of kindness which led to the awakening of Sergeant Snips. All the friends he made, human and spirit beast and tree spirit. Gormona's prince, Trent, attacking the village. The hellhound's arrival. Tropica creating a church. Breakthroughs, awakenings. The hellhound, Borks, returning to join the pack.

Fischer was also sharing the visions with everyone else on the shore. Laughter bellowed from Sven when he saw Tropica's assault on Gormona. His mirth was a balm to Aletheia's frazzled soul.

More memories. Gormona's return attack against Tropica. Fischer's acceptance of leadership. More breakthroughs and awakenings—too many to count. The arrival of an amalgamation of earth elementals and his abyssal brother, both thousands of years old. Knowledge. Realization. The truth of the war between the water and divine gods. The justified unmaking of Dolos and Apate. The divine betrayal.

The divine betrayal.

The divine betrayal.

Fischer only showed it once, yet Aletheia replayed it over and over, ignoring the rest of the memories as she sought a flaw—anything that would prove the vision false. Thin cracks started to form on the mask.

She might have been watching the hundredth loop by the time Fischer finally spoke again. "You'll find nothing, Aletheia. No matter how hard you try, you already know I'm telling the truth. I showed your followers that memory earlier while my wife patched up your core. Took her over an hour, by the way. Bit rude of you to rip it back open."

"I forgive her." There was a flash of light, and God-Queen Maria appeared at Fischer's side. She gazed down at Aletheia. "You're as much a victim of the betrayal as anyone else is, Aletheia. Maybe more so. Try not to be too hard on yourself."

Maria was right. Aletheia's entire life—and the lives of her ancestors—had been based on a lie. She felt numb. The mask's cracks became fissures, its surface crumbling as its influence receded. She had wanted to be free of it for so long. Had wanted to escape its confines. Yet now she feared losing its certainty.

Who was she without the mask? It had done horrible, *horrible* things, but its intentions had been pure. Even if some of the divine gods had betrayed this world, the heavens could still be trusted, couldn't they?

The heavens had chosen her. Had set her on this path. Had given her a *quest.*

Her ideal, silent thus far, came boiling out. It latched on to the broken mask, using golden light to connect the gaping chasms in its surface. That same golden light shone within her, filling the gaps in Aletheia's core, creating something entirely new from the pieces.

With her blessing, the repaired mask slipped back into place.

"How?" asked both Aletheia and her mask. "How can I possibly believe you?"

Her light beamed out, creating bridges from her to anyone with a divine core, subjugating them under the heavens. Damaged cores were ripped back open, the invisible sutures splitting one by one, thin needles of light connecting them all. Even Eustace and Fern were drawn in, though they resisted more than the others.

"I wish I could trust you." Aletheia stood, her chi cutting through the tendrils of unaspected essence binding her wrists and ankles. "Really, I do. But your tale is *too* perfect. Too enticing. And no matter what you say, no matter what proof you present, I cannot believe your words."

Fischer schooled his expression. "I showed you what happened to the king who didn't let me cleanse away his corruption. You know I'll have to destroy you, right?"

She took a step forward, ignoring the agony in her soul as she channeled a divine spear into her hand. Her core wasn't as repaired as she had hoped. "I know you'll *try*."

"Uhhh, I can tell the *actual* Aletheia is helping man the fort right now. You're not the mindless force of nature that screeches like a banshee whenever something goes wrong."

"So?" she spat.

"So you're not an idiot. I don't know why you seem to have two personalities kicking around in there, but I can tell you're the kind one. *And* the smart one. You know how powerful I am." He pointed at Maria. "You know how powerful she is. And you know that you don't stand a chance, especially with the state of your core."

He was right, of course, but that was irrelevant. "Yet I have to try. It is my duty."

A sliver of despair wormed its way onto Fischer's face. "I can't save you if you unleash that spear, Aletheia. I'm *stupid* powerful, but even I have my limits." He pointed at her abdomen. "Any more chi leaves that, and there'll be nothing left to weave back together."

Again, he was right.

What if he is also right about the divine gods . . . ? a small, pathetic part of herself wondered.

Her ideal called out then, bubbling up from within. She hated it. How long had she dreamed of finding one? She'd found it, all right. And it had led her down a path that ended up hurting everyone around her. Yet it gave her the strength to do what needed to be done. For that, at least, she could be thankful.

"If something does not serve me or humanity," she quoted, "it is my obligation to burn it away."

She drew back the bridges of chi from her followers. Connecting to them had been the mask's doing, and it had been a mistake. There was no need for them to join her in the afterlife. They dropped to their knees in the sand.

Doing her best to ignore the searing pain in her own abdomen, Aletheia reabsorbed the bridges. Some strands escaped through the wounds in her core, but she pushed them back in and willed them to remain.

"Aletheia . . ." Fischer tried. He took a step forward, dismay and regret leaking from him, just as golden light leaked from her. "I'm sorry I let things go this far. There has to be *something* I can do. I'll make an oath if that's what it takes. On my own unmaking. Would that convince you?"

"Don't," she grunted. "If you *are* telling the truth, I need you to take care of my friends . . ."

Fear and guilt radiated out alongside his regret. "This isn't the answer, Aletheia. Please."

"Ah, but it is." She forced a smile onto her face. "Either you are lying, and the heavens will assist me in your destruction . . . or you are telling the truth, and I will be burned away."

Kill the few, save the many, she recited in her mind, seeking strength. She could do this.

Someone fell against her back. Aletheia almost launched her spear, assuming it was an enemy come to stop her, but then he spoke.

"Please, Your Holiness." Evan tried to wrap his arms around her. His pain brought him up short, so he leaned against her back, clutching his own torso. "Don't."

Despite the mask's comforting certainty, a soft whine escaped her. She wanted to tell him she was sorry. Wanted to demand that he call her *Aletheia*. Instead, she snarled. "Get away, Head Mage." Her lip quivered. She thanked the heavens he couldn't see it. "That is an *order*! Get away from me before—"

Somebody fell against her left side, followed by another.

"God-Empress . . ." Grace groaned.

". . . Empress," Esmond grunted. It was all he could get out.

Eustace embraced her from the right, having ambled over from the bench. Fern was there, too, hugging Eustace from behind, glaring at Aletheia with baleful eyes. Anius growled like a cornered wolf, arms against his knees as he forced himself upright, only to collapse into the sand. He lifted his head and clenched his jaw, then started clawing at the ground, dragging himself closer.

"Please . . ." Aletheia took deep breaths to keep the sobs at bay. "I love you all." A single whimper made its way out. "But you need to get away from me. Your chi . . ." Even now it was streaming from their perforated cores. Her ideal and the mask were sucking it in, pulling the holes in their cores wider.

None spoke. They were in too much pain to utter a word. Yet they all shook their heads, refusing her.

She glowered up at the blurry shape of Fischer. "Why?" she demanded, wiping her eyes. He tried to answer, but she barreled over his reply. "Why did you let them come to me? You could have stopped them. Now I *know* you were lying about everything, you cruel, spiteful, heretical—"

"Okay," he interrupted. "Things are getting heated, and there are some big feelings going on. Before any of us say something we regret, let me . . . *There*."

He'd not moved a muscle, but the chi from her friends had stopped flowing into her. Aletheia blinked. It wasn't just their chi that had frozen. He was exerting his will over the entire shore. Even her spear of divine chi was affected, feeling lighter, sapping less of her essence over time. It was a staggering show of strength. And he claimed to only be at half his usual capacity . . .

"Sorry for letting them get close. I thought you might be able to hug it out. You know—the power of friendship and all that. As far as I'm concerned, you're my allies, so I won't coddle you. I mean, unless you want me to?" He rubbed his chin in thought. "Actually, now that you mention it, I probably should have asked you beforehand. My bad. Would you prefer I just save you, or do you wanna work for it?"

Aletheia wasn't sure if she wanted to slap him for babbling or thank him for saving her friends. "What are you talking about?"

"You're right. Now is hardly the time to make such a decision. I'll just save you this time, okay? Then, when you're not all evil or whatever, we can discuss it properly."

She focused on the golden spear in her hand. Why hadn't she launched it? The mask was screaming for her to let it fly, and her ideal agreed. She held them both at bay for now. The mask had tried to drag her followers along on her suicide mission—it couldn't be trusted. Not completely.

"Silence means you agree, by the way," Fischer said. "Them's the rules. That's reasonable, isn't it, Claws?"

The otter was perched on the sand beside them. She nodded vigorously.

"Wonderful. In that case, let's . . ." Fischer trailed off, his head drifting toward the otter. "I shouldn't be using you as a moral touchstone, should I?"

She shook her head with even more vigor, a grin splitting her face.

Fischer sighed and cupped his hands to his mouth. "Sniiiiips!"

Aletheia felt something shift on her leg. She looked down to see a crab crawl out of her pocket.

"Yes, Master?" hissed the crab as it hopped down onto the sand.

"Oh. I forgot I asked you to keep an eye on the god-empress. You heard all that?"

"I did."

"Thoughts?"

"I trust your judgment, Master. If you deemed the god-empress a threat and decided to remove her head, I would assume you knew best."

"That's . . ." Fischer pouted, considering how to reply, and decided to change the subject entirely. "Initiate plan D!"

Corporal Claws reached into her pocket, rummaged around, and removed a jacket with a large rip. She raced over and helped her master put it on.

"Well?" Fischer asked. "You've seen my memories, and now my sweet threads let you know my genuine feelings. Is it working? Have you realized that I really am . . ." He trailed off, looking behind Aletheia. "Uhhh, Fern?"

"What?"

"I kinda forgot that this jacket lets me know how others feel about me, too—why am I getting the vibe that you want to throw me off the edge of a cliff?"

Fern gave him a look of unbridled disgust. "Because you're a terrible person. You're acting like this is all a game. There's no love lost between the god-empress and I, but there's no reason for you to be so cruel. She's one second away from launching her spear and ending herself."

Fischer rubbed the back of his head. "Okay, I get that this might look bad, but I promise there's a method to the madness. I'll cut the shit for a second. I have a mate named Ellis. You haven't met him yet—which might be a good thing, because he can be a real prick—but he's the one who's kinda been running the show around here. He's an archivist, and one of his abilities is a personal library that nobody else can access. I finished this massive string of quests to defend Tropica, right, and the reward was a whole bunch of history books. Before I could even touch them, he stole the books and put them in his personal library—like I said, bit of a prick.

"Anyway, because he yoinked the books, he has access to all this ancient knowledge or whatever, and he gave us this big, vague speech about an ominous threat on the distant horizon. We weren't fighting you guys for shits and giggles—he told us that if we don't get stronger, we're basically doomed. We're desperately trying to grow and improve, and you should be doing the same. If I robbed you of a chance to ascend, how would you feel, Aletheia? If the end of the world came, and you were one breakthrough away from saving everyone you loved, would you be glad I didn't make you feel like . . . five minutes of discomfort?"

Aletheia barely heard the question. Her mind was caught on something else he'd said. "The System gave you quests?" she asked. "And you completed them?"

"Uhhh, yeah. I'm guessing I completed all of them, because it didn't give me any more. Why?"

"I . . . I have a quest. It's the reason I came here."

His head rocked back. "It is? Wait . . . when did you get it?"

"A couple of months ago."

Fischer groaned and rubbed his face. "Is that why I didn't get any more? I completed my last one around the same time. With power returning to the world, it probably only has enough energy to hand out a few at a . . . *Whoa.*"

Aletheia glanced to the side, following his gaze toward Eustace and Anius, the last two Seers of Phostheia.

Their eyes were glowing.

Even Fischer stopped talking as thick beams of golden light shone down on the seers.

Aletheia knew what this was. She'd read about it a thousand times in the royal library. The wisdom of the heavens was flowing into the seers, granting them a vision.

When the golden beams faded a few seconds later, Eustace and Anius looked at Fischer, then at Aletheia, then at Fischer again.

"What . . ." Aletheia licked her lips. Only the mask stopped her from immediately dismissing her spear. "What were you shown?"

Eustace looked at her with joy- and tear-filled eyes. "Dear . . . we were right all along. You *are* the divine bridge between Kallis and the heavens."

"That— You're lying. You're just saying that so I don't unleash this spear."

Anius's stomach started shaking. It took Aletheia a moment to realize he was laughing. His amusement dragged on for a long while, the seer chuckling silently. "If you think that was a bit too convenient, you're going to hate what else we have to say."

As Eustace nodded her agreement, tears ran down her face.

"Tell me," Aletheia said. "Please."

Anius sighed and shook his head with a smile. "You're the divine bridge, God-Empress, the one who will connect Kallis to the heavens." His amusement returned, and he grinned as he turned back toward Fischer, pointing a single finger at the god-king. "And you, Fischer . . . you're the heavens."

"Uhhh, come again?"

Eustace shrugged. "That's all there is to it. The vision told us that Aletheia is 'the divine bridge,' and that you're 'the heavens.'"

"No thanks," Fischer said. "I'm good."

Anius gave him a sly smile. "I understand you might have some reservations, but I'm afraid that's not how it works."

"Sure it is. I decline. I refuse. Unsubscribe me from the mailing list."

Sergeant Snips scuttled forward, patting his thigh with one mighty claw. "This is to be expected, Master. The universe has acknowledged your might."

Corporal Claws crept up to join Snips. Aletheia didn't like the way the otter's eyes were sparkling. She looked like she was scheming.

"This is my karma for dragging this out." Fischer stood and brushed off his pants. "You said you had a quest, Aletheia? What's the requirement?"

"Why do you want to know?"

"Because I'm about to call in the spirit beast who will help save you from yourself. I already have an idea of the angle she'll take, but you said the quest is the reason you came here. It will help."

"It's . . . It's not—"

"Doesn't matter," he interrupted. "Hit me with it. You want to be able to trust me, right? Or would you rather throw that spear and die for no reason?" He gestured to either side of her. "You're surrounded by friends. We both know you're not gonna let them see you die before you at least try to do it my way. Chop-chop, God-Empress. Share the quest description."

After only a moment's hesitation, she fought down her doubt, gathered her will, and ordered the System to share her quest with him.

Sweat sprouted on her brow as his gaze went distant, the description appearing in his field of view. He shook his head to dismiss the words, then slowly turned to look at her.

In his defense, she was fairly sure he tried to hide his amusement. But his damned jacket was still broadcasting his emotions out.

"You find this funny?" Aletheia demanded.

"This bloody jacket, I swear . . . I was trying not to be a dick, but yeah, it's pretty damn funny. I'm honestly surprised you haven't worked it out yourself."

She felt her face flush. "Haven't worked what out?"

He was still amused, but stronger emotions were piling overtop his mirth, beaming out into the world. "Wondering why I'm so happy? It's because I know for a fact that you can fix yourself." He cupped his hands to his mouth and yelled at the top of his lungs. "Plan S!"

"Plan S . . . ?" Anius asked. "You really had that many different plans prepared?"

"What? No, I literally used all of them. Plan S is the final one. Don't worry about it not being sequential. You'll understand soon." He turned to look at her again. "The ideal. Say it again for me."

"What are you—"

"Come on. Indulge me. It's important."

Aletheia lifted her chin, meeting his eyes. "*If something does not serve me or humanity, it is my obligation to burn it away.*"

"And the other bit?"

"Kill the few, save the many."

"Right. So your ideal is about remaining dynamic. It's about shifting your perspective and rapidly letting go of things that don't serve you. Perhaps even killing them, if such a thing is possible."

"Yes, but I don't really see what you're . . ." She trailed off as an idea struck, starting as a vague possibility that gained traction the more she considered it.

Fischer's grin was almost as devious as the elemental otter's. "It just clicked, didn't it?"

"It can't be . . ."

"Can't be what? That simple?"

She gave a faint nod.

"Well, it is." He raised one finger. "You have an ideal about letting go of things that don't serve you." He raised a second digit. "Your quest is to identify and eliminate a 'severe' threat to your kingdom, and humanity as a whole." A third finger went up, but he twirled this one around, not letting it sit still. "Now, if only there were something that no longer served you, that was also a severe threat to your kingdom, and humanity as a whole . . ." He raised his other hand and stroked his chin histrionically. "Such as, I don't know, a second presence in that divine noggin of yours? A personality that is literally driving the Kingdom of Light's god-empress to annihilate herself, which would leave the kingdom—and humanity as a whole—without one of its strongest cultivators when some ill-defined, looming threat eventually comes to Kallis."

Everyone was staring at Aletheia now. She could see the hope on their faces. She looked away before it spread to her. "What if it doesn't work, Fischer?"

"It will."

She clenched her fists. "You can't know that. What if it *doesn't* work? What then?"

"You know, I've learned so many lessons during my time in Tropica. I'm a *really* good learner, you see. I'm so good at learning that I sometimes learn the same lesson over and over. Today, I learned—for like the sixth time—to trust my friends again. You should try it out."

"Trust, you mean?"

"Yep." He leaned toward the ocean, shielding his eyes from the sun as he looked at something. "Any other questions?"

"Do you always babble this much?"

Fischer laughed. "Only when I'm trying to stall for time."

Aletheia squinted as a shadow approached the shore. A giant lobster exited the waves a moment later, scuttled up onto the beach. There was a smaller, more reasonably sized lobster on its back.

"You've not been introduced yet, but this is Pistachio." Fischer bumped the giant lobster's claw. "And this is Shelly. She's plan S."

Aletheia gave the lobster an assessing look. How was a sea creature supposed to help her . . . *Oh.*

"Shelly had her breakthrough not long ago," Fischer said. "I find her ideal super fascinating—you can feel it, right? It's so broad that no matter what I ask her to do, I feel like I'm wasting her potential, you know? Just once, I'd like to be able to point her at someone and say, 'Off ya go, Shelly! This person needs help with *change!*'"

His grin was just as devious as before. Corporal Claws leaped up onto his shoulder and started aggresively waggling her eyebrows.

"How about it, Aletheia?" Fischer asked, scratching his familiar behind the ear. "Can you think of anyone that needs help with change?"

CHAPTER FIFTY-FOUR

Farewell

Two weeks later

It was a beautiful morning on the shores of Tropica, even if it was almost time to say goodbye. Maria and I strode toward the ocean in comfortable silence. A breeze swirled around us, carrying with it hushed conversations and the quiet roar of distant crashing waves. The sounds grew louder as we crested the final dune, catching sight of the shore and the hundreds of people gathered there, milling around the ships that were moored to Tropica's latest construction: a new dock.

Aletheia's Prime Cadre of mages had created it for us, insisting they'd replace the wooden jetty the god-empress had obliterated upon their arrival. Rather than extending from the village, the dock was built midway between Tropica and my home, ensuring ships sailed nowhere near the forty sunken vessels now forming an artificial reef beneath the bay.

The dock extended over a hundred meters into the ocean and was wide enough to handle two wagons abreast. *Theoris* was moored on its north side, Bob the boat was moored on the south, and the hundreds of coconut boats were stored in various cubbies along the wooden walkway, hidden and protected, yet easy to retrieve if needed.

Aletheia had forbidden Tropica from helping. Naturally, we disobeyed via peaceful protest, providing snacks and cold drinks that we just so happened to serve right by the new dock. We'd only meant for it to be temporary, but after Sue and Sturgill opened up a coffee and pastry cart, the area had turned into a social hub of sorts.

From there, Tropica had gotten even more obstinate.

Brad, Greg, and the rest of the woodworkers had descended upon the shore, leaving decking, stalls, and tables with long benches in their wake. There had been a minor and good-natured dispute over what constituted working on the "dock" when Greg tried to connect his deck to it. In the end, Theo had mediated a third-party solution. He'd brought in Fergus and Duncan to create a foot-wide, four-meter-long metal plate, which functioned as the border between both projects.

Steven and Ruby had made shade sails for the stalls and umbrellas for the tables. As a result, Maria and I adopted Fin for almost an entire day, only bringing her back from our forest and beachside adventures whenever she needed to feed.

The shade sails were currently lowered, letting the sun's warm rays kiss my skin as Maria and I strode down the dune and onto the wooden deck. We joined the end of a long line for coffee and pastries. Sue arched her back to lock eyes with me, and I shook my head at her questioning gaze—I'd wait in line like everyone else.

Now that we were close, I could smell the scents of coffee and fresh pastries. They assaulted my senses every time the breeze changed direction. After a particularly strong gust, the wind suddenly died down, leaving me wreathed in the enticing aromas. I closed my eyes and imagined washing down a bite of buttery croissant with a swig of hot coffee.

"Is he okay?" asked a calm, feminine voice.

"Don't mind my husband," Maria said. "He gets a bit excited about breakfast."

I opened my eyes and turned around, facing the newcomer. "Mornin', Aletheia."

"Good morning. Mind if I join you in line, God-King?"

I narrowed my eyes at her. Two weeks ago to the day, Shelly's ideal had helped the god-empress change her perspective almost immediately. It hadn't resulted in a breakthrough, though, so Aletheia's core remained wounded. The damage was so severe that it still wasn't completely healed. We'd spent plenty of time chatting over the past couple of weeks while Maria helped restore her channels . . . which meant Aletheia knew I hated formalities just as much as she did.

"Only if you stop calling me God-King," I said.

"As you wish, Traveler Fischer."

I groaned.

Maria beamed at me and wrapped an arm around Aletheia's shoulder. "Can we keep her?"

"I reckon we have enough disobedient strays already." I nodded toward Claws, who was squatting atop a nearby dune with most of my animal pals, so preoccupied by a feast of clams and fish that she hadn't noticed our arrival.

"Yeah, but *this* stray wields divine chi!" Maria squeezed Aletheia tighter. "She can hold the other strays in check!"

I absentmindedly wondered how her recovery was coming along. The moment that thought occurred, tendrils of chi rushed from me, assessing the state of her health.

With the help of Maria and Slimes, the channels lacing Aletheia's body had been completely restored. Her core was no longer riddled with holes, but neither was it completely restored. Patches of my wife's pink chi remained, keeping the core stable while it continued to strengthen and regenerate.

"Sorry," I said, grimacing and forcing my chi to withdraw. "Still getting used to having all my strength back."

She gave me a lopsided smile and a quizzical look. "Are you apologizing for checking on my health?"

"Nah. I'm apologizing for doing it without asking permission first."

"Well, don't. We're friends now, remember? As are our peoples."

She gestured all around us, and I slowly spun, taking in the myriad conversations and animated exchanges, though I actively suppressed my sense of hearing, not wanting to intrude.

"You win this round," I said, turning back to Aletheia. "Same order as usual?"

"Oh, absolutely not—didn't you hear? Sue stayed up all night making a special syrup. It's all anyone has been raving about."

I scanned the surrounding people again. Sure enough, many of the conversations seemed to be centered around the mugs they were holding. I craned my neck, trying to catch a glimpse of the golden liquid within, but Maria's exclamation arrested my attention.

"Adephagia's gluttonous curves!" she swore. "Fischer. Over there!"

I followed Maria's gaze to find a bulbous bunny slumped atop one of the dock's posts. She was lying on her back, her rotund stomach greeting the sky. The sun's golden beams shone down upon her. She looked like the subject of a renaissance painting. The fur surrounding her mouth had been dyed a deep purple, giving me a good idea of what the syrup's main ingredient was.

"The syrup *must* be good," I said with a smile. "I've not seen Cinnamon overindulge like that since she first tasted Barry's chi-filled sugarcane."

The queue before us slowly dwindled. Just as Aletheia had joined us in line, so too did she join our comfortable silence. All three of us—a god-king, a god-queen, and a god-empress—simply enjoyed each other's company as the pleasant sensations of a morning by the ocean washed over us.

Before I knew it, the way before us had opened up, and Sue's radiant face was beaming at me. Calling her radiant wasn't an exaggeration—she was practically glowing. She gave Maria and me a wink, gave Aletheia a curtsy I hadn't seen coming, then became a blur. She poured milk with one hand, tamped down ground beans with the other, and used a slight exertion of will to ready the espresso machine.

As the shots flowed from the portafilter and into separate glasses, she set three mugs in a line. Then she picked up a white jug, which she swept past the mugs, pouring a viscous, dark-purple syrup into them with a practiced flourish.

I pursed my lips as she started steaming the milk, giving it all of her attention. "Aren't you gonna ask what we want?"

She didn't look up from her task, but the corners of her mouth curled up into a victorious grin. "Don't need to. I already know what you need."

Fifteen seconds later, she tipped the shots into each mug, then swiftly added the frothed milk, letting increasing amounts of foam through as she went from my cup, to Maria's, to Aletheia's.

Though they looked like our regular orders when Sue slid them forward—a flat white, a latte, and a cappuccino minus the chocolate powder—they started transforming before our eyes. I leaned closer, my brow furrowing in confusion before rising in surprise. The dark syrup seeped up from below, slow at first then all at once, coloring the golden crema a vibrant purple, leaving the white froth untouched.

The System tried to make me inspect the drink, but I swept it aside without reading it. I passed Maria's and Aletheia's to them, then grabbed my own, breathing deep of the fruity notes. I raised the mug to my lips, paused for a moment as I appreciated the purple and white latte art of a swan, then took a slow sip.

The unmistakable flavor of passiona husk exploded across my awareness. Its hints of passion fruit and strawberry danced over my tastebuds, almost too sweet. The flavor of the passiona husk was so strong that I wondered for a moment if she'd also infused the beans with it. But then the taste of the coffee came crashing down, bitter, earthy, a touch burnt. Alone, either ingredient would have been too much. Together, they perfectly complemented the other, the bitter and sweet notes weaving across my awareness. A shiver rocked my upper body, my arms breaking out in goose bumps.

"I roasted the beans twice," Sue explained, confirming my suspicions. "All the test batches were too sweet until I used a plain dark roast."

"Sue . . ." I held up a finger, took a sip, and shimmied my shoulders in delight. "Normally, I'd have called you doing test batches without me a capital offense, but I'll forgive you this time." I went to take another little sip, but it turned into an indulgent swig, the deliciously hot coffee leaving me no other choice. "Damn. It's *so* good. Filled with chi, too."

To my side, Aletheia upended her mug and sculled the rest of her passiona latte. Maria, Sue, and I all watched her as she shook her mug, ensuring she got every last drop. In that moment, I was struck by the difference between the god-empress who'd arrived on our shores, and the one who would soon depart.

From maniacal tyrant to a woman embracing her inner child—who was now using a finger to scrape any remnant foam from her cup—Aletheia was unrecognizable. I couldn't help but smile, the change somehow making my own latte taste all the sweeter. Maria squeezed my arm, also seeing the contrast.

Sue, however, had a very different reaction.

"Silly girl," she said as Sturgill stepped forward with three pastries. "Now you have nothing to wash your croissant down with. I'll make you another."

Despite Sue's words, I didn't miss the gratification plastered across her face while she swiftly prepared another beverage for Aletheia.

The god-empress was much more reserved with her second mug, sipping it slowly between bites of steaming-hot croissant. "My resolve to sail back home is diminishing with each meal. I can't believe how good you have it here."

"I wouldn't worry about that." I nodded toward *Theoris* and *Elegos*, whose hulls were packed with crates of produce. "They might not be as skilled at first, but I'm sure your citizens will advance quickly with the ingredients and farming methods you're taking home with you."

She turned to lock eyes with me, her expression suddenly serious. "Thank you, Fischer. Really. I am at a loss for words with how much you've done for me and my people. We—"

She was cut off as the ground shook, followed by a deafening *boom*. Already knowing what I'd see, I glanced up, finding a mass of muscle and outrage sailing toward us.

"Incoming," I called, raising a bubble of chi around everyone.

Lucky I did. Barry created globules of molten glass when he landed on the nearby dune, anger radiating from him in waves of boiling heat. He took a step toward the animals, who all gazed back at him with varying levels of curiosity and fear.

"Uhhhh, Barry?" I said. "You good, mate?"

"Not now," he hissed, steam billowing from his mouth.

"Mate, I'm not trying to tell you off, I'm just letting you know . . ." I pointed at his semi-glistening torso. "You're only half oiled. I thought you might wanna go finish the job, then redo your dramatic entrance."

He ignored me, instead jabbing a finger toward my animal pals. "You went too far this time."

If there was any remaining doubt as to who had angered him so, it was cleared up a moment later when a grinning otter pointed at herself.

"Who, me?" trilled Claws, feigning ignorance. "I have no idea what you're talking about."

"You put *dung* in the bottom of my *moisturizer*! I've been using it for weeks! I put that on my *face!*"

She rotated one forepaw dismissively, the other discarding an empty clam shell. "That could have been anyone. Besides, you should probably thank them, whoever it was. Your muscles need all the help growing that they can ge—"

Barry exploded forward so swiftly that he almost caught her by the scruff. Cackling with laughter and scattering shellfish all over, Claws fled, zapping toward the southern mountain. I raised another protective barrier as Barry took off after her, displacing half a ton of sand from each dune he stomped across.

Theo had come running through the crowd, ever keen to mediate. Now that the disagreeing parties had departed, he came to a stop between Maria and Aletheia, gravitating toward the god-empress.

Aletheia avoided looking at him. "Tropica is always so . . . *energetic.*"

"Sorry about that," I said. "I wish I could say it was a rare occurrence, but—"

"Lie," both Theo and Aletheia said at the same time.

In tandem, they glanced at each other, then at the ground, hints of red rising in their cheeks.

I barked a laugh. "You two are *terrible* at this. How are we even supposed to tease you if you make it so obvious?"

"Stop it, you." Maria gave me a soft *whap* on the arm, and them an apologetic smile. "We think your budding romance is cute."

If my comment had added a stroke of color to their cheeks, Maria's added the rest of the paint tin.

"Well, uh, yes. It was lovely seeing you." Clearly panicking, Aletheia grabbed and shook Theo's hand. "Bye now!" With that, she disappeared in a streak of golden light, appearing back on her repaired galleon, *Theoris.*

An immature man would have pointed out how similar *Theoris* was to the name *Theo*, so I did. Theo put his head in his hands, doing what he could to hide his face. It earned me another smack on the shoulder, but I knew Maria was enjoying herself just as much as I was.

Someone cleared their throat to my side, and I turned toward Eustace and Fern, both women giving me a meaningful look.

"Don't worry," I said. "Already on it."

I reached for my power, wrapping twin tendrils of chi around a Truthsayer and a god-empress, preparing to teleport them both to the other side of Tropica, far from prying eyes. It wasn't like they'd never see each other again—Phostheia's fleet already had plans to return in a month—but I was too much of a romantic to let them part on a damned *handshake*.

Before I could finish moving them, however, Aletheia shoved my essence aside. She streaked back over, crashed into Theo's chest, and kissed him square on the mouth.

Apparently, it wasn't just Maria and me who'd noticed how much time they were spending together. The crowd of cultivators erupted, cheering and whooping and flaunting good-natured taunts. Loudest of all were Eustace and Fern, who celebrated like their lives depended on it.

Aletheia stepped back, her shoulders squared and chin high, refusing to look at the ground despite how much she was blushing. "Bye, Theo," she said, departing once more. Only a ribbon of gold marked her passage back to the deck of *Theoris*. "With me, Kingdom of Light!" she called.

Her followers rushed to obey, only pausing long enough to hug their new friends goodbye—or grab some croissants for the road, as three enterprising young cultivators did.

Of the entire fleet that had come to assault Tropica, only two women remained ashore.

"Are you sure you don't want to go back?" Maria asked Eustace and Fern, leaning against me.

"You know," Eustace said, "maybe it would be nice giving some people a proper goodbye, but not if I have to spend one more minute with a certain *old toad!*"

"Let me know if you change your mind, hag!" Anius called from *Theoris*, where he lounged on a bench that had been the topic of many a debate over the last fortnight. "If you decide to come, you won't have to deal with my company—I'll throw myself overboard!"

"Hmmm. Maybe I *should* go. What do you think, Fern? Would you come with me?"

"I'm good here. I have nobody to say goodbye to. Besides, I'm only *just* getting the hang of fishing."

"Here, here!" I said, raising my empty mug in a salute.

"Then it's settled."

"Bye, Tropica!" Aletheia called. She waved enthusiastically as the sails of two galleons unfurled, the only ships remaining of the grand fleet.

We all called back, a chorus of goodbyes, wordless cheers, and animal noises. Only one of us infused his voice with chi, and I flinched, pressing a hand to my ear.

"Bloody hell, Ellis. Glad you're feeling better, but give me a heads-up next time you do that."

The archivist had denied Maria's healing and refused to elaborate on the matter. He'd still been under the weather yesterday. Today, he actually had some color in his cheeks. Not as much as Theo, though, who was glowing beet red from Aletheia's kiss.

Ellis smiled at me, his wooden pipe clenched between his teeth. "Lots to be happy about, Fischer."

"Does that mean you're finally gonna tell me what the frack you did in the alchemy workshop? Or where the first sister is?"

"Oh. You noticed that?"

"Pretty hard to miss the disappearance of a lava slug, mate. And don't change the subject. What in the divine hells were you doing in the alchemy workshop?"

"Sorry, Fischer. I—"

"—cannot tell you," I finished for him. "Yeah, yeah, mate. Loud and clear."

"Speaking of loud and clear . . ."

I frowned at him, but he just nodded out to sea, grinning as he puffed on his pipe. All of those who had come to attack Tropica—an entire fleet's worth of people—crowded the decks, hands cupped to mouths. I felt chi building in their cores.

"Wait. What are they—"

"All hail God-King Fischer!" they droned with the slow, inflectionless cadence of students addressing a teacher.

It triggered a panic response in the depths of my core, reminding me of the time Tropica had conspired to turn me into a god-king. When nothing happened in my abdomen, I let out a weary sigh. "Oh, ha-ha, Ellis. Very funny. I hope this little prank made you feel better about—"

"All hail Tropica!" they continued, and my world shook.

No, really. The entire world shook, the ocean going still in stark relief. When the tremors subsided, the waves returned, lapping at the shore as if nothing had happened.

I whirled on Ellis. "You dastardly, conspiring, rat-lookin' son of a goat—"

"Fischer!" Rubes chided, covering Fin's ears. "Not in front of your chosen champion!"

I rubbed my temples as I felt the network below shifting. I groaned when I felt hints of divine chi flow into it. "Mate . . . why are you like this? Can you not just . . ." I squinted at Ellis, his eyes distant, some of the world's chi connecting to him. "Hold up. Did you just finish a quest?"

He shook his head, returning to the present. "No."

More chi connected to him, its signature unmissable as it flowed through my Domain. His eyes went vacant again.

Mine went flat. "And you just got a new one, didn't you?"

He puffed his pipe as his vision cleared. "I have no clue what you are talking about, God-King."

I groaned again as it all snapped into place. "*That's* why you've been leaving me in the dark, isn't it? I thought it was odd that I got no more quests after the last ones. You've been getting them? Is not telling me one of their conditions?"

He took his time, circulating his chi as I continued to spiral. Finally, with a great exhalation of smoke, he looked over at me with the air of a sage addressing a rowdy disciple. "If that were all true, which I am absolutely not saying is the case, confirming it would only hamper said quest, would it not?"

I gazed out at the departing ships, their forms already growing smaller, great gusts of divine chi hitting their sails. "Maria?"

"Yes?"

"Did George and Geraldine ever dig those latrines?"

Understanding me better than any other, she snapped to attention. "No, sir! I believe they assumed you were only joking, sir!"

"Good. Mark Ellis down for latrine-digging duties."

"Yes, God-King!"

"And it has to be the best damned latrine I've ever seen."

"Yes, God-King!"

"One more thing," I said, giving Ellis a pointed look. "If he doesn't actually do it, instruct Corporal Claws that she is forbidden from further pranks unless Ellis is the target."

Though he was trying to play it cool, his eyes darted toward the southern mountains and the lightning crawling through the sky above them. Claws's chittering laughter reached our ears a moment later, only cutting off when Barry leaped into the air after her, swinging an uprooted tree directly at her head.

Epilogue

I was sitting on the rocky shore of the headland, dangling my legs over the edge and delighting in the incoming tide that was lapping at my calves, when a pulse of abyssal chi washed over me. It was a common enough occurrence lately, so I ignored it, resolving to ask about it later.

But I couldn't ignore what happened a minute afterward. Maria—who'd left not long ago to fetch some ingredients for seaside sandwiches—abruptly sent me her love, then closed our connection. I'd been staring down at the waves, and my head whipped around, facing the center of Tropica where I'd last sensed her.

A spike of alarm seemed to come from outside myself, but I pushed it down, choosing instead to remain calm by focusing on the sensations of my body: the fitful breeze flowing past, tickling the hair on my arms; the midday sun beaming down from up high; and the refreshing ocean below, whose lapping waves made it impossible for me to be anything other than grateful.

There had to be a good reason. There always was when it came to my wife. Maybe she was preparing a surprise for me.

That outside source of alarm receded, but it flared back to life a moment later when I heard someone approaching on foot.

Oi, I thought at Claws, who was swimming around in the river mouth, openly broadcasting her emotions into my mind. *Cut it out.*

She chittered at me. Or maybe she chittered at a fish. It was hard to tell.

"Hello, Fischer," Ellis said, deftly striding into view across the rocks.

"G'day, mate." I lazily pointed toward Tropica with my thumb. "Was that your doing?"

He nodded and came to sit beside me on the shore, lowering his legs into the water. "It was."

When it became clear he wasn't going to apologize, a hint of anger joined the lingering alarm from earlier, but I pushed it down. "So what can I do for you, mate? What's so secret that you can't tell Maria, and what makes you think I won't just tell her the second you leave?"

He smiled at my question, an unreadable glint entering his eyes as he removed his pipe and packed it with dried plant matter. Before he could light it, however, he sighed and let it fall into his lap.

"I fully expect you to tell Maria most of it, Fischer, but it is important to me that this conversation happens between just us. Some of it *must* be kept secret." He turned to face me. "I am not worried about you telling Maria, because once you understand the stakes, you would not dare. I have already told Maria this, which is why she so readily agreed to close your connection, even if only temporarily."

Again, surprise and a touch of anger flared from Claws. Again, I pushed it aside.

My mind raced. "Okay. Point taken. Will you warn me before you tell me that bit, though? I don't want someone overhearing by accident."

"I will. You were correct, Fischer. I *have* been getting quests, and I was explicitly forbidden from telling you, and anyone whose power was directly needed."

"What's changed since this morning?" I asked. "You and the squad have kept us in the dark for months. How come you can tell us now?"

"Because I just completed a quest, and started a new one, which only forbids me from telling the others about some of it."

I frowned, swirling my legs through the water. "Is that what caused the pulse of chi earlier?"

"Indeed."

"Okay. That all makes sense, but I have a question."

"Which is?"

I turned toward him, watching his expression closely. "Are you telling me because you want to, or because the quest ordered it?"

He gave an easy shrug. "Because I want to."

"Good. Follow-up question: Do you want to tell me so that you don't have to dig a latrine?"

Ellis scoffed. "No. I am afraid of neither physical labor, nor Claws's pranks."

"In that case, thank you. I appreciate you coming to me right away."

"You should not be thanking me, Fischer. I owe you an apology. I will not lie and say that I derived no amusement from confounding you, but if not for the explicit stipulation of the quests, I would never have kept it from you. This, I swear on my core."

It wasn't exactly an oath, but Ellis didn't need to make one. I believed him.

"Apology accepted. So . . . what have you been building?"

"Oh, that is easy to answer. Tunnels."

I gave him a flat stare.

"To the very center of the Kallis realm," he continued.

"Come again?"

"The tunnels we carved—they go all the way to this world's core."

I stared down at the swirling water, imagining the network of power extending all the way into the center of this planet. "I knew they were vast, but . . . damn."

"My thoughts exactly."

"How did you know how to do it?"

He gave another easy shrug. "Many have attempted something similar. There are multiple records of such events within the history books in my library. I simply recreated their workings, but with the cultivators we had on hand: abyssal cultivators to expand and fill the network; Alchemists, whose concoctions stabilized the tunnels; and a lava elemental, without whom, our efforts would have come to naught."

That outside source of shock returned, seemingly stunned by the revelation of the first sister's active involvement.

"Damn. *Damn.*" I chewed the inside of my lip as I considered it all. "That's where the first sister has been? I felt a hint of her chi when Geraldine busted down the door, but I'd assumed she was just lending power."

"Oh, absolutely not. She was integral to the operation. So that's the how. As for why we did it . . . I can only tell you once you've guaranteed our privacy."

I nodded and created a bubble of chi. It was so thick that even if Claws snuck up and dealt it a full-powered hit, she wouldn't be able to breach all its layers.

"Okay, mate. Nobody else can hear us now. Why did you do it?"

"Because, Fischer." He thumbed the end of his pipe. "I believe that someone *did* succeed in suffusing the entire world with chi. Even in the records I possess, it is not explicitly stated, but the connections are obvious." He glanced over at me, his eyes severe. "After all, I believe that's how the divine gods began their reign."

The implications of his words crashed down on me like a tidal wave. It took me at least half a minute for my mind to calm enough that I could speak. "How sure are you?"

"It's still only a theory, but all evidence seems to support it. In the early stages of the expansion, we found vast pools of divine essence underground. I partially lied earlier; the abyssal cultivators were not just expanding the network—they had to simultaneously combat the remaining divine chi. The first sister helped them in that regard, separating it from the magma it had become more or less fused with."

"No wonder you were all so fatigued . . ."

"It was certainly trying." He raised his arm out before him, his hand trembling like a leaf in the wind. "I do not believe I will fully recover for at least another fortnight."

I rubbed my chin in thought. There were so many questions I wanted to ask. I could sit here and grill him for hours and still not have all the answers, but that wasn't the kind of day I wanted to have. I wanted the one I'd already planned, which involved dangling my feet in the water, making seaside sandwiches with my beautiful wife, and watching the tide come in.

I looked at Ellis, deciding to cut to the chase. "You still haven't answered why, mate. What was the goal?"

He allowed himself a small smile. "You already know, Fischer."

"I think I do, yeah, but I need you to say it."

"Very well. The goal was to spread your influence. Initially, I hoped to tunnel as far down as possible, then redirect it back up in a giant cone, spreading your Domain. But now that we have successfully infiltrated the world's core, our goal is to spread your Domain across the entire planet, perhaps even into the heavens. That is as much as I can tell you for now."

I nodded along, dismissing the bubble of chi.

Ellis gave a tired grin, the end of his pipe held between his teeth. "It feels good to get that off my chest." He snapped his fingers, somehow creating a flame in the center of his bowl, lighting the brown plant matter within. "So, what do you think of my tale, Fischer?" He exhaled a thin cloud of smoke. "Pretty salacious little story, if I do say so mysel— *bleglrlebeblgblegler!*"

The torrent of seawater blasted him directly in the face, filling his mouth and making water explode from his nostrils.

"You dare keep secrets?" demanded Claws, her head bobbing above the waves. "From *me?*"

Ellis coughed and sputtered, then shot to his feet, beard wet, clothes drenched, expression promising vengeance. He forced himself to take slow, deep breaths.

"Corporal Claws, I understand your frustration, but I hardly think I am a deserving outlet for your—"

He ducked the torrent of salty water, expecting it this time.

"Corporal! Claws! I must insist that you— Where are you going? Claws? Claws! You get back here! I am not done talking about this!"

Only one of Claws's forepaws reemerged from the ocean, giving Ellis a single-digit salute before sinking back beneath the waves.

Author's Note

Join my mailing list to get notified about new releases and more! You can find the sign-up button on the bottom of the page at HaylockJobson.com. I promise I won't spam you.

If you can't wait for the next installment, visit Patreon.com/haylock to read advance chapters and whole books ahead of their release. You can also follow me on Instagram (@haylockjobson) and Facebook (Facebook.com/haylock.jobson)!

Acknowledgments

Thank you to my loved ones, who had to put up with me while I wrote and revised (then wrote and revised) this book.

Thank you to my team—Danny, Matt, Seth, Teagan—for helping take care of the business side of things, and for always having my back.

Thank you to my beta readers, whose advice and feedback sharpened this manuscript. The book wouldn't be what it is without you.

Thank you to my editor, Crystal, whom I bombard with accidental (and intentional) crimes against the English language.

Thank you to the members of my Patreon, some of whom have been with me since I started publishing Heretical Fishing there back in 2023. All this might not have been possible without your initial support.

Thank you to my writer friends for always being down for side quests, shop talk, and shenanigans. There are too many of you to name.

Thank you to the fine people at Podium—Brian, Julie, Kendall, Keara, Leah, to name a few—who always put the story first and were nothing but understanding when I yoinked back an already-submitted manuscript.

Thank you to my friend and narrator, Heath Miller. No small amount of my success, and the success of the series, is a direct result of your skill and performance on Heretical Fishing. I'm sorry that I stole the killer valediction you were using when signing Heretical Fishing books (but not sorry enough to stop using it). Hugs & fishes, Heath. Hugs & fishes.

And last but not least, I have to thank you, the reader. This was my first series, and it has been challenging to navigate at times. This book was tough in particular, which is why I revised it so heavily (and repeatedly). Though I wince a bit when I look back at certain parts of the series, I wouldn't change a thing, because each misstep was a valuable lesson that got me to where I am today. Thank you for going on this ride with me. It's such a blessing to have so many people consume something I've created, and I don't know what I did to deserve it. From the bottom of my heart, thank you.

About the Author

Haylock Jobson is the author of the Heretical Fishing series, originally released on Royal Road. He lives on the beautiful shores of Australia's Gold Coast and spends his days writing in local cafes, drinking what some might refer to as "too much" coffee, and annoying strangers by asking if he can pet their dogs.